I0819578

Wait for Me

Also by Amy Jo Burns

Mercury

Shiner

Cinderland

Wait for Me

A NOVEL

☼

Amy Jo Burns

This is a work of fiction. All the characters, organizations, and events portrayed in this novel are either products of the author's imagination or used fictitiously.

Printed in the United States of America. For information, address Celadon Books, a division of Macmillan Publishers, 120 Broadway, New York, NY 10271.
EU Representative: Macmillan Publishers Ireland Ltd., 1st Floor, The Liffey Trust Centre, 117–126 Sheriff Street Upper, Dublin 1, D01 YC43.

www.celadonbooks.com

Designed by Michelle McMillian

Library of Congress Cataloging-in-Publication Data

Names: Burns, Amy Jo, 1981– author.
Title: Wait for me : a novel / Amy Jo Burns.
Description: First edition. | New York : Celadon Books, 2026.
Identifiers: LCCN 2025009473 | ISBN 9781250399304 (hardcover) | ISBN 9781250399311 (ebook)
Subjects: LCGFT: Novels
Classification: LCC PS3602.U76486 W35 2026 | DDC 813/.6—dc23/eng/20250506
LC record available at https://lccn.loc.gov/2025009473

First Edition: 2026

10 9 8 7 6 5 4 3 2 1

For Louise DeSalvo, who will always be the greatest of all time to me

Wait for Me

What Happened to Elle Harlow?

August 27, 1991, *Nashville Noir*

This December marks the eighteenth anniversary of famed country-folk singer Elle Harlow's strange disappearance in 1973, just after her first and final performance at the Grand Ole Opry in Nashville, Tennessee. Eyewitnesses outside the concert hall claim they saw her drive east in her Studebaker, bound for her next concert in Sunset Park, Pennsylvania.

Those witnesses were the last to see her alive.

She never arrived for the show. After that night, she was never seen again. Her Studebaker was never found, nor was the custom 1970s pink-and-white guitar she always traveled with. Her final album, *Wounds from a Lover*, remains the bestselling female folk record to date.

The album's message about the rapture and the regret of falling for someone—about love and ghosts in the eerie Appalachian hills—ignited a generation of singer-songwriters to follow. But Elle Harlow had a dark side. As much as she's remembered for her creative genius, she's also known for her mercurial moods, her vengeance, and her violence.

Now almost two decades have passed and recollections are fading from those in attendance at Elle Harlow's last concert. Some think she put on the show of her lifetime; others say she ran offstage. Some swear she took her guitar with her; others claim she left with nothing, not even her shoes.

Is she dead? Why did she disappear? Theories are rife with claims of foul play. Her fans believe she left clues in the lyrics of her final songs—but the more time passes, the less likely it seems Elle Harlow will ever be found.

She was only twenty-two years old.

Missing

A farmer swore he saw it first, while rocking on his front porch. His wife flickered behind the screen door, about to tell him to get his third can of Rolling Rock his own damn self, when the house began to shiver. One windowpane broke, then a second. Then a third.

Not a mile away, at the edge of the forest, a boy tossing a flat football through a tire swing heard a great peal of thunder. A murder of crows flew south from the hemlocks and did not return until morning. They knew what one woman on the run had learned almost twenty years earlier: Once you fell into Lenora's woods, you didn't come out.

It was a warm Sunday night, late August, a lavender sunset yawning beyond the farmer's fields. And then, just as he popped the tab of his beer—

I've never seen smoke like that before, the farmer said. *Like God dragged a cigarette across the sky.*

No, other witnesses claimed. *It looked like a brush fire caught in the clouds.*

You're wrong, still others said. *The heavens tore in two.*

Some, closer to the point of impact, never saw it at all. Instead they heard an otherworldly groan, then felt the earth trembling beneath them. A stench like dead bodies rose from the dirt. Observers grasped for an explanation they'd already seen—an earthquake, perhaps. Another dynamite truck got lit. An old oil tank, living on borrowed time, had finally blown.

Every testimony was wrong, in part. The meteor whirled into view at sunset, shooting straight across the northern pocket of Appalachia toward a small, overlooked town called Lenora. It struck the earth thirty seconds after it appeared. A minute later, everyone in the river valley heard its roar.

No two recollections of the event are alike because facts never tell the whole story.

Can something be missing if it isn't lost? The answer is yes, because the thing that disappears will never tell you where it's gone.

Part I

The Last Night of the World

(1991)

Knowing what you would say
Ain't the same as hearing you say it
All this music you left with me
Ain't the same as hearing you play it

—"SING IT SLOW," THE *MERRY* ALBUM

Shut Out the Light

Ever since she was born, Marijohn Shaw could hear the dark sing to her.

It was an unusual truth, as darkness didn't have a voice. Yet she'd always loved the inky pitch of things like nightfall and dreamless sleep—the mystery of it, the privacy, the music. Eighteen years ago, she'd slipped into the world with a swirl of dark hair and even darker thoughts. Her earliest memory wasn't sight but sound—a crooning in the dimness, low and certain, like the whisper of a beloved ghost she'd known forever.

Marijohn was not someone who got frightened by things she couldn't see. The ghost was a comfort because its voice had always sounded like the words to her father's favorite song. They went like this—

There's three ways to fall in love with an outlaw
The first is quick and dirty
A flash of heat on a cold night

These were the lyrics to Elle Harlow's most famous ballad.

On the day the meteor struck, those words hounded the rusty loudspeaker outside Shaw's gas station along a forgotten stretch of highway in western Pennsylvania. The sound was an echo of the air that held it, hypnotic and hot. The music had that simple paradox Marijohn looked for in any song she loved—part savior, part sin.

She hung up the gas pump's nozzle for the last time that afternoon, the metal clicking like a gun. She'd just pumped a full tank into a Jeep Cherokee, bone white, the body propped up so regally on its monster tires that the undercarriage reached her hips. The musk of gasoline bit the skin around her eyes.

That scent, sultry and smoked, smelled just like home to her.

It was 1991—the year of Pearl Jam and Keanu Reeves, Desert Storm and apartheid—and Marijohn had no idea what was coming for her. She didn't realize how young she was, how guarded and bold and stallion-hearted. What she did know was that tonight was a night for last chances, and she was itching to take them.

She didn't think of herself as someone with courage. But her best friend Lazarus was leaving town in the morning—and she was hell-bent on confessing she was in love with him before he did.

Marijohn's father, Abe, watched her from his perch inside the station, mouthing along to the words of "Third Outlaw" just as he'd done every damn day that she could remember.

The second way is a slow smolder
Like a cigarette you can't quit
All glory, all pain

The song itself was an open wound. It didn't rhyme. The tune haunted any ear that heard it. By then, Elle Harlow had been missing for seventeen years, eight months, and thirteen days—almost longer than Marijohn had been alive. She knew how long Elle had been missing because her father kept track on a chalkboard behind the register. His tallies looked like the cigarettes Elle sang about, lined up but never once lit.

The Shaw family's blue-and-white gas station played little else but Elle Harlow songs, just shy of an hour from I-79 and buried in the hemlocks. They had only one pump, which customers weren't allowed to touch. They weren't self-service, and they weren't easy to find—unless you knew what you were looking for.

"You'd get more business if you changed that idiot sign," Mr. Jeep Cherokee observed.

He wasn't wrong. The whitewashed marquee planted in the dirt by the road boasted more than just gas. THE LAST PLACE ELLE HARLOW WAS SEEN, it hailed, the block letters placed as an act of worship by Abe's hands so long ago that the final letter tilted far right, as if it were running away.

Abe swore this station in the middle of nowhere was the last place Elle Harlow had been before she disappeared. Problem was, no one believed him.

Not even his daughter.

"I'll be damned," Marijohn replied. "Our mighty deliverer has come in a Jeep Cherokee."

The driver spat brown juice at her feet. "Your old man is a kook."

"There are worse things to be."

Marijohn was used to this: the drive-by, pitying dismissals of her and her father. Since 1973, Abe had sworn he was the final person to see Elle alive when she stopped to gas up her Studebaker. She was barefoot, so the story went. Abe begged Elle to sign the pump, and she never showed up for her set that night—or any night after.

The old gas pump still stood at the same station, supposed proof of Abe's story—except it wasn't. The route from Nashville to Sunset Park didn't go through Lenora, and Elle's signature didn't have her telltale heart for the double *l* in her name.

"That's one shitty copycat autograph if you ask me," the man said.

Marijohn ran her fingers across the cursive loops, their color slowly fading. The inscription next to Elle's autograph said:

Try to heal everything, and you'll heal nothing at all.

Mr. Jeep Cherokee caught her looking. "See what I mean?" he said.

She did.

The words proved that the "Elle" who fooled her father had been a fake.

"Heal Nothing" wasn't her song. Abe knew this. Marijohn knew this. Even Mr. Jeep Cherokee's wad of chew knew this. But Abe was the sort of person who could hold two conflicting truths without needing them to reconcile. The kind of person who cheered for the Pirates from the sovereignty of his couch, certain they'd still win the season opener when they were down by seven against the Expos in the bottom of the ninth.

They didn't.

Marijohn gawked at the man, who was gawking at her. The sign stood before them, sad and eternal, and she couldn't stop herself.

"Can I run something by you?" she asked.

Mr. Jeep Cherokee sniffed. Leaned his elbow out the window.

"I have a theory that this gas station marquee is the grim reaper," Marijohn said.

The man's elbow retreated inside his truck.

"Hear me out," Marijohn pressed. "It's not a grim reaper for people—but for time. Every few days I go up the ladder and change the price, because the cost of gas hasn't really gone up or down until the sign announces it. Everything else in the world can fall to shit, but you can count on gas prices fluttering for the rest of eternity, like the sign itself will still be breathing without a heartbeat, long after you and I are dead."

"Honey." The Cherokee's driver drew down the bill of his hat. "You've been sniffing too much gasoline."

He tossed a twenty out the window, not wanting to look her way as she twisted the gas cap back into place. He was uncomfortable—she could sense it in the way he forced the pads of his fingers into the meat of his forehead.

"It bothers you," she said softly. "Thinking about death."

The spray of blood vessels on the end of his nose twitched. He finally squinted at her, as if she were an eye chart he couldn't quite make out. "You must be real fun at parties."

Marijohn leaned for the squeegee to swipe the dead bugs off his windshield. "If I'm ever invited to one, I'll let you know."

He used the bill of his ball cap to wave her off. "You should be out, seizing the day and shit," he said. "Ain't you got dreams bigger than pumping gas?"

She had dreams, plenty. But she couldn't tell him what she really wanted was to find the source of that dark voice in her head.

He fumbled for the cigarette lighter below his dashboard just as Marijohn pinched his receipt between her fingers, far enough away that he'd have to look at her before snatching it.

"Been a real pleasure," she said, just as the scythe of Elle's voice sliced through the speakers.

"I hate this got-damn song," the driver called as he peeled out of the lot.

Marijohn bent, fetched the twenty, and tucked it into the back pocket of her Levi's. It was nearing five o'clock, and the sun held strong beyond the tree line, plump and round.

There was no breeze, still hot as hell, and Marijohn couldn't help it. She was excited for tonight. She prided herself on the thick candy coating that protected her velvet heart, but that summer it had started to crack.

Inside, Marijohn was a bubble bath. A melted bonbon. A baby bird.

She walked toward the marquee, to the mailbox by the road. The lid had buckled a year ago when a pickup knocked into it, so she had to use both hands to pry it open. Three months back, Marijohn had run here every day while waiting for college acceptance letters. She'd gotten two, to major in music—but no scholarships, and Abe couldn't afford for her to attend.

It's all right, she'd sworn when her father peeked into their bank account and despaired. He got a particular look about him when he was bereft, as if he were being forced backward by an imaginary wind, and it took all his strength to remain upright. He pinched his eyes shut and tucked his chin into his shoulder, and Marijohn couldn't stand it. She wanted to swallow that wind in her throat, will it to disappear.

I didn't want to go anyway, she'd said.

It was true, and it wasn't. Marijohn specialized in aching for the impossible. What she really wanted was to stop time itself, down to the second. To keep her favorite song from ending, to keep her father from aging, to keep Lazarus from leaving.

Marijohn hated that she always wanted so many things she knew she'd never get.

Now she fanned through the mail: bill, bill, grocery flyer, bill. And a tiny package from Kentucky, throned in packing tape, that made her excitement wilt.

"Shit," she said.

Elle Harlow's voice shot through the stillness as she walked back toward the station. Her voice scratched against the quiet—the words riding the eerie melody Elle strummed on her guitar.

To learn the third, she sang, *you'll have to wait.*

A bell chimed when the glass door swung open, and Marijohn stepped inside the cramped shop. It smelled like rubber and vinyl, and a little bit like the macaroni salad they'd brought for lunch.

Abe looked up.

"Depressing the customers again?" he asked.

Marijohn grinned.

She set the pile of mail on the counter, and Abe tore open the package.

"Look at this." He held up a rhinestone barrette. The gems were styled in the shape of a cat, its tail curling at the edge. "Came from that guy in Kentucky I talked to last week. It's got to be Elle's—it matches her first album cover. Don't you think?"

Abe looked at Marijohn with such unsullied faith, oil-slick and sunburned, with a graying five-o'clock shadow and a jaw that could chisel the face of a rock. The jewelry glittered in his palm, looking like fresh snow against the grime that had settled into the lines on his hands.

Abe closed his beloved repair shop on only three occasions per year: to attend church on Christmas Eve, to man the french fry vat at Lenora's annual "ox" roast that hadn't served ox since 1967, and to celebrate Marijohn's birthday on December 15. Her father was her first love and her favorite thing, tied up with fishing line and nostalgia.

He also got cheated, over and over.

"How much was this one?" Marijohn asked.

"Just forty-five."

She felt the loss of that money like a fist around her neck. "Next time," she said softly, "I'll take the call."

He was so fixed on the barrette she couldn't be certain that he'd heard.

Marijohn loved her father so much that it made her hate anyone who dared swindle him. As the self-appointed curator of the country's only Elle Harlow museum, situated next to his repair bay, her dad was a man who cared for hurting things, missing things, torn things—even when everyone called him a fool for it.

A few of his favorite relics—

A stray lyric—*Jaclyn, in her iris fields*—written on a bloodied linen napkin
A stuffed calico cat
A single turquoise earring
A tube of rose-pearl lipstick
A set of cowboy boots with golden toes

There was a reason no one was allowed to touch the pump out in the yard. It was the first item of Abe's to become an artifact after she had disappeared. He was known to pay just about any price for something that might have belonged to Elle Harlow.

The song resolved on a hollow note, and Abe—handsome and muscled and blue-collar down to his blood—looked up at her.

"Been meaning to say," he said.

Abe wasn't known for his speeches. He had a quiet way, most of his sentiments boiling down to two words—*love you*—which he used on all occasions: when she'd changed her first flat, when he'd forgotten to apply for financial aid, when Marijohn went to sleep every night. Those words meant everything: *I'm proud of you, I'm sorry, I'll see you in the morning.*

"Even though Laz is leaving tomorrow," he said, "it don't mean you ain't still you."

She looked away, taking the cold bottle of water her father had offered from the cooler and touching it to her forehead. The unruly wave of black hair on top of her head had been tamped down by sweat.

The record player in the corner skipped, and Abe rose from his seat to right it. He lifted the arm, the shush of the spinner filling the small space. When he set it down, "Shut Out the Light" began to play.

Marijohn turned the rhinestone clip over in her hand. It looked feeble and used. She pushed on the clasp and the metal bucked against her skin. Inside, a small golden sticker appeared with one word on it.

CLAIRE'S.

Her eyes flitted toward her father, who had his back to her as he eyed the pink-and-white pattern on Elle Harlow's first album cover that hung on the wall. Swiftly, she pushed her thumbnail against the sticker. It wouldn't budge. She dug again, but this time Abe saw her.

"What are you doing?" he asked kindly, always innocent of what she hid from him. He had such hope in her, such trust.

"Something's stuck. I almost—"

Abe freed it from her hand, squinted to inspect it. "Oh," he said as he saw the sticker. The music seemed to slow, and a tear of sweat lingered on Marijohn's back. "Oh."

She felt it—Abe had plummeted between those words. *Oh, oh.*

"It isn't real," he said.

He clutched the barrette for a moment before letting it clatter onto the counter. He looked at Marijohn as if he'd caught her in a falsehood like a fly in amber, which he had.

Abe ran a hand down his face. "That money could have gone toward tuition, couldn't it?" He cast a glance toward the record player for solace, as if it were a window. As if it were a wife. "Will you play for me?" he asked.

She nodded.

"You're real good, Marijohn—college degree or not. Good enough to play for other people," he said. "And not just your dad."

"I like playing for you."

She reached beneath the counter and took out a slim black case with a zipper. Her father might have loved his tiny artifacts, but here, in her hands, was what she treasured.

Her broken mandolin.

It was mortally old. The teardrop face of the instrument had splintered long before her time with it. When the bridge of "Shut Out the Light" hit the loudspeaker at the gas station, Marijohn started to play. The mandolin's rosewood sounded ghostly when played alongside Elle Harlow's old folk records, like it always should have been there.

The strings sank into her fingers as she played the progression:

G-D-Em-C

"Nobody plays it like you," Abe said. "Except for Elle."

The sound flew out the open door like a specter. Abe and Marijohn courted their own solitude, especially at the edge of the forest. Their house, not a half mile from the station, stitched a scant hem along the skirt of the woods.

When the song had finished, Abe's eyes were trained on his artifacts trapped in glass. He didn't blink, and he didn't look away.

"Marijohn," he said, her name like an idling engine. "How many."

She knew what he was asking. He was asking her to break his heart.

"Dad," she said, slipping the mandolin back into its case. "Come on."

"How many of these are fake?" He scanned each relic as if it had betrayed him. "And you knew?"

"What does it matter, Dad, whether it's hers?" Marijohn's elbow smacked the counter as she tried to cross her arms. "It's just old junk someone threw away."

"Marijohn." Abe's voice went quiet. He never raised it at her, even now. "You know it's so much more than that."

Marijohn couldn't answer, not when he was looking at her like that insidious wind had returned, and it took everything he had to withstand it. Abe loved Elle Harlow's music not just because she was a once-in-a-lifetime talent. It was because her music had granted Abe a family when he had none.

This was why every time Abe pulled out a thick cloth to shine the pump, Marijohn would ask him to let her put her hands on it. Let him believe that she believed his story of Elle, too. When she was a child he'd pick her up and hold her close to his chest, even when she was old enough to reach. Marijohn treasured the tender nearness of that motion even after she'd grown, the citrus scent of upholstery cleaner that hung on to his flannel. She'd stretch out her palms and run her fingers over the hills and valleys of Elle's fake signature.

She did it because she'd always known what her father couldn't bring himself to accept. What would crush him if he ever reckoned with the truth.

Elle Harlow was dead.

Abe called the gas pump his first artifact, but that wasn't exactly true.

The woman who stopped for gas that day was searching for something, Abe had said. *She just didn't know what it was.*

December 15 was the best day of his life, he claimed—and not because he met a faux Elle Harlow. It was because that day, he met his daughter.

The only real thing the imposter left behind was Marijohn herself, tucked into the dark while "Third Outlaw" played on the radio. When Abe had run inside to find a permanent marker for her autograph, this woman left an infant in a wicker trunk on the far side of the pump beneath a giant Christmas wreath. Abe was too enthralled by the prospect of Elle's signature to notice the trunk when he returned.

The woman was long gone by the time Abe heard the baby cry.

Namesake

One hour before the meteor struck, Lazarus Wright skidded his dusty blue Chevy to a stop in the parched earth of Marijohn's yard and let the truck idle as he climbed out.

"Marijohn!" he called.

The glare of early-evening sun poured through the living room's picture window. When she spotted him through it, she pressed a flat palm to the pane.

Give me five minutes.

She didn't need five minutes. Marijohn had already cleaned the gas station grit from her hands, crammed a scalding microwave pizza into her mouth, found a rubber band for her long black hair in the tangle of twist-ties and paper clips she and her father kept in a junk drawer. She'd also peed about a dozen times—and practiced what she was going to say. Then practiced it again.

Lazarus.

I know this is terrible timing, and unfair, and selfish. But I've loved you for a very long time.

I've never not loved you.

The speech was set. What Marijohn hadn't done was plan enough time to panic about it.

Her palms itched as she sank down against the floor beneath the window. She and Laz had been honest with each other in every single way—sharing their first-draft song lyrics, their college rejection letters, even their weird ideas about death—every way except for this. Sparkles of dust skated through the air in the sunlight, and Marijohn knew she had monumental things in her heart. She didn't care if she pumped gas every day for the rest of her life. What she wanted was to be able to risk herself for someone, because of someone.

Marijohn wanted someone to sing for.

It was a quarter past six when she finally stepped out of the yellow house she and Abe lived in, with moss-green shutters and forget-me-nots draping the windowsills. The stones she'd painted as a girl still lined the walkway in innocent colors like seafoam and poppy and cerulean.

You're grown now, Marijohn tried to convince herself as she looked at every evolution of bicycle she'd ridden stacked against the far side of the house. A tricycle, a Huffy, a white ten-speed with a friendship bracelet woven around the spokes.

Her mandolin clung to her back.

In his Chevy, Lazarus was sweating in the late-day heat. His wire-rimmed reading glasses slid down the edge of his nose as he examined the accounting textbook he'd kept in his car all summer, half of it rolled up like newspaper. A wave of golden hair fell into his eyes, and he combed it back with a wide hand that also held a mechanical pencil.

Lord, he was handsome. Laz had that devastating hint of next-door godliness, both approachable and unattainable. He was blond, bronzed, brawny—and he remained perfectly unaware of it, no matter how many shiny-eyed young women packed into Reverend Wright's pews to ogle him each week. The beauty looked easy on him, someone so cuttingly handsome yet still human enough to sweat just like everyone else.

Watching him toss the textbook onto the dashboard, Marijohn felt pale, but she didn't flush or blush or sigh, or any of those other things young women do in storybooks. Even as her world tipped, she'd learned how to steady herself.

What she wanted now was to tip it back.

When he saw her, Laz tucked his reading glasses into the sun visor. Marijohn walked to his truck's passenger side and eased her mandolin through the open window as if this wouldn't be the last night she rode in his Chevy for a very long time.

"Hey, Marijohn," Laz said.

She lingered in the way he'd said her name, the way it fit like a favorite shirt. Most people who had known her since childhood still mispronounced it.

She used to correct the mistake—*MARE-ih-john*, she'd say, *not Mar-EE-JOHN*—until she realized it didn't matter. All her life, she'd been misspelled and mistaken for a lot of things she'd never been. It had made her tougher and wiser. She had swelled inside the reality of being misunderstood. She'd risen to its call.

Laz gently wedged the mandolin against the stick shift. Between them on the bench seat sat a Sony Handycam. Its gold lettering glimmered against a sheen of black.

"What's that for?" she asked.

"It's a surprise." He pointed toward the road at the end of her driveway. "Let's head to the woods."

The woods were a place no one went alone. Lenora natives swore there were sinkholes there that would swallow a steamroller. The nearby farmer insisted he'd lost a cow or two. For Lazarus and Marijohn, it was the perfect place to make music: eerie, abandoned, alive.

They'd dreamed themselves as a duo, just like Emmylou and Gram. June and Johnny. Stevie and Lindsey. They weren't going for popular—they were going for immortal. Music that lasted beyond its generation always had a nick of torture in it, Lazarus said.

The two of them had tried to write a song together that summer. It began like this:

Your shadow stuck around / Long after you left home
Pictures on a lonesome wall / Are all but buried bones

The hook was as far as they got, because they couldn't agree. Marijohn wanted to write a murder ballad like "Long Black Veil." Lazarus heard it as a love song. All he wrote were love songs. Each slap of a basketball hitting pavement was a love song. His mother working in her summer garden was a love song. Even Marijohn could have been a love song then.

Lazarus wrote like he was dreaming. Marijohn wrote like she couldn't fall asleep. They agreed on only one thing: The best songs were always the ones that hurt.

So they fought, and bickered, and dug their heels in, and never finished what they'd started. Now summer was ending, and Lazarus was about to leave home—headed to a small college forty-five minutes to the north, which to Marijohn might as well have been a separate galaxy.

He looked at her and opened his mouth—then his eyes shifted toward the road, coasting like a hawk hunting for a place to land.

"One last night," he said. Like a firing squad, his fingers tapped rapidly against the wheel.

"One last night."

Not a bad song title, she thought.

Laz was antsy. His knee bobbed as he turned the ignition, and a piano rendition of "Be Thou My Vision" flooded the cab. The melody was wavering and melancholy. He reached for the cassette button and turned it off.

"My dad's been driving the truck," he said.

"And here I thought this was your favorite song."

When he didn't laugh, she asked, "Is that your mom playing on the tape?"

Laz nodded. His fingers finally rested on the wheel. "My dad said he fell in love with her the first time she played the piano at church. Did I ever tell you that?"

Marijohn shook her head. "That's romantic," she said, then wished she hadn't.

Lazarus sighed loudly, as if Reverend Wright were riding shotgun and had just turned up the volume. "I swear to God if you cut me open, you'll see hymns tattooed all over my insides. I just want—"

"Something of your own," Marijohn supplied.

"Yeah, I do."

He seemed tired and defeated. As if his whole life were a hymn already written.

She eyed the textbook on the dash. "And you plan to create something of your own as an accountant?"

His cheeks looked a little more sunken into his jaw than they had the day before. "Numbers can be creative."

She looked skeptical.

"Maybe it's not the most exciting thing." He'd worn a shirt with the sleeves cut off, and he fiddled with an unraveled thread as he leaned back in his seat. "It's still an important job."

"*Super* essential." Marijohn kept trying to prod the dregs of honesty out of her friend, and it wore away at him.

"Super essential," he repeated, yanking the thread free. "Like a gas station attendant."

The words took a slash at her. In the distance, a calf let out a longing moan.

Laz's mouth dropped open.

"Marijohn," he said. The firelight in his eyes flickered. "I didn't mean it."

"Yes." She backed away from the truck. "You did."

The evening already wasn't going how she wanted it to. She wanted to flee for the porch. For the attic. For her bedroom.

"Please." His whole face pleaded with the word. "Let's not fight tonight. Not when I have to leave tomorrow."

Marijohn looked back toward the house, and then the gas station beyond it. She couldn't hear it, but she knew her father was probably listening to "That Don't Mean You Ain't Lived" for the third time in a row. And here Laz was, trying to actually live, and he was afraid.

Which meant he needed her not to be.

So Marijohn tilted her chin toward the sun and gathered her hair into a high ponytail before tying it back with the band at her wrist. She drifted back to Laz's Chevy and let herself in. They didn't speak as he pulled out onto the main road.

Laz was a force, his voice a covenant of tempered and gripping heat any time he sang. But he was timid in his own skin—and he'd remain timid until he had reason enough to be brave.

Lazarus was Marijohn's best friend. Her only friend, truly. She didn't attend parties, didn't speak up in class, didn't feel the need to cut silence with small talk. She liked old country records and busted-up paperbacks and owning a single pair of good Levi's, just like her dad.

She and Laz met one summer right on the edge of the woods by the ravine. It was June, the air smooth and sweet, and Marijohn had gone for a long walk by herself in the dark. She cherished that feeling of solitude, of letting the landscape of the dark cloak her, the whisper of the water and the sigh of the owls and the stars thrown across the sky.

But that night, she wasn't alone.

She'd almost tripped on Lazarus, who was lying flat on his back in the grass, his eyes trained on the jagged black oak branches above him.

"What are you doing here?" Marijohn asked, firm in her belief that these woods belonged only to her.

Back then she'd known Laz as the young point guard with a wicked three-point shot, the preacher's son who was unfailingly polite. He seemed like a communion wafer—flat, perfunctory, flavorless. Marijohn didn't think it would take much to scare him away until he spoke.

"Oh, you know," he answered. "Just thinking about death."

"Death?"

What an unexpected and delightful answer.

"I'm a preacher's kid." Laz stretched his arms behind his head. The bubble of his biceps peeked out from behind his ear. "It comes up a lot."

"Funny," Marijohn mused. "It comes up at the gas station, too."

Lazarus tilted his pretty head toward her. She took a step closer, her foot dangerously close to his thigh. Quietly, he looked back at the hollow sky.

"Heaven and hell are things to believe in," he said. "But death is a certainty. Death just *is*."

After years of trying—halfheartedly—to relate to classmates who collected miniature trolls with hot-pink hair and concealing her addiction to anything related to *Sweet Valley High*, this was a conversation Marijohn could sink her talons into. She sat down beside him, the grass curling around her ankles.

"Did you ever wonder if when you die the first thing you'll see is a collection of every plastic container you've ever used, and you're left to sit with what it means to have left behind so much emptiness, and yet so much trash?" she asked.

Lazarus sat up. Dirt had gotten caught in the lifeline on his palm. "Or what if you're forced to read through a binder of every bad thing ever said about you behind your back? Maybe the binder's there in an empty chair beside you, and every day you're fighting with yourself over whether to read it or not."

Marijohn considered it. "What if it's a binder of mean things you've said about other people?"

A delicate line formed between his eyebrows. "How many mean things have you said?"

"Enough that I don't want to read a book about it."

Laz grinned, devilish. "I'm sorry, but that would be your only reading material." He paused. "And the air smells like your favorite food, but you can't ever figure out where the smell is coming from."

"Let me guess." She thought on it. "Pork chops?"

A wave of disgust hit his face. "Have you ever seen the way a pig races for an Oreo at the county fair? Those things have *feelings*. Hell no."

"Oreos, then? That's your favorite?"

"Guilty."

Marijohn frowned. "That's a fairly prepackaged smell to follow you into the afterlife."

"It's better than concession-stand nachos. That's your meal of choice, right?"

She looked behind her, as if someone had leaked her dirty secret. "How could you know that?"

"Because I've seen you stuffing your face with them before football games, all by yourself at the fence."

Marijohn reddened. She'd been found out—and somehow being seen didn't feel as fatal as she thought it would.

"So if you're here, rhapsodizing about death, what do you need that for?" She pointed toward his guitar case, flipped open with a Gibson gleaming inside.

"That"—he grinned—"is to piss off my dad."

"He wishes you had a Martin?" she joked.

"He wishes I played the organ."

She laughed, but he was serious.

Marijohn had seen Lazarus at church on her annual Christmas visit, dressed like Presbyterian royalty in a crisp denim button-down and pressed Dockers, his hair slicked to the side. He held the door for every widow, lit the Advent candles with the single swoop of a match, turned the pages of his mother's sheet music as if that sanctuary were the only place he belonged.

And yet he'd felt stifled the whole time.

"You're not how I thought you'd be," Marijohn said.

"People rarely are." He took two Jolly Ranchers out of his pocket and offered one to her. "Like you."

"Oh?"

The crinkle of plastic shocked the wooded quiet as he popped the candy in his mouth. "I'm guessing there's more to you than that day you melted all those dolls' eyeballs in metal shop."

Marijohn's lime-colored candy glimmered in her grip. "I didn't know the blowtorch would fuse the whole thing to the table," she said. "It was *really* hard to get off."

She'd had to borrow her father's putty knife to pry free the molten mound of eyes. Then Abe had placed the monstrosity as a centerpiece on their dining room table.

"But you're right," Marijohn said. "There's more to me than that." She tucked the Jolly Rancher into her pocket and kept her hand there. "I play, too. The mandolin."

His grin was a wide and glorious thing. "Do you write?" he asked.

Marijohn squeezed the candy. She'd never admitted it before—not even to her dad.

"I try," she said.

"If you ever want to play together," Laz said as he reached for his guitar, "this is where you'll find me."

That moment had been the start of their long duet.

On warm nights for three summers now, Laz drove them to the western reaches of the forest, his guitar in tow and a heap of Jolly Ranchers in the cup holder—watermelon for him, green apple for her. There, they played songs together in the bed of his Chevrolet. He reversed his pickup to the edge of a cliff covered with white pines and black oaks, and they played their instruments beneath a sky full of stars.

She still had that first Jolly Rancher he'd given her stowed away in her jewelry box.

In the woods, Marijohn and Laz played their own music; they played the music of the greats. Bonnie, Joni, Dolly. Linda. They played anything that wasn't Elle Harlow. It wasn't that Marijohn didn't love Elle's songs, but that her father loved them too much. Elle was the third member of the Shaw family—silent observer of weeknight freezer meals and Lake Erie day trips and their annual holiday screening of *Ernest Saves Christmas*—but it wasn't even Elle who lived with them. It was the idea of her, the ghost, the legend, the illusion, when what Marijohn truly needed was a real, palpable mother. One who had bad days, and a wealth of outdated but covertly useful advice, and a cupboard full of oil-stained recipes, and a signature laugh, and a closet of high-waisted jeans, not to mention her own favorite songs to share with her daughter.

For a long time now Marijohn had wished Elle's body would be found, if only so her father would finally lay it to rest.

She'd imagined the facts of Elle's death a thousand different ways. That she'd died in the back seat of her car like Hank Williams. Gasping for breath like Jimmie Rodgers. In a small plane crash like Patsy Cline. Maybe she'd left behind a lover who soon followed, the way June Carter Cash had.

Never a simple death did Marijohn imagine for Elle, because she had never lived a simple life. This was why Abe loved her. Lonely and forlorn, Abe was a folk ballad in the flesh. He'd lost both his parents when he was young. Since the day he found his daughter, Abe had never married.

Didn't even date. Instead, he abandoned himself by tending to lost things in case their owner ever returned.

And he did it all because he believed in his bones that Elle Harlow was Marijohn's mother.

Marijohn had never been able to make herself believe it, too.

She had no memory of this woman, whoever she was. She hadn't left Marijohn completely alone in that wicker basket, though. The broken mandolin had been tucked beside her, along with a note.

Call her Marijohn, it read.

One of her tiny arms clutched a bottle, Abe said, and the other little fist had grabbed a tuning knob. She wouldn't let it go. Now, the mandolin bore her marks, too. Her sweat on its neck, her skin on its frets.

This not-quite memory formed the words to the first song Marijohn ever wrote—

My mama gave me my name / I guess you could say
She left, and left me a better namesake
Words better than a gun / I ain't never shot one
But I am a song and I'll pull that trigger
Till I'm done

That note had left behind a hole. Marijohn felt it grow every time she read about Elizabeth and Jessica Wakefield's mom in Sweet Valley, every time she clipped her father's gas station nozzle into place, every time she changed a string on her mandolin.

Call her Marijohn.

She was worthy of three words only—*call her Marijohn*—and nothing else.

Her own mother hadn't wanted her—and it was this, more than anything, that she'd built her sense of self upon.

Laz pulled off into a patch of dirt by the guardrail of a sharp elbow turn in the road, right up against a farmer's meadow that led to the woods. Paula Abdul's "Rush, Rush" played on the radio, and Lazarus turned it up.

"I love this song," Marijohn said.

Laz pressed on the brake. "The violin part gets me every time."

"Me, too."

Cows lowed in the distance as sunlight feasted on the early-evening sky.

After Lazarus backed up his truck to the edge of the ravine, they climbed into the bed and lay with their heads at the tailgate. The coming sunset looked like its own solar system—swirls of lilac and gold, and a distant, cosmic rust. Sitting at the brink of the hemlocks had always felt like teetering on the edge of an unseen world. It reminded Marijohn of why she loved to sing.

It gave things back to her that she thought she had lost.

Laz reached for his Gibson and played a ballad in G for her. She felt the notes course through every part of her body. Folks in Lenora thought Laz's hands were made for dribbling a basketball, but it wasn't true. His hands traveled the strings at gentle speed, every melody like a wave lapping a shoreline. Marijohn ran her fingers along the neck of her mandolin.

"What's the camcorder for?" she asked.

Laz's skin was tan and silken in the dusk. "I thought we could record your song," he said. "And I'll make two copies of it. One for you, and one for me."

It was such a thoughtful, kind gesture that it sent a savage disappointment straight through her. The two of them were about to become a thing to remember, just like Elle and all her relics.

"What's wrong?" he asked.

"Lazarus," she began. "I know this—" Marijohn couldn't get the words out, no matter how many times she'd practiced them. "I just wish I were a braver person."

A single dimple appeared on his cheek. "This, from the girl who puts bowls over spiders in the house until her dad comes home."

"That was *one* time." She hit him in the shoulder.

"You think you aren't brave because you're not going to college?" Laz's fingers slowly thrummed against the strings of his guitar.

"No." College was the furthest thing from her mind. "It's because I have trouble telling the truth."

"Marijohn." He stopped his guitar flat. "You're the bravest person I've ever met."

"Me?" She laughed. "I've never done anything that matters to anyone."

"That isn't true." He gripped the waist of his guitar. "You matter to me."

But you're leaving, she couldn't get herself to say. *And you might never come back.*

Laz pushed his thumb against the Gibson's bridge. "You've also written a song."

"I can't find the nerve to sing in front of anybody else but you."

"That doesn't matter," he answered. "You're brave when it counts. When you think no one sees."

His brown eyes looked wild and skittish, as if it hurt to let such a confession go. He wasn't someone who much valued his own feelings outside of the songs he wrote. He found safety in stockading them between chords like a prince in an impenetrable tower.

"What have I done that's so brave?" she asked.

He didn't even have to think about it. "You stand by your dad, no matter what anyone says."

Abe got called a rube, a sap, an easy mark—often behind his back, but loud enough for Marijohn to hear. She'd developed her own razor-sharp tongue to defend him.

"He's easy to stand by," she said.

"But you let him be who he is, folk fantasies and all," Laz said. "Most people have a love that comes with conditions."

Laz had a kinder estimation of her than Marijohn had for herself. "What if I've had to lie to him to do it?" she asked.

"What do you mean?"

"He found out today," she said, "that some of the relics in his shop aren't real."

Laz slid his guitar pick beneath the strings. "Maybe it's time. You can't do that forever, Marijohn. He wouldn't want you to."

"It feels like—" She paused, caught in something, unable to name it.

"Like he saw the real you," Lazarus said. "Not the one you wish you could be for him."

Laz knew. He always did.

"My father's never felt like he was enough for me, and I've never told him that he is." This was Marijohn's original sin: She loved her father yet still felt that something was missing from their life together, the very one she feared was going to change. "That's the opposite of courage, if you ask me."

Laz watched her, his eyes following the outlines of her cheek. "I think courage never feels like courage in the moment."

Lazarus somehow understood lots of things that Marijohn didn't. She felt safe in his orbit, deep in their woods, even as they stood on tender and haunted ground.

"Let's record your song," he said.

Suddenly, she was terrified.

"No," she said. "It isn't any good."

They both jolted when Lazarus clamped a hand around her wrist. He wasn't one to grab; she wasn't one to let him. And yet the moment held. He pressed his fingers into her pulse, as if her arm were the fretboard of his guitar.

"Marijohn," he said. "I want to take a piece of you with me."

He felt it, too, this painful severing between them. It struck Marijohn then that perhaps she'd never needed words at all. Maybe all she needed was a last chance.

This was her moment, and she took it. She leaned toward Lazarus and closed her eyes. Her lips found his. They were supple, open, awake. Divine. She was sinking into him with all she had, her heart this pure and tender harmony, right there in the back of his truck.

And then Lazarus stiffened.

"Marijohn." He pulled away. Laz wiped his mouth with the back of his hand and looked at the sheen on his skin—part of her, part of him. "What are you doing?"

Marijohn held strong. "What's the point of putting everything into a song if you never let yourself feel it, Laz?"

He sat his guitar down on the truck bed, and the strings cried out.

"You know I have to leave tomorrow, right?" His voice was abrupt and flat, but his eyes cut through her. The ardor there, the need.

"Yes," she whispered.

"I don't want to be somebody who leaves you, Marijohn." He picked up his guitar again and clutched it to his chest. "I don't want to repeat what your mother did."

He wasn't wrong. What he'd said was brutal and true, and it crushed her.

People in Lenora had always assumed Marijohn was in love with Lazarus, even if they didn't know the truth of it. Marijohn loved that he never flaunted his strength. She loved that he always took the long way home. And she loved that he spent his summer nights sneaking beneath her window, spiriting her away to the woods. They'd always known it couldn't last forever.

"I have to leave, Marijohn," he said softly. "And I think you should, too."

"You know I can't," she answered, part truth, part lie. "My father won't survive it."

She watched him as he stared at the curve just beneath her neck, his eyes dark and hungry. He was accustomed to denying himself, feeding off the echoes of gymnasium crowds and his favorite songs on the radio. A pendant dangled from a chain nestled on Marijohn's chest: a golden replica of Elle Harlow's signature. Abe had given it to her. The double *l* in the pendant took on the shape of a heart, listing to the left as if it were trying to listen for her pulse. Laz saw it so often that he must have found its imprint on the backs of his eyelids before he fell asleep at night.

That was the consummate and quiet way he loved her—no difference between the waking and the dream.

Could Lazarus fear Marijohn's way of loving would hollow him out, just as it had with her father? She couldn't help but see the likeness between them. She and Abe were both incendiary with want. Abe wanted the past to return. He wanted a fable to turn into truth. Marijohn wanted a mother. And she also wanted things from Lazarus—his fingers on her fretboard, his songs in her throat. She wanted the way he said her name, like it was the first word he'd ever learned. It gave her a mirror image of power in a world where she had none. So to ask if she loved Lazarus was to ask if she could trust herself.

To that, she had no answer.

There was nothing else to say. The trees praised a sky bright with stars. The white pines parted ways, just for them. Marijohn spread Lazarus's spare sweatshirt across her body. Laz was as close as he always had been, but now he felt so near that she wanted to hide.

"It's going to rain," he said. "These rocks we're sitting on will be down in the river tomorrow."

He jumped off the tailgate and set up the camcorder on a tripod on the ground. For the recording, they sat back-to-back just like they always did. But this time Lazarus was the only one who sang "Namesake." Marijohn was cut too deep. Afraid of always wanting too much and never getting any of it. When she opened her mouth, nothing came out.

"Sing for me," he said.

"I can't." Even though she wished she could.

After a moment, Laz nodded.

Marijohn let her broken mandolin sing for her instead. It sounded like a fairy in the dusk—a tone high enough to travel down pikes and swim through trees. To her it was a woodland sound, golden birdsong, the chirr of creek water in the half-light.

Lazarus began:

My mama gave me a name / I guess you could say

The recording kept on, as if it were the reason Marijohn and Lazarus would remember this night for the rest of their lives, no matter what had happened before it.

It wasn't.

Just after sunset, an extravagant ray of light shot through the night sky. It was so searing Marijohn had to shield her eyes. She heard a rush of wind around her, leaves and sticks and stones whipping into the air. The Chevy started to shake.

"What is that?" Marijohn asked, the tremor so volatile that she bit her tongue.

"Wait here," Lazarus said as he leapt out of the truck.

When he staggered toward the clearing, the sky caught fire. The clouds rippled, and a starry stone headed straight for them. The night turned from gray-blue to purple to marigold. It was bright as day by the time Laz ran to the tailgate and covered Marijohn's body with his.

"Marijohn!" he screamed, just as the earth began to quake.

This was it—the moment he would be brave. But it was barely a moment, so fast had he run to her. The meteor arced just beyond the fields, tore into the woods, and slashed the ravine behind the truck. In the distance, a cow shrieked. Around them, trees fell to their knees. Laz didn't look to his left or right. He tightened his hold on her and didn't let go.

Marijohn had always been more than just a friend to Laz; she was a home. No matter what else happened, there would always be this—when Lazarus thought the world was ending, what he reached for was her.

Take Me to the River

Marijohn never saw the meteor. She felt it punch the earth while pressing her face into the stack of blankets Lazarus kept in the bed of his truck. The Chevy's wheels shuddered. Then the guardrail by the road's elbow turn spiked into the air and the metal screeched. Tree roots hung from it like anemic teeth. The woods Marijohn had known all her life twisted around her in the wind. The brilliance that had lit the sky seconds ago darkened into a track of white smoke, splitting the clouds.

Her bottom lip had begun to bleed, and her head throbbed. *Steady,* she said to herself. *Steady*. She heard a voice nearby, but she couldn't make out the words. When she opened her eyes, Marijohn saw only a haze, and a shadow eclipsing the most radiant light she'd ever seen.

Of course it was Lazarus, still shielding her body with his. His breath sank warm and heavy into her skin.

"Marijohn," he said, over and over. "Marijohn."

"I'm all right," she finally answered. "I'm all right."

In the ravine, a tree cracked. Branches fell. Then Lazarus lifted himself off her like gravity had shifted and he was floating away. Marijohn flinched in the cool air and tasted blood on her tongue.

"Lazarus," she said. "What the hell happened?"

"I don't know." He reached out a hand to help her sit up. His knuckles had been rubbed raw.

Marijohn still couldn't see much, except for a field of yellow rocket at the edge of the cliff. The blossoms were like a sea of fireflies in twilight. Marijohn looked at Lazarus's palm in her own.

It was then that Laz remembered himself. He dropped her hand.

"Oh no," he said. "The camera."

The camcorder had toppled into the dirt, its red recording button still lit.

Laz hopped from the truck to retrieve it, and Marijohn knew she was about to be sick. On hands and knees, she crawled to the side of the Chevy. Then she vomited into the dirt while Lazarus flipped out the camcorder's viewer lens, rewound the tape, and pressed Play.

One minute passed. Then another. Laz's milky voice filled the stunned woods. The guitar and the mandolin had never sounded lovelier—the mandolin shimmered when the guitar moaned. Together, they ebbed and flowed—four hands, but one body. One heart.

Then the wind hit the video, violent as an ocean wave.

"Marijohn," Laz whispered. "We caught it."

"Caught what?" she asked, wiping her mouth on the hem of her shirt.

"That thing in the sky," he said, squinting at the tiny lens. "I think it was a meteor."

"Bullshit," she said, taking the camera.

Then she held proof of it in her hands—not just the meteor, but everything that happened before it. She rewound the film and watched the spear of light spiral in reverse, soaring straight away from them. She saw Lazarus's face in the easy dusk, her lyrics in his mouth. The shattered look she gave him while he sang, jagged with longing. His blurred hand as he pressed Record, and the screen went black.

She closed the viewing lens and handed the camera back to Lazarus. Marijohn didn't want to watch it. She only saw one devastation on the tape, only one once-in-a-lifetime, and it wasn't a falling star.

Together, she and Laz stood at the lip of the ravine and stared into the chaos of downed limbs, rushing water, and earth.

"Lazarus," Marijohn said, "it's down there. The meteor."

The air was eerily silent. It had started to smell like a tire had burned.

"It'll be gone soon," she said. "Sunk beyond anyone's reach."

He turned to her, sudden panic strewn across his face. "No." His voice was dry. "We're not going down there."

"I definitely am."

"You just puked off the side of my truck," he said.

"I'm the bravest person you've ever met, right?" she asked. "You said that."

He gently took her wrist. "I didn't mean it like this."

"Isn't there any part of you that wants to be the bravest person you know, even for just a minute?"

They were talking about the meteor, and they weren't.

"You know that's not fair," he said.

"It's the oldest thing you're ever going to see, Lazarus. The oldest thing you'll ever touch."

He watched her, and she could hear the sad melody in her voice, the wistful plea of it. She sounded like her father.

"Are you coming or not?" she said.

Marijohn could have been the kind of girl who believed she didn't get to play hero. Didn't get quests of her own. Every country music murder ballad she'd ever heard had promised that girls turned into women by blood, by a broken heart, or by betrayal. But Abe—lonesome as he was—wasn't the kind of father who let his daughter believe folktales like that.

He'd told her stories of Dolly Parton and Sara Carter and Elle Harlow instead.

"You're gonna be the death of me," Lazarus said.

He went to the truck bed and fetched the stack of thin blankets. Then he knotted them together to form a makeshift rope. "Here," he said, handing her an end. "Tie this around your waist."

He took the other end and secured it to the hitch below the tailgate. "If you're trying to prove that you're brave, there are better ways."

She shot him a side-eye. "You said I was already brave."

His cheeks went pink, his only tell that he was getting mad. "Is this brave?" he asked. "Or stupid?"

"I'll be careful," she said. "I promise."

Marijohn headed over the edge of the ravine. The sound of trickling water led her deeper, toward the spine of the woods. The slope was slick, muddy, steep. She had to slide down the roughest patches, the blanket rope tugging at her waist. The meteor's vestiges lay everywhere she looked—split rocks, overturned earth, the black water below a magnetic swirl of pine needles and blighted leaves.

"Your sandals," Lazarus called from the ledge. "They won't protect your feet."

"From what?"

"From whatever toxic shit is in the swamp."

She hooked her chin over her shoulder and smirked. "Like that time you were convinced you had toe cancer?"

He pointed a finger at her. "Someday somebody is actually going to get that, and you're going to feel *really* bad about it."

"Laz," she chided. "I'm fine."

But as soon as she said it, she stumbled against a fallen tree root at the bottom of the cliff and her foot got stuck. Mud—warmer than it had any right to be—seeped between her toes. The river hummed a few feet away, and she felt the ground beneath her leaning into it, as if being drawn by a tide. Silt had formed into stiff ridges at the water's edge. Then suddenly, the river's humming stopped.

Marijohn crouched, Laz's tether tight in her grip. For just a moment, the water was achingly still. Then it began to gurgle. It coughed and spat like someone choking on a chicken bone.

"What was that?" Lazarus called, but Marijohn didn't answer.

It was too late. The meteor was already drowning down the river's throat.

She knew enough to be light-footed and quick. Sinkholes beneath the water could swallow her, too, fast as a steamroller. A sewer of decay slowly sputtered up from the water, thrust toward the surface as the meteor sank down. Glass, rusted metal, parched white matchsticks that looked to be the bones of a squirrel. A sparrow called out overhead as Marijohn dug into the mud to free her sandal.

That was when she saw it.

A small piece of plastic nested in a puddle, with a pink-and-white gingham pattern and a heart drawn right in the middle.

She'd never witnessed anything like this before—the forest, finally sated from swallowing things, had begun to vomit them out. She bent to inspect the plastic. At first it looked like a lovelorn emblem someone would hope to find if they ever returned.

That wasn't quite it.

Marijohn had seen this gingham pattern every day of her life on the cover of her father's second-favorite record album—Elle's first, *School Girl Crush*. The checkered snippet also matched the gold necklace resting at her throat. Elle Harlow's trademark double *l* in her signature mirrored the shape of the gingham heart. It came from a 1970 model of her signed custom guitar.

Only one had been made.

"Holy shit," she said.

"Did you find it?" Lazarus called.

"The meteor's gone," she yelled back. "The river took it down."

She clutched the piece of plastic to her chest as a crow cried out from the trees. The day was still warm, but she felt a chill rising from the water. It was true that though the guitar had belonged to Elle, it didn't mean that she'd fallen down the ravine in these woods almost eighteen years ago.

But maybe she had.

Lazarus drove back to Marijohn's house at careful speed, windows down and glasses on, tales of wreckage all around them. Downed telephone poles lay next to a fat, furious slash through the farmer's fields, as if the poles themselves had threshed the grain and then lay down and died. Belligerent cows held court right in the roadway. Radio static played, and neither Marijohn nor Laz reached to turn it off.

The camcorder sat between her and Lazarus, a dented rectangle. Marijohn's mandolin was nestled at her feet. She clutched the piece of plastic gingham so tightly that it bit into her skin.

"Marijohn," Lazarus began, his eyes trained on the roadway covered in saplings and debris. "Are you all right?"

She turned toward him. His profile was hewn into the auburn sunset beyond his window. "What do you mean?"

His eyes shot to the plastic shard, the hand that held it. "You're shaking."

She'd been waiting so long for some gentle way to help her father see the truth about Elle Harlow. Only now could she see that it was she who was afraid of it.

"What if the myth isn't a myth?" she asked.

"Marijohn, that plastic could be from anything."

She knew it wasn't. "But what if?"

"It would prove Abe's story," Laz allowed. His right hand left the wheel and rested on the stick shift.

"And it would prove that Elle Harlow is probably dead."

Laz finally turned the radio static off. "You already thought she was dead."

"I thought *Elle Harlow* was dead," she corrected him. She wanted so badly to be understood, even if she couldn't fully understand herself. "Not my—not my mother."

Marijohn felt ridiculous saying the word. Needing it.

"She might not be your mother," Laz said gently, as if she were at risk of waking from a dream.

He was being too careful with her. She felt the wound and the weight of not being believed—that same hurt her father must always have felt.

"Just say what you mean."

Laz slowed to veer around a chunk of asphalt.

"*Say it.*"

"This is why you won't leave town." Laz's hand pushed the gearshift. "It's not because of money, or your dad. It's because deep down, you've always believed the story."

"And you never have?" It was a silly question. No one did.

"It doesn't matter what I believe."

"It does to me, Laz."

In that moment it was the only thing that mattered.

"Laz," she said.

He looked straight ahead and didn't equivocate. "I think you need to guard your heart. Otherwise this folktale will swallow you."

"*Guard* my heart?"

It was a proverb Reverend Wright had offered countless times from the pulpit, but Marijohn had never needed to be preached at. There had been no one more guarded than her, more vigilant, more steadfast—until tonight.

She was never reckless or thoughtless. All she had done was find her honesty and give it a voice.

A stilted laugh escaped her mouth. "This is because I kissed you. Because I broke one of your invisible, suffocating rules that you think will get you out of here. This is because I showed you that I have a beating heart." Her eyes dug into his. "And you liked it."

Laz took a swift left turn into Marijohn's driveway, and the neck of her mandolin tilted against his leg. She reached for it, and her fingertips brushed the fabric of his jeans. She felt the heat of him, the tension, the burn.

"I hate fighting with you, Marijohn," he said, his voice lonely and lost. "But sometimes it seems like that's all you want."

It wasn't all she wanted. Not even close.

The screen door thwacked against the side of her house as Abe came running toward the Chevy.

"Marijohn! Lazarus!" he called. "Are you all right?"

She didn't have time to pull herself out of the truck before his head hung through the passenger-side window, inspecting the two of them with a repairman's stare.

"Are you sure you're all right?" he asked again. "I was watching television and all of a sudden the world ripped apart."

"We're okay, Dad," she answered, as his eyes scoured her shoulders, her elbows, and then stopped. She'd forgotten what she was holding in her hand.

Abe didn't even have to ask what it was. He already knew. This was Abe's meteor, his long-traveled treasure, so desperate to find its way home.

"Marijohn," he said. "Where did you get that?"

"At the bottom of the ravine." Marijohn paused. "Buried in the river."

"Buried?" Abe said, his eyes wide as if before him stood a fearful new world.

"Yes, near that—" She paused, about to break her father's heart for the second time. "That section of mangled guardrail."

Marijohn could see it now, the way a car could have flown over the railing into the river below and no one would have known.

"We have to call the police." Abe's voice cracked. "To search the swamp."

"Dad." Marijohn kept herself level. "It's been eighteen years. You know they won't."

There was no use in calling the police. No one would believe the pink-and-white plastic had come from the woods. No one believed any of Abe's stories anymore.

"Oh," he said. "Oh."

His body leaned into the dusty Chevy. Then his gaze sparked as it met his daughter's, and they made a silent vow. It had always been the two of them who had shared this legend, truth or not. As soon as they were able, they'd go into the woods and search that river themselves.

Their stare held for so long that Lazarus leaned over and touched Abe's arm.

"Mr. Shaw?" he said, glancing at Marijohn. "I'm worried about my truck."

Abe blinked. "What happened?"

"There was debris all over the road. I drove over some pretty rough patches."

Abe nodded. "Think you got a flat?"

"I can't be sure—can you take a look?"

"I'll follow you to the shop." Abe patted his pockets for the keys to his Sierra. "Must have left the keys in the house."

He trotted inside, and Marijohn took off her seat belt, took her mandolin by the neck. "Why did you do that?" she asked.

"I didn't want to lose two Shaws to the same sinkhole in one night," he answered.

Marijohn rested a palm on the door handle but couldn't get herself to pull.

"I probably won't see you again until there's snow on the ground," she said.

An unadorned hurt laced her words, simple and raw. It wasn't anyone's fault, just the natural disaster of growing older, of getting left behind.

Abe appeared on the porch. He slid into his Sierra, turned on the engine. Flicked on his headlights.

"You think it's so easy?" Lazarus asked. "Being the one who leaves?"

Laz fidgeted with the steering wheel, then wiped his hands against his jeans. He was flustered and angry, and about to be gone.

"Yes," she answered. "I think it is."

Abe flashed his lights.

"I have to go," Laz said, as he shifted the truck into reverse.

Marijohn stepped away from the Chevy and saw how late it was. Early evening was gone. The moon was out. Thunder clouds formed beyond the tree line. This had been their last night, and now Marijohn had lost it. Their summer together, this time that was only theirs, was over.

"Play one more time with me," she said through the window. "After you're done at the shop."

Laz slowly began to back out. "Camcorder's battery is busted. It won't record again."

"I don't mean for the recording." Marijohn didn't want something to remember this moment—she wanted the moment itself. She wanted to bring him back to her. Back to the woods. Back to what held them together. "I mean for you and me."

The muscles in his neck jumped as he looked over his shoulder. "It's too late," he said.

It might have been romantic, this meteor. A lit match skating across the sky like a vaulting, throbbing heart. Instead, it shot out of the sky like a predator. A bullet, hunting for things fragile enough to destroy.

Lazarus turned onto the main road. Marijohn watched until his taillights disappeared, the red burn of them still a scar when she closed her eyes. They'd always been running out of time. Any moment Marijohn had with Lazarus, she had to steal.

Her heart had turned her into a thief.

The Last Night of the World

Marijohn sat on the front porch of her yellow house well into the night after Laz had driven away. He'd been right, partly. She did like to argue. Even with strangers, Marijohn went on the attack at the slightest sign of threat. She'd always been able to readily see all the things at her fingertips that were worth fighting for—but this was different. It felt as though they were fighting over something already gone.

Laz had left her alone in the kind of late-summer silence she'd never heard before. There were no crows in the forest, no crickets in the grass. No instrument in the attic.

Her mandolin still comforted her, even in its stillness. The more she'd learned to play it, the more its timbre opened beneath her fingers. It gave her a reason to believe in love, because she loved that cracked mandolin, and it loved her back.

Laz was the only person who'd witnessed this devotion reach its full measure. He'd watched her tentatively press her fingers into the strings, back when she was young enough to believe her mother might return. *G chord, C chord, D chord.*

"I love the way you play," Laz had said one July night when the fireflies came out. "Like you've got nothing to lose."

He'd been there while she learned to pick out one melody after another, as she realized that her mother—whoever she had been—was gone for good.

"I was wrong," Laz had admitted a year later, when it had rained in the woods and they hid in the cab of his truck. The windows had fogged, and the two of them were rimmed in mist. "You play for all the things you wish you could keep."

Marijohn's transformation into a motherless daughter, over the course of many summers, was probably the truest song her mandolin would ever play.

But Marijohn didn't fend off the absence. She'd learned how to thrive in it—to take that emptiness and treat it not as a tomb but as a drum. A medium that called out its own echo, one that set rhythm to the world around it. That was what her mandolin gave her. She didn't even know she'd learned to play left-handed until she tried to strum a guitar in music class at school.

That's backward, the teacher said—even though it was natural to her. Marijohn wondered if her mother was left-handed, too. It was a game she played in her mind, this wondering where shavings of herself had come from, as if she might be able to reassemble the pieces into a kinder message her mother had left.

Marijohn stayed on the porch until the rain came. These were her favorite summer moments—the slap of lightning in the sky, the proclamation of rain behind it. On the far side of the woods, the trees swayed through the storm. Lightning blistered. The branches of the spruce in the front yard groaned in the wind like they were in pain.

True to Laz's prediction, it rained until morning. Marijohn didn't sleep the whole night. Instead she watched the cavity of her father's truck fill with rainwater from her bedroom window in the dark. The mud tracks Lazarus's tires left on the lawn had washed away. The clearing where they'd spent their summer together in the woods had likely bled into the river below it. Saplings trampled, footprints gone. Nothing left to prove what they'd shared there.

The sun hadn't risen yet and the world was still inky blue when Marijohn crept into the living room and turned on the television. The local news blared with updates about the mystery that lit up the sky the night before.

The farmer who owned the field by the ravine called in to the station. "I got me a piece of it," he said. "The meteor."

He'd been sitting on his porch when he felt a windy roar like an airplane rushing toward him. One of his heifers screamed, and he ran to the sound. The rock had sliced through the side of her fur, leaving a swipe of a burn. Beside her, two feet in the ground, a small stone had tunneled through the soil. It fit in the palm of his hand.

"It was hot as hell," he said.

"What are you going to do with it?" the anchor asked.

"What do you think?" The farmer laughed. "I'm going to sell it."

Meteors, it turned out, were worth a fair amount of money.

By late morning, the thunderheads cleared and the sun emerged. The news prattled on. A second piece of the meteor had been claimed after it shot through the roof of a hunting cabin on the east end of the woods. Abe spent all of Monday in his repair shop, fixing dents and busted tires because of the storm, and Marijohn worked the day for him at the pump. When she returned in late afternoon, there were three messages on her answering machine.

They were all from Lazarus, asking her to call. He'd left a new number, the one to his dorm room.

On the six o'clock news, coverage of the meteor expanded across the nation. The station had finally secured video footage of the shooting star, and Marijohn held her breath as they began to air it. The first reel showed a blurry view of the meteor in black-and-white from the camera on Lenora's water tower. Like a brilliant comma, it soared through the twilight. It looked stunning and holy, like an omen of luck.

The next reel came from a video camera. This one had sound and color. Marijohn recognized the murky profile of the woods, the familiar melody that scraped the air. It was her song in Lazarus's mouth, her mandolin escorting his guitar.

On Marijohn's television screen, the sky brightened with electric orange and azure and lavender, like a kaleidoscope in the atmosphere. The date and time blinked in the corner. She found herself wishing she'd witnessed it, even though she had.

But she hadn't seen this: a black silhouette cutting through the light. The shadow of a young man running toward someone, reaching out to shield her as the meteor crashed, the ground shook, and the feed went dead.

Laz looked roguish and valiant on camera as he towered over the lissome body beneath him. Marijohn didn't recognize herself—the way her head leaned toward his until their shadows melded into one, the way they fell together as if timelessly rapt. The video showed only the simplest of opposites: light and dark, danger and safety, strong and weak.

It didn't show that Marijohn had strength and heat of her own. It couldn't illuminate every moment that had come before.

The caption at the bottom of the screen read:

METEOR IGNITES YOUNG LOVE

At the video's last second, when the shooting star burned brightest, Marijohn could see the expanse of Laz's back. The squall in the sky left a trail of heat on his neck, and broken leaves sparkled like emeralds against his shirt. It was the kind of image that held the weight of a song, one that could capture a generation of hearts and break them all at once.

Lazarus had given their video of the meteor to the news, the one where he'd sung only to her. It was the best of them all.

By Tuesday morning, the clouds vanished and the hills dried out.

Lazarus continued to call, though Marijohn didn't know it. She'd unplugged the phone from its jack. For two days, she'd watched the tale of the meteor unfold around her, as if it were some natural wonder and not an uninvited, ruthless herald of the end. It wasn't her world that had ended, but who she was in it.

Marijohn had thought she'd raised herself to be unflappable. What a joke. When she pictured the way Lazarus had wiped his mouth after she kissed him, her heart flapped like a bird that had never been told it was flightless. A desperate flailing despite the tether of truth.

Her mother placing a basket by a gas pump? *Flap*. A car flying over a guardrail with someone inside, and no one ever knew? *Flap, flap*. She couldn't find the right word to express the absolute madness this had caused her from the minute she spied that tiny pink-and-white piece of plastic. The past wasn't formless anymore; it had shape. This intricate unknowing made her feel helpless and small.

Her world had somehow ballooned now, even as it shrank in on her.

The rest of Lenora basked in the glow the meteor had left. As word had spread of the flash in the sky, a professor at a geological institute in Pittsburgh quickly chartered a small plane to fly over the woods. Marijohn had heard its incessant buzzing as it swept back and forth above the trees.

After the meteor, Abe's gas station didn't play Elle Harlow songs anymore. They listened to AM news radio instead. Flickers of the outside world filtered in—Latvia had declared independence, Gorbachev had resigned. Bonnie Raitt had given music fans something to talk about. News of the meteor mingled there like glitter. While Marijohn pumped gallon after gallon of unleaded, she heard an interview with the professor on KDKA 1020. All of Lenora clung to his words.

On the farm by the woods, the professor took measurements and photographs. He concluded that the farmer's piece of space rock was dug too far into the ground to warrant the velocity with which it hit the earth. He did the same with the shard that broke through the hunting cabin.

Both pieces were too small for that kind of speed.

"What's all this mean, Doc?" the DJ asked.

"It means . . ." The man paused. "There's a third piece of the meteor somewhere nearby, and it's large."

"How much is a meteor worth?" the DJ prompted.

"Depends on the meteor," the professor answered. "Could be a couple hundred dollars, could be a couple hundred thousand. The only way to know for sure is to find the rock."

That settled it. Lenora now marked an X on everyone's treasure map. By Wednesday, men had set out on foot to comb the woods like they were searching for a dead body—but the woods had other plans. The topography of the forest had changed overnight, as if the face of it had wept with the rain. Near the western edge of the trees, most of the thin birches and black oaks had slid into the water below, damming themselves against the ground.

When Marijohn finished work on Wednesday evening, Lazarus was sitting on her porch. Swinging on her swing, trying to pick a soft tune on her mandolin, as if he had never left. She hated how handsome he looked, hated how much she longed to sit next to him and fold herself beneath his arm. He was all comfort: silky and broad-shouldered in his worn cotton shirt and Levi's, his hands both solid and soft. She hadn't seen him in three days. It was the longest they'd been apart since summer had begun.

They stared at each other for a moment—him from the porch, her from behind the dashboard of Abe's Sierra. Lazarus looked strong but sheepish. He knew she knew he'd given their recording to the news and hadn't saved it for her. The song itself seemed so trivial now.

She stepped out of the truck.

"What are you doing here?" she asked.

"Nice to see you, too."

The air between them was charged, thick with the miracle they'd both witnessed.

"How's—" she tried. She'd already forgotten how to talk to her best friend. "How's college?"

"Lonely." He drew a thumb down the strings of her mandolin. "I never really had to meet people before."

She nodded like she knew, even though she didn't.

"Everyone is searching for it now," she said. "The meteor."

"I know."

"Is that why you came back?"

Laz glared at the way Marijohn had asked a question she knew the answer to. "I already know where that meteor is."

"You could have told anyone about it, or gone to get it yourself. Why didn't you?"

"Why didn't *you*?"

Here it came again, honesty forcing its way out of her mouth. "Because I'm scared of what else I'll find."

"You and Abe haven't gone digging yet, then."

"No."

Laz must have felt it then, how things were changing between them, because he looked tortured and thirsty—just as he looked every Christmas Eve once the candles had been lit and he'd started to recite the gospel of Luke from the pulpit. Captivated by his voice, Marijohn had attended each year, sitting in the last pew. She'd memorized the hook of Lazarus's back while he bowed his head in prayer. After it was through, he scanned the sanctuary for her face, always finding her at a distance. He knew that she knew he hated being on display—as if it took something away from his faith every time he had to perform it—and that had been the first of many secrets between them. Sharing them was a little like sharing love, if love couldn't be found.

She used to think Laz reveled in how much he wanted to leave home. As he stood before her now, she realized he wished he'd never needed to.

Laz had never been eager to disappear. He was sad.

"Of course I had to come. You wouldn't pick up the phone." He tossed the words at her now, from the porch. "I've been calling for days."

"The last time I saw you, you told me all I want to do with you is fight," she said. The swing creaked in the quiet. "And I've been trying to decide if I agree with you."

"Do you?"

"No."

He let out a sigh. "This is why we could never finish a song together."

"Maybe it's exactly why we should."

"Marijohn," he said as they sat down together on the swing.

The way he said her name made her tremble. Like a wind chime, or church bells on Sunday morning. If this were a dream, he might have told her he loved her.

"Something good happened," he said instead.

Marijohn watched him, expressionless, as he told her how beloved a hero the video of the meteor strike had made him—not just in Lenora anymore, but beyond it. She didn't slump or frown or shudder as he spoke. Ever graceful, she kept herself. Ever even.

"I'm going on a national news program tomorrow morning," he went on, until Marijohn interrupted.

"Why did you do it," she said, though there was no hint of a question in her voice. She already understood, even if Lazarus didn't.

"Give the video to the news?"

"No."

He tucked the pick beneath her mandolin's strings and set the instrument aside. "What, then?"

"Why did you shield me like that when the meteor hit?"

He laughed, confused. "You wish I left you to fend for yourself?"

"You know that's not what I mean." Her black hair drifted from her shoulders in the breeze. "I want to know why it was me you ran for."

Laz paused, lowered his gaze, then lifted it. The hungry hurt in his eyes penetrated her entire body.

"You know why," he said. His voice was the slow tick of a clock, the measured tuning of a guitar.

"I want to hear you say it."

"Why do you need to know you were the only thing I saw that night?" A flush of red painted his neck. "You're always the only thing I see."

There it was—the reason he had returned, and the reason he thought he had to leave.

"I want to know whether you're afraid to love me," Marijohn said, "or just afraid to say it."

Lazarus looked gone, like the heart of him still lay in a truck bed with a rock tearing the sky. It was unfair, and Marijohn knew it. Laz didn't owe her the kind of promises he put in his country songs. They were eighteen, ready to spend their ideas of love that ran flush like dollar bills in their pockets.

"You're jealous." His voice faltered. "Jealous that I left. That I tried something new. That I *did* something with that tape."

She felt a deep severing between them then, even as they sat side by side.

"This has worked out well for you, being a hero," she observed. "Hasn't it?"

He stood so abruptly that the swing shook. He clutched her mandolin like a dead animal. "What do you mean?"

"That night in the back of your truck when I kissed you and you didn't kiss me back? It belonged to us." She stood, too, the edge of the porch swing lapping the backs of her thighs. Slowly, she took the mandolin from his grip. "Only to you and me until you gave it away to the rest of the world."

"You don't understand." Laz drew a hand down his face as he cursed. "I don't give a shit about the meteor. What I care about is that it gave the rest of the world a chance to hear your music. I knew you'd never do it on your own, and you know it, too."

She didn't answer, so he tried again.

"Can you admit I'm right, just this once?"

"No."

"Forget it, then," he said.

He stalked to his truck and slammed the door after he climbed inside. His hand hovered over the ignition before he turned the key. Marijohn could tell he didn't want to leave. He sat in his cab, watching her, his mouth parted. She liked seeing him this way, riled and real. Golden hair mussed, at war with himself. They stared at each other until he sighed, threw the truck in reverse, and backed out of the driveway.

Maybe Marijohn should have seen it coming early the next morning, the same way she could sense a thunderstorm along the beaches of Lake Erie when it was still a ways off. The air gathered a peculiar heaviness to it as Marijohn switched on her television—the kind that made it hard to breathe as the sky purpled against the horizon.

Lazarus stood on the studio floor of a newsroom in Pittsburgh, a halo of light around him, his guitar strapped to his chest and his striped polo tucked into his Levi's. Laz sang "Namesake" as a solo without Marijohn, and without her mandolin.

The tune was slippery, would fit itself against any voice. The words

Marijohn wrote flaunted themselves in Lazarus's throat, prettier than they'd ever been in hers.

My mama gave me my name
I guess you could say
She left, and left me a better namesake
Words better than a gun
I ain't never shot one
But I am a song and I'll pull that trigger
Till I'm done

When the final chord resolved, the news anchors' clapping curled around Lazarus's neck like the smoke of a cigarette. In that ephemeral fifteen seconds, Marijohn witnessed his metamorphosis—Laz's coming into being as he slung his guitar over his shoulder. The creamy makeup they'd caked onto his face smeared onto the collar of his shirt.

An anchorwoman approached him, and the camera lens zoomed in. She was glossy and tan, her smile fixed and white.

"What was it like?" she asked. "Seeing a meteor strike?"

Marijohn knew the right answer to that question could launch a lifetime of music played on a radio, with Lazarus Wright's name in neon. It was what they'd dreamed of, so close he could taste its sweetness in his mouth.

All Lazarus had seen the night the meteor crashed was Marijohn, but that wasn't the truth he wished to turn into song. He reached elsewhere, toward what he imagined the world longed to hear.

"There was a fireball—brighter than you've ever seen," Lazarus said into the microphone. "And I swear to God I thought it was the last night of the world."

Leaving Song

Marijohn's sinking woods were full of people now, hunting the meteor. Each of them had that gold-rush gleam in their eyes. She could see the hunters from her attic window, how they invaded the forest like a locust swarm. They entered the woods with chins lofted and emerged from it empty-handed. Her town never felt full like this except when disaster struck. It was the only time the outside world seemed to care about towns like Lenora—another mine collapse, lead in the water. Bodies in the ground.

Marijohn hadn't spoken to anyone but her father since Laz's television performance. Abe's head was clearing, though his heart still lagged. The world looked different to both father and daughter now, even if it was the same as it had always been.

Together they stood at the ravine just beyond the gnarled guardrail, while looters scoured the woodlands to the east.

"I'll tie a rope around my waist," Marijohn offered. "And go into the river."

Abe shook his head. He'd never played an instrument, but his hand grasped his fishing rod as if he were aching to hold one, just this once.

"We're gonna fish," he said.

Marijohn nodded, and the pair of them slid down the steep incline toward the water. She looped the rope around her waist and tied it to one of the few trees still standing after the storm.

"Just in case," she said.

With that, Abe cast his line. For two hours, all they caught were a handful of darters and tangled chicken wire.

"Patience," Abe cautioned, just as Marijohn put on his waders and stepped into the water.

Instantly she felt herself sinking as the earth shifted beneath her feet. In the middle of the river, she fell to her knees. The current caressed her neck, and she let her hands comb through the silt. She moved left, then right. Back again. Forward, and then a little more. At last her hand grazed something smooth; Marijohn followed it but couldn't find its end. It had a curved edge, and she wrapped her fingers around it and pulled.

"Dad," she said, but Abe was already splashing into the water, thrusting his hands beneath it to find his daughter's.

Together they leaned back, using all their might to free the object from the mud. It made a giant sucking sound as they wrested it from the silt. By the time they'd towed it to the riverbank, both Marijohn and Abe were doused in dirt and sweat.

The piece of metal they'd rescued was oblong and bent like a crooked smile. Abe used his shirt sleeve to wipe down one of the ends.

"That," he said, leaning his hands onto his knees, his back heaving as he caught his breath, "is the chrome bumper of a Studebaker."

Marijohn bent to inspect it. "How can you tell?"

"The shape. And it's tarnished, but not rusted out."

Marijohn took hold of it as if it might still sink beyond their reach. This shard of the past, barreling into the present. "It's hers, isn't it?"

A slash of mud settled into the wrinkles next to Abe's eye.

"No one ever bothered to solve what happened to a once-in-a-generation talent like Elle Harlow," he said. It was the first time he'd come close to admitting she was no longer alive. "People are combing our hills for a piece of space rock more than anyone ever looked for her."

Marijohn sat down in the leaves at the top of the embankment, and Abe joined her. Their fingers were puckered and ridged in filth.

"You ever wonder if some things are just meant to be lost?" she asked.

"Things, yes. People, never," he answered.

"You've spent a lot of your life searching for missing things," Marijohn said softly.

"Well," he said, his voice tangling with melancholy resolve, "I think I might be done with all that now."

This was the moment Marijohn had hoped for, and all she felt was a tidal wave of guilt.

"I wish I'd been honest with you about the artifacts," she said. "It wasn't you I didn't trust. It was everyone else in the world."

Abe scratched his jaw with the knuckle of his pointer finger. "Turns out I'm the idiot everyone thinks me to be."

Marijohn thought of herself scaling down the ravine, clutching Lazarus's blanket, hoping to touch that meteor herself in just the same way Abe had held on to his relics.

"Not all your artifacts are junk," she said. "Some of them have to be real."

He raised his shoulder. "Most of them probably ain't, though."

The bumper sat before them like a gilded snake.

"Thing is," Abe said. His damp shirtsleeve had a stripe of grease on it, and he rubbed it with his thumb. "It was never myself I was collecting them for anyway. It was you."

"Me?"

"I've been trying so hard to create a past for you that it kept us from making your future."

"Dad," she whispered. "It's not your fault. I never wanted to leave."

"Either way, you deserve to make the choice yourself."

He came to his feet and pulled Marijohn up after him. "So here's what we're going to do. We're gonna come back with a pulley rig and tow this bumper to the police station. And then we're going to see about getting financial aid for next fall."

"Dad, you don't have to do that."

Her father, ever beautiful and careworn, looked like everything Marijohn loved in life—safety and home and music and firelight.

"I want to," he said. "What I don't want to be is someone in love with a lie."

"I know what you mean."

Lies were intoxicating and sweet, and they demanded total surrender. Marijohn had spun her own myth by believing her mother left behind a broken mandolin as an heirloom for her daughter. But the myth wasn't what Marijohn truly needed.

She needed to know whether the voice behind the darkness in her head belonged to the woman she'd come from. And now she knew she never would.

The mandolin might not have held her mother's voice, but it had come to hold Marijohn's, because the instrument also knew the pain of being left behind. The two of them were shredded, but they rang out clear and whole. This mandolin had seen things; it had lived a life. It harbored secrets, and that was why it captured Marijohn's heart. It dressed all her music in its own dulcet pain.

"Do you think my mother ever sang to me?" Marijohn asked once they reached the top of the ravine. The yellow rocket along its edge had flattened in the rain.

"I know she did." Abe slipped his arm around her shoulders, stable and firm.

"How?"

"Because no one could meet you and not want to sing to you."

They leaned against the grille of Abe's Sierra and watched the onslaught of afternoon sun as it slowly gave way to the shadows in the woods.

"What was it like," her father finally asked, "seeing a shooting star hit the earth?"

Marijohn thought on it. "Is it weird to say it revealed all the things that I never wanted to see?"

Abe shook his head, pensive. "Like what?"

"Like Laz wants to be with me, but he won't let himself."

"I saw the video," Abe said. "He must love you a lot."

"I don't think love is worth much to Lazarus," she answered.

She wanted to be that rare wonder to satisfy what her best friend needed, a delicate key made only for his lock, but Marijohn had never thought of herself as anyone special. So she told her father everything she'd want to tell her mother, if she had one: the kiss, the song, the video. Abe listened not with a repairman's focus, but a father's ear.

"I feel like an idiot," she said.

"There are worse things to be."

She'd offered these same words in her father's defense only days earlier, and she wasn't certain she believed them anymore. "I doubt it."

A crow crossed the sky and disappeared into the trees.

"There's a difference between bravery in heart and bravery in deed," Abe said. "Maybe Lazarus hasn't figured out the heart part like you have."

After a beat, he continued. "But that don't mean the love between you isn't real."

Marijohn watched the clouds shift west so slowly she wouldn't even realize when they'd traveled beyond her eyesight. If she could trace the feeling back—before the meteor, before the music, before the first chords they'd ever played together—where would she find the start of it? She couldn't remember a time when Lazarus hadn't held a piece of her.

"I don't know what love is," she said. "And neither does he."

But it wasn't true. Marijohn did know what love was—more than anyone. She just didn't *want* to know. Love hadn't fed her, and it hadn't fixed her father. It hadn't made her mother return, and it hadn't been enough to make Laz stay.

One week passed after the meteor strike, and already the crowds had thinned out. Hunting for a lost object took more than desire—it took a threadbare commitment to reason, the ludicrously divine devotion of a shepherd who would leave his flock of ninety-nine in search of the single sheep that had run away. For once, Marijohn was glad no one else seemed to have this depth of loyalty but her. It was useless, and chronic, and lonely.

After sunset on the seventh day, she climbed to the attic perch in her bedroom and pushed open the window. Then Marijohn picked up her notebook and pen and tried to write a song for her mother. What else could she do with the dark voice singing in her head?

She sang back.

Marijohn hadn't played her mandolin since before the meteor, and it felt at home snuggled against her chest as she slipped her arm through the strap.

Lazarus came again that night. Stared up at her from the worn patch of grass like a country Romeo, handsome and tragic. This night was like so many others they'd shared, but the two of them were different now. He hadn't brought his guitar.

"Come down," he called. "Please?"

Marijohn didn't know why they did it. When she came outside, she and Lazarus climbed into the back of his Chevy and lay with their faces to the sky instead of sitting on her porch. His stack of blankets had returned to its post in the corner, laundered and neatly folded—the mud and the memory of that night now ghosts.

"I know I should have asked if I could sing your song on television," he said. "I just wanted the world to hear it."

Her chest felt like it might break. "I know."

Laz looked broken, too. "Then why are you upset with me?"

"I'm not upset with you," she said. "I envy you."

He groaned and laid his arm across his forehead. "You have more talent in a single eyelash than I have in my whole body. Why envy me?"

"Because you never doubt yourself." She looked past the trees into the darkness above. "You have a basketball, you shoot it. You see a meteor, you run away from it. You have a song, you sing it. The things that are so simple for you turn me in circles."

He lifted his arm, and his eyes followed hers into the woods. "You don't need to question yourself."

"I do, though." She turned to look at him. "There's something in me that feels like it's never been whole, and usually I don't mind it. I prefer the emptiness—except when I'm with you."

His voice quieted. "Maybe you're better off without me, then."

"That's a shitty thing to say," Marijohn said. "And you know it."

They said nothing, then, for a while.

"There's one more thing I need to tell you," he offered finally. A heavy cloud hovered, and they couldn't see the moon or the stars, only the thick spruce branches that threaded the sky. "A lot of people saw the clip of me singing your song—not just our video, but the news program, too."

"I know," she said.

It was happening, their wild, secret, star-in-the-sky dream becoming his.

"A record company in Nashville heard it, and they want me to demo a few songs in their studio."

At that, Marijohn's heart leapt like a windblown leaf. "They want my song?" she asked. "They want 'Namesake'?"

She hadn't allowed herself the glory of this truth—her music had been heard across the country, in houses and cars and storefronts. Her words, her melody, her heart.

Lazarus looked as if the truth had skinned him. "It isn't the song they want." He uttered the words so hoarsely that Marijohn turned her head to watch his mouth move. "It's me."

She started nodding, just for something to do with her body. She couldn't stop. A gutting sensation revisited her, like a week-old shadow—her kissing Lazarus, his pulling away.

"So my song isn't good enough to leave town," she said, "and neither am I."

Laz looked at her like he didn't know her at all, and she couldn't blame him. What was it that she really wanted—to leave or to stay? To remain hidden, or to be heard?

She'd told her father that the meteor had revealed things just as they'd always been, and here was another moment that proved it. Marijohn knew the second she saw Lazarus on television, her words in his mouth, that she'd desperately wished it had been her. The music, the lights, the audience—she wanted it all.

"I don't know if it was the song that got their attention, Marijohn." Laz covered his eyes again with his arm. "Or the meteor."

"Which they wouldn't have seen without the song."

"Which they wouldn't have heard without the meteor."

He didn't sound triumphant or proud. He sounded trapped by the good favor he hadn't earned.

"What about school?" Marijohn asked.

"I told the studio no, Marijohn." They both flinched at the volume of his voice.

"You what?"

"I said no. You and I write songs together. We sing for each other."

"Lazarus," she said, but he hadn't heard.

"I can't do this without you." His eyes burned through hers as he offered the words she'd always wanted him to say. He hadn't given them as an ultimatum, or a curse, or a way to martyr himself. Lazarus had just allowed himself to tell the truth. So she did the same.

"You know you can't stay," she said.

Marijohn understood something then that she hadn't before. Loving someone wasn't only a brazen kiss in the back of a truck or secret longings written in a diary. Sometimes loving someone was letting them leave you behind.

"Call them back, Lazarus. You have to go."

"I—"

Marijohn pushed the heel of her hand into his chest. "You know I'm right. You don't want to be an accountant, and maybe this is your one chance not to be."

A bit of her spirit shattered as she said it, the way she'd sent her own dreams into exile as if she'd blown on the white head of a dandelion. Lazarus remained silent, his face already haunted by what he was about to do.

"It isn't fair," he said.

"Life usually isn't," she answered.

Marijohn sat up and climbed out of the truck for the last time. They parted ways without saying goodbye because she didn't know how. Lazarus stood with her in the tall grass and took her wrist in his hand just as he had the night the meteor struck. Any time she'd miss Lazarus in the cooler nights to come, she promised herself she'd return to this moment when she felt the flame in his grasp as he held her, and the moment the burn waned as he let her go.

The next morning, Lazarus left town for good. Abe stood on his porch and announced he was ready to change the lettering on the gas station marquee. Marijohn's days filled with her father, and she wouldn't have traded it. After they delivered the Studebaker's chrome bumper to the station, the two of them attempted to complete a Magic Eye puzzle, only to find they were missing the final piece. They did not talk of meteors, or the future.

On the third day after Lazarus left, she heard a knock at the door. It was early evening, and they hadn't had any visitors since Laz had gone. Marijohn opened the door, and there stood a woman with a sheen of auburn hair and a delicate necklace at her throat.

A lesser heart might have thought Marijohn barely took a breath in that moment, but it wasn't so. Marijohn had always been breathing, had always been singing. Had always been waiting for someone to sing back.

There was power behind true music—not just accidental chords thrown together, but the kind woven to meet an inmost need or ignite the keenest regret. The kind that gave rhythm to the broken and bone to the downcast. Music was an apostle for the lonely. It cut teeth with harmony, all chipped nails and rough fingers pressed to the supple side of a wrist with a voice that promised there was life here yet. There was life here, still.

This was what Marijohn had been waiting for.

The woman wore a faded plaid shirt and jeans, well-worn cowboy boots. Weighty silver hoops in her ears. Time had run its rivers across her forehead and through her hands, but there was no mistaking her identity.

It was Elle Harlow.

She was alive and staring at Marijohn like she had something to confess.

"You're not dead," Marijohn said.

"Not today."

Marijohn couldn't stop herself. The words flew right out of her mouth. "Do you have a kid?" she asked.

"Jesus," Elle said. "Buy me a drink first."

Marijohn gaped at her until Elle grew impatient. She could tell by the way Elle twisted the ball of her boot against the whitewashed boards of the porch. Then she put her hands on her hips and pushed past Marijohn through the front door. She stalked through the entryway only to stop in the middle of the room and point her finger at the mandolin hanging on the wall.

"I saw you on the news," Elle said. "And I want to know where you got that mandolin."

"You don't play the mandolin," Marijohn said.

"No shit."

The instrument hung between them in the low light, a teardrop made of rosewood that held all the music Marijohn had ever played. But this instrument had always been missing a piece of itself—a whisper she couldn't place before she fell asleep at night, a flame burning from the dark side of a wicker trunk. All this time Marijohn had been playing a nocturne for someone too far away to hear it.

Until now.

She hadn't been prepared when she'd been a baby abandoned at a roadside gas station, or when a shooting star hit the earth. But for this moment—after a lifetime of Elle's voice on salty records and Abe's stories in her ear and *Wounds from a Lover*'s chords pressed into her fingertips—Marijohn was ready.

She reached onto the living room shelf for the pink-and-white piece of plastic with a twisted heart scrawled on it and placed it in Elle's hand.

"I'll tell you," Marijohn said, "but first, tell me where you've been."

Marijohn had her then. *I in her palm, she in mine.* Even from the beginning, it felt like they were writing a song.

Part II

What Happened to Elle Harlow

(1964–1972)

How far back must a woman go
To tell the truth of her life?
The beginning is end, the story is slow
The day a daughter turns into a wife

—"Daughter to Wife," *Wounds from a Lover*

TRACK 1

When she was a girl, Elle Harlow learned how to sing from a mountain healer who didn't speak.

Merry was her name, and songs on her mountain didn't come from mouths. They came from silver creeks and West Virginia grassland, broken hearts and blood spilled on dirt roads. Spirits and devils when no angels could be found.

Some called Merry a witch, some called her a haint. Everyone called her when they were sick. Fevers, rashes, wounds that kissed the bone—those eerie, quickfire illnesses that seemed to hunt only the people living in her hills. Merry kept a leather notebook of her remedies, slept in her Ford, and played a rosewood mandolin.

Mountain folk swore that a good story could build back the blood, and here was Merry's. She'd found that mandolin smashed to pieces during a red sunrise in 1932 when she was young. Its fretboard had looked serpentine in the crimson light. Like a hinterland Moses and his slithering staff, Merry knelt and took it up.

The instrument felt rigid in her grip, this creature that—like Merry herself—was silent. No one knew why Merry had been born this way, yet the inability to speak was no weakness. Merry's strength was found in the way she listened to the whistling crows that signaled a storm, to the burr of a cough settled too deep in a set of lungs.

Shard by shard, Merry pieced the mandolin back together with clothespins and carpenter's paste. Hung it on the drying line like the skeleton of a fawn. Sanded its curves until it took the shape of a woman and had the tremolo wail of one, too. Gave it a blond finish, a shimmering topcoat. Merry breathed life back into its severed grain, and it gave her a song in return.

It was the only immortal thing she'd ever healed.

As she aged, Merry never let the mandolin out of her sight. Seasons passed; the earth flushed and shriveled. Merry turned fifty. She kept her mandolin strapped to her chest all the while, its neck hailing the sky.

Now it was 1964, deep in the woods of West Virginia, and Elle Harlow was thirteen years old. She was rusty-haired, terse, and hungry as hell. Her father had been away at war for months, and her family had just eaten the last of the potatoes in their cellar. They had no relatives, no money, no reason to believe they'd ever be the object of someone else's charity. So Elle did as her father taught her—lifted his Winchester rifle from its catch above the fireplace and skulked through the frozen meadow that spread across their hill.

In the vale by the cherry tree, she flattened herself against the snow and peered into the Winchester's sights. She saw nothing, just like the day before.

"Well, motherfucker," she said to no one in particular.

Elle loved to hunt. It wasn't the chase she craved, or even the victory. She loved that she never felt ashamed of her hunger with the butt of a rifle flush against her shoulder.

"Tough as hell, so you are," her father, Hosea, had told her as he'd demonstrated how to gut a buck one month before he left. His fingerprints were marked in deer blood on the handle of his blade when he gave it to his daughter. "Anything I can do, so can you, Elle."

At the time he'd said it—early fall, coppery and cozy—the words felt more like a blessing than a curse.

It was winter now, and a haughty afternoon hung in the air. The hill should have been quiet, most of the wild game hibernating or dead, but it wasn't. Elle heard Merry's mandolin—sweet, soulful, slick—before she ever saw her coming.

The sound filled her with dread.

A doe, dainty and agile, leapt from behind a stand of balsams. Elle hefted the rifle. The mandolin clucked in the distance, and the deer fled. Elle tossed the Winchester into the snow.

"This witch is going to starve me," she said to the barren cherry tree.

Elle had never seen Merry, but as a child she used to hear the instrument's golden notes at dusk. The sound wept clear through her skin.

Truth was, the music made Elle smell the stench of her own loneliness. She hadn't heard even one melody since her father left four months earlier. The mandolin made her remember happier times, when she'd been a better version of herself.

"Every hello is a love song," Hosea had sung to her on the day he was scheduled to report for duty in Charleston, his thick, glossy hair tied at the back of his neck. Rain spent itself on the porch roof as Hosea worked his banjo. "And so is every goodbye."

Elle had always thought of the song as hopeful before her father was drafted. Now she stepped into the rain to veil her tears. She didn't want to make it harder for her father to leave when he had no choice, didn't want him to worry about them while he was gone.

Save your own life, she'd wanted to say to him, but didn't. *And I'll save everyone else's.*

Hosea pulled her back, a rough and warm hand on her elbow.

"How long is a country song?" he asked. His voice was gritty, and she knew he was holding back tears of his own.

Elle wiped her eyes and shrugged.

"Three and a half minutes," Hosea said. "That's all it takes to fall in love, meet your death, lose your mind."

Elle blinked, and her father's handsome, blurred face appeared between the fan of her eyelashes. "So?"

"Your best and worst moments can pass in the length of a good song." He took his hand and ran it along her braid. "If you start to miss me, have Reuben play one of my ballads. You'll feel better by the end."

Elle didn't believe music had that kind of power.

"If I start to miss you—" she began.

"Don't," Hosea finished.

It was the last word he spoke to her before he'd ridden away in the passenger seat of his buddy's two-tone Ford, his head in his hands.

Less than six months had passed, and Elle was already failing him. She missed him so much she could barely breathe.

On the hill, a quail dove into a tuft of snow. Elle gripped her rifle and trained the barrel of it on the bird. It was a shit way to kill such a tiny animal. The mandolin played on, tickling like laughter.

Merry didn't visit families for happy reasons. She'd come to this crag in the mountain because Elle's younger brother, Reuben, had pneumonia. His cough was a persistent, urgent alarm that woke Elle at night in the lofted bed they shared, set a rhythm to her day as she skinned squirrels and shot at birds in their nests.

That was Elle Harlow back then: fearsome enough that even illness cowered in her wake. Her body had fought off the pneumonia, but her brother's hadn't.

It had been this way since Reuben's birth nine years earlier. He was a slight boy who played his mother's dulcimer and had the voice of a seraph. He also caught every virus that skated on the wind.

"You're gonna play at the Grand Ole Opry," Elle had whispered to him on many evenings in the drafty attic they shared, his frail body shivering alongside hers. "We just have to get you there."

The healer's silhouette climbed the valley as Elle's prey hit the field at her feet. Elle grunted when she bent to pick it up. It was light in her grasp, dangling and dead.

"You cost me a doe," she said, by way of greeting. Then she turned her back, and Merry followed her inside.

If Hosea's words spoke truth—that three and a half minutes could change the course of a life—then these were Elle's. Merry stepped into their cabin, and a cloud passed over. The quail's feathers skirted the planked floor as Susannah reached for it. The moment held: a mother, her children, a lifeless bird. They all looked so gray-skinned, Elle thought. But not Merry.

Her eyes were the color of rain-swept seashores. The kind someone would want to look into every day for the rest of a life—the eyes of a firm and nimble friend. Yet Merry had no kin, but for her mandolin.

Kin or not, it was Merry who set the cadence of their hills. Elle felt it then for the first time, the quickening that drew everyone else on the mountain toward the healer. Merry's very body seemed to say, *Put your heart in beat with mine*—and folks complied.

She was a woman in black: black wide-brimmed hat, black denim with black boots that clipped the wooden floor as she strode toward Reuben. Merry pressed a fleshy palm to his face, then studied him. Peered inside his mouth. Watching her work was like wind skimming a meadow. Soft, silent.

She reached for the satchel on her back and revealed a sack of butterfly weed. Reuben coughed as she crushed it with a single hand. After she brewed a tincture with boiling water, she made a poultice from the stems. She wasted nothing—not even time.

Reuben fell asleep in a rocking chair, his dark hair drifting across his forehead. Merry's boots rapped as she headed for the door until Elle's mother, Susannah, took her by the elbow. The mandolin's strings shushed against her arm as Merry turned.

For the first time that day, Susannah looked panicked. Her face, once round and pink, now looked dredged. She felt the need to pay. To give from what they lacked.

Susannah thrust the dead quail toward Merry, and a fatal itch let loose all over Elle's skin. *You'll have to be heartless,* she heard her father command, *in order to survive.* Elle yanked her mother's arm backward with such force that the quail fell. It hit the floor like a sigh.

"This is for Reuben," Susannah said, her hand resting firm and warm on her daughter's back.

"The medicine won't mean shit if he don't have food to eat," Elle shot back.

"Elle."

Susannah was no hunter, but something much fiercer: a mother. The way she said her daughter's name—a warning, a demand, an incantation—shaved a year right off Elle's life. Elle wouldn't defy her, even for Hosea.

Merry looked from Elle to Susannah. The dead quail still lay on the floor. Elle knelt and handed the bird to her, and Merry grabbed it by the neck. Their fingers brushed; Elle felt the chill of being known by a stranger. In less than ten minutes, Merry had witnessed that Elle's hunger was the worst, most achingly tender part of her.

It left her feeling in need of a fig leaf to cover her nakedness.

Merry left as swiftly as she'd come, but Elle watched her footprints in the snow long after there was no starlight by which to see. Merry was a shadow, beating back the dusk. What they shared that afternoon was a silence so full that Elle didn't realize until Merry was gone that she hadn't spoken a word.

After a dinner made largely of onion broth, Elle stepped out onto the porch. There against the clapboard siding sat the quail they'd surrendered to Merry, cold and plump. She hadn't taken any payment after all.

The house smelled like ramps for days afterward. The only sound Elle would remember later was the wooden creak of the porch rocker when it caught the wind. For the first time since Christmas, Reuben wasn't coughing. The weed had worked.

Merry left behind a bag of dried herbs with instructions to drink the tea no more than once a day. Such a small amount of powder, tasked with saving a life.

"Everybody wants something," Elle's father had warned when he first taught her to shoot. "And if you ain't careful, they'll take it from you."

She'd learned to be shrewd from Hosea, who had ordained her as the man of the house in his absence.

"You are the man of the house," he'd whispered over and over in her ear as he stood behind her in the field, their hands joined on the trigger of his rifle. She shot at a buck and grazed it. Shot again, then again, until it lay mangled in the grass.

"I am the man of the house," she repeated.

Her father pointed at what they had killed.

"You're like me, Elle," he said. "Doing the ugly thing so the beautiful things can live."

It hurt him to say it, all brutal necessity without any of the shelter his broad shoulders once loved to provide. Back at the house, Elle's mother had watched them from behind the thin curtain. Susannah was all hips and nurture, biscuits on the stove and candles burning bright after dark—but she wasn't weak. Most of her life was dedicated to raising her chickens and keeping Reuben safe from the harsh wild outside their door. It was Elle who would break ruthless ground with the meat of her hands, Elle who would shoot to kill.

When her father left well before Christmas, Elle took ownership of Hosea's Winchester, his overalls, his empty wallet, his eternal worry. She wanted Hosea to come home safe, of course. But it wasn't what she wanted most. When he returned, she wanted to point at their home and say—

Look at this good life I protected. Look how ugly I became for it.

Elle couldn't name the need growing inside her, even then. Had no idea that sometimes the best kind of healing comes from a desire planted instead of one fulfilled. Elle Harlow didn't see herself as a reflection of beauty. She was coarse, basic, necessary. She didn't know that what the healer wanted that day had nothing to do with payment, or with Reuben at all.

As soon as Merry set foot in the Harlows' slipshod cabin, she wanted Elle to learn what it meant to sing.

TRACK 2

The morning after Merry's visit, Elle stood in front of the fire and strangled the butterfly weed with her fist. Its pistil fell like cinder into an empty mug.

Steam hissed as hot water hit the cup. She took a sip of the tea and spit it right into the flames. It was cloyingly sweet, with a hint of spice on the back of the tongue.

"Told you it was bad," a voice said from behind her.

Reuben had crept down the stairs and waited by the counter, indignant and waifish.

"Where's Mama?" he asked.

"Bartering eggs down the hill," Elle answered. "Maybe we'll finally get some beef."

"I don't like beef," Reuben said.

Elle thrust the cup toward him, relieved that he had the strength to complain. Reuben held on to the mug, staring into it like it told his future.

"I'm sick of being sick," he said, his eyes big and brown. "I miss you."

"Miss me? I'm right here."

Elle gave him an indulgent smile, as if she didn't know exactly what he meant. She'd lost her playfulness since her father left. They didn't shoot rotten apples with Reuben's bow and arrow anymore. Didn't trick

Susannah into thinking her chickens had sprung loose again. Didn't laugh the way they once had.

"Just drink," Elle said.

She watched until he finished the tea, swiped the back of his hand across his upper lip.

"Elle," he began, but he didn't finish.

"What?"

"Never mind."

"What." Elle was stern. Fatherly.

Reuben looked deeply pained, but not his usual kind. "I think when Daddy left, he took you with him."

Reuben might as well have reached into her chest and torn out her heart—but she feared it wasn't there anymore. *You'll have to be heartless to survive,* Hosea had said. He hadn't told her how much losing it would hurt.

Three days later, Reuben no longer needed to stay in bed. Susannah opened the windows, and cold air rushed through. In a few weeks, winter would end. Elle wouldn't be so trapped by her solitary thoughts. Her caustic moods. She hadn't spoken to anyone but her family in months—and she hadn't been able to make it down the mountain for school or church in over six weeks.

Once summer came, Elle could be fun again. She'd bust out the bow and arrow. Tease the chickens. Walk with her mother to Sunday service. Wade through the tall grass on Saturday nights and listen to the Grand Ole Opry from the signal that radiated off the barbed-wire fence on the other side of the stream.

Elle had never thought of music as her own to make. She believed she was too mean for it, too bloody from deer hides and dull knives scraped across her knuckles. Leave melodies for those who were meant to inhabit beauty like Reuben, she figured, and not destroy it like her.

A week after Merry's visit, Reuben sat on a low wooden stool and strummed his mother's dulcimer. It was a tiny thing, crafted from creamy pine, with two heart-shaped holes on either end. It sat in Reuben's lap like a cat.

His lungs weren't strong enough for him to sing, but the dulcimer's gilded notes set the house on wings. Joy had come calling, and all three of them knew to welcome that rare stranger in from the cold.

Then, without warning or fanfare, the butterfly weed ran out.

In a day's time, Reuben took ill again. Couldn't breathe, had a rasp trapped in his chest and chills chattering his teeth. Someone needed to seek out the healer, but Susannah remained bolted to Reuben's bedside, dread fixed on her face.

"Mama," Elle said once, then twice. "*Mama.*"

She got no answer, and so Elle donned her father's thick overalls, then rolled up her pant legs and stuck extra socks in the toes of Hosea's old boots. She tromped toward the bluffs, where Merry was said to make her winter camp. An old hunting cabin stood at the foot of the mountain, with a tail of smoke curling from its chimney. It took Elle half the morning to reach it.

The snow kept on. Even so, Merry sat rocking on the front porch, mandolin in hand. She played a syncopated lick but chopped it dead when she saw Elle from afar. Merry leapt so violently from her chair that it sputtered behind her. They needed no words between them. Merry already knew why Elle had come.

"I don't want your charity," Elle spat into the snowfall.

She left her true feelings unspoken: *But I need it.*

"I'll pay you in firewood" was the only thing Elle said as they hiked, even though she knew her family couldn't spare it. Now was the time for desperate gifts.

When they reached the steps of Elle's house, they knocked the ice from their boots.

"I can brew the tea myself," Elle said. "Just give me the weed."

Merry took hold of Elle's wrist. Her skin was warm against Elle's raw-boned hand. Elle looked up at her, and Merry shook her head. In the downy snow, Merry wrote two words with her finger.

No more.

She'd already given Reuben everything she had left.

Elle wanted to spill herself across the ice.

Reuben needed a doctor. He needed penicillin. A miracle. Merry didn't pretend otherwise. But there was no way off this mountain, and no way to convince a doctor to come in this deep.

"Why did you come all this way?" Elle hated the reedy split in her voice. "If you ain't got no more?"

Merry brought the fingertips on both of her hands together and turned them in a circle. *Together*.

"We don't want your company." Elle blew into the cabin, the screen door snapping behind them as Merry followed her inside.

Elle learned two things that day. First—harvesting butterfly weed will kill the whole plant. Once it was gone, it was gone. And second—not everyone, or everything, can be saved. Reuben lasted two more nights. Then he passed on, asleep in his mother's arms. Susannah had carried three hearts in her lifetime. Now one of them was silent.

What can be done when no father can be found to dig a grave in the cold?

A daughter will dig it herself.

Elle put on her father's overalls once again, along with her mother's oven mitts. Then she traced the overgrown path through the white pines, to the orb in the middle her grandfather had cleared fifty years ago when he'd been a young husband. He was buried there alongside his wife. More of Elle's family would be gathered below ground now than above it.

She and her mother brought Reuben in the sled, tucked in a blanket that Susannah had knitted from fine wool. Elle gathered the firewood. She lit a match from their scant supply, and then she took up her shovel.

The ground in the clearing was solid as stone. Elle and her mother took turns boiling two black pots filled with snow over the fire to douse the frozen land. Once the steaming water fell, Elle dug for her life. She cried out and thrust her spade into the dirt.

The hole Elle and Susannah dug was not deep enough, nor wide. But Elle had done what she'd done, and they laid her brother to rest along with his mother's dulcimer. Neither of them wanted to see it lie still in a chair.

Susannah helmed the empty sled, unthinkably light now, and followed their fading footprints back home. That day she and Elle joined the legion of women in their hills who had lost—a father, a brother, a sister, a son.

They said nothing by Reuben's grave site, so tired were they from digging it. There was no music to soften the winter bearing down on them, only the canine howl of the wind.

TRACK 3

One week after her brother's death, Elle began to follow Merry in secret. Grief, Elle found, caused roaming. Merry also drifted on foot. She had a quiet way, slipping into the houses of the sick, then slipping out.

It made Elle wonder what it was Merry had lost.

Ten days after Reuben's death, Merry paid them another visit. The morning snow had started to melt. Everywhere, a soft trickling fell from the trees like distant rain. The sound saddled Elle, same as the knowledge that soon she'd have to send her father a letter and tell him what had happened to his son.

It took brute strength to bear terrible news, and Elle didn't have it anymore.

Merry came early, before the sun had risen, in her black overalls and wide-brimmed hat. Elle answered the knock at the door because her mother hadn't gotten out of bed since the burial.

"What are you doing here?" Elle asked, not kindly.

Merry handed her a piece of paper. On one side, it said:

I sent word to your father about Reuben.

And on the other:

May I come in?

Elle would never claim to need healing or help, not with a whole hillside ravaged by another ruthless winter. Yet Merry had completed the task that filled Elle with dread. She'd already hunted the broken spirit inside Elle and reached in, bare-fisted, to splint it herself.

It was something one friend might do for another.

Silently, Elle stepped to the side and watched with awe as this woman, mountainous in stature, came in, hung her black hat on a peg, and sat on Reuben's stool. Then—of all things—she started to knit. Long johns or a sweater, Elle couldn't tell. The legs—or arms—were pink and crooked. Merry's needles ticked. Ten minutes passed before Elle realized she'd never shut the door, and a wind dampened the hearth. She heaved the heavy door closed, and Merry put aside her knitting.

She turned her head to the left, then the right, then back toward Elle. As if to ask:

Where is your mother?

Elle looked at the dark stairwell, and Merry nodded before entering it.

Half an hour passed.

Elle crept toward the instrument tilting against the wall and ran her fingers along the crack in its face. Her hand hovered over the strings. She didn't dare touch them.

The flames crackled, yet the room grew cold.

Elle stole up the steps. She found her mother lying flat on her back in bed, with Merry lying beside her on top of the coverlet. Of all signs and wonders, there was this: Her mother let out a laugh and wiped her eyes. The heat in her face had returned. The life. Elle learned another secret then from watching Merry work. She wouldn't use medicine when empathy would do. *Incarnation,* Merry might have called it. A sharing of pain to lighten the load.

Yet it took something from Merry—that intensity of communion with Susannah, that depth of sight. After she left the house, Elle followed her to the river, where floes of ice traveled south toward Kentucky. Merry lay herself on a flat rock. Cried there while making no sound. The sun peeked from behind the clouds and shone softly on Merry's face—her rosy profile, those slate irises. Merry stood and stretched to the sky. It was a kind of mutual resurrection, watching this woman gather her strength.

A rally—one that Elle, young and alive and bright with loss—longed to do for herself.

And then Elle heard it for the first time in her life—

Be who you say you are
Don't let me down
Give me what I'm longing for
Don't shackle me and call it a crown

What was this whisper beckoning her—a ghost? Some specter in the wind? A certain alchemy of loss had come to life, one born not from Elle's joy but from her sorrow.

These were the words to Elle Harlow's first song.

TRACK 4

A month passed, and that haunted voice that visited Elle at the river didn't return.

It was April now, and her mountain was eastering. Supple shoots of bloodroot and butterfly weed had begun to push through weary soil. Every time Elle trailed Merry through the woods, she felt a gravity pulling her out of her own skin, reshaping her. Like Elle, Merry had nothing at all, except for her mandolin and her herbs, which she gave away. Everything else she borrowed—her Ford, her winter cabin, her time.

The difference between them was simple and vast. Merry was content with what she couldn't do. She'd never pretended to be a doctor. Merry didn't speak, yet everything about her seemed to say:

Try to heal everything, and you'll heal nothing at all.

Elle scribed these phantom lyrics into her notebook. She hated the truth behind these words, how arbitrary it was. Unlike Elle, somehow Merry had made her peace with what she could not save.

The warmer weather brought rain that veiled the whole mountain in mist. Elle stood in its thrall, water falling in sheets from the cuffs of her sleeves, as she watched Merry on a spring afternoon through the slats in a barn door. The barn stood on forsaken property in the lowlands, abandoned by its farmer years ago.

Elle had witnessed since she was young how a landscape told the story of its people. How a bad storm could wash it away overnight, stripping the face of a homeland until it looked like a stranger.

Living, Elle was coming to see, was an act of losing. She had once basked in the expanse of this life, before Reuben died. Before her father left. Mountain springs cooled her when she was hot, bushes of wineberries fed her when she was hungry, mountain music comforted her when she was lonely. All that wonder turned to dust when winter came. They say seasons come and go, but winter didn't just come. It took. It took every last tender thing.

As Elle focused her eyes through a knotted hole in the barn wall, she saw that Merry was staring back. Elle staggered away, her heartbeat a flurry. Then she dared to spy again.

A boy about Reuben's age writhed on the floor inside one of the horse stalls, coated in filth. He screamed; he wouldn't be calmed. His voice scratched the air—not with gibberish, nor in a tongue Elle had ever heard.

She hadn't seen an ailment of this ilk. And by the tumult on Merry's face, Elle reckoned she'd never seen it either. Merry tried to embrace the boy, but he slapped her so hard her lip began to bleed.

A pony inside the barn brayed at the noise trailing from the boy's mouth. Not a moan or a cry, but a low, guttural urging. The boy coughed and vomited in the dirt. Then he lay in it.

"He's been like this all night," his mother said. "It's like a demon got him ever since his pa passed."

Elle knew of this boy. His name was Malachi. He delivered flat boxes of cigars all throughout the hills, and his father had left for Vietnam over a year ago but didn't return. The war was a hovering illness, and the whole mountain was sick with it.

Merry closed her eyes for a spell, then opened them. Her head whipped to the crack in the barn wall where Elle hid. Merry pointed at her, her eyes glossed and gray like the day Elle's brother had died.

Mountain folklore swore that a peculiar exchange must take place between a healer and her apprentice. A covenant to bind them, a wordless vow—less like a conversation, more like a kiss. Somehow, Elle knew that Merry was calling her forth.

She wanted Elle to sing.

Merry wanted Elle to sing, and not in a pretty way. The boy's darkness needed Elle's darkness to shelter it, to say, *Oh, you hurt? So do I.*

He trembled when Elle stepped through the barn door. She started to sing Reuben's favorite song, "Wayfaring Stranger." The boy roiled, but Elle kept on. She was no great soloist then, but her voice knew how to haunt.

Elle understood her brother wasn't inside this child who writhed in front of her. And yet, when she looked into his wild eyes, she saw Reuben's. The moss beneath his nails, the curt smell of sweat and creek water on the edges of his clothes.

More than once, she'd wondered where Reuben had gone while his body became earth. Elle feared he'd gotten trapped somewhere, aimless and alone, trying to attach himself to a luminary the way a moth rams itself into a lightbulb until it burns. But it was Elle who was restless and roving. Elle who had never said goodbye to Reuben, who didn't know the time had come to sing his favorite song so it could be the final sound he heard.

She could do it for Malachi. A meeting of two sorrows so they might find solace in each other. The child took hold of the deeply unknown parts of himself, while Elle called the bitter things out, and he settled.

This was the first time Elle healed someone.

Malachi's mother collapsed at Elle's feet, begging pardon for having no money to give. She offered what she had, strapped to the back of her pony—an old classical guitar with a glittering mother-of-pearl inlay.

At first, Elle refused. Hosea would have said that strength was found in Elle denying herself such a lovely thing.

"Please," the mother said. "Take it."

Elle felt then what Merry must have felt when her mother thrust a dead quail into her palms. The act of giving can be reciprocal. The right gift, when bestowed, begets another, and another, and another.

This was how their mountain did more than survive. This was how their mountain lived.

And this—singing her own hurt, turning her pain into tonic—was how Elle began to live again, too.

TRACK 5

For five years, Elle and Merry worked side by side. Together they composed the prettiest, most peaceful of ballads—Elle carried Merry's paper sack of wildflowers in the fall and helped her forage for herbs in the spring. On late-summer afternoons, they'd sit in the sun at the riverbank and watch the water bleed over the stones while Merry studied her notebook of mountain remedies. Elle found rest in letting Merry lead. It kept her from examining the bruise she'd become.

Elle's father, Hosea, had returned one year after Reuben's death. He came home with a soiled canvas knapsack on his shoulder, a smoking habit, and a missing finger. His long hair was shorn, and he looked younger—as if layers of him had been peeled off, laugh lines and dimples and sunburnt skin.

He did not look like anyone Elle recognized.

When he walked through the door, he tossed his bag and took up the banjo in the corner that had been waiting for him like a dog. He threw the strap on, a snarl on his face as if he knew what was coming.

Hosea strummed, trying to press the D string without the pointer finger on his left hand. The sound was dissonant and sour. He let out a mangled cry as he took the banjo and smacked it against the fireplace. It clanged and broke, the tiny pieces crackling against the floor. Susannah and Elle watched in silence, afraid of this stranger who was also someone they loved.

"Daddy," Elle tried, her voice sounding like it belonged to child—which it did. "Let me show you where Reuben is buried."

"I know where he's buried." Hosea took up his broken banjo and stomped out the door.

Elle followed like the shadow she'd always been until he spun on his heel and shoved her. He'd never put his hands on her before.

"You can't come," he said.

Then he lit a Winston and hiked toward the pines, leaving his daughter on her knees. The shove hadn't hurt, truly. Elle had withstood worse—a kicking mare, a crashing stack of firewood, even a fall from the loft onto the unforgiving planked floor below. What had slayed her was the cold, assessing glare her father served that said, *You aren't what I want.*

It had always been this way between them, Elle saw then. The war had only revealed what was true—a father who had tried and failed to turn his daughter into a better version of himself.

Hosea hadn't brought Elle's heart back with him. He hadn't brought back his own, either. Elle lay on the porch, feeling like every breath had been thrust out of her. She could hear the swish of a broom as Susannah swept up the leftovers of Hosea's instrument inside the house. She was so immediately *good* at it—collecting her husband's pain into something she could contain and send outside. Even in his absence, Elle's world had spun around her father's dreams and demands. Susannah deserved someone to comfort her, a set of solid shoulders she could press her tears into, and she'd never gotten it. The iniquity of it felt endless and chilling, like one long winter night.

Elle already knew she hadn't been what her father needed, but now she realized she hadn't been what her mother needed, either.

A year earlier, Elle would have gone hunting. She would have found something dead to feed this maw inside her, to offer up to her family rather than her own beating heart. Instead she took her guitar and fled toward Merry, who always seemed to say in the breadth of her eyes—

Be with me.

When Elle found Merry at the river the day Hosea returned, she said, "My father wishes it was Reuben he came home to, and not me."

It was the truth. It gutted her because she wished it were true, too.

Merry pressed a palm to her cheek and looked at her, just as she'd studied Reuben on the day they'd met—scouring for pain, smoking it out. She took hold of Elle's hand and pressed three of her fingers into the fretboard of her classical guitar. A G chord. Then she migrated to the bottom strings—a D chord. That day Merry also taught her how to set loose a melody from the strings.

Sing it slow, Merry wrote to Elle in her notebook. *That's how you begin.*

By the time Elle was eighteen, her father had returned to work in the mines for months on end, Merry was fifty-five, and Elle figured she'd grasped all the healer's secrets. Elle dried the yarrow, dug up the juiciest ginseng without damaging the root. She brewed teas, pulverized florets, placed them in paper bags. Mostly, she sang. Together she and Merry created the finest duet—the low croon of a guitar mated with the sweet cry of a mandolin. Everything they did was an aria for their whole mountain to hear.

So it stung in a very intimate way when Merry opened a fresh page in her notebook and wrote that there was one place Elle could not come.

The forbidden spot was a blind cabin atop a ridge where a cigar maker hermited. Elle had never set eyes on the woman, so dedicated was she to her craft. Everyone had seen her tin boxes as Malachi ferried them around dirt paths and docks, tightly packed with spiraled leaves of tobacco pulp. For all the years that Elle had followed Merry, Merry had visited every mountain home, except for that one on the ridge. Elle hadn't asked why. She reckoned when they needed help, she and Merry would go.

The day arrived in 1969—a July potion made from thunderstorms, flash floods, and the height of summer's heat—but Elle wasn't allowed. Merry's refusal felt like a swift, heartless jab in Elle's gut. A spiral of red smoke cut through the spine of the treetops just beyond Merry's riverside cabin, which was the mountain's signal for the healer to come quick. When she spotted it, Merry threw her bag into the bed of her truck and cranked open the driver's side door. Then she wrote in her notebook:

Stay here.

And yet Elle made to follow, as she always did.

Merry thrust out her palm, as if to say *STOP*—just as she'd done when Elle was thirteen and she wanted to brew a cup of butterfly tea for Reuben when Merry already knew there was none left. Just as her father had done when he returned home and wanted to sit alone at his son's grave. The memory burned in Elle's chest of everything she hadn't been able to do, of the life she hadn't been able to save.

The red smoke kept on, a rusty billow against the blue sky. Elle stood behind the truck's tailgate and blocked the path Merry needed to reverse. Merry laid on the horn, and a clot of sparrows fluttered. Elle hadn't felt angry at Merry since Reuben died—but just then she remembered she did have a temper, and it had been too long since she'd flaunted it. So she threw Merry's satchel on the ground, took up her guitar, and turned her back. Then she stomped home to cook dinner with her mother and play her a song.

Elle didn't see Merry for a week. She grew fiery and agitated as she thundered through Susannah's creaky house, thwarting dust, stabbing biscuit dough, pounding her guitar. Silently, her mother watched her from her rocking chair. Pipe in hand, Susannah observed her daughter nurse her slight by shooting accusations in every direction:

"After all this time, Merry still pities me."

"I'm *almost,* Mama, and that's it. *Almost* pretty, *almost* smart, *almost* good."

"Why am I not enough?"

She'd said it all about Merry, but she'd felt it from Hosea, too.

What Elle started to believe once the sun went down on the seventh day was that Merry would never come after her. Not the way she had for Reuben, or Susannah, or the way she would for anyone who fell ill.

How quickly her daily life had splintered without Merry's tasks to anchor it. With a crimp in her heart, Elle realized she needed Merry to thrive. Merry did not need her.

It caused chaos in Elle's mind to have her utility questioned. She turned feral. She didn't bathe herself; she started to stink. Susannah opened the windows and pointed to the tub.

"No more of this," her mother said. "Clean yourself up and go ask Merry what you've done wrong."

And that was just what Elle did.

It was sundown by the time she approached Merry's cabin. A storm threatened from the far side of the pines. Fading light smeared shadows across the ground. The campfire had gone out, and nothing moved but the rushing water. Merry's Ford was gone, its tire tracks scratched into the dust.

Elle caught that same feeling of dread she'd had the day she held up the quail and offered it to the healer—like there was an inescapable peril at hand that Elle desperately wanted to defeat. How viciously easy it was to surrender all she had in the name of that quest until she became nothing but carrion discarded just outside her own front door.

But that wasn't Merry's way. She didn't discard things, or trample them, or leave them to decay.

Elle paused in the summer stillness. Listened, just the way Merry had taught her. Not too far off, the storm hovered. The healer didn't like to drive the hills in the rain, and she never took the truck out after nightfall.

Something was wrong. Here, finally, was Elle's chance to right it.

TRACK 6

Few things are creepier than a blind cabin in the middle of the night. Elle risked the deadly switchbacks on the hike toward the ridge, over some of the deepest patches of stream, through brambles and downed balsams. The moon hung above, no wider than a sickle. Thunder rumbled as Elle passed Merry's Ford parked in a mess of grass at the foot of a steep ravine.

She forged onward into the black, unable to see the hands in front of her. Slowly, she counted her steps after she crossed the creek.

Elle brought nothing with her—no guitar, no lantern, no knife. The ancient trees, thick and untamed, conjoined overhead. For a length of the journey, she had to crawl on her knees. That was her only guide—*a trail so small no man can ford it,* so the stories went. A path meant for women and children, and no one else.

Last summer, Reuben had ventured up this far before he'd gotten sick—trailing Malachi, the courier boy who delivered the cigars in their tins.

"You'll smell it before you see it," he'd said.

Back then Elle had brimmed with envy—but she hadn't scolded her brother for climbing the ruthless pike. She hungered as much as anyone for details of what lay inside that cabin without any windows.

"It's just a house," Reuben had said, to Elle's disappointment. "With a woman inside who don't want to be seen."

Not even Malachi had spied anything beyond her arms, according to Reuben. The woman slipped her tins through a small, hinged door meant for dogs. After taking his cut, Malachi surrendered the money he'd collected, and a pair of gloved hands gave him a fresh load of cigars to sell.

Reuben's words rang true—Elle caught the sultry scent of tobacco in the air before she spotted the squat house. When she pushed through a final stand of scarlet oaks, the tip of her nose brushed the maple planks on the cabin's back wall. She leaned an ear to the wood and heard the din of a transistor radio playing Jimmie Rodgers's ghostly yodel.

She felt her way around the broad side of the house. Elle had no plan, other than to demand an answer for why Merry had left her behind. She couldn't see anything beyond her own need, wouldn't allow Merry's frontiers to lie beyond her own.

Slowly, then quickly, it started to rain.

Around the front of the house, Elle came to the hinged door meant for animals, right at her feet. The boards above it had spread over the seasons, allowing a slim slice of firelight to escape. She lifted her eye to the crack and caught a glimpse of shadows sailing toward her.

It was Merry, swathed from head to toe in thin sheets with only a small sliver as an opening for her eyes. Another woman sat bandaged on a makeshift bed, letting Merry tend to a seeping wound on her arm.

When the music stopped, Merry pulled away from the woman and Elle saw she looked so very much like the healer—the heart-shaped face, the onyx eyes, the long sterling hair.

This was Merry's sister, and she was very ill. Leprosy, maybe. Hemophilia. Tuberculosis. Something that had turned her either contagious or easily contaminated.

It was Elle's turn to pull away. She fell to her knees. Ravenously, Elle had chased after Merry's company when all Merry had asked for was solitude. All at once she understood: Merry hadn't told her of any sister, any hidden life, any dangerous, incurable disease. Even though Elle had shared every broken and holy piece of herself, Merry hadn't chosen to do the same.

Merry didn't need her, and she never had.

A bloodred shame washed over her as she stood and peered again through the hole. The cigar maker's arm bent at an angle, tightly wrapped in a sling. An ugly bruise spread across her left cheek. This must have been the cause of the smoke signal; the hermit had likely fallen. She seemed flimsy and unsteady, easily breakable. Something precious Merry had wanted to shield. The healer's hand cradled the injured arm, but her eyes shot straight to Elle's on the other side of the maple. Just as she had the day Elle spied on her through the barn door five years ago, Merry knew she had come.

This time she was angry.

The cabin door flew open and Merry charged out. Elle had never seen her so furious. Merry hated storms—what they did to her people, and what they did to her land. Only someone as bedrock as a sister would cause her to reckon with driving in such ruthless rain. But now Elle was her burden. She couldn't go into the cabin, and she couldn't stay outside in the storm.

Merry pointed down the mountain, then drew her fingertips from her mouth to her temple.

Home.

Rain slapped against the tin roof.

"Merry," Elle tried. "I'm so sorry."

But the words held no meaning. Elle hadn't obeyed, and now she'd thrust all of them into danger. Merry wasted no more time. She drew her fists to her chest and pointed straight in front of her with each hand.

GO. Merry hadn't spoken the word, but Elle still felt it like a rimshot cracking against the night. Merry pointed down the mountain. The fury in her features had turned her into a stranger.

Go!

Elle slid down the narrow ridge until she reached Merry's Ford. She was covered in mud and leaves, her skin slashed by rocks and bark. As she crossed the tailgate, she heard it—the rhythm of another set of feet in the downpour, twigs breaking, branches shivering. Elle spun, and her heel slipped on a trio of moss-laden stones.

As she pitched forward, she saw that Merry had trailed her, her keys in hand. She'd taken the covering from her face, though her body was still wrapped in a damp sheet. Merry grabbed Elle by the elbow to break her fall and thrust her toward the Ford's passenger door.

She was going to drive Elle home, even in the storm.

Elle climbed into the Ford and watched Merry round the truck in the rearview mirror. Lightning flashed, and in an instant Merry vanished. A terrible, singular throb caused the truck to tremor.

Elle waited for Merry to reappear, but she didn't.

When Elle climbed out of the Ford and lumbered to the tailgate, she saw Merry's legs jutting out beside the exhaust pipe, and then her body lying with half her face in the mud.

"Merry!" Elle ran to her and lost her balance on that same stretch of mossy stone, the one that had also caused Merry to slip.

Elle had fallen forward, but Merry had tripped to the side—and she'd cracked her right temple against the Ford's steel hitch.

A crimson orb swelled beneath her head, which had bent at an unkind angle. Her eye was fixed on the sky, but it could not see.

Merry was dead.

Lightning shot into the woods; trees began to crash. A nearby pine smashed into the riverbank, not ten feet away. Elle didn't think. She took Merry beneath her arms and dragged her to the open passenger-side door. As gently as she could, she lay Merry's body onto the bench seat. Then she flew to the driver's side and pulled Merry in the rest of the way.

Elle took the keys from Merry's grasp and shoved them into the ignition. The engine sputtered. Coughed. She tried again and again, her fingers gripping the metal, her foot jamming the gas. The engine ticked, and then it flooded.

Elle slammed her fists against the wheel, rain and tears sluicing down her skin. What had she done?

She looked toward Merry, who had told her to do one thing. *Stay away*. Elle had disobeyed her once, and now surveyed the destruction doing so had wrought.

Go, Merry had ordered, and so Elle did. She ran all the way home, leaving her friend's broken body behind.

TRACK 7

What is any mountain healer's origin story? Always and only this: the failure to fix someone you love. Elle had believed Merry was as immortal as her mountain. But even she had wounds that wouldn't heal. Even Merry still searched for pearls she'd lost.

Elle waited until the storm cleared at dawn before rushing back to the water. When she arrived at the riverbank, Merry still lay on the bench seat inside her Ford. The mandolin rested beside her like a lover.

With fingernails biting into her palms, Elle dared to look into the healer's eyes.

Elle knew that she was dead, but she clapped a hand against the glass. Slapped softly once, twice. Then found herself slamming a fist against the window and yelling out Merry's name. The louder she screamed, the less she knew the sound of her own voice. Merry's body was a statue, even as the truck shook.

Of course Elle blamed herself. Her own wanting, her own hunger, had led to destruction. Elle hadn't lost the healer, like everyone else in the hills. She'd lost her only friend.

The truth rested there, a downed vessel in her heart. Merry had saturated Elle's world, but Elle had occupied only a small part of Merry's. The amount of love Elle had for her now turned exorbitant and unrequited. Showy and pathetic. Indulgent and naïve. Elle felt like a child and an old woman, all at once. She'd learned this too many times for someone so young: the heart finds a thousand new ways to break when someone dies.

Elle wanted to turn to dust. She felt chafed, and sunken, and minuscule. She needed to find something to fix, and quick—and she thought of what Hosea would do, the questions he would ask when the blood of another hadn't yet dried on his hands.

What was she going to do with Merry's body?

Take me to the river.

Elle thought she had imagined it. She held her breath and listened again.

Take me to the river.

She hadn't heard that spectral whisper since the first time she'd spied Merry at the water's edge when Reuben died. Merry had cherished the water, the way it petrified against winter's onslaught until it rebirthed itself in the spring. It wore away even the strongest stone. *Water is a woman,* Merry had written many times in her notebook of mountain law. And Elle knew it was true.

All Elle would need to do was put the Ford in neutral and push. The river ran deep enough to engulf the truck. Elle and Merry had searched for its bottom on countless Sunday afternoons, never once finding it. They'd spent so many throwaway moments together, and Elle had loved every single one.

As she had when they met at the lowlands barn, Elle began to sing the words to "Wayfaring Stranger," but halted before the final verse. The water danced at her feet.

This would not do.

Merry deserved something wholly original, a song that belonged to her alone. And she didn't just deserve a song—she deserved to be sung to.

Take me to the river, Elle sang.

Take me to the river
Don't wash me white as snow

I'll take my chance with darkness
For everything I owe
Darkness ain't a blindness
For someone wise as she
Night gives dawn its new eyes
That's where she first found me

It was an ode to Merry as much as Elle's hymn of herself. She gazed at Merry's broken mandolin, mute in the Ford. Before she shoved the truck toward the water, she reached into the cab and rescued the instrument. Elle had buried Reuben with his dulcimer, but this time she couldn't bear it.

The mandolin held Merry's voice. Elle would not kill it while it still lived.

A Song for My Mother, Draft 1

BY MARIJOHN SHAW

Of all the things you left with me

Why a broken mandolin?

Of all the things ~~you took from me~~ I cannot see

Your face, your name, your ~~kin~~ sin

TRACK 8

Elle remained faithful to her work for a month after Merry died. She brewed spearmint tea and boiled pig suet. She sat with the infirm and prayed by the water. Elle even buried a lock of her hair beneath a dogwood tree for a young woman about to be wed. These mountains bred superstition, and Elle trusted in it now that she no longer trusted herself.

She was bottoming out. Her world had a giant crack running through it, like lightning splitting an elm. Just as it had been with Reuben, there was no fixing Merry's death, no return to what once had been. Elle stayed away from the deepest part of the river where she'd laid the healer to rest. The act seemed a hateful thing now.

The shock of Merry's death, and trying to understand the life she'd left, became Elle's private illness. She couldn't play Merry's mandolin, because it was crafted for a left-handed player, as Merry was. Still, it lay next to Elle in bed.

Eighteen and penitent, Elle mistook honoring Merry's memory for polishing the heirlooms of the dead. And so she vowed to practice healing on their mountain. One day, she'd find an apprentice of her own.

She would become a song-saving woman, a keeper of history in hill country.

All these things were true until a fire swept through.

Had the fire been a folk song, "if only" would have been its hook. If only there'd been more rain in the summer of 1969, and the huckleberry leaves hadn't been so brittle. If only most of the mountain hadn't gathered to shuck dry husks from bushels of corn. If only they hadn't insisted on a fire to beat back an army of mosquitoes. If only a spark hadn't caught the wind and landed on the heap of parched crabgrass by the woods.

Thirteen people burned, two of them children. They fought off the flames with dampened blankets and pails of river water. Elle had never encountered burns of this magnitude. Every wound reached the bone. Her soothing salve did nothing. Flank by flank, the injured staggered toward her. Never had she needed Merry more.

Merry would have known what to do. Elle did not.

At sunrise, the fire showed no signs of slowing. A great thunder resounded, and Elle looked up to see three crop dusters dousing the flames. They accomplished in an hour what Elle's mountain hadn't done in eight. Planes landed in an open field, and rescue workers filed out in tangerine jumpsuits. They rushed in and pushed Elle aside.

No one could breathe the air. Gray ash flitted like fireflies. Medical helicopters landed and whisked away the worst of them. Five in total, taken from home. Mountaineers took direction from no one, and yet each of them was ordered to clear out. Let strangers save their hills.

Elle did as she was told. She went home. Sat naked in the tub while her mother poured water over her, washed her hair. Wiped soot from her cheeks. Then she sat alone until the water grew cold, her skin pebbled and blue.

Now, at last, grief took hold. When there was no work to be done, when most of their mountainside had gone bald from flames. In a day's time, the rescue team left. The air still stank. Elle couldn't bring herself to leave her house. She settled into bed the way her mother had when Reuben had died.

Merry's work had stopped, and Elle could not continue it for one simple reason: she was not Merry, and she never would be. Elle couldn't heal the way Merry healed, couldn't hear the things Merry heard, couldn't love the way Merry loved. Bitter foretellings of failure masked the harder truth to reckon with. Elle missed her friend, and she was at fault for her death.

There was only one thing to do.

Elle sat up in bed. She took Merry's mandolin and set it in the rocking chair across from her. The instrument sat there with its neck arched like a scarecrow. Elle watched it as she took up her own guitar, tuned each string by ear. E-A-D-G-B-E. The vibration consoled her, the thrum of a beloved. This small thing, she could set right.

Elle set out to play Merry's old favorites, beginning with "Barbara Allen" and ending with Kitty Wells, but that wasn't what came out. Elle's heart brimmed with minor chords. She heard a fierce melody that called forth the lowest notes of her range. Her guitar was lonesome without the mandolin; it cried out as she slid her fingers down the strings.

From that moment onward, Merry was the ghost in every note of an Elle Harlow song.

Let it be known—this was not catharsis. This was reckoning. A calling to account of everything Elle had loved and lost, and everything she would always regret.

She wrote about the day she met Merry, and the day Reuben died. The moment Merry called her out from the other side of an abandoned barn wall. She wrote about the work of Merry's hands, and all that Elle had taken from those hands into her own.

She did for Merry what Merry had done for a generation of mountain women. Elle gave her a history not told, but sung.

After two weeks in her bedroom, Elle had written ten songs. She rose from her den of sheets and washed her face. Put on a clean pair of jeans and a checkered shirt, stole a bit of the rose-pearl lipstick her mother liked to wear when she fed the chickens. Elle found Susannah drinking coffee on the porch, in her own set of jeans, a cherry pout printed on the tin ledge of her cup.

"I decided something," Elle announced, and her mother looked up. "I'm going to get a job."

Susannah scanned the horizon. "Oh?"

"In one of the mines. I'll come home on the weekends to treat anyone who is feeling poorly."

Her mother tilted her head, squinted in the late-morning sun. Then she took up her pipe.

"That," Susannah said, "is a terrible idea."

The words hit like a slap.

"I'll come home," Elle swore. "You know I will."

Her mother laughed. "Leaving home ain't the problem. It's the looking back that will kill you."

"I don't understand."

"Elle," her mother said, plain. "You sat up in this house for two weeks, seeing no one but that guitar."

"I—"

Her mother held up her hand, and Elle shut her mouth.

"You spent half a month hiding out, writing and singing." Her mother exhaled a plume of smoke. "And damn if they aren't the best songs I ever heard."

Elle's throat started to itch. She wasn't accustomed to compliments.

"The way I see it," Susannah said, "you got one choice. And that's to go to Nashville and sell your music."

"What about you?" Elle could barely whisper. "What about everyone here?"

"Listen." Her mother set down her pipe. "This life you've been putting on since Reuben died? It ain't yours. You rode Merry's wings in the wake of grief, and there ain't nothing wrong with that. But you don't have to anymore."

Elle looked at the soft wooden planks at her feet.

"Besides," Susannah went on, "this mountain ain't moving. We'll always be here for you to come home."

Here was the magic of mothers—the simple reminder that the same road a child travels to unknown lands can also be used to return. That day,

Elle decided to grant herself respite from the ghosts hounding her. Merry, Reuben, her burning hills. Later, after everything to come, she would write a chorus about such an illusion.

Run from what you came from, baby
Never too far, always too fast

But first—before these words would return to haunt—Elle and Susannah began to pack a suitcase, save their money, and dream of kinder things.

TRACK 9

Elle left her mountain on a Wednesday with her whole life packed in the back of a wide Studebaker Wagonaire. One of Merry's old patients won the station wagon in a barroom bet and gifted it to her. The new tires came from another of Merry's friends, and an oil change from yet another. An entire hillside helped Elle on her journey. She had her mama's red suitcase, her own guitar, Merry's mandolin, and a hundred and fifty dollars from selling off the ginseng she'd dug.

She'd also made a crude recording of her music in the barn where Merry had first called out to her. Merry's absence hung there like an old winter coat, her fury frosting the air. This was the scar Elle would carry with her—that Merry had been angry with her when she died.

Elle had never felt worthy, and that knowledge settled into the cracks of her skin like dust. It didn't make her ache anymore. Now she felt terrifying instead.

And she wanted to be.

Elle liked the barn's malty acoustics, the way the spirit of the young boy she'd sung to, Malachi, still clung to the air. Even Elle got spooked by the raw edge in her tone.

She didn't want to be another pretty voice. Elle wanted to sound the warning knell. She spread out a map on her mama's kitchen table and circled West Virginia with a red heart. Then she did the same around Nashville and drew a vein of routes between them. She drew an X over cities with radio stations along the way: Winchester, Knoxville, Chattanooga. She planned to swipe a fresh coat of red lipstick across her mouth and ask the disc jockeys to listen to her album.

She left her mountain with its peak in the rearview, unsure when she'd come home again. Elle vowed she wouldn't return empty-handed. Somehow she'd find a way to give back all she'd taken. All she had killed.

Elle stopped at five different stations on her trip, each of them run by men. The first DJ said he'd consider her, and then she watched as he threw her recording in the trash. His office was no bigger than a closet, and he looked—and smelled—as if he hadn't left in weeks. A recording of "A Boy Named Sue" lay on the floor by the door. It had a chunk missing from its rim, as if a dog had taken a bite out of it.

The second DJ reeked of cheese curls and could only stare at the buttons straining at the bust of Elle's blouse. The third refused her outright.

"Didn't you hear? Everybody's into Woodstock artists now. Hendrix. Joplin. Don't need no more female country singers," he said, his muttonchops dancing as he chewed a wad of dip. "Especially if you ain't blond."

Elle speared him with the arrow of her stare—ready to point out that Janis Joplin wasn't blond, either. But he acted as if she'd already gone, flipping through stacks of padded mail, hopes packaged with postage stamps, full of women with voices and ambition just like her.

The whole day felt like screaming into a pillow.

Elle camped outside Nashville's city limits on the bank of the Cumberland River. She slept that first night in the back seat of her car, cramped like an accordion. Of course she thought of Merry, the way she'd slept in her Ford, the way she'd been buried in it.

The next morning, Elle rose at dawn and washed herself in the river. She'd likely have more luck snagging one of the three-foot stripers she'd heard could be caught in the depths of the Cumberland than she'd had at any of the radio stations. Elle had one more recording to give away, but she was tempted to toss it in the river, too.

This plan wasn't working.

Lord knew she'd stared down plenty of harsher things. But Merry had taught her how to listen for the pulse in any living being, and when Elle inspected the anatomy of the plan she'd hatched at her mother's kitchen table, she couldn't find a heartbeat. The recording was a dead, static object. A bird fallen from its nest. What Elle needed then, more than anything, was to prove to herself that she was still alive. That her heart hadn't gone missing but was hiding instead.

Elle needed to find someone who also felt the keen risk and the wilding thrill that she felt every time she strummed her guitar. Music had always been life and death to hill people. Elle had to lock eyes with a man who had his finger on the trigger. She needed to sing live for someone on Music Row.

So Elle perched herself at the corner of a crosswalk and a string of manicured pine trees outside the entrance to Weston Studios at 6:45 A.M. She began to tune her guitar. Every string of the instrument was sharp. The street sat empty then, cool and gray beneath her feet. Vanderbilt University stood a handful of blocks away, and although Elle couldn't see it, a few miles to the north the Cumberland River arched above the city like the hump of a camel.

At the studio entrance, a secretary swept the welcome mat. A citified sound—the shush of bristles meeting concrete like a brush on a snare drum.

Before leaving her hills, Elle had imagined the famed studio into a skyscraper. But this squat building was formed from rust-colored brick, with a planetary red-and-white sign stuck just below the roof. In a word, it was plain. Small.

Elle let the sweep of the secretary's broom set her tempo, and then her guitar took flight. She played every song she knew, from honkytonk to hymns. Her scalding voice razed the comely city—from the musician-for-hire ads stapled to the telephone pole to the famous Ryman Auditorium and its wooden pews less than two miles away. *This* was the center of it all, the lifeblood of country music itself, right where Elle stood.

Problem was, Elle wasn't the only one singing. Two other intrepid troubadours also auditioned on the same street. One of them had cymbals strapped between his knees, and the other sang the wrong lyrics to Merle Haggard's "Hungry Eyes." Together, they sounded worse than a runaway jug band.

Men with curated mustaches and bolo ties skirted past them on their way inside. Studio musicians cast them pitying glances. Soon, taillights lit the street. A Mason-Dixon delivery truck double-parked across the road, and the driver of a Trans Am leaned on his horn. Diesel exhaust polluted the air. The blaring hearkened back to the day Elle's mountainside had burned—the stench, the noise, the chaos. In an instant Elle knew she was about to be sick. She stumbled to the side of the building and spilled the biscuits her mother had baked all over the alleyway.

She sank to the asphalt and pulled her knees to her chest. Her guitar, still clamped against her, clanged in protest. She pressed her cheek into its strings, just to feel them push back.

"Rough morning?" a voice said.

Elle raised her head. A Black man in bell bottoms and a red turtleneck stood at the far end of the alley, smoking an L&M. His banjo stood pertly against the brick.

Elle nodded. "There's still time to step in shit before noon."

The man laughed and flicked the end of his cigarette. Took his banjo by the neck and walked toward Elle.

"I'm Leo," he said. "I'm guessing you're new."

"What gave me away?"

"The puking."

It was Elle's turn to laugh as she rose to her feet. "I'll try again at quitting time."

"The lunch hour isn't bad, either," Leo offered. "You could try stumping in front of Tootsies. It's not far from the Ryman."

"I will. Thank you, Leo." Elle's voice broke. This was the first person who'd looked her in the eye since she left her mother on the porch where they'd watched every sunset together. "I'm Elle."

Leo opened his mouth, shut it, then opened it again.

"Listen," he said, "it won't matter how well you play if you don't have a place to stay." He peered at Elle's mussed hair and the creases in her sleeves. "You look like you're sleeping in your car."

Elle flushed. "That's obvious, too?"

"You smell like the Cumberland," Leo said. "You got any money?"

"Some."

"There's a room for rent in a boardinghouse about ten minutes from here. I'll talk to the landlady if you want."

When Elle asked if Leo lived nearby, he coughed. "I don't live in that neighborhood. I mow the lawns."

Elle thought she understood all that Leo was saying, even though she didn't. She recognized the familiar need to work two jobs for every life that counted on you—even if it was just your own.

"Thank you," Elle said. "How do you like working here?"

Leo smirked. "Pay is shit for somebody like me. But at least I get paid to play."

"Ever get to record your own music?" Elle asked.

"These fools think they invented the banjo." Leo lit a second L&M. "I'm someone who gets written out of his own songs."

"That's awful," Elle said, slowly beginning to grasp what Leo had meant.

This was an everlasting loss that Elle had not known.

She grabbed her bag, wrote down the address of the boardinghouse in her notebook. Together, she and Leo ate the last of Susannah's biscuits while the bell of the Methodist church at the end of the block chimed nine times. Leo's break had ended, so he disappeared inside the brick facade. The door closed with a smack behind him. Elle took up her guitar, took a breath, and went to sit in Tootsies' alleyway until it was time for the lunch-hour rush.

One day in late September, Elle ran out of money. For three weeks, she had stumped morning, noon, and dusk. She turned not one head. An auburn-haired wraith, she withered in her cowboy boots while Nashville passed through her. She might have found the city unkind, if not for Leo. If not for a tiny room up in a garret with checkered curtains, all her own.

Elle lazed on the sidewalk outside Weston Studios. That afternoon, she would have to head home. She had no cash to pay her weekly rent and barely enough gas in the Studebaker to get her back up the mountain. The secretary pushed her broom by the entrance, but Elle couldn't hear its rhythm anymore. She'd entered a land of Kodak cameras and lava lamps, steel guitars and autoharps. Nothing here had an edge that hadn't been sanded, sculpted, and glossed. She didn't fit in. Elle felt more akin to the street itself, dusted in gravel, made from gutters and dirt.

A kid slumped by and kicked a stone right at her that landed in the well of her guitar. She overturned it, thumped its back until the stone fell out. The E string snapped, and Elle cursed.

The boy stuck his tongue out at her.

"*So* sorry," the boy's mother said. "He's just hungry."

"I'm sure that's it," Elle replied.

The woman unbuckled her candy-red wallet and tossed a tidy roll of bills into Elle's guitar case. Elle fanned through the cash when the woman walked away, her go-go boots ticking on the concrete. Thirty-five dollars. The most—and only—money Elle had made as a singer in Nashville. It would buy her another week at the boardinghouse, but not much more. She threw the bills into the case and dropped her head into her palms.

Spotting Elle's distress, the secretary set her broom against the brick and knelt beside her. She smelled like lilies, and her hands looked like they'd never had to haul firewood, never had to dig a grave. Elle had paid her no mind as she'd been singing her guts out for weeks. The secretary was Nashville-nice: eyes like a July sky, pale blond hair with waves that didn't frizz. Rhinestone earrings that twinkled. Someone who understood this city, someone who belonged.

"Hi," she said.

The word had a sorry melody all its own. Elle had felt invisible every morning on this corner, and now here was someone who had seen her at her worst.

"Hi," Elle returned.

"I have a confession." The secretary grinned with a dimple deep enough to stick a penny in. "I've been coming out here every morning just to hear you play."

"Oh?" Elle was allergic to pity. "I thought you were working."

"They pay me to answer the phones, not sweep the doormat." She pointed behind her, and Elle saw something she didn't expect. Calluses like Elle's on the tips of her left hand. "If I keep this up, I'll be fired."

Elle laughed for the first time in a long while. She hadn't laughed since before Merry had died.

"Listen," the secretary said. "You're singing at the wrong entrance. Not many musicians know that Arlo uses a private entry in the back, just behind the garden with a willow in it. All these people who use the front door? They have no say in who gets to make a record here."

Elle revived at the words.

"The man you're looking for—Arlo Weston—drives a baby-blue Cadillac. He's the one you want to hear you sing." The secretary thought on it. Her face held a depth Elle hadn't noticed at first blush. A hustle, a heat. A flash in a mirror. "Get him a cup of black coffee with a splash of whiskey in it, and it'll double your chances."

"I ain't got any whiskey."

The young woman smoothed her plaid skirt, and Elle caught the small sweat stains beneath her arms. The flared muscle in her shoulders. She liked to work, just as Elle did. To push. To wear a blouse at least three times before paying for the laundromat. This woman was pretty in every way Elle was rough, but they shared an animal kind of vigilance. It took spunk to balance at the edge of this Music Row world. To pull out your claws to hold on to it.

"Just the coffee then," she said, combing her fingers through a shiny pearl of hair at the crown of her head. "You don't need extra luck."

Elle had always figured she wasn't susceptible to flattery. The boys she'd known all her life didn't use words to prove affection. Theirs was a language of skinned rabbits and draft cards, money sent home in envelopes. They were blood to her, a bond deeper than words—flesh of my flesh, so the Old Testament said. But now, Elle had emerged on the other side of a great flood as Noah had, her past life sunk at the bottom of a river. The wonder of it unfurled before her like a golden scroll.

"Arlo comes in early, so you'll want to be by the back door tomorrow by six fifteen. When he rolls down his window, sing for your life."

Elle offered her hand to the secretary. "I'm Elle," she said.

"Josie," she answered, like the call of a dove.

TRACK 10

The next day, Elle followed Josie's directions with precision. A cup of coffee in her hand and a guitar around her neck, she waited in the morning half-light. Only a circle of ravens joined her, forming a black diadem in the soft willow tree on the far end of the lot. As Josie promised, a Cadillac purred as it turned the corner and idled in a parking spot. Elle emerged from the shadows and crept toward the car. She hesitated, then chose to leave the coffee behind. She wasn't here to serve. She was here to sing.

The man in the Cadillac—Arlo—looked her up, then down. Not in a leering way, but as an assessment, like counting the change in his pocket. He ran a long finger against the wave of his mustache, and then raised a hand in salute. Elle took it as her cue. Her hand found the frets, and the cut of the strings into her flesh steadied her heart. She began to play "Wayfaring Stranger" in honor of her mountain, in honor of her own wandering, and in honor of Merry who had given her the power to sing.

But it wasn't truly power, was it? It was Elle's weakness, her sorrow, her joy, tangled together in the gallows of her chest. All she'd lost, and all she hoped to find. That was what it meant to sing—to cry out for kinship, and to answer that cry herself.

When she finished the song, Arlo stepped out of his car. He was tall, wiry.

The red socks beneath his dress shoes caught the light of a meager streetlamp. He and Elle exchanged no introductions, no pleasantries. Arlo sat on the concrete steps, lit a Marlboro, and blew smoke into the gray morning.

"Play it again," he said.

He closed his eyes and listened, and once more, Elle played that guitar for her life.

Arlo Weston, it turned out, was from the woods himself. Deep in Kentucky, and Pennsylvania before that, he said. He'd fashioned a career out of the music he'd longed for since his daddy played the fiddle while Arlo sat at his side.

"Damn," he said, sitting there with his eyes still shut. "You make me think of home."

Home: It spoke of loss and comfort and kitchens and things that no longer were. Arlo inhaled, as if he could smell the sound of Elle's voice. His cigarette fell into the gravel, still lit. "Music ought to feel just like that, don't you think?"

"I do."

"It's the best feeling in the world, turning that dial and hearing your favorite song." One of his eyes opened. "Every day I fight like hell to get good music on the radio, and you'll have to, too. I can't make it easier for you than it is for me, you understand."

"I don't do easy," she answered.

Arlo began to rub his hands together, as if he were warming himself at a campfire. "Let's see if you can perform for a room full of men and not lose your lunch. You ready?"

Elle nodded. She wanted to sing for women, but there might be no end to the list of men she had to impress first.

Two hours later, Arlo bustled past everyone in the office, leaving in his wake a shuffle of papers and shoe polish, a scuttle of sideburns neatly trimmed as if the barber had used a ruler. In fifteen minutes, an unremarkable boardroom lot had gathered. Potbellies and wristwatches, subtle patches of chest hair and comb-overs. Elle was nervous and unimpressed. These were the minds that chose the score to American life: the songs an entire generation would listen to as they fell in love, as they got drunk, as they danced, as they cried.

Elle stood in front of them, feeling like a pinup girl in a small, windowless room. She'd not often been in the company of men. They smelled faintly of meat and orange sherbet. Elle felt alone, but she wasn't.

Dauntless country women had carved the path that lay before her. Patsy Cline, Odetta, Loretta Lynn, and even Sara Carter back in 1927, who had first sung for her life while nursing an infant. These starlets had reversed the order of a world that would not listen to them unless they set their voices to music.

The room had quieted. Men stared at her, dull-eyed. Elle's voice had never mended itself since that spell of pneumonia she and Reuben had shared. It rasped like trees creaking. Like the tailwind of a ghost. It was haunting, Elle knew, because she'd heard the echo of it through the holler where fishermen said it brought a chill to their bones.

Elle had never wanted to sing for anyone but her people. She'd never imagined that Merry wouldn't be at her side. Truth was, she wouldn't be standing in a room full of strangers, one word from stardom, if she'd never met Merry.

If Elle hadn't been the death of her.

Arlo had told her to sing "Wayfaring Stranger," but Elle understood then that this moment demanded her own words. She wanted to brand their minds, set fire to their skin. So she sang a song she'd written for Merry, one she wrote with smoke and ash still in her hair. No one but Susannah had ever heard it.

This don't work without you
Believe me, honey, I've tried
We never talked of things you wanted to
Now it's bleeding me out inside

I should have asked the question
Should have made you speak
Thought your heart couldn't be pressed on
But it was mine that turned us weak

Elle hit a G chord on her guitar, then sang the final verse a capella:

I took you to the river
Took your mandolin as mine
A new song I couldn't give you
But believe me, honey, I tried

If Elle thought the room had fallen silent before, now it had lost all other senses, too. It was blank and bottomless. Not one man looked her in the eye. She'd shown them the barest, hungriest part of herself, and each of them couldn't stand the sight.

The clock above her head ticked. She glanced at Arlo, who tipped his head toward the exit. She left without a word, her guitar jangling softly as she walked out the door.

Josie waited in the hallway, where she fiddled with the seam of her miniskirt.

"How'd it go?" she asked, her eyes wide—but not seeking. She seemed so certain already of Elle's presumed success, so accustomed to deciding for herself the way things should be.

It was because she was beautiful, Elle thought.

She let her hair fall into her eyes. "Terribly."

Josie frowned, a delicate crease denting the smooth skin on her chin. "Did any of them smile?"

"Not one."

She nodded, put her hands on her hips. Tried to set things right. "That's good. It means they didn't pity you."

"Doesn't mean they liked me."

She took Elle's elbow and squeezed a bit too hard. "At least they didn't laugh."

Elle started to walk. "You've got a piss-poor way of making me feel better."

Josie stepped in front of her, and Elle let her take the lead as they passed album after hit album posted on the beige walls. Connie Smith. Eddy Arnold. Charley Pride.

"What will you do now?" Josie asked as she strode toward the exit.

"I—" Elle paused. "I have to go home."

Josie stopped dead and looked over her shoulder. "Why?"

"I have no money."

"Money can be found. Talent can't." Josie resumed her walking, quickened her pace. "If you go home now, you'll always regret it."

They'd known each other less than a day, and somehow Josie understood the risk of this new life even better than Elle did. Most of the other eighteen-year-old girls Elle knew were betrothed to boys who hadn't yet returned from Vietnam. There was no going back to that for Elle. She couldn't now, not when she'd felt this freedom, even when it ended in defeat. The thought knocked her sideways, and the headstock of her guitar cracked against the wall.

"Hey." Josie touched her shoulder. Her eyes were searching, defiant. In them, Elle felt her own strength begin to gather. "You okay?"

"I am." The truth sat on her tongue, itching to be released. "I was just imagining a future I don't want."

The panic she felt at the thought of becoming a wife was biblical in its intensity. Elle couldn't help it—she started to laugh.

If Josie found her strange, she didn't seem to mind. "You want to see your future?" she asked. "Come on."

She pulled a ring of keys from her pocket and slid one of them into a door at the end of the corridor. Together they stepped into the dark. Josie turned on the lights, and the wonderland before her brightened in soft pink-and-gold tones. A plastic pine tree strung with tinsel sat right in the middle of the room.

"Elvis just recorded a Christmas album in here," Josie said. "He likes to set the mood."

The studio was only a rectangle framed by cinderblocks, but all of it was magic. A 1942 Steinway piano sat against the near wall, and folding chairs littered the rest of the black-and-tan-checkered floor.

"If you stand just here"—Josie took Elle by the shoulders and settled her five paces from the door—"you'll hit the vocal sweet spot."

"I can't sing in here," Elle whispered. "Every man in that boardroom looked at me like I'm a backwoods witch."

Josie crossed her arms. "Just what this place needs, if you ask me."

Elle trained her eyes on the Steinway, the gloss of it like the skin of the water on her mountain's rivers.

"Come on, Elle," Josie urged. "Sing."

Elle looked down at herself—her torn jeans, threadbare blouse, worn boots. She looked hard, used. Emptied. And yet when she sang out the first line of "I'm Thinking Tonight of My Blue Eyes," the hypnotic swell of her own echo surprised even her. She had grown up madly in love with country sunsets and fresh snowfalls and fires in the dead of night. But here was the sound of Elle, resounding. The beauty of this space rivaled them all.

Josie looked on beside her, mutually transfixed. "Nothing like it in the world, is there?"

Elle shook her head. She ran her fingers against the strings of her guitar.

"You play, don't you?" she said to Josie.

They were sharing the shadow side of a dream, each of them staring into something they wanted and might never get. Josie didn't look away.

"I've been trying for my shot, too," she said. "I'm trained in classical piano, but country music is my dream."

"What if you don't get it?" Elle asked because she feared it for herself. "Will you head home?"

"Hell no," Josie said, plain as day.

Josie was self-assured, decided, and persuasive in her patent-leather heels and ivory pointelle sweater. Elle couldn't remember ever owning any item of white clothing. She and Merry wore shades of dust and earth to cover the blood, dirt, and grass stains of their daily work. There was a pastel simplicity to the woman who stood before her now, so unlike the darkness Elle kept in the catacombs of her memory. Josie breezily declared things with nothing to withhold, no stain to disguise. There was quickfire courage in that *Hell no*, as if it were a handgun that could be stowed in a clutch and brandished at any moment, the very kind of courage Elle used to have.

Elle had traveled far from home to do this thing alone. She'd found peace in living half a life, with half a heart, while leaving the rest of her drowned at the bottom of a river. But now, Elle felt the fevered spark that ignites when half a heart meets its match.

TRACK 11

Elle and Josie couldn't help themselves. They snuck back into the studio that night after Elle's failed audition, and they played their hearts out for all of Nashville to hear. Suddenly city life teemed with locked doors and treasure chests—from the fifteen-cent hamburgers at Red Barn to the backstage of the Carousel Club on Printer's Alley—and Josie held the key to them all.

Making music with her in the dark was like a comet shooting through the sky. Thick and gritty, Elle's voice smoldered through every beloved old-time country hit Josie asked to play.

"You have a *Martin,*" Elle said, praising Josie's gleaming guitar when they finally took a break.

She'd never seen one before. Josie's guitar had abalone tuning pegs, the plates filigreed in gold. Most of the instruments on Elle's mountain were passed down through generations, crafted from salvaged wood.

You want an instrument that has seen *things,* Hosea used to say to Reuben every time he asked for a new dulcimer. Elle loved her old classical and would never trade it. Yet watching Josie hold her guitar to her chest, Elle understood what it meant to own something that had only ever been hers. To grow up with it, like a twin.

Josie ran her fingers along the strings, the dissonance breaking the air. "I could never afford it on my own," she said. There was a flash of pain in her eyes. "It was a gift."

Elle nodded, feeling seen. "So was mine."

"So you've never been trained?" Josie asked, her pick sticking out of her mouth. "At all?"

"Trained?"

Elle didn't know how to answer. Merry had taught her how to pull a song out of her own blood and guts—but Elle doubted that was what Josie meant.

"Like solfège. Music theory. Sight-reading."

Elle hadn't heard half those words put together in such a way before.

"I just play how I play," she said.

Josie grinned, dimple on full display. "A natural, then."

She was a sun-rinsed photograph in the flesh—Josie had traded her secretary's bun and heels for flowing blond hair with a thin leather headband, a short denim skirt, and cowgirl boots. She tapped her foot as she strummed, and Elle could hear the strings of her Martin lament as her fingers traveled the frets.

"I'm not much, compared to you," Elle whispered.

She reveled in the Martin's soft sounds, the emotion caught in the instrument itself. But here was the paradox of any light-washed photo—it was beautiful because it was fading. Elle and Josie time-traveled so sweetly through songs—from Jimmie Rogers to the Carter Family to Hank Williams, casting them all in Josie's cotton-candy glow—that Elle forgot the seminal sensation that still dominated everyone she knew on her mountain.

Hunger.

Nothing could replace the urgency of making music with Merry. Music was memory on her mountain. It served as a record of their people who worked endless days and lived abbreviated lives. She and Merry sang because they had nothing. And even that, they gave away.

With Josie, it was different.

With Josie, Elle no longer felt the friction between buttery Nashville and her savagely lush mountain. She had long feared losing time—ever since Reuben died, ever since her father left for war—and singing with Josie gave time back to her. Every moment found its pause in that dark studio. Even midnight rebirthed itself. Nothing ever seemed to run out in the city—not the people, the color televisions, the Cadillacs, the creativity.

Elle got high on the opiate of abundance.

"What's your favorite song?" she asked one October night after they'd finished playing "Always, Always" by Dolly Parton and Porter Wagoner. Josie had sung Dolly's part while Elle did Porter's, the harmonies wistful and lovesome.

"No contest," Josie answered. "'Long Black Veil.'"

Elle's brow lifted. "I didn't take you for a Johnny Cash fan."

"Johnny Cash didn't write it," Josie shot back.

Elle would never best her when it came to musical intelligence. She didn't dare try.

"What's your favorite song?" Josie asked.

Memories drifted to the surface of Elle's mind, unbidden. Merry's mandolin. Elle's guitar. The music they made.

"My favorite songs are ones no one has ever heard," Elle said.

"Play one for me, then."

"No."

Josie looked surprised and not a little hurt. This was the first time Elle had ever refused her.

"Why?" Josie asked.

"It's—" Elle swallowed. "It's private."

Elle hadn't given even half a reason, but it was all she would allow herself.

"Is it even a song if no one's heard it?" Josie asked.

A tear pricked Elle's eye. "Absolutely it is."

Elle had no idea what she was doing here—a mountain girl on the run, playing pretend in a fancy room. She took up her guitar and headed for the door. Josie stopped her with a hand on her arm.

"Elle," she said softly. "What is it?"

Elle hunted for a safer truth she could share. "My brother," she said. "He passed away when I was young. That's why I learned to play—because he couldn't anymore."

As she said it, Elle wondered if she'd ever been young, thirteen with a rifle in one hand and a lifeless quail in the other.

"I'm so sorry," Josie said. "Please don't leave."

Josie had started to look a little riled and panther-like, as if Elle's past was a kind of living prey she could pin down. She had no idea there was so much inside Elle that was already dead.

Josie played a baleful chord progression on her Martin, Am-C-Am-G, and it seemed to set her at ease. Her blond hair had gotten trapped beneath her guitar strap, and she stopped strumming to shake it free.

"How do you know so much about country music?" Elle asked. She'd grown up on murder ballads and old folk tunes, but she knew nothing about music as an industry—a way to make a living, like working the mines. Like going to war.

"I grew up here. This is all I've ever wanted," Josie replied. "There's never been anything else for me but this."

It was Josie who knew how to get to Arlo, Josie who had been inside Nashville's most powerful studio and held the key. Elle doubted those rights could be given. They had to be earned.

"Tell me," Elle said, "why you don't have a record deal of your own yet."

Josie played a waterfall of notes on her guitar. "Arlo says I'm pretty and blond enough, but my songwriting needs work. He lets me sit in on their recording sessions and gave me a job in the meantime."

A dream indeed, to be so invested in. Elle might have envied Josie, if she hadn't been this marvel Elle could harmonize with, note for note.

"What do you think it's like?" Elle asked. "Getting to record?"

"I think it's the closest we'll ever get to stopping time," Josie said. Her face was devout in the studio light. "It's miracle and madness, strapped together."

"Play one for me," Elle said, quiet. "One of your songs."

Josie regarded her, assessing the risk of sharing her own nakedness, her own need. This time when Josie began to play, her fingers found a darker progression: F-C-Am-Em. Then slowly, she began to sing.

Josie finessed her guitar like it was a lovesick man. Her hands charmed laughter from its body, sighs and moans from its mouth. It fluttered, it exclaimed. Elle witnessed the magic of it, just as she had with Merry and her mandolin. Josie knew the guitar as an instrument in a way Elle never could. Elle's style was utilitarian and blunt. Josie's lyrics were a simple ornament to the tapestry she spun with her Martin. The notes were intricate and symphonic, and the song Josie sang for Elle had only one verse, over and over:

Jaclyn, in her iris fields
Jaclyn, in her iris fields
Jaclyn, in her iris fields

It was stunning. The same words had a thousand different moods. Elle had never heard anything like it, and it bewitched her.

Josie's light eyes went gray in the shadows. She watched Elle as her final chord resolved. Her stare was a baring and a burning.

"Your turn." She stood and motioned toward her stool. "Play one of your ballads for me."

Elle grew instantly shy. Her songs seemed plain now, and simple.

"They ain't any good," she said.

"Bullshit," Josie said.

"It's true."

"Do you want your own name on your songs, or don't you?"

Elle did. Direly. She took up her guitar and began to pick an arpeggio of the opening notes to "Leaving Song."

Where you were going
You said I couldn't come
Then you left without a note
Like I was just anyone

It kills to know your life
Was bigger than just me

You didn't want to be a wife
But weren't we still family?

I waited days for you to show
Then I went in search of you
That search became my leaving song
Because now I see what's true

It kills to know your life
Was bigger than just me
This song still cuts me like a knife
Even leaving won't set me free

"Who is this song about, Elle?" Josie asked.

Memories flashed, deadly as lightning. Merry at the creek, sunning herself. Merry holding a hand to Reuben's cheek. Merry with a blossoming stain of blood beneath her head.

Elle thumbed through the melody again, her guitar granting her voice its silence. While she played, Josie watched her hands with careful attention. When the room fell silent, she closed her eyes and leaned forward.

"Play it again," Josie said. "I'll sing the second verse."

Elle began the arpeggio, and Josie coupled the rhythm with her own pounding run. She sang a counter-harmony on the chorus and took the second verse in a hummingbird tone, then added an instrumental bridge at a higher octave by choking up on her guitar.

Elle never knew her music needed to lift its anchor until Josie set wind to its sails. When the song resolved, Josie finally looked into her eyes, and Elle knew she felt it, too. What had happened between them was intimate and explosive and unforgettably rare. Their two visions became one.

It wasn't just a song. It was a hit.

TRACK 12

Elle hadn't thought much about fame before she met Josie. It seemed impractical and needy. All she'd wanted was music of her own and money to send home. But Josie made her crave more than contentment. Bold and brazen, she pushed them both to grab hold of all the jewels Nashville had to offer.

Josie lived in a cramped apartment on Second Avenue, not far from the Silver Dollar Saloon where they topped off her cola for free and gave her an unlimited supply of olives. She'd hunted down the cheapest stores for discount shoes and peasant blouses, and she also knew the best spot to view the Belle Carol riverboat as it passed, its lights flickering against the water at night.

Elle loved it. Loved every inch of how this dream made her feel.

If the world spun for just the two of them, the friendship between Josie and Elle would have been a carousel of color. Josie never tired of Elle's songs about her mountain. After "Leaving Song," Elle played every tune she'd written for Merry, but hadn't told Josie the full truth. She'd told Josie about Reuben's death, but not who she was deep down—someone who could not save anyone. And Elle hadn't told Josie about Merry at all.

By Thanksgiving, Elle had been making ends meet in Nashville for three months. She'd gotten a job at Tootsies—where Tootsie slipped Elle a free meal or two—and introduced herself to every executive who came in for a drink. Elle used Tootsie's hatpin to poke any stragglers who refused to leave after last call. She covered rockabilly hits at dive bars, and she and Josie still met in secret at night.

Those nights when they sang and dreamed until their fingers bled were the only thing Elle found in Nashville worth staying for. She longed for her mountain in the fall: the amber hues, the frost. But she couldn't afford the gasoline for the trip home. Besides, she was determined to return with good news. This remained Elle's vow, even though she'd left home—to somehow heal her mountain.

"I've been thinking," Elle said one night in late November. "Maybe we should audition for another record company." She paused. "Together."

Josie looked at herself in the studio's windowpane and readjusted her leather headband to cover a curl of hair. "I've been wondering, too."

Elle came to stand beside her at the window. Down the street in both directions sat at least five other studios the two of them could try. "So let's do it. First thing after the holiday."

Josie dropped the strings of her headband and turned toward Elle.

"I don't want to rush," she said. "The bridge on 'Believe Me, Honey' still needs work. So does the ending on 'Shackle.'"

"Really?" Elle was doubtful. "A song just needs some verses and a chorus, and somebody to sing it."

"Not if we want to stand out. The music has potential, but it's raw, Elle. It's better to wait until it's too good for anyone else to say no."

"I hate waiting," Elle said. "It feels like dying."

It was the truest thing she'd said since arriving in Nashville.

"We have time to do this right," Josie said gently. "Let's take it."

Taking time wasn't something Elle had ever done before. The air in the studio began to feel thick, and it was getting late. Josie thrust open the door and sized up her friend.

"I know what's bothering you," she said. "You're homesick."

"I'm not."

She was.

"It's okay if you are." Josie headed toward the exit and gathered up her guitar. "Here's what we'll do. Come home with me for Thanksgiving. Then next week we'll decide what other studios to try." She swung the strap of her guitar over her shoulder. "*After* we fix the bridge on 'Believe Me, Honey.'"

Two days later, the pair of them left the heart of Nashville behind. Josie had no car, so she drove Elle's Studebaker in the late afternoon, her hand riding the breeze out the open window. Elle hadn't thought to bring a fancy gift for her hosts, other than an earthen salve Merry had taught her to make that she kept in small jars. It extracted splinters, disinfected wounds, and cooled a burn. It also smelled strongly of tar and suet.

Elle felt no need to impress. She wore her russet hair long and loose, a navy shirt, and denim bell bottoms that a girl from the boardinghouse had lent her. Elle's body thrummed. She ached for Josie's family, if she couldn't be with her own.

"When were you last home?" Elle finally thought to ask as they headed southwest, away from Music Row.

But Josie's hands were tight on the wheel. "It's been too long."

Elle smiled. "I know what you mean."

Thing was, she didn't.

Just before seven in the evening, Josie pulled Elle's dusty station wagon onto a brick drive that led to a pillared mansion with a fountain. Light blazed from a crystal chandelier in the wide windows like a tiny sun.

If Elle took every house on her mountain and put them all together, the result still would have been smaller than the palatial monster in front of her.

"Josie" was all Elle said.

"Listen," Josie started.

Elle pushed her back against the window, as if she needed to escape. "I thought you were a secretary."

"I am."

It was hot, and Elle's jeans stuck to her thighs as she ground her hands against them.

"My parents wanted me to be a classical pianist," Josie said. "They disowned me when I told them I wanted country music instead."

"*Disowned* you?" Elle snorted. She'd never heard the word.

"They got me the job at Weston Studios." Josie's long hair had gotten stuck in her seat belt. "And then they wrote me out of the will."

"God forbid."

Josie reddened as she unclipped her safety belt and her hair fell free. She'd never been nervous before. Or embarrassed. Or contrite. "We're the same, you and I."

Elle laughed, but she was mad. "We are not the same."

Elle's father had taught her that money would never bring her happiness. He'd also taught her that money ruled everything. He'd gotten his physical for the army with two other young men who had funds to bribe the doctor into claiming they weren't fit for duty. But they'd been strangers—a part of Hosea's story one moment and gone the next. Elle wondered if money ought to matter between friends.

Josie worked as a secretary. She slept in a tiny room in a shared apartment, full of young women hoping to lasso the spotlight with their voices. Elle had seen Josie in only three different blouses—all of them well-made but worn. She'd assumed that like her, Josie was poor. But she wasn't.

Josie was broke.

"If we're the same," Elle said, "answer me this. Did your parents pay to get anyone out of the draft?"

Josie shifted in her seat, and Elle's face grew warm.

"Did they?" Elle repeated.

"It's complicated," Josie said.

"Explain it."

"Technically, my older brother is a student at a university near here."

"So your parents are paying for classes he isn't attending to keep him home. Can I go to college in his place?"

"He attends the classes," Josie offered. "I think."

Elle reached for the handle of the passenger-side door.

"Elle," Josie said, touching her forearm. "Please."

"Why did you bring me here?" Elle pulled her arm away. "You know I won't fit in."

"I don't fit in here either." Josie's voice snapped. "Do you think anyone here asked me if I thought it was right to pay for James to avoid the war? Do they ask what I think about anything at all? They think supporting me means buying a fancy guitar so they can decide when and where I play it. Maybe I had more money than you, but I also know what it's like to be a constant disappointment. To try and be married off at eighteen. To always be compared with a perfect brother."

"Brother?" Elle seethed. She couldn't help it—the only loss she could feel was her own. "At least you've still got yours."

"Stop it," Josie whipped. "You know that's not fair."

"You're sure as hell right, it's not fair."

Elle wanted to scream.

"Look." Josie drilled her fingernails into the plush seat between them. She looked agitated, and nervous, and desperate. "You hate being judged for having so little. Don't judge me for all of this." She pointed toward the house. "It was never mine, anyway."

Elle remained unmoved. Beside her, Josie sagged in her seat, Elle's keys in her hand.

"I didn't want you to be alone on Thanksgiving," she said. "That doesn't make me a villain."

Elle looked at Josie, still so vibrant even in the November gray. She saw now why only Elle had brought her guitar. Josie's talent—her heart-stopping, sinewy music—was scorned here. Elle felt the hard lines of her principles slip, and she squared it with herself: If she had the money, Elle would have spent it getting every mountain boy she knew out of that terrible war.

And her father, too.

"All right." Elle sighed. "Cry your golden tears."

Josie laughed. The sound was brash and too loud for the small space. The studio magic Elle and Josie shared felt threatened here, and fake—like they'd imagined the whole of it.

"Here," Josie said, taking out one of the turquoise studs from her ear and handing it to Elle. "For shared strength."

Elle fastened the earring in her left ear. Then the pair exited the Studebaker and stood before the brick behemoth. The second secret Josie had kept was that they were already late for a dinner party. The gruff and stately house towered over them with holly boughs dripping from its eaves.

Elle feared this would be the most boring night of her life.

Until midnight, it was. Elle drifted through orbits of chiffon and cigars, crystal and champagne, and constellations of appetizers on hand-painted porcelain. Minnie Pearl was there, making guests laugh from the wide staircase. No one spoke to Elle. Josie's parents, outfitted in matching hunter green, didn't greet her. Elle handed Mrs. Starling a jar of salve, and her whole face pinched at the smell as she placed it on a passing server's tray. Then she and her husband whisked Josie toward the attentions of a young man dressed in a threatening amount of corduroy.

Elle wanted no part of it.

She took up her satchel and stepped into the cool night. The gardens in the backyard were lush, even in autumn. Chrysanthemum, magnolia, iris, and snapdragon. Glad for her sleeping bag, Elle breathed deep and vowed to spend the night outside.

Somewhere, a grandfather clock struck twelve. Upstairs in the great house, a bedroom light flicked on. All at once—a crash, a scream. Ten seconds passed. Twenty. Then Elle heard a familiar name called into the dark.

Jaclyn.

The sound of it was angry and rushed. Laden with fear.

Elle ran toward the noise, toward a back stairwell that led to the third floor.

Up a hidden staircase, down a white hall, into a white bathroom, Elle found petal-pink water in the bathtub and a young woman bleeding at her wrist. A razor floated above the drain. Josie's mother stood transfixed before her, holding a stack of soiled linens.

"I can't stop the bleeding," she said.

All Elle could think of was Merry.

With one hand, she took a towel and pressed it against the wound. Then she opened the satchel at her hip and dug through it until she found a bag of Merry's yarrow root, which she carried with her always. She spit into her palm and made a paste from the powder. Josie rushed in just as Elle climbed into the tub.

"Jaclyn," Josie said.

Elle had never heard anyone say a name with such terror and heart.

This was Jaclyn—Josie's sister. Elle peered at her face as she pressed the salve into the cut. She had Josie's eyes, her nose, her cowlick.

"You're twins," Elle said.

Josie nodded. Couldn't move, couldn't speak. Elle knew that feeling like the shadow it was in her mind, the way she'd stood over Reuben's body and felt helpless as hell.

"There has to be a doctor downstairs." Elle pressed harder into the wound. "Go find one."

Josie ran from the room. Her mother knelt on the floor and white-knuckled the edge of the tub.

Elle held fast. "Why are you keeping Jaclyn in the back of the house?"

"She's always so dour. I thought"—Mrs. Sterling swallowed—"it was better this way."

"Is it?"

Elle fixed her stare until Josie's mother looked away. Then she pulled the plug on the drain and ran a hot stream of water. She was covered in Jaclyn's blood.

Jaclyn wouldn't stir, and dread settled in Elle's gut.

What would Merry do?

A phantom voice, a beckoning, a leading. Always, Elle would heed it.

"What's her favorite song?" Elle asked.

Mrs. Starling blanched. She didn't know. Yet in that moment, Elle did. In a heap on the floor, she spotted a napkin that had a familiar lyric written on it in permanent marker. She could picture Josie scrawling it for her sister, joyously defying her mother's immaculate linens. Elle began to sing—

Jaclyn, in her iris fields
Jaclyn, in her iris fields
Jaclyn, in her iris fields

It didn't sound the way Josie's version did. Elle's voice was ragged and wired. But she'd never needed it to be pretty, and she didn't need it now.

Jaclyn's eyes fluttered. Music, Merry had taught, offered the best medicine when every other balm failed.

"I need you to speak, if you can," Elle said softly. "Even with your hands."

The girl moaned. Her breath was coarse and her pupils bloomed, but she took Elle's hand.

"There you are," Elle said, a shiver in her throat.

The doctor burst in then, with Josie close behind. Elle lifted herself from the tub as the doctor felt Jaclyn's pulse and eyed the bloodshed on the floor.

"What is this paste you used?" he asked.

"Yarrow and saliva," Elle answered.

"Strange," he mused. "A backwoods remedy?"

He said *backwoods* as if she'd cast some spell.

Elle took up the linen napkin and used it to wipe the blood from her hands. She offered it then to Mrs. Starling, who still gripped the soiled towels to her chest, but she backed away.

"Keep it," she said.

"Looks to me," the doctor continued, his ear to Jaclyn's heart, "that the yarrow saved her life."

"It wasn't the yarrow," Jaclyn whispered from the tub. "It was the song."

Josie and her mother gaped at Elle.

"What—" Josie's voice wavered. "What did you sing?"

"'Jaclyn in Her Iris Fields,'" Elle answered.

"That's my song," Josie said lowly, as if she were cleaved by guilt—and a snip of jealousy—that she hadn't been the one to sing it. "Mine and Jaclyn's."

"It still is. I just borrowed it." Elle tucked the napkin into her back pocket. "I learned to sing this way when I was young. My own sorrow reached out to Jaclyn's. Held it till she could pull herself out."

"Sorrow?" Mrs. Starling acted as if she'd never heard the word.

"Darkness, then."

They looked at her as if they'd welcomed home a conjurer.

"What *are* you, Elle?" Josie asked.

There were many answers to that question, but Elle could only think of one.

"A mountain healer," she said. "I used to be."

It was the first and last time Elle would refer to herself as such.

"You never told me that," Josie said, a spear of betrayal in her stare.

"Did you use witchcraft?" Josie's mother cut in.

"Don't be ridiculous."

Mrs. Starling's jaw dropped at Elle's impertinence. So did Josie's.

"Go get Pastor Roberts," Mrs. Starling told the doctor. "Now."

"I doubt that's necessary," he said. "She's just a country girl."

"I'll get him, Mama," Josie said, and Mrs. Starling took hold of her daughter's hand.

Together they gazed at Jaclyn.

Elle caught the look of shared loyalty between them, the bond of blood. A loneliness sliced through her, just as it had the moment Elle discovered Merry had a sister, and she'd been left outside in the storm.

"Please don't tell anyone about this," Elle whispered to the doctor.

He nodded, and Elle moved toward the door. Josie cast her the rattled glare of a stranger—which Elle wondered now if she'd always been.

"We'll pay you," Mrs. Starling stated, "before you go."

"Pay me?" Elle asked.

"For saving her life."

Mrs. Starling may as well have slapped her.

"Mountain healers don't take money," Elle said.

"There's no shame in it," Josie said.

"In what, exactly?"

"Charity."

Josie's expression held both relief and fear, which Elle understood. But her gaze also had a distant kind of disdain that made Elle reexamine the invitation she'd been given back in the studio. Josie hadn't wanted to bring a friend to her family's mansion. She'd wanted a safeguard. A sacrifice. Someone to send into the chasm between her and her mother.

Now she'd seen Elle for what she truly was—a mountain healer's apprentice, poor and troubled—and Josie didn't like it.

Elle pulled her into the hallway.

"Josie," she said. "I'm still me."

Josie beheld her, covered in her sister's blood, eyes sunken, her own ghosts brooding just beyond her shoulders.

"Elle," she said. "I don't think you're all right."

Elle dropped Josie's arm. "What's that supposed to mean?"

"There's something—off about you. It's in your songs, in your eyes, even in the way you're standing here right now." Josie's eyes went small as they raked over her. "I don't know what it is, but I can't help you."

"I never asked for your help," Elle said, but Josie didn't hear.

She disappeared down the hall, and Elle was gutted that Josie—her friend, her confidant, her partner—had seen the hurt in her, named it, and backed away. Elle had always strayed toward darkness, toward sorrow, toward pain.

With soiled hands, Elle left Josie behind that night. The next morning she rose from the yard before dawn and drove back to Nashville alone. When she made it to the boardinghouse, she took out the turquoise stud Josie had lent her and tucked it away in a drawer. Tossed the dirty linen napkin in there, too.

It was Thanksgiving Day, and at the side of the porch, Leo was trimming a bush. When Elle came down and collapsed in a sad heap on the steps, he was kind enough to put down his shears and play Elle's favorite music on his banjo. Before the first verse of "Wildwood Flower" was through, Elle knew she never wanted Josie Starling to speak her name again.

TRACK 13

A week went by, then two. Winter sank its teeth into Music Row, and still Elle hadn't seen Josie. She thought she'd spot her from afar during her shift at Tootsies or on one of the street corners where she still stumped. She could nod—or not—and act as if they'd never made music in the dark. As if they hadn't made each other stronger, made the dream of Nashville so real it lived at the edges of their eyelashes and on stray pieces of paper with scribbled lyrics.

This was the easiest way, Elle figured. A measured and immediate parting, numb and final. It wasn't the way of her mountains, but the way of the city. A death in its own right. Elle mourned what she'd believed to be true about their friendship with everything she had.

She'd believed in herself when she was with Josie, for one thing. Her confidence was seductive and contagious, so much so that Elle had come to think of it as her own. But Josie had been granted things Elle had never gotten in life—and they had nothing to do with money. Josie never questioned herself. She never felt empty. She remained openly allegiant to her own vision and grit. Josie was trained, and cultured, and beloved. Men parted ways for her when she strutted down the studio hall. They gave her the final slot at every open mic. She understood music not as a series of heartbreaks, as Elle did, but a consummation of strings and walk-down scales and pedal tones and high harmonies Elle could not hear. And Josie—when all the finery had been stripped away—thought Elle was stained, just as she was.

Christmas arrived, and Elle returned home with nothing in her pockets, the opposite of all she'd promised. She folded herself in her mother's arms, her blue-and-green patchwork quilts. Breathed in the wood smoke and listened to the crackling of biscuits on the stove. That ache for home had eased, but a fresh one took root. Josie hadn't come to make things right. Elle hadn't been enough for Josie to even try.

Truth was, Elle hadn't tried, either.

Once again, the inertia of loss set in. Elle's grief drew her deeper into the bed she'd slept in as a girl. Once she climbed beneath the covers, she didn't come out. For the first time, she was grateful that life in these hills stopped when the cold came. She was sick of how the world elsewhere kept spinning, no matter its lattice of broken hearts.

"Not this again," Susannah said on the fourth day Elle wouldn't leave her bed. "Get up and sweep the snow off the porch, at least."

Elle knew her mother was worried—about her husband, who arrived home from the mines on Christmas morning and spent most of it in the woods with his Winchester, and about her daughter, too. Elle hadn't touched her guitar since she'd come home. It had turned their cabin eerily quiet, just as it felt after Reuben's burial. Each morning Elle looked deep inside herself for a reserve of strength and found nothing.

"Tell me," Elle said to her mother, "what Merry told you when you couldn't get out of bed after Reuben died."

Susannah's hands rested at her waist as she shut her eyes. She looked a little like her son just then, the way her lashes fanned across the tops of her cheeks. "She wrote four words in her notebook. *Tell me about Reuben.*"

"And it helped?"

Susannah let out a breath. "Nothing helped."

Elle reached for her mother's hand.

"I think it reminded me that his name wasn't a curse, just because he was gone," Susannah said. "That he was more than just his death."

"I'm sorry," Elle said, the words slipping from her like water. "I wasn't here for you when you needed me."

"Excuse me?" Susannah clamped Elle's hand hard with both of hers. "You held this house down, as I recall. You cleaned and cooked and dug a grave with an old, shitty shovel. Forgive the language, honey, but you're strong as fuck, Elle."

Elle covered her mouth with her free hand in mock horror. "Mother," she said with a peek of her lost playfulness. "What would Reverend What's-His-Face say?"

"You mean Reverend *Barnes*? Really, Elle. He's been the preacher here since you were born. He married your father and me."

Elle shrugged. Here in a drafty bedroom, her mother had lifted her up, had shown Elle something true about herself. "I only keep track of the people I love. My brain doesn't have room for much else."

"A good quality." Susannah gave a single nod. "Apologies to the reverend, though."

The house stood quiet around them, built for four, now cared for by two.

"What does it get us hill women," Elle asked, "being strong all the time?"

Susannah sat down on the bed. Outside the window, fresh snow began to fall. "I don't know what you mean."

"A baby needs birthing, we do it. The sick need healing, we do it. A body needs burying, we do it. For what? We're still treated like we're invisible."

"You're not invisible to me," her mother said.

The look on Susannah's face was so plainly earnest, so wholly focused on her child that it stitched up one of the snags in Elle's chest. She didn't often consider all her mother had lost in her life. A son, an itinerant husband. A daughter she'd encouraged to go out into the world. So much of a woman's life was this relentless unspooling.

Elle couldn't think what to say. All her words, all her lyrics had fled. Susannah lay down beside her in bed, just as Merry had done with Susannah after Reuben had died.

"Elle," she said softly. "What is it?"

Together they stared at the ceiling while Elle told her everything that had happened in Music City. Of Arlo, Leo, Josie and her family's fortune, and of Jaclyn, too.

"Seems cruel," Elle said, mostly to herself. The quilt had worked its way around them into a nest. "Jaclyn was holding her sorrow, all alone, even with all those people there. I'll never forget it."

"Memory bears a heavy weight at times, doesn't it?" Susannah said.

Elle nodded. She was still young, and already she had plenty of hurts she'd rather not remember. Memory was both a blessing and a blight—a twin Elle had brutally thrust into a closet.

"I saved Josie's sister," Elle said. "And she still didn't want me."

Just as had happened with Merry, it seemed Elle should have chosen to love someone best by leaving them alone. It hit Elle with the kind of hunger that couldn't be satisfied with a meal.

She hated how much she missed Josie Starling.

"Did you think"—Susannah slipped an arm around her daughter's back and gave her a squeeze—"how terrible it must have been for Josie, seeing her sister like that?"

Elle had thought about their friendship. She'd thought about losing Merry and Reuben and what it meant to be an unwelcome guest in a rich family's house. But she hadn't considered all the things someone like Josie might lose that no amount of money could replace.

"No," Elle answered. "I didn't."

"Can't help where you come from. Everyone deserves clemency now and then," Susannah said, and Elle knew it was true.

They sat with it for a beat.

"You know what I like about being a woman?" Elle's mother asked when the silence weighed too heavy. "Lipstick."

Elle hadn't forgotten how to laugh. She welcomed it.

"Truly, though," her mother continued, "what women know is how to begin again. We do it a hundred times a day. Every meal we cook, every bit of dust we sweep. It's what Mother Nature does, sun up, sun down. She'll set fire to her own house, rip herself down the middle, wash herself clean just so she can do it over. Mark my words—she's doing it, even now." She pointed at the snow falling outside the window. "No man has ever known something as fierce as that."

Susannah sat up and took Elle's hand. "The best thing for you to do is something you've already done before, Elle. Today you get up and start again."

It didn't fix things, but as Merry had taught her of their healing work a long time ago—

Try to heal everything, and you'll heal nothing at all.

The world was not all right, and Elle's heart was not all right. But that day she did the one small thing she could. She got out of bed, put on her boots, and took a broom to their porch, where she throttled the snow.

In time, spring came again to Elle's mountain. Sparrows sang, violets grew plenty, and Susannah bought herself a radio. They'd had months of quiet, and nothing to soften the harsh wind—not even the sound of Elle's guitar strings.

All winter, she hadn't wanted to listen to any country music. Not even her own.

But now the sun floated in the sky on buttermilk clouds, and Elle was ready to prune her ghosts. She could try again in Nashville, if she wanted. She could become a miner, a teacher, a seamstress. There were infinite ways for her to have a voice.

She and her mother huddled around their new radio like it was an infant, squealing at every little noise it made. They twisted the knob until they caught the bright notes of a bluegrass mandolin. Susannah cranked the volume as high as it would go and opened their windows so the neighbors in the holler could hear.

The radio serenaded them from morning into late afternoon while Elle turned a vat of potato soup on the stove. Each song was a long-lost friend bestowing its secrets. Reminding Elle of who she was. Breathing life back into her one note at a time.

Then came a melody Elle had never heard on the radio before. A lonely guitar, a lonelier voice. It sang to her prettily at first.

I'll write you letters when I'm gone, though you won't write to me
A message in a bottle, getting lost inside your sea
No pretty words will keep you, no picture on the wall
Try to heal everything, and you'll heal nothing at all

Elle listened, but her ladle of scalding soup splattered on the floor. She didn't feel the burn on her legs.

You came up my mountain
Not one word you said
You couldn't save my brother
But you saved me instead

"What in the holy hell?" Susannah asked.

This verse had its origins long ago when Merry was still flesh and blood, with breath in her lungs. This melody was the ache that formed the first ballad Elle had written for the woman she'd loved. This song belonged to her alone, but she wasn't the one claiming it on the radio.

It was Josie.

Elle had lost her friend and her shot in Nashville all at once. And now she'd lost her own music, too.

The song resolved, and Elle had to force herself to move. She turned herself in a circle and ended up where she began.

"'Heal Nothing' is the first hit by newcomer Josie Starling," the DJ said. "She wrote and recorded an album of ballads for her beloved soldier before he left for the war."

Josie had written the song to remember him by, the DJ went on. Luke was his name. *Her beloved*. Elle had never heard her mention him.

The kitchen seemed to tilt on its side, and Elle sank to the floor. Found one breath, then another. She took up the spoon she'd dropped, wiped the stain.

As the burn on her legs began to sting, Elle reckoned with what had been taken from her long before she knew it was gone. There was music and the dream of stardom, but a far more penetrating theft had taken place, with Elle a willing part of it. She'd surrendered her untold history with Merry—all the pain, love, and sin—and now Josie wore it like the pelt of a fox when it was Elle who had gutted the beast and turned it into song. Elle who had formed its ribs and tendons and teeth. Elle was its creator, keeper, and captor. Josie deserved none of it.

She'd made Elle think less of herself and her music, and Elle had let her.

This was the first time Elle didn't ask what Merry would do. Merry was too deferential, too mild, too meek for a betrayal of this breed. Instead Elle peered deep down, beyond the black hole inside her, and that was where she found it.

Her heart.

It had woken, and it growled like thunder about to swallow a drought. Her father had said she'd need to be heartless to survive, but he was wrong. Elle's heart was a wild ghost, and it rose from the dead the minute her song came on the radio.

Elle stood, smoothed her apron, and drifted toward the radio to shut it off.

"I will *never* speak to Josie Starling again," she said.

Then Elle did only what she could—that next small thing. She climbed the stairs to her room and began to pack her essentials. A change of clothes, her mother's rose-pearl lipstick, and her guitar.

Elle had spent her winter in melancholy, but never again would she waste any sorrow on Josie Starling.

Now she was mad as hell.

A Song for My Mother, Draft 2

BY MARIJOHN SHAW

~~*A shooting star hit the forest floor*~~

~~*Now a song I wrote isn't mine anymore*~~

~~*What did I steal from you?*~~

~~*What about the things you stole from me, too?*~~

CUT. TRY AGAIN.

TRACK 14

Elle had one task in mind when she arrived in Nashville. She'd left West Virginia before midnight, driven through the dark until she reached Weston Studio's hidden back lot several hours later. There, she planned to wait beneath the willow until Arlo rolled through in his Cadillac. Once he stepped out, she'd let loose the demon of her fury.

This time, she'd skip the coffee altogether.

Elle drove along the city's empty streets, the lamp lights casting crowns into the heather. So much of it remained the same—the record store still stood with a larger-than-life guitar tilted against its red-and-white sign, the arched windows on Tootsies' second floor were still thrust open in the cold, and the telephone pole on the corner where she'd first noticed Josie's light hair as she worked her faithless broom still had countless slips of paper stapled to it with phone numbers of musicians looking for gigs. Some of them floated in the wind like snowflakes. The city hadn't changed, but Elle had. Music Row's sweet tooth rotted in her mouth. Elle wanted to spit it out.

As the Cadillac pulled into the lot, Elle pinched her waist with her hands. Like a vanguard, her guitar hung around her neck. She was cold, but she wouldn't let this man see her shiver.

Arlo stepped out and squinted at her beneath the streetlight. His face looked skeletal in the shadows.

"Do I know you?" he asked.

Elle almost lost her nerve. She hadn't seen him in months and had spent less than an hour with him, even then. He'd likely never thought of Elle again after her audition ended. She'd thought of him every day since.

Her rage blistered.

"Arlo," she spat. "Josie Starling stole my song."

It wasn't the grandly piercing speech she'd planned, but the words got the job done. Arlo sighed and eased himself down on the concrete steps. His pants were too short for his long frame, and the hems rode up above his red socks.

"Which one?" he asked.

At this, Elle froze. She'd never considered that Josie might have taken more than one.

"'Heal Nothing,'" she answered. "What about 'Leaving Song'? Did she record that, too?"

Arlo stilled his body. Elle knew she wasn't wrong.

"'Take Me to the River,'" she kept on. "'If Only.'"

Ballad by ballad, Elle listed all ten of the tracks on her *Merry* album. Arlo fixed his gaze on an inchworm pulling itself from the crack in the concrete. Elle gripped her guitar and strummed the opening notes of "Believe Me, Honey."

"That song," he said, his eyes meeting hers. "It sounds different when you play it."

It cut, that comment. Josie's version had the low harmonies, the delicate riffs, the smooth build on the bridge, but none of the heart.

"You think her shallow version is so much better?" Elle asked.

He reached out a hand, as if to soothe her. As if he understood what it was she had lost. "Not better. Just different." Arlo paused. "You auditioned for me?"

"I sang every verse of it to your room full of men," Elle said, her voice like a razor. "*My* song."

Arlo blinked. His mustache twitched. Finally, he remembered. "I told you to sing 'Wayfaring Stranger.'"

"I didn't want to."

"And now here we are." He took a Marlboro from his shirt pocket and lit it. Smoke twirled into the air. "I told you this was war, and you didn't trust me."

"I haven't had reason to trust many people, as of late."

He exhaled, conceding the point. "How do I know *you* ain't lying?"

"You know I'm not." Elle waved the smoke from her face. "You've heard her songwriting."

"Did you get a copyright on your work?" His eyes circled the lot.

Elle couldn't help it—she flinched. She didn't know what a copyright was.

"If not, then it's your word against hers." The Marlboro bounced in his mouth. "And honey, you ain't gonna win. Her family's like royalty around here."

"Don't call me honey."

Arlo groaned softly. He looked bereft, swimming in his large wool coat made from buffalo plaid. Arlo must have seen what stood in front of him—a nineteen-year-old girl with bags under her eyes, a threadbare utility jacket, and teeth chattering in the cold.

"What do I call you, then?" he asked.

"Elle."

"Elle." He pawed around for his wallet. "I can give you five hundred dollars for your trouble."

"Do *not* pity me," she snapped.

"It ain't pity." The words were strong in his mouth. True. "This is me paying what they're worth. Five hundred."

She dizzied at the sum. It was more money than she'd ever held at once. But Elle's heart would not be seduced.

"I want my name on the songs," she said.

Arlo clenched his cigarette and rubbed his eyes. "I got daughters of my own, you know. They'd like you."

"Put my name on the songs."

"Thing is," he said, "it ain't my daughters you got to impress."

"Put my name on the songs." Elle began to tremble. The louder she spoke, the less weight the words seemed to have.

Arlo rose to his feet to signal the argument's end. "I can't" was all he said.

"Why?"

He leaned against the railing. The look in his eyes was sad and final. "You got people relying on you, Elle?"

"Of course I do."

"So do I."

The neck of Elle's guitar pointed at him like the spear of a bayonet. "I'll go to the press."

She knew this last-ditch effort wouldn't work in her favor. All of Nashville worked like a country club, a term Elle had heard because of Josie. The city ran on gossip and family trees, and she'd trash her own reputation instead of that of Josie, who was now pitied across the South for sending an imaginary boyfriend off to war.

Arlo watched her with that assessing glare, though this time it had nothing to do with potential and everything to do with risk.

"You could go to the press," Arlo responded. "Or."

"Or?"

"You could record an album of studio songs. With me."

Elle sneered as she stuffed her hands in her pockets. "One album is the price of my silence?"

"Not the only price," he said. "You'll need to girl yourself up. Coif your hair. Wear a skirt. That kind of thing."

"You think I can't wear a skirt?"

He held up his hands in surrender. "I have yet to see it."

"Don't patronize me."

"I ain't." The sides of his mouth drew down as he dropped his cigarette on the concrete. "There's one thing you can count on. When it's just you and me in the room, I'll always shoot straight."

"And what if we're not the only two in the room?"

He lifted an eyebrow. "Even the devil's got to dance some days."

"My answer is no." Her guitar held steady as she clutched it, a breastplate against the allure of his offer.

He touched her shoulder, then started up the stairs. "Think about it," he said.

The door made a soft click behind him, and once again Elle was alone. She'd just gotten the opportunity of a million lifetimes, and it soured her stomach. This was not vengeance, or justice, or retribution. This was an act of defanging.

She wanted no part of this world anymore, with its rhinestone jumpsuits and its silver microphones. What of it was real, what held even a portion of the joy she'd felt while singing at Merry's side? She hated how often she was reminded of what and who she missed.

Elle took the alleyway to return to her station wagon, which was parked on the street. She spied the spot of gravel where she'd vomited on her first day in town. It wasn't even a year ago, but Elle felt like a shell of the woman she'd been then.

Just as he had that first day, Leo appeared with his banjo and an L&M in hand. The bell of the Methodist church chimed nine times, and Leo was about to start his first session of the day.

"Hey," Leo said, and offered a pull of his cigarette.

Elle took it. "Hey."

"Your room's still free," Leo said, "if you want it."

Elle watched the end of the cigarette burn, and then handed it back. "I ain't staying."

"It might be worth another shot here." Leo took a drag. "They've been known to grant deals on the third or fourth try."

"Oh," Elle said, knitting her hands together. "They offered me an album."

Leo didn't hide his surprise. "You turned it *down?*"

"They only offered it because Josie stole my music."

Elle couldn't look him in the eye. Instead she kicked at a small tuft of snow in the alley. She sounded spoiled and ungrateful, all the things Elle claimed to hate.

"Tell me," Leo said. "What is it on this mountain of yours that you're so eager to get back to? Is it gonna heat your mama's house the way a record deal would?"

"No." Elle thought back to what Leo had said when they first met. "I didn't want to get written out of my own songs."

"You're luckier than most, Elle." Leo stamped his L&M against the asphalt and took up his banjo. "Be pissed if you want," he said. "But take the deal."

Leo pulled open the thick door to the studio. Elle made the move to follow, but he turned around.

"Where do you think you're going?" he asked.

Elle flushed. "To tell Arlo I'll take the deal."

Leo laughed. "Wait at least a day before you accept. That man deserves to sweat."

And that was just what Elle did.

TRACK 15

It put a hex on Elle to watch her dream come true.

In May of 1970, she stood in the vocal sweet spot of the recording studio that Josie had shown her the previous fall. Entire careers had been birthed there—Elvis, the Everly Brothers, Patsy Cline—but all Elle could remember was the shipwreck of Josie's stare as she'd watched her sister pass out in a tub. That emotion had been real, Elle thought. The fear, the love. The loyalty.

Which of them would become a legend in this space? she wondered. And which of them deserved it?

As she waited for Arlo to confer with the studio writers in the corner, Elle felt bits of herself—her real, find-me-in-the-dark self—begin to flit around the room. Shavings of who she was—the daughter with a rifle aimed at the sky, the sister with a shovel dug into frozen earth, the apprentice in the cab of a truck on a stormy night—peeled away from her. All of Elle, all over the floor, each piece too tiny to be rescued or inspected. She wasn't made new, exactly, or old. She was now liminal, temporary. Masked.

It wasn't what she'd dreamed of. But at least it didn't hurt.

The group of writers inspected her as they volleyed song ideas back and forth.

"What's her angle?" Hal, the lead writer, asked. He stroked the calico cat he'd brought along and stuck a pencil behind his ear. "Naïve? Broken-hearted? Man-eater?"

In unison, they spoke back to her what they saw. *Naïve.*

Before Elle had turned eighteen, she'd witnessed what mountain living could strip away over the course of a life. It dried out the fathers and drowned the mothers. Already Elle had built a life's work and had it taken from her.

She grew rightfully indignant when a room full of blowhards—who wrote ballads of love, each of them on their third marriage, at least—found her naïve. They couldn't have meant naïve in the ways of a woman, of self-sacrifice and betrayal. But in the ways of men: sex and money.

The next day, Elle recorded a fast-tempo number titled "School Girl Crush."

June, July, and August, too
I spent my summer waiting on you-oo-oo

If her mother had heard it, she'd have laughed and laughed. Elle longed for the sound.

On her first few takes, Elle fuddled the opening verse. The phrase *sweet, sassy sunrise* tripped her up again and again. Who on earth would ever say such a thing? Only a room full of men who wrote soapy song lyrics while eating baloney sandwiches, that's who. On the seventh take, Elle went sharp.

Arlo cut the whirring track and fiddled with the mixing console. The bassist coughed. Hal's cat wound around Elle's legs, catching its tail on the back of her knee. Every person in the studio looked at Elle like she was a mistake.

"Maybe"—Arlo fumbled with the lighter in his pocket—"we can try again tomorrow."

A low hum of voices filled the air, the sum of their expectations turned true.

This country girl ought to go home.

"No," Elle said.

"Pardon?" Arlo shot back.

"No."

Arlo was so shocked he couldn't even blink. He must have had some woman in his life he allowed to tell him no, but it surely wasn't Elle.

"Hey, now," Hal whispered, holding out a hand toward her. His thumb had a dollop of mayonnaise on it. "I think you misunderstand—"

"I need a guitar." Elle's head swiveled toward Arlo. "You said you didn't want me to play, but I need it."

"That don't fit the image of a cutesy girl," he answered. "She wouldn't have calluses."

Elle's palm shot up. White ridges crusted the fingertips of her left hand. "This one would."

Arlo stroked a hand against his stubble. His eyes were squirrely and black. "I just don't see it."

"Then don't look."

Elle strode to the light switch panel and turned each of them off.

"I can't see," whined the bassist.

"Wing it." Elle lifted a spare guitar from its stand along the wall. "Arlo, press Record."

"Well . . ." He hung a finger off his collar as if he might choke.

"Press it."

Arlo obeyed, and Elle began by strumming a C. The studio drummer caught on and set the tempo, and Elle finished the track in one final take.

When they listened to the recording in the control room, all the pieces married. The voice, the guitar, the drum, the bass. The sugary lyrics in concert with Elle's raspy alto created a kind of musical paradox that hadn't appeared yet in Nashville. The record was novel, even if the song wasn't.

The only blip was the soft mewling of Hal's cat in the background after Elle's last chord.

"Got-dammit, Hal," Arlo spat. "I told you not to bring that thing in here. Now we have to record all over again."

"That cat is good luck, and you know it," Hal shot back, and the two began to toss insults back and forth.

"Leave it," Elle said, quietly at first. The boys continued to squabble. "Leave it," she said again, louder, until the fighting stopped.

"Fans will love it," she finished. "You'll see."

Elle picked up the cat and pet its gleaming coat. "She and I would look pretty together on an album cover, don't you think?"

It was something Josie would have said—and the thought made Elle falter, just the tiniest bit. Truth was, she'd never have been so bold if she hadn't met Josie. Hadn't spent so many nights with her in this very studio. If Josie hadn't shown her how a woman can step into a room and own it.

Now Elle let everyone else in the studio fall for the appearance of her confidence, even though she was still nervous enough to puke again in the alleyway. A trail of sweat had worked its way down her spine, hidden by a thick denim jacket.

But Elle's self-doubt was short-lived. Arlo's glare sprang from her to the cat and back again, and then he started to nod. "All right," he said slowly as he grinned like a raccoon. "I see it now. A schoolgirl with a guitar and a calico cat. She's got layers."

Elle nodded. "*Layers*."

The cat purred in Elle's arms, and that was the moment she became a recording artist. Once again, she'd changed over the course of three and a half minutes. Elle had always loved the way writing music undressed her, laid bare her most intimate moments. But "School Girl Crush" was an act of dress-up, a costume for the world to consume, and Elle was great at wearing it.

Nothing had ever felt so lonely.

After that recording, Elle did as Arlo asked. She flounced in a checkered skirt. She spun up her auburn hair. Blew kisses into the audience and left a print of her pink pout backstage at every venue. She even giggled each time a crowd meowed at the end of "School Girl Crush."

The crowds loved her. They tossed little stuffed calico cats on stage, pink and white roses, fake diamond rings with phone numbers attached. At the end of each show, Elle took the roses. A custodian swept the rest up with a long-handled push broom and mailed it in a box to the studio.

It went on and on like this for weeks. Then months.

Elle learned to smile when incandescent rage flared between her ribs—when she wasn't allowed to tour without a chaperone, when she got stiffed her payment at a seedy gig. Still, she kept a trove of her own lyrics in the notebook she stowed beneath her bed. It didn't take long for them to get buried beneath kitten heels, fringed jackets, pantyhose. She'd never been able to pretend while she wrote music. It was the truest part of her, a pool of still water now troubled by the reflection of someone shimmying in a short skirt.

There were worse fates than recording an album of shallow songs, and Elle was determined not to be downcast about it. It wasn't as if she'd gotten sent off to war, for heaven's sake. Her classical guitar, on the other hand, harbored its own opinions. It squawked every time she plied the strings with another bubblegum bop.

Like water skipping over rocks, she whispered to the instrument. So she and her guitar would be.

It was a balm to send cash home in envelopes, to keep that promise she made. She remembered those envelopes every time she stepped into Ernest Tubb's record shop and saw *School Girl Crush* on display. The record was black and shiny, like a crow in the moonlight on her mountain.

"When are you coming back, Elle?" Susannah asked the last time she'd called home.

It was fall; Elle hadn't been home since spring, when she'd left in the middle of the night. She held a copy of her album's cover art in her hand. At first Elle wanted to describe it to Susannah so they could share a laugh. In the photo, Elle's hair looked like twirled macaroni. It was a close-up shot, Elle's cheek flush against the kitten's fur because the cat had scratched Elle's arms and legs so badly it left a spattering of blood on the floor. But Elle found she couldn't tell her mother about it because this girl in the picture was not Susannah's daughter at all.

The phone connection was poor, and someone had left a melted nougat bar in the corner of the phone booth down the street from Elle's boardinghouse. Ants swarmed her feet.

"I'll come back when it's done," Elle answered her mother, but even as she said it, she knew she'd never be done.

Not when beside her own stack of records at Ernest Tubb's sat her *Merry* album with Josie's name plastered on it. Not when she heard her ballad on the radio sung in Josie's sickly-sweet soprano and folks went moon-eyed over it. And not when Elle had propped up this scarecrow cutout of herself so the real Elle could hide in the weeds.

She'd thought money would soften the edges of her pain, but it took the opposite effect. All she wanted was Merry back, playing her mandolin as the summertime stalks of lavender came into being.

How Elle still longed for that kind of hope. For that kind of company.

Watch how quickly a life changed:

Elle's album topped the charts for the rest of 1970. *School Girl Crush* was a crossover hit. Country, mainstream, young women, and mothers, too. Everybody loved it—even if Elle didn't. To celebrate, Arlo drove Elle seven miles south of the city. His Caddy wasn't built for the tight turns near Radnor Lake, so he slid off the road and cut the engine.

"What is all this?" Elle asked as Arlo grabbed a bottle of champagne and tossed a bag over his shoulder. She'd expected him to throw her one of the schmoozy parties he liked to host at his grossly lavish mansion on the outskirts of town.

"You'll see," he said.

They hiked for the better part of an hour. Elle's fingertips grew numb in the cold. She didn't mind, it turned out, even though her buckled tan heels weren't right for a hike. She hadn't felt this kind of shiver since—

"Wait a minute," she said.

"I know it ain't home, exactly," Arlo offered as they reached a waterfall, the force of it crashing against the distant call of wild turkeys. Sweat had darkened the back of Arlo's flannel. His mansion stood a few more miles south in Brentwood, easy enough to reach from Nashville now because of the new interstate. "But this can feel like your mountain if you let it."

Elle scanned the horizon and found no city skyline, heard no roar from trucks on the nearby highway. The air was mossy and wet as she brought the bottle of champagne to her lips.

"I don't want this to feel like my mountain," she said.

"Nashville weaseled into your heart that quick, did it?"

The bottle dangled in Elle's grip. "Can I shoot straight?"

"It's just you and me."

"I think if I let myself miss home—even a little—I'll fall apart."

The trees were such a lovely gold above them that it hurt Elle to witness something so regal, so fleeting.

"Let me tell you a secret." Arlo ran a finger down his mustache. "Everyone here is one step from falling apart. They just have newer clothes."

Elle smiled, though she was sad. Suddenly she felt the need to grip Arlo by the elbow so she wouldn't be left in this city alone.

"Thank you," she said. "For bringing me here."

"Other girls would want the white tablecloth as a celebration," Arlo said. "Diamonds and pearls. But not you."

"I thought you forgot about the real me."

Arlo took the bottle and drank. "Didn't forget. Just put her on a shelf. And it was the right choice, you'd agree."

Elle stole the bottle back.

"I got one more thing for you." He swung a cactus-shaped bag off his back and unclipped the cover.

Inside the silk-lined case lay a limited-edition, pink-and-white-gingham vanity guitar with her name scripted on it, complete with a heart for the double *l* in *Elle*.

"It's one of a kind," Arlo explained. "The only one made."

"It's ugly."

"Because it's cute?" he scoffed. "What you got against pink?"

"Nothing. Red just suits me better."

"Buy yourself a Corvette, then," Arlo said, fluttering a hand in the air. "A red T-top. Bought with this pink thing."

Elle slipped the strap over her head. It was lusciously smooth, and Elle felt like she was cheating on her Taylor—which waited back in her attic bedroom like a faithful first wife.

"Figured you could learn to sign your name like that," Arlo said, pointing at the signature, "'stead of that chicken scratch you do."

"Screw you, Arlo," she said, even as she followed the cursive script with her finger.

He laughed. "You're welcome."

Aside from that hike, Elle didn't celebrate. She didn't take days off, she didn't say no to appearances. She received desperate invitations from radio stations, where the same DJs who had thrown her demo in the trash now played her singles and asked her, unapologetically, to unbutton the top of her blouse. She toured festivals and opened for headliners like George Jones and Lefty Frizzell. She declined endless requests to cover "Let It Be" after the Beatles disbanded; she pulled off the highway and wept when she heard about Janis Joplin's death from an overdose. Elle ricocheted through a hundred different hotels, often drove through the night over potholes that looked like the craters she'd seen on television during the moon landing.

She also bought her mother a Dodge with a fat wad of hundred-dollar bills and had it delivered; she grew accustomed to strangers calling out her name. Elle got buckets of fan mail at the studio, some from little girls who were just like the girl she'd once been—young, defiant, and hungry. She didn't feel young. It felt more like coasting through an afterlife where her true music hadn't joined her. She missed the teeth of that music, the scrape.

Elle had considered on many sleepless nights what she'd do when she saw Josie Starling again. How much shame she could impart with only the fire in her eyes since she'd vowed never to speak to her. Their paths would have to cross when Josie claimed her spoils—a multicity tour for her wildly popular *Soldier* album, a recurring slot at the Opry.

The war drew toward its agonizing end, and folks at home had no sympathy left for army men. But Josie Starling had maintained the gem of curiosity. She'd sung an entire album for the soldier who'd left her behind, and a whole nation of country and folk music fans were waiting for them to reunite.

A war-weary country craved a love story to quell them, even if it wasn't true.

Elle's popularity continued to skyrocket, yet there was one thin snag in the tapestry of lies Arlo had spun for her. It didn't matter how much money she earned, or how many people meowed at her music, or how many autographs she signed. Elle still yearned to perform a song of her own in front of a crowd. To find that writer inside her, sunk into the watery darkness, and yank her toward the light.

At a festival in Texas in 1972, she found it.

It had rained relentlessly that day. That was all Elle could remember. The festival's sound system shorted out, and evening clouds threatened to roll in across the flat plains. The audience stayed eager, though, shouting Elle's name. Backstage, she unveiled her Taylor with the mother-of-pearl inlay, the one she hardly played anymore. It struck her—not like lightning but like a slap—that she was no longer the Elle who had written those words for Merry. She was someone fiercer now.

She was the Elle Harlow who wanted her words back.

Elle kicked off her heels and swiped the lipstick from her mouth. It left a trail of red across her right cheek. As soon as she stepped onstage in her bare feet, Elle knew she'd sing "Heal Nothing" without accompaniment, dressed down, just as she'd intended it to be.

She came out rugged, she came out tired, she came out angry, she came out true. She sang from the place deep inside her that longed for things that would never be.

I'll write you letters when I'm gone, though you won't write to me
A message in a bottle, getting lost inside your sea
No pretty words will keep you, no picture on the wall
Try to heal everything, and you'll heal nothing at all

She'd thought the crowd would help her along and add strength to her voice. But as she crowed low and loud, Elle could no longer see anyone beyond the edge of the platform. Storm clouds shut out the setting sun. Thunder cried in the distance; a raven landed at her feet. She finished the final chorus, and a crescendo of silence threatened to knock her down.

As she was ready to fall with no one to catch her, someone in the audience yelled the phrase she'd come to hate, now baptized anew in her own music.

Play it again.

A royal tide of applause surfed over her, and the chanting gained force in the heat. *Play it again, Elle. Play it again.*

And she did. The rain hit, and the real Elle Harlow sang her guts out. The audience loved her just as she was, just as she'd always been.

TRACK 16

In a pathetic display of happy greed, Arlo begged Elle to record her own version of "Heal Nothing" after the festival, where he waited in the rain. It came at a price, though. She'd have to pay royalties to Josie for the pleasure of recording her own song.

She wouldn't do it.

"Thing is," Arlo reasoned, "you're going to have to record another album sometime."

"Why don't you start with Josie?" Elle asked, fluttering her eyelashes, sweet and full of spite. "See what kind of songwriter she is."

Arlo dared to suggest they record a duet.

A thunderclap, a deluge of water.

"Over my dead body," Elle replied.

"Listen," Arlo said tenderly, "country music will always love someone like Josie Starling."

"You mean because she's blond?"

Arlo didn't deny it.

Elle wrapped her Taylor in a poncho. "Good thing I'm not only a country singer, then."

He threw up his hands.

"People flock to damsels in distress," he said. "They recoil at vindictive women."

Well, Elle thought. *We'll see about that.*

When she returned to Nashville, she changed the strings on her old guitar. It wheezed as she ran her fingertips along its length. She used her thumb and forefinger to pick out the melody to "Long Black Veil," the song that Josie had loved. Merry would have liked it, too. The guitar smelled like Elle's old life: mountain frost, hemlock, and yarrow.

Elle felt as splintered as the face of Merry's broken mandolin—afraid to revisit her past, shaking at the wheel of her present. She still missed home so terribly that she'd started to find comfort in punishing herself. Elle still lived in the boardinghouse, although she could afford a bungalow of her own, even as other Music Row hopefuls came and went.

Leo had moved to the West Coast a while back to join a band in Bakersfield.

"Nashville only wants one flavor of ice cream," he'd said to Elle before he boarded a Greyhound. "And I don't like vanilla."

Vanilla. There was no better description of the first album Elle had made, this machine that provided for her and crowded out her life.

She hadn't forsaken her roots, even if she dreaded returning to that riverbed where Merry's body lay. It was for Elle's roots she kept on playing the same songs night after night, even when her fingers bled. The music didn't fulfill her, but the money served its purpose. She'd paid to patch her mountain's school roof, bought acres of land to keep sawyers at bay. Elle also sent books, and every kind of record she knew her people would enjoy.

She only hadn't gone home to visit.

Elle couldn't help but wonder about the kind of woman Josie had become.

But back to the task at hand—a new album, a true album. Full of Elle's own songs. Music fans were eager for it now that word had spread of her wildfire performance at the festival. Elle had long feared her songs about Merry were the best she'd ever write. Now, she set out to prove herself wrong. She didn't want to be so Merry-haunted anymore.

But when she sat down to work, nothing came out.

Her guitar gaped at her. It also had nothing to say. Three years ago, she'd written ten songs in a matter of two weeks. After four days in her small bedroom, she had nothing but half phrases she'd written in pencil on the wall.

Desperate, Elle headed for the comfort of Tootsies on a Thursday afternoon. The lounge had been painted purple by mistake, and the building lit up Broadway like an Easter egg. Weston Studio's glut of songwriters was known to hold court at the upstairs bar, where they were merry and ruby-cheeked when Elle arrived. Hal slapped the graffiti on the counter as she walked up the stairs.

"Elle!" he shouted too loudly. "Our favorite girl!"

"You say that to everyone," Elle answered as she took a stool.

"But I only mean it with you," Hal said.

Down the bar, someone passed him a napkin and a pen. "Write that down!" he called out. "For your next top-ten hit."

Hal obliged, made his note, and stuffed the napkin in his pocket. "Now," he said, turning to Elle. "What ails you?"

Elle itched to come clean. "I can't write worth a damn," she said.

"I'll tell you what you need," Hal said, knocking back the rest of his whiskey. "Get married. You could make a man very happy, if you wanted."

Elle snorted and stood to leave. Of course these men saw her as a lonely girl, hunting for a husband to fill all her empty spaces. They'd written "School Girl Crush" for her, after all.

Hal touched her shoulder, guided her back down into her seat. "Hear me out," he said. "You don't only need to get married. You need to fall in love, then get married, *then* get a divorce. Write a few songs about each of them—then, bam! Your album is done."

"This is why you're on your fourth marriage," Elle observed.

"And over thirty top-ten records to prove it." Hal raised his empty glass.

"Which part of the cycle were you on when you wrote 'School Girl Crush'?" Elle asked. "Love, marriage, or divorce?"

Hal considered it. "That one sounds like divorce to me."

Elle laughed, traced her finger over Kris Kristofferson's signature scrawled on the bar.

"Straight shooting?" Hal asked.

Elle nodded, and he scratched the side of his jaw.

"You've spent the last two years in a station wagon, driving from gig to gig. No one wants to listen to a song about that. Let yourself live a little."

Fall in love.

After a month, Elle still had little to show for her efforts. Arlo, who was resistant to impatience, assured her the music would come in due time—but he wasn't short on suggestions.

"I'll tell you what your problem is," he said to her in his stuffy office, late on an August afternoon. The city heat had subdued every living thing, and they both languished as an oscillating fan spat hot air at them in shifts.

"You've got too much Nashville in you." He slammed a palm on his desk, causing his shelf of Grammy awards to clatter.

Elle flipped him the bird. "That's your fault."

Arlo remained undeterred. "Where'd you write those first songs of yours?"

"In my bedroom," Elle answered. "Out in the country."

"So go back."

Elle blinked. Arlo blinked, too. She thought of how she'd sent Merry's body down to the river's darkest place. She still didn't know how to forgive the girl who had run, and how to become the woman who returned.

"There's no going back there, Arlo," Elle said. "Not for me."

It was the most honest she'd been with anyone in months.

Arlo's eyes shut as she said it—as if he'd stumbled on the naked, true version of Elle and he needed to avert his eyes. Then he looked out the window toward the sidewalk, where a hopeful musician in seersucker strummed a terrible version of "Eleven Roses" on his guitar. The sour clang made Arlo remember himself.

"The country, is it?" He banged his palm again. "I know just the place."

Arlo grabbed a travel map from his credenza and wrote an address on the front. Then he circled a spot on the map itself and wrote a few notes.

Abruptly, he paused. "You scared of bears?"

She didn't answer. Instead, she snatched the map from his hand and headed for the door.

"Also," he called to her back, "bring a sleeping bag."

"Trust me," she said, "I'll last longer out there than you would."

He patted his shirt pocket for his cigarettes. "No doubt, no doubt. But you'll be done in a week. Two, tops."

Elle climbed into her Studebaker and checked for her guitar in the back seat, where it nestled against Merry's mandolin. Then she unfolded the map and found that Arlo had circled a knot of dense forest in the southwestern corner of Pennsylvania.

Lenora, it was called.

A Song for My Mother, Draft 3

BY MARIJOHN SHAW

I have two fathers

One I met in '73

The other I never met

*And I wonder [if he ever knew about me]**

**Keep this as a song title. Scrap the rest.*

TRACK 17

If Elle had set that road trip to music, the first verse would have gone something like this:

> *Love's dotted yellow line led me deeper in the dark*
> *Long drives and interstates are made for ruined hearts*

Elle's everlasting love had always been her music. Somehow Arlo had known Elle would need to disappear to find it again. He'd needed the Elle who wrote the *Merry* album to vanish so she could become the Elle who performed "School Girl Crush." Now, he wanted to call the true Elle out of hiding.

Often she resented Arlo for the disappearing act he'd forced on her. She didn't want to admit all the ways she'd also forced it on herself. Aside from her mother, Arlo remained the only constant in Elle's life. People passed through her like water through a sieve, except for this man who had built a new Elle from her broken pieces.

Arlo, the trickster, was honest about his schemes. Elle didn't want to like him as much as she did, but she couldn't help it. He was safe for one reason: he had seen both the real and the fake versions of Elle Harlow, and he hadn't flinched at either. Elle could be her worst, and Arlo would understand because he remembered what it was like to have nothing at all.

Elle wasn't the only one who never returned home yet bought up property to keep it from harm. Arlo had done the same in the spooked marshes of western Pennsylvania that held the shack where his grandmother was born. She'd raised a brood of steelworkers there—including Arlo's uncle, who could no longer play the fiddle after he lost three fingers in an accident at the mill. Arlo revered good music because he knew what it meant to lose it.

Arlo also understood that Elle needed solitude. To live without comfort. To recall what it felt like to be cold. To cast off her titles: daughter, woman, starlet. Elle had been consumed, down to her studs. Now she wanted to burn like an ember until she took everyone's breath away.

She couldn't wait to be alone.

As Arlo's notes directed, just after Shaw's blue-and-white gas station, Elle took a turn down a dirt path that wasn't marked on any map. She was accustomed to steep switchbacks in the woods, but this road jackknifed around pockets of sinking earth. Arlo's family shack stood on stilts and leaned next to a tender bend in the creek. A boat floated there, tethered to a railroad tie.

Any other woman might have feared these haunted woods would be her undoing, but Elle yearned for such a gift. She prepared to behold herself as a folkish Eve—ageless and austere—beginning again as her mother had bid her.

Then she turned the cabin's doorknob and saw that she was not alone after all.

A bleak, creaking moan rang out when Elle opened the door. Shadows hovered, flickering like windless kites. Tendrils of wood skittered across the floor. A light switch on the wall—Elle flipped it. A buzz and a flutter.

At first, they resembled skeletons. Then sunlight swept in. Gently carved pieces of curly maple hung from hooks in the ceiling, each curved in a Florentine scroll to make the face of a mandolin.

The telltale heart of a carpenter ghosted the whitewashed room. Bins of tuning pegs sat in the corner next to a stack of rosewood fretboards. Beside them, a bending iron and a travisher, a jigsaw. Everywhere, the scent of sawdust and paste.

This was the old workshop of a luthier.

Elle hadn't touched a mandolin since she'd tucked Merry's into the back seat of her car over two years ago. It lay there, alone, through all of Elle's performances. The watershed tones of Merry's music flooded the tombs of Elle's memory. The birdcall of it, the ache. For the first time, the sight didn't flatten her. Arlo couldn't have known what mandolins meant to Elle. She'd told him so little of her life before Nashville.

Elle lay on her back and watched the mandolins twirl. Planetary, they spun, each stained with a sunburst finish. Merry would have loved it here. Elle would never have been so awed by such a place if it hadn't been for knowing the healer. Loving her, losing her. The thought fatigued Elle. She couldn't write because she was still running—always running from the way Merry had died.

When was the last time Elle had truly slept? She couldn't remember. The sun had set; it was barely past eight in the evening. She had no musical epiphany. But for now, she would rest.

Elle woke to the barrel of a gun in her face. Cold steel, a breeze. The startled breath of a stranger. Elle couldn't recall where she was, but she could tell it was about to rain. The air smelled like moss and lichen.

"Get up," a voice said.

Elle stood, the vision before her hazy in the moonlight. A trimmed beard, russet hair darker than her own. The woodsy scent of pine oil. The man hadn't asked, but she raised her hands above her head.

Her father had taught her how to be steady when faced with the deadly end of a rifle.

"This place is supposed to be empty," Elle said.

"Did you touch them?"

"What?"

"The mandolins." His voice was like a train leaving the station—certain, rushing closer. "Did you touch them?"

"No."

"Seven hundred and fifty dollars. That's the price for each. They won't be ready for six weeks."

Elle realized she was waiting for him to turn on the light and recognize her. Softly, rain began to fall. "Can you—"

"No."

"Turn on the light," she said.

"No."

She risked it and dodged for the switch.

"Watch it." He dropped his rifle and steadied the swinging planes of wood with his fingertips.

A soft glow warmed the room. The mandolins looked like carcasses. The stranger squinted at Elle in the lamplight. Elle waited, as he waited on her. There was no flash, no smile. He didn't recognize her.

"The place was supposed to be empty," Elle said again.

"Says who?"

"Arlo Weston."

He sighed as a hand trailed his beard. "That piece of shit."

"So you know him well."

The man laughed loudly—a chorus of notes that bellowed into the night. His face looked too young for a laugh like that. A laugh that knew how to make the most of itself.

Elle noticed then that he was handsome. Green eyes, a bright smile that didn't often come out of hiding.

"He's my cousin. Helps sell these in Nashville." The luthier motioned toward the instruments.

"Why wouldn't he tell me you live here?"

He paused, searching for his bearings, cocksure about his instruments and nothing else. Elle wondered when he'd last seen another person.

"I don't live here," he explained. "I'm just behind schedule."

"Still, he should have told you."

The luthier held her stare. "I ain't easy to get in touch with."

A story there, a history, lingered between them. Elle found herself leaning in, wanting to lure it out of him. Every inch of him was lithe and rough, except for his amber eyelashes.

He had the rusty patina of a mountaineer, the kind that guarded some inner secret. Elle wanted to strum it like a guitar.

"Do you play?" She pointed above her head.

"Of course I play." He looked toward her Taylor propped against the wall. "I'm not rough on my mandolin the way you brutes are with guitars."

"*Brutes?*" she repeated.

"I said what I said."

She noticed it then, the mandolin case strapped to his back.

"Can I—"

"Who did you say you were?" he interrupted. His eyes flew to her notebook, her satchel, her lips.

"I didn't."

He waited.

Anonymity was a buried treasure Elle had lost. She couldn't remember the last time she'd had to introduce herself. "I'm a songwriter," she said.

That did it. The man nodded as if he understood. He found a broom and began to sweep stray sawdust out the door. "Arlo sent you here for some find-yourself bullshit."

"I'm not the first, I see."

"You're the prettiest," he answered.

It wasn't flattery, merely observation. A silent recognition that anyone who'd come through this door before had been a man.

"You should know," he warned, stilling the broom, "this is a terrible place to write."

Elle didn't want to stay. She also didn't want to forfeit. Her head ached. She'd driven nine hours to get to these forsaken woods and couldn't do nine more. Not tonight.

"And you should know," Elle answered, "I do my best work in shitty circumstances."

The mandolin slid off the man's back. It landed softly on the floor.

He stepped toward her, reached out. Elle bit her lip and held her ground. He grabbed a blanket from a hook on the wall.

"Don't ask me to change your strings." His voice lost steam the closer he stood to her. "I don't have the time."

"I change my own damn strings," Elle answered.

"I'll sleep outside," he said, watching her lips.

"It's raining out there."

He blinked. "It'll pass."

"You don't have to."

He frowned. "Your breath is already warping the wood in here."

"I'll sleep outside, too, then."

"No." He took his mandolin and whisked the door shut behind him.

Elle didn't waste time. She strolled around the room, blowing a hot tunnel of breath on each piece of suspended wood. Fair payment, she thought, for his skinflint gallantry. Then she lay back on the floor, but she couldn't sleep. After the rain cleared, the smell of ashes wafted from a campfire. At the window, Elle caught the arc of the luthier's torso, the mandolin at his chest.

He was beautiful, this stranger, rugged and sharp-jawed. Grumpy and meticulous. Light-eyed and copper-haired.

And then he began to play.

Elle felt the sky break. She'd heard other mandolins from her time in Nashville, but this was bespoke. Beguiling. Beloved. The luthier played an instrument he had made—just as Merry had—but it was more than that. His voice was so purely lonesome, so exquisitely intent, Elle could have sworn he was singing just for her.

He strummed the melody of "Sam Stone," adding a quivering tremolo at the end of each verse. He loved this music, lived it, longed for it. The intensity of his devotion traveled the breeze from his campfire to the cabin's open window, and Elle drifted to sleep while wondering about his name.

An hour later, she woke in the pitch-black of night with the first song lyrics she'd had since she sent her friend into the river.

Don't tell me your name
And I won't tell you mine
The less I know about you
The more I'll be just fine
Because we both know
Before it's time to go
I'm not the holding-on-to kind

TRACK 18

For three days, Elle and the luthier obeyed an unspoken treaty. She rose early and took to writing down by the creek. Her thoughts were not lyrical—not yet. They were guttural, full of instinct, stops and starts. She paced, she threw rocks. Asked questions that had no answers.

Elle was troubled by how strange she felt in her own skin. It was tight and unyielding, like she'd grown into an unwieldy monster who could no longer string a few chords and words together. But she'd always had to work so doggedly at every single thing, hadn't she? Shoveling snow, keeping her brother alive, gathering eggs, falling asleep at night. Elle knew it would be written on her tombstone: *She tried too hard.*

Elle stank. She stank with sadness, with anger, with envy, with struggle. She caught the odor of her own flailing on the edges of her clothes, on her every sigh, on the case of her guitar. She figured the anonymous luthier could scent it on her, too, and chose to stay away.

On the first day, Arlo's cousin worked in his shop until sunset. The air smelled of burned wood, fresh paint, phosphor bronze. It had been endlessly hot that afternoon, and he hadn't even taken one break for a drink at the water's edge. Maybe, Elle mused, he'd rushed it when she went to relieve herself in the woods. But he didn't watch her the way she'd started to watch him. At first, she'd merely spied. Now, once the bright of daylight eased, she let herself witness all of him.

Up at the cabin, the luthier had built a carpenter's bench by the porch. Sweat darkened the soft plaid beneath his arms, and he grunted gently as he lifted a heavy slab of maple onto the bench. Wiped his palms on his thighs. The forest took on the blues of dusk, every branch a shadow. Finally, the luthier looked up from his work.

Exerted, panting, alive.

His eyes found Elle's; the heat of them felt like no spotlight Elle had ever stood beneath—but the heat from an abandoned home fire, a broken hearth. He made his way to the water without looking at her again, and Elle climbed toward the confines of the cabin. The luthier seemed to want to cage her away from his wildness, the bits of sawdust that feathered his hair.

When they passed each other in the cattails, their knuckles brushed.

"Sorry," she whispered, and he recoiled as if she'd committed a sin in her apology, in speaking at all.

She took to calling the man Weston in her mind, as he and Arlo shared a surname. The mystery of it swelled inside her—this carpenter who looked at her with wounded wisdom, as though he'd survived the end of the world and yet was somehow still waiting for it to begin.

The sky went dark after they parted ways. That night Elle dreamed of Weston's tenor coming toward her at dawn. His voice—plaintive and wistful—splayed the whole forest while he worked. Elle had never heard a more hypnotic sound. Like hands gently tied behind her back, it arrested Elle to hear his mournful falsetto. She found she could learn a lot about a man through the songs he loved. Weston liked Townes Van Zandt and John Prine, with a dash of Joni Mitchell. It was a wonder that Arlo hadn't signed him.

Arlo, Elle suspected, wasn't the reluctant one. Weston was.

Elle considered herself a loner, but she'd never seen anything like this. Weston took no interest in her. Instead he granted all his fair attentions to the bird's-eye maple maidens swinging from their hooks. He preferred early morning, when he shaved thin planks of spruce along the grain until they fit together as if they'd always been destined to meet. He made the travisher look like it was slicing through butter. Everything in that shop bent to his will. It took a singular sorcery to sever a tree and remake it anew. Elle was spellbound by it.

Softly, Weston sang his instruments to life. He saved so much of his tenderness for them that it appeared he only looked upon Elle with scorn. It took the opposite effect of an offense—his disregard felt complimentary, an equality that didn't fuss with deference. Strangely, she'd never felt more like someone's partner.

Even though they never spoke.

The second day, Elle caught a melody in her mind down by the river that wouldn't quit. So she started to write:

Run from what you came from, baby
Never too far, always too fast
Give some when you have none, maybe
All that you are—

She sang it through, then stopped at the next-to-last line every time. Elle couldn't find the right ending for the lyric. Over and over she sang throughout the afternoon until her voice gave out. When it faded, she heard the faint tumbling from Weston's throat as he finished the chorus.

Ain't gonna last.

He'd been singing along—and he'd found the perfect final note.

At sunset, they each ate dinner alone. Weston huddled by the fire, Elle spying him from the cabin stove where she cooked cornbread. She turned her back when he washed himself in the water. The cabin's only light remained off, and Elle stood by herself in the dark and stared at the wall. She felt the river trickling through Weston's fingers, dousing his hair. An hour passed, and Elle didn't want to sleep. The mandolins hung over her, mobiles without a lullaby.

She was waiting for him.

Elle pressed her hands into the sill beneath the open window once

Weston began to play his mandolin. This was the part of night she loved, the very thing she didn't know she'd been missing. As Weston's melancholy tenor tied her in knots, the keening of the instrument's upper octave undid them.

It was heaven and hell, all in one.

Merry's style had been backwoods and front-porch mandolin, the kind that accompanied country chapel confessions. If she was Sunday morning, Weston was Saturday night. His signature was a stark baying, every musical run like jumping off a cliff. His voice, his face, his everything had a forlorn filter. An owl calling out in the night, needing no sound in return.

For two days, Elle wrote mostly about Josie. Her first attempt was a tune in E minor titled "How Do You Sleep (All Right at Night)." It was a song that might not keep, but it was a start. She wrote about Josie as a way to return to herself—to call the old Elle back into being.

She'd been inside her all this time, waiting until it was safe to emerge.

When Josie stole her music, Elle feared she'd reached the end of her own territory—that she'd never become someone larger than what had been taken from her. She didn't know what else to do but follow Arlo's map. Now, Elle was beginning to see that *she* was the map.

On the third night, Elle was startled awake by Weston cursing at the water's edge. She dashed to the window and saw him clutching his wrist as he knelt by the fire.

Instinct took her. She grabbed her bag and ran toward him. Blades of grass, cool on her feet. She didn't ask permission, didn't say a word. Just took his hand in hers as blood ran routes down their fingers. A bottle cap rested on top of his mandolin by the fire. Weston had been using it to slide over the strings as he played. It must have slipped and sliced open the sensitive part of his wrist. Elle pressed a piece of muslin against the cut. When the bleeding eased, she spread an antibacterial paste made from goldenseal that Merry had taught her to make.

No shame in it—she held on to Weston's hand longer than she needed to. She liked the scrape of his fingers, the rifts on their tips. Hands that built, hands that birthed. Hands not unlike her own.

Elle hadn't healed a stranger since the night she found Jaclyn. Everyone in that upper room had averted their eyes from the bloodshed, even as it held a miracle. Now it was Weston who beheld it, and he didn't look away.

She hadn't heard Weston speak since that first night, when he'd pushed his rifle into her neck. She'd only heard him sing. Slowly, achingly, eerily, he'd courted her through folk song. He let her dress his wound. When she'd held his wrist too long, she looked up and caught him watching her in the firelight.

"Where did someone like you learn something like this?" He held up his bandaged arm.

"Someone like me?"

"Someone who sings a song like 'School Girl Crush.'"

Elle nodded. She resigned herself to a familiar kind of dismissal, just as she'd received in the city when a man assumed he'd figured her out. "So you do know who I am," she said.

"I like a summer bop just as well as the rest. Sue me."

It was a kind word Elle hadn't known she'd been desperate for, and it made her want to spill all her frustrations in the dirt at his feet. Josie's ghost loitered, warning her to back away.

"That song belongs to Arlo, not to me," Elle said.

Weston batted a hand. His light eyes looked like sea glass in the night. "Let him have it, then."

"Why haven't you recorded an album?" Elle asked. "You know you could."

He laughed. There was that sound again, languid and luring. "Nashville is worse than hell, Elle. Everyone there wants to make you into someone you're not."

Those words slashed at Elle's pride. The hard choices she'd made to let her *Merry* album go, knowing she'd lose if she fought for it. She'd made her fortune at the hands of a mirage because no one wanted her for the woman she was—just as her father hadn't.

Elle took a stone and tossed it into the fire. "I am not what those men made of me."

She said it, even though she didn't believe it. A deeper truth hid behind the words. Elle *was* what she'd made of herself, and she didn't like it.

Silence sat like an interloper between them. Weston remained unaware of it.

"What are you doing all the way out here, all alone?" Elle prodded. "You ain't got a life?"

Weston picked up his mandolin and held it close. "I'm living it."

Elle had posed the question as if Nashville and all its accoutrements were the only sights in her rearview mirror. Maybe Arlo was right. Music Row had infected her. Hadn't she once longed for a life in the woods, just like Weston?

"Ain't *you*?" he followed. "Living a life?"

Elle hadn't felt like she was living for a long while.

"Someone once told me that writing music is the closest we'll ever get to stopping time," she answered. "Do you think that counts as a life?"

"I think it's a pretty phrase, but there's not much truth in it."

The burning logs before her flickered into ash. "Maybe not."

He studied her, his legs loosely crossed at the ankles. "What is it that's bothering you?"

There were so many right answers to his question, but Elle wanted to give one that began and ended with her. One she couldn't blame on anyone else.

"I think maybe all my songs arrived too late," she said.

He thought on it for a minute. "Too late for what?"

"For them to matter."

"What do you want them to do?"

"I don't know." She felt foolish as the words spilled out of her mouth. "I think I want them to undo the hurt I've caused. Or stop the hurt from happening at all. But they never come on time."

"Too late for you," Weston said as he toyed with the bottle cap in his hand, "might be right on time for someone else."

"Now *that* sounds like a pretty phrase without much truth in it."

Weston let it out again—that glorious, riotous, gorgeous laugh. The sound touched the tops of the trees and spread itself across the water. She couldn't believe he'd been here so long without anyone to hear it.

"Are you"—Elle halted at the word—"happy?"

A minute passed, and still he hadn't answered. All at once, Elle felt she'd overstayed her welcome. Here, at the fire, in the cabin, all through the woods. She rose to leave, and then Weston spoke.

"For a long time, I got to thinking," he said as he began to play. Elle recognized the tune—"Sweet Summer Blue and Gold" by the Stone Poneys. "That it's possible to be self-sufficient. That independence is what it takes to be happy. But here I am, proving it's not."

She knew that feeling of wanting to be whole within herself and failing at it. Weston looked at the muslin on his hand as he clasped the fretboard.

"I only bandaged your cut," Elle said, watching his fingers move. "You could have done just as well on your own."

Weston looked beyond the fire and into the smoke. "That ain't what I mean."

The music stopped.

"What, then?"

"The best part of my day starts when you open that door and come out in the sunrise and start to sing." His voice trembled at his truth, and Elle's tin of goldenseal fell from her hands into the dirt. "As if you're singing to me."

"Oh," she said.

Weston set down the bottle cap in the grass.

"You came out here to be alone," she continued, "and I've been in your way."

He gazed at the fire, acting as if he hadn't heard.

"And you like it," Elle finished.

Elle had once stripped herself bare in her music, and now she'd done the same to Weston as he listened to it. It couldn't have happened in any other place, at any other time. Elle needed to find her voice again, just as Weston needed to hear it.

"I do."

He drew a hand down his face, and then locked his eyes with hers. It kindled every muscle in her body.

"How long are you going to hide in the woods?" she asked, her voice soft.

His voice went soft, too. "Who's the one hiding, Elle?"

Elle wondered how well she could truly understand a person when she didn't understand herself. Every relationship she'd known had this tension between intimacy and anonymity, pursuing and retreating like a tide. Merry, Josie, Arlo. She and Weston circled each other like two thirsty, wounded animals. Wiry and unwilling to make the first move—until Weston did.

"You can't get mixed up with me," he said.

It wasn't a threat. It was a confession, and he was right. She couldn't.

"Thank you," he said. "For fixing my hand."

Elle nodded and turned to leave. And yet her feet wouldn't move, even though it was late. Even though she'd hoped to spend the night sleeping beneath the window, pressing her hand to the wooden wall, knowing he was somewhere on the other side.

"Weston," Elle said, "I need something."

She needed to feel other truths in her body, besides this constant ache. His eyes slid over the length of her, and she shivered. Elle hadn't known how much she wanted to be hungered for. A failing, she thought, to be so human.

"Name it," he said.

"I need to go swimming."

His gaze swept to the creek. "Now?"

She held out her hands, covered in his blood. There was no bath in the cabin, and she hadn't been able to wash herself since she'd come to the woods. Elle gave him no answer. Instead she walked down the hill, where the full moon blossomed. Fireflies gleamed like city lights. She peeled off her shirt, then her pants. Waded in, unafraid. After two years traveling every highway in the country, her body didn't feel young anymore. But it still wanted. It was still so very much alive.

This was the moment Elle would uncover all she needed to write another album. She might have stripped Weston's heart bare, but he'd done the same to her. She shed the Elle Harlow in the checkered skirt, with the glossy guitar, who sang "School Girl Crush" and kept her real lyrics hidden beneath her bed. She shed the Elle Harlow who hurt so much she couldn't stay in any present moment without bracing herself for whatever tragedy might come tumbling after.

Weston followed her to the creek. Took off his shirt as Elle forced herself to look away. He came up behind her, touched the silk of her hair that skated on the water.

"I'll give you credit as a cowriter," Elle began, "for the lyric you gave me on 'Run.'"

"Please." His body tensed. "Don't."

"What do you want, then?" she asked.

"I think I've been waiting," he said in her ear, "for someone to be here. With me, just as I am."

Elle turned and looked up at him as a shooting star burned a scar in the sky.

"I'm here."

TRACK 19

Elle wrote through all her Josie rage. The songs first surged in anger, then melted into grief, then opened toward this new world in front of her—one with a gray cabin and a rope of smoke in a sinking forest, the embrace of night swimming in the creek. Elle could see it as an album of her own, each track appearing in the order she wrote it, as she experienced—in real time—a kind of rebirth. And on the other end of it was Weston.

Elle had scoffed when Hal told her she needed to fall in love again. *Good for the heart,* he'd said. *Good for the art.* She'd never admit how right he'd been—even if he hadn't known the person she needed to fall for was herself.

Her faults, her regret, her resolve.

The studio songwriters liked to tease Elle that she was married to her music, but it wasn't quite true. Marriage implied a legal binding, a written record, courts and such. It belonged, in some ways, to the public. But Elle's work was all her own—it circled back on itself and grew into its own evolution.

Weston listened to Elle rehearse while he fit sliding dovetails for the necks of a dozen mandolins. After Elle had been there for a week, he told her his thoughts one night at the campfire.

Elle had been working on "Run," and the chorus was set. It was the verses that gave her trouble—

I took off after you
Because you took my dignity (you took her away from me)
And I want it back now
I want it back

"Melodically, it works," Weston said, and then pinched his pick between his lips.

"But?" Elle led.

He took the pick and gently pointed it toward her. "But I think you're stopping at what this person took, when really it's about what you lost."

Elle felt like he'd cleaved her in two.

"Aren't they two sides of the same coin?" she asked. "Taking and losing?"

"Maybe. But you're not writing about thievery. You're writing about hurt. You're writing about the losses you carry with you."

She'd never had anyone consider her art so deeply, so tenderly. "Is that what you see when you look at me? My losses?"

"I think—" Weston paused, searching for the right words. The taut muscles in his shoulder jumped. "It's not about *your* loss. It's that when I listen to your music, I feel less alone in mine."

She couldn't help herself. "What did you lose?"

He watched her keenly, his instrument tucked into his chest, as he wrestled with himself. "The chance to be with someone."

Elle leaned closer, just slightly. "What happened?"

"I said yes to the wrong things, and no to the right ones."

His eyes shuttered, and Elle decided not to press. She looked at the water glittering at the bottom of the hill, like pieces of silver and slate. "Has anyone ever told you the biggest regrets in life come from things you didn't do?" she asked.

"Yes."

"It's total bullshit, isn't it?"

"Spoken by someone who's never needed forgiveness."

"For something terrible they can't take back."

His fingers grazed the cut Elle had bandaged on his wrist. "That might be what I amount to, in the end. A series of irreversible decisions."

"I know the feeling."

It felt so bare and true that she couldn't look at him. She began the song again, with a new verse in mind—

Loss is what I know
Love is what you took
I could never tell you no
Just let me off your hook

Weston closed his eyes as he listened. "I feel that." He placed his hand on his chest. "In here."

"Then it's yours."

He opened his eyes. "Can I play?" His face was earnest, imploring. "With you?"

Elle hadn't known what a gift it was to be asked until then.

"Yes."

He played the melody on his double strings, and the beauty of it made Elle hungry for him. The moment held everything she loved about making music with Merry, and something wholly new on its own. Not a partnership, but a meeting. A commitment to all this moment brought, and nothing after it. Elle had decided she'd never sing another duet, because of what Josie had done. Weston had no interest in such things—and that freedom set Elle's spirit to flight. She only saw how much she enjoyed having an audience when she witnessed how much Weston didn't. He played for himself, and for her.

"Elle," he said one night as a soft, late-summer rain came pouring down, and they ran to the cabin for cover. She'd been in the woods for two weeks by then, but time felt as if it were reversing itself. As if those days were undoing the hurt of every hour that came before.

"This man you write about in your music," Weston said. "What did he do to you?"

"It wasn't a man," she answered. "It was a woman."

Elle took a cloth to her neck and arms, wiping the rain away. At the open window, she could see their fire smelting to ash. The night went black, and the only sound was the sigh of the storm.

"She stole my music," Elle answered as the smoke disappeared. "And called it hers."

Weston let out a low whistle, and Elle's heart clenched.

"Does Arlo know?" he asked.

"The only reason I got a record deal was to keep me quiet."

It stung, stating the truth so simply.

"That's bullshit, Elle."

"You know what the worst part is?" Elle felt both strong and weak. "They were songs I wrote for my friend after she died. The whole album was for Merry, and someone turned it into a storyline about her sweetheart leaving for war."

"'Leaving Song,'" Weston whispered. She loved him for not saying Josie's name.

He looked gutted, as if it were his friend who had died. "It's a goddamn beautiful ballad, Elle."

"Thank you," she said, and leaned her forehead against the raised windowpane. "I've never been anybody's beautiful thing, but those songs were mine."

He didn't try to fix it, didn't try to convince her that brighter trophies lay ahead. Soberly, they sat with the loss.

As they spoke, Elle saw a truth she'd been avoiding. Merry's album was the loss she carried with her, but it wasn't what she was running from.

"That isn't the worst part," Elle said. "Though I wish it was."

"Then what is?" Weston's eyes were steady, safe.

"It was my fault she died," Elle began. "Merry."

Weston listened as she told him everything.

"It will always be the worst thing I've ever done," Elle said.

"You liken yourself to Josie, then?" Weston asked as a trail of rain slipped down his temple. "Someone who took what wasn't hers?"

"That isn't it," Elle answered. "It has nothing to do with her—just what she revealed when I lost all my music. Every time I look inside myself now I find nothing. I feel dead. And maybe it's not my fault, but it just lingers, like I have nothing left. All that's there is this voice that says, *You don't have it, you don't have it, you don't have it*. And it's the loneliest fucking thing."

"Don't have what?" Weston asked.

"Whatever it is that makes someone want to hold on to me," Elle answered.

Weston nodded. He was so close, so warm, so real.

"I can feel her," he said. "Your friend. In all of your music."

Elle smiled, though it hurt. "I wish I'd used her name in a song, at least once."

Weston stared at her for a beat, his fingers drumming against his thigh. "It's not too late."

"How so?" she asked.

"Maybe you can write some hints into your next album. Clues that lead us to the true woman hidden in the songs Josie sang."

"You mean like a riddle."

"Exactly that." He touched the windowpane with the flat of his hand.

It was a good idea, Elle thought, one that wouldn't give back what she'd lost, but would create something new instead.

"All my songs about Merry are so sad," she said slowly, "but Merry wasn't sad at all."

She wanted lyrics now that stoked a fire, brought heat to skin, burned through the night.

"There are three ways to fall in love with an outlaw." Elle let a new lyric play in her mind.

"The first is quick and dirty," Weston offered.

"The second long and slow."

"And the third?"

"The third is all Merry, all over that album no one will ever know was mine. The third way to fall in love is to lose it, I think."

Weston looked toward the storm, and then they watched the rain fall.

"You play the mandolin like she did," Elle said, after a spell.

He turned toward her at the window. "Is that why you have a cracked mandolin sitting in the back seat of your car like a dead body?"

"It is."

Just as soon as Weston started to say, "Can I—" Elle began with "You can't. Play it, I mean."

"Oh." Weston's voice wavered. "I wasn't—"

"No, no." Elle touched his arm, let her hand remain. "She was left-handed. The mandolin is left-handed. That's why you can't play it."

"I see," he said. "I could restring it for you. Polish it, patch up the grain."

"I—" She couldn't manage the words. Those strings were the last thing Merry had touched.

"Instruments are meant to be played," he said. "Not kept in back seats."

Elle nodded, and a curtain of rain fell through the trees. She was coming to understand the silences between them. They existed because there was so much that Elle didn't need to explain. Somehow, Weston already knew. He must have seen how desperately she wanted to know him—body, mind, spirit—and be known by him, too.

"There's something else," she said, "I should tell you."

Weston's hand fell from the windowpane.

"I've never been with a man." She confessed it as a blight, a bruise. Elle hated that it made her look naïve, when all she felt was worn.

She hadn't trusted anyone in so long. Maybe never.

He used his fingertip to lift her chin. "That don't mean you ain't lived."

Elle flushed at being seen, just as she was—beating heart, true lyrics, weary blood. "That's a good song title."

He stepped toward her. "I daresay."

"Can I use it?"

His eyes traveled from her eyes to her mouth. "It's already yours."

Elle recalled her favorite adage: It only takes three and a half minutes to change a life. The words were true in these woods, though not how Elle expected. Everything Weston said was a song waiting to be written.

She ran her fingers up the back of his neck into his auburn hair. He exhaled heavily and wrapped his hands around her waist. Pulled her close.

Buried his face in her neck. The scratch of his beard against her skin set her pulse to his.

Elle had seen him watching her, wanting her, and resisting. *You can't get mixed up with me,* he'd said. But wasn't it a miracle to bare your sins to someone who would listen? Elle wanted him, all of him. She didn't care what someone else called evil or good.

Weston pressed her into the wall, kissed her long and slow, like he wanted to make it last for the rest of his life. Elle ran her nails down the slope of his back. His muscles tensed beneath her touch; he started to shake.

"Elle," he said.

She slipped her fingers beneath his soaked shirt, pulled it over his head. Ran her calloused fingers along the tightrope of his spine as he brought his lips to her jaw, her neck, her shoulder.

He kissed her, held her like he played that mandolin, lips and fingers everywhere, all over her. Soft enough that there was no telling where they were going, only where they'd been. Elle heard herself crying out from the joy of it, letting her voice be loud, reveling in how it drowned in the tempest.

This would come to be the final song on Elle's next album, a mournful, eerie display of longing and truth finding each other on a dirt floor. Begun the first night she and Weston met, she'd call it "Love Beneath the Mandolins."

Don't tell me your name
And I won't tell you mine
The less I know about you
The more I'll be just fine
Because we both know
Before it's time to go
I'm not the holding-on-to kind

Love beneath the mandolins
No need to know whose heart this is

I'm holding, no scolding
From past lives, other sins

The instruments swayed above Elle and Weston as they tumbled to the floor, riding the breeze through the open window long after they'd fallen asleep.

Elle had planned to stay no more than a week or two but remained with the luthier for six. Wrote enough music for three albums' worth. Together, she and Weston saw the first signs of autumn come to pass—a slight crimson frosting the edges of the hardwoods, a trio of bulldozers loudly flattening the eastern edge of the woods. If summer were infinite, Elle and Weston would have lingered in the forest forever. But there was a truth they'd both left unspoken. The cabin had no heat, and once winter came, they wouldn't be able to stay. Elle would have to return to Nashville and deliver what she'd promised.

The future stood in front of her like a hatchet waiting to fall. She didn't dare speak of what was to come because Weston hadn't. He'd finished his mandolins, branded each one with his personal insignia of an Omega symbol. And yet he made no mention of what his plans held.

A cold front prevailed in the distance. Like a scavenger, Elle had pieced together bits of Weston's life beyond this clearing in the forest. Weston was a prominent family name in Kentucky, she had surmised, and yet her Weston seemed to have no people of his own. She wondered, even as she knew the answer for her own life—how someone so young ended up so alone.

She relished the music she'd created, and she couldn't wait to share it first with Arlo, and then with the world. It was everything she'd put into the *Merry* album, and even more—it celebrated the strength that came from loss, the intimate art of grieving something back to life. The volcanic risk of falling for someone new.

Tentatively, she did only what her heart could.

She asked Weston to come with her.

"Elle," he said, once, then twice. "Elle, Elle."

The sound of her name, like the ringing of a warning bell. His hair shone like copper in the afternoon light.

He hadn't said no; he hadn't said yes. There was a reason he'd gone into hiding, she knew. Once again, she'd revealed her deepest secrets to someone who only concealed their own. Elle and Weston fell asleep by the fire on their last night together, limbs and hearts tangled into one.

He was gone in the morning, which to Elle had not been a surprise.

What had shocked her—for which she only had herself to blame—was that he'd left without a note, and he'd taken Merry's mandolin.

Elle wept, because she thought she'd never see that instrument again. Yet buried wishes have a way of finding their way toward the sun, same as a wildflower pushing through tar and stone. Merry's mandolin, lost for almost twenty years, reappeared when a meteor struck the ground in that same haunted forest in 1991, and a news broadcast revealed it in the hands of a young woman Elle did not know.

Her name was Marijohn.

Part III

Third Outlaw

(1973–1991)

Those we can't save tell us who we are.

—"Heal Nothing," the *Merry* album

HEAL NOTHING

"Give me the mandolin," Elle Harlow demanded the night she appeared on Marijohn Shaw's porch.

Each of them waited there in the dark, viper-still, so fearfully ready to snatch the miracle standing right across from her. A mother, an instrument, a friend, a history. A lost treasure, finally getting found.

Slowly, Marijohn beheld the marvel standing beneath the porch light. Elle was forty years old, her jeans at least twenty, and the hunger in her eyes was nothing but timeless. She was breeze-blown and angry and the most beautiful fucking thing Marijohn had ever seen.

There was no moon that hot September night in 1991, no firelight. Only the raspy etch of Elle Harlow's voice.

"I'll pay you for it," she said.

"I don't want your money," Marijohn replied, just as she was—staunch, weary, and resolute. It was the first time in her life that the dogged emptiness inside her didn't feel like a stain. It had been guiding her to this moment, whispering the secret to remaining on her own two feet.

She had her own hunger, and she let it lead.

A breath seemed to catch in Elle's throat at Marijohn's response. *I don't want your money*. She tilted her head as if a memory had beckoned her, as if she'd just heard her own echo.

Marijohn's fingers fidgeted with a coil of her black hair. She was wildly nervous. There were so many things she needed from the woman in front of her—answers about where Elle had been for the last eighteen years, where Marijohn had come from, and whether she and Elle had ever met before.

The day the meteor struck, Marijohn had sensed that the coming autumn would be a season of last chances, and she'd been right—but it had never been about Lazarus. It had always been about her.

Abe had taught Marijohn how to handle an artifact: curiously, gently, steadily. But she had no idea how to approach a legend that had come back from the dead. Elle looked reckless, a thoroughbred who had just broken free of her fences. Marijohn did not want her to run.

"Can you even play it?" she asked.

Elle didn't answer. Her eyes kept drifting toward the tree line, her whole body tilting toward the wooded darkness as if she'd caught a melody coming from the heart of the forest that no one else could hear.

"You've been in these woods before," Marijohn led. "Haven't you?"

Elle looked disturbed—pupils in bloom, bottom lip trapped between her teeth. "Is anyone living in there?" she asked.

"I don't see how anyone could."

Marijohn waited. The folk singer was rooted to the threshold of the house, her fingernails digging into the wood above the doorjamb.

"Elle," Marijohn said. "Are you all right?"

Again, Elle didn't respond.

"Answer me this, at least." Marijohn had a list of questions and aimed for the easiest one. "Who was the third outlaw in *Wounds from a Lover?*"

Elle's face scoured Marijohn's. Then her eyes trailed the mossy boxes on the windowsills and the colored rocks on the pathway. The slew of bikes, the forgotten rolls of local newspapers huddled in the corner and blanched by the sun. She must have seen the split-open life Abe and his daughter lived, the way they welcomed the world by painting over all the empty spaces a wife or mother might have filled.

"I didn't come here to sate your curiosity," Elle said.

"Why couldn't anyone find you?" Marijohn pressed.

At that, Elle laughed. The sound knocked against the eaves of the house. "People could have looked for me plenty. They just didn't *see*. Now give me the mandolin."

Her gaze flew to the woods for a second time, as if she believed Marijohn had hidden it there, even though she'd already seen it hanging on her wall.

Elle's demands seared like a burn. If the meteor hadn't hit Lenora, if Lazarus hadn't set off on his own—maybe even if Marijohn had ever had a mother—she might have surrendered it. She might not have needed the instrument so furiously. This mandolin was all Marijohn had left.

Fate had not brought them together. This was one woman recognizing another woman's longing because it looked so much like her own.

"I can't give it to you," Marijohn said. "It deserves to be heard."

And she deserved to be the one who played it.

"Oh?" Elle's brow raised. "And there's so many people out here in the middle of nowhere, waiting to listen?"

Marijohn felt them then—all the questions she'd ever wanted to ask her mother. Every lyric she'd written in her notebook, longing to give definition to the shape of an absent woman. But truly—all this time, she'd been searching for how to create her own contour, her own silhouette, her own shadow. She'd been sifting through everything she didn't have, rather than what she did. Until then Marijohn hadn't yet thought of how she might define herself, but in the wake of Elle's question, she knew.

She was the wind in the woods after midnight. She was the blade in a back pocket. She was the final note of her favorite song.

And she was someone who loved that mandolin.

"There's me." Marijohn's voice held strong. "That's enough."

Elle's eyes narrowed as if what she had once seen through a glass, darkly, she saw now face-to-face.

"It's not yours," she said.

"I have a feeling"—Marijohn squared her chin—"that it's not yours, either."

Elle stood her ground, that shard of pink-and-white plastic deep in her grip. They were at an impasse. Marijohn recognized a glimmer of herself in the wiliness of Elle's gaze. Elle teemed with so much defiance that she gathered force from it.

Telling her no would not work. Marijohn needed to find another way.

She needed the mandolin to speak.

"Wait here," she said. "Please."

Inside the house, Marijohn fetched the mandolin from the wall. Then she did what she'd done every summer night since the weather had turned. She went to the attic, opened the window, and began to play her favorite Elle Harlow songs.

When Marijohn finished "Love Beneath the Mandolins," she peeked over the ledge of the roof to see Elle hunched on the front steps, her head in her hands. As the last chord hung in the air, Marijohn started to understand who Elle Harlow was, at heart. She was no starlet, no folk-singing heroine who had disappeared. Elle was a woman who had lost something she loved.

Marijohn couldn't help wondering what it was.

"I can't tell you," Elle said, "how long I've been waiting to hear that sound."

And then she said what every dauntless musician hopes to hear.

"Play it again."

So Marijohn did.

After she finished the final chorus, a soft round of applause came from the porch. Elle whistled when Marijohn stepped through the screen door a few minutes later. She sat on the swing, her guitar now in her grip.

For a moment, they stared at each other.

"You—" Elle tripped over the words. Tried again. "You astonish me."

Marijohn's heart flared. "Why?"

"It's how you play."

"What do you mean?"

"You play soft and somber, but not weak." Absently, Elle began tuning her guitar. "Like you're the morning after a storm. Like you survived three days in a tomb," she said. "And you also play just like her."

"Who?"

Elle didn't answer.

"Play with me," she said instead. The words seemed foreign in Elle's mouth, as if she hadn't spoken them for many lifetimes. "The rest of the album."

Marijohn smiled. A sudden lightness hung in the air, the mandolin fitting neatly against the cradle of her hip—as if things were just as they always should have been.

Neither of them slept that night. One by one, they played through each track on *Wounds from a Lover*—"Daughter to Wife," "Shut Out the Light," "That Don't Mean You Ain't Lived," and the rest. The attic ritual Marijohn had practiced every summer evening while listening to Elle's records and clutching her mandolin to her chest came to life in front of her. This Elle was no fable. She had hands and feet and red lipstick that left an imprint on the guitar pick she pinched between her lips.

When they'd finished, Elle balanced her guitar on her thigh and said, "Play 'Heal Nothing' with me. I'd love to hear it on the mandolin."

Marijohn's fingers stilled. That song had been a part of Abe's folklore for as long as Marijohn had known him.

"Wait a minute." She recalled the inscription on her father's gas station pump, the one attributed to Josie Starling. "That's not your song."

Elle's head tipped toward Marijohn, her eyes two slits. The sight was subtle and terrifying. Marijohn couldn't help the tremor in her hands. She'd heard of Elle Harlow's famed moods, her temper. Her violence. Elle kept the cold stare so long she seemed to shed an outer skin, as if the song itself had scaled her.

"Just play it." She paused, settling herself. "Please."

Marijohn shook her head. She ran her hand down the neck of the mandolin, and the strings squealed. "I don't know how."

"I'll teach you," Elle said, simple as that.

It was the first time a woman had taught Marijohn a song.

Elle played through the verse and called out the chords to a tune that ran like a waterfall:

I watched you bleed from behind the door
Rain came down, didn't care what for
Your gaze held mine till I felt the scar
Those we can't save tell us who we are

As Elle's fingers moved across the frets, Marijohn remembered how the air had quickened in the moments after the meteor hit the ravine, like the veil separating heaven and earth had been torn in two. The charge between Elle and her felt just like it—atmospheric and atomic, solemn and sublime.

Miracle and muscle and madness and metamorphosis.

When Elle sang the chorus to "Heal Nothing," it was plain that the words were hers alone. Her voice brayed with candor, a glorious and chilling sound. The inscription on Abe's old gas pump—*try to heal everything and you'll heal nothing at all*—a lyric everyone knew as Josie Starling's, obviously belonged to Elle.

Marijohn understood then why Elle was so desperate for the mandolin. It was a memory, a solace, a confession. A whole life.

"Tell me," Marijohn said, "why this song is no longer yours."

And Elle did.

She told her about Reuben and Merry and Arlo and Josie and Weston—each person that she'd loved and lost. She said nothing about where she'd been since 1973.

She said nothing about leaving an infant behind.

If any joy could be found in the wicked miracle of the meteor, it was the shock on Abe Shaw's face when he woke before sunrise the next day to find his favorite folk singer sitting on his front porch.

"I knew you weren't dead," he said.

At dawn, Elle fell asleep on the porch swing. Her Taylor lay like a blanket in her lap. Abe and Marijohn regarded her with awe from behind their screen door. Queenly and haunted, legend-in-the-flesh Elle Harlow snored softly in the day's first light.

Abe couldn't look away from Elle's face. "Did she say anything about leaving a baby at a gas station?"

"Nothing." A sadness like lead settled between Marijohn's ribs. "Maybe it wasn't her."

But they both knew it was.

Together they stared at the broken mandolin, wishing it would speak.

Later that morning, Marijohn returned to the porch with a cup of tea for Elle. They sat in the damp air, dew drawn across the grass. The day was cool and gray, the kind meant to be spent writing a song.

Marijohn couldn't help it. She had to begin somewhere.

"Was Arlo the third outlaw?"

"He wishes," Elle grunted, then she turned. Steam from her cup dissolved in the air. A sass colored her countenance along with the new day. "What is your name?"

"It's Marijohn."

"Marijohn." Elle cast a glance over her shoulder and eyed the mandolin in its case at the bottom of the stairs behind her. "That instrument's been cleaned up since I last saw it."

"Has it?"

"In 1972 it was in such terrible shape it couldn't even be used." Elle held her teacup with both hands. "I haven't heard anyone play the mandolin so well in a very long time."

Marijohn tried to thank her, but Elle kept on.

"How did you learn?" she asked.

"I taught myself."

"So you've never had a teacher?" Elle lifted her mug to her lips but didn't drink. "Any kind of mentor?"

"No."

No mother, either.

"Christ." Elle finally took a sip. "It can't be true that you want these woods to be your only audience for the rest of your life."

It was like a bird taking flight, hearing the truth spoken back to her. Marijohn met her stare. "No."

"What are you doing here, then?"

It was a question without one answer. Marijohn was licking her wounds.

Looking after her father. Languishing in the trench of half-written choruses, laboring over the fear that she'd already missed her only shot.

But here was the balm. Before her was a woman who understood.

"I think I ruined my chances," Marijohn said, "before any of it even began."

Elle frowned. "What do you mean?"

"I should have sung on that video of the meteor, but I didn't. I held myself back. Now it kills me every time I think about it."

Elle waited, raising her chin. "Go on."

She already knew about the shooting star. Marijohn told her the rest about Lazarus, her song, his ticket to Nashville. When she finished, Elle looked as if she smelled rot in the air.

"He played my best song," Marijohn said. "And they still wanted him instead of me."

"First of all"—Elle's pointer finger spiked the air—"it ain't your best song."

"You haven't even heard it."

"I don't need to. You have to believe any song you're writing is your best one yet. Otherwise you'll never finish it."

Marijohn's eyes were hooded in disbelief. Elle continued.

"Second," she said, "if you're not careful, every song you write will end up in the fist of a man."

After a night of hearing the story behind Elle's betrayal, Marijohn didn't know what to say. Lazarus didn't have it in his heart to steal, but that had never been the fear holding Marijohn by the throat. With Laz or without him, Marijohn had never stood up to claim what was hers. Had never shouted it from her attic window for anyone to hear. Had never examined her own prowess, that dark and sonorous voice in her head, and said, *This is mine.*

"I can see your mind straying," Elle said.

"How can I take back things I already gave away?" Marijohn asked.

"I can tell you only this." Elle held open her hands. "You have music, and you have men. You can't serve them both."

All her life, men had been an affliction to Elle, even as she'd loved them. Her father, Arlo, Weston. So Elle had hidden her memories in her music, where no man could reach. But Marijohn could.

Elle's body of work, her whole life, lay before her—a testament, a promise, a call.

"The song is yours," Elle said. "The heart. The fire. Even the regret. So the question is, Marijohn—what are you going to do with it?"

Here they were—Marijohn Shaw's three and a half minutes to change her life. One answer and nothing would be the same.

"I want to sing," she answered. "I want people to hear my songs."

Elle looked so keenly at Marijohn, so dearly and so direly, it was as if she'd said the words herself.

HUNGER

In 1972, Elle busted out of the woods in western Pennsylvania, feeling like she'd been born with a hole in her pocket. She left Arlo's cabin with less than what she'd brought with her. Elle's guitar held the memory of the new songs she'd written, but Merry's mandolin was gone. With it went the belief that Elle might have some good left in her—and only one thing remained. It had been her companion in the frozen fields with Hosea's Winchester, trapped at the back of her throat when she sang with Josie, knocking on the window to her room in the garret as she wrote lyrics on the wall.

It was hunger—induced by her own vulnerability—and now she was ravenous.

Elle had given lavishly of herself to Weston, and it had left her defenseless. In those woods she hadn't surrendered her pride or her loyalty, but her love. So few people were granted it. Devotion—whether for a mentor or friend or man—always turned Elle stupid. It scavenged her like a tireless fever until it left her smaller, weaker, emptier. Now Elle knew why she never felt like she'd had enough. She loved too loudly and gave too much of herself away.

After Weston stole her mandolin, Elle returned to Nashville in autumn with the teeth of defeat at her heels and a triumphant album laying waste to her heart. She took no notice of the crimson hills shepherding her route, the state prisons tucked behind tree lines, the clouds fluffed like Susannah's biscuits that floated across the sky. Elle wanted to bury herself in a song. She never felt ashamed of the honesty in her music the way she did with her skin-and-bone self.

In her rearview, the back seat was bare. Merry's mandolin had lain alone there so long the sun had faded the black vinyl around its edges, leaving a darkened shape so that even its absence was a present object.

Instruments ought to be played, Weston had said to her as rain poured down the windowpane and his eyes held a quiet fire. He'd played her like a mandolin, and he'd done it beautifully. How tenderly, how savagely he'd pried her mouth open and all these lyrics had spilled out. How deeply, how completely Elle had misunderstood him, even as he'd tried to warn her.

Now, once again, this album of hers was half owned by someone else. It stood testament to her fear that she scared people away. Weston had witnessed her becoming and then he'd chosen to leave. What truth had he found in her so terrifying that he hadn't said goodbye? Elle had written the songs for herself, but she'd sung them to Weston. His was the face she saw when she closed her eyes. His eyelashes fluttering on the chorus of "Shut Out the Light," his lips silently mouthing the words—

The truth don't always set you free
I don't want to fight no more tonight
Think of all the selves we'd be
If you'd just shut out the light

Elle hummed the tune. It was almost as if she'd written the song for this very moment in her Studebaker, like her body knew she would need it once Weston was gone and took a piece of her with him. She could perform her music for any adoring crowd, but Weston would claim the soul of this record. Elle had created these melodies for an audience of one.

Don't you dare feel ashamed. Elle fought with herself. The yellow lines on the road began to haze as she pressed her foot on the gas. Shame wasn't an emotion born from excess, but scarcity. Elle believed she hadn't been that hungry mountain hunter in a very long time.

Nashville's skyline came into view on the last leg of Elle's journey, the Life and Casualty Tower sticking up among the other buildings like a middle finger. Elle slept one last night on the bank of the Cumberland before she rose early to meet Arlo by the willow just beyond the studio, as was their way. That parking lot kept them true. There, he had never refused her.

She saw his cigarette before his face broke through the dark.

"Well, shit," Arlo said, as he sprang from his Cadillac. "I'd started to think you weren't coming back."

"That cabin you sent me to," Elle began, "was occupied."

Arlo's expression remained fixed. "I warned you about the bears."

"Not the bears. Your cousin."

Arlo laughed. "You'll have to be more specific."

"The luthier."

Elle watched him carefully. She'd glean the truth not from what Arlo said next, but how he said it.

"Shit," he said again. He fumbled into his breast pocket for another Marlboro. "Who else did you tell?"

"Why?" She stepped toward him, the heel of her boot clapping against the brick walkway. "What did he do?"

"He ain't—" Arlo fished for the right words. The night faded away around them like a sigh, and Arlo's eyes skittered in search of a place to land. "He ain't supposed to be at the cabin. He still there?"

Arlo slipped into *ain't*s on only two occasions. When he was trying to sweet-talk, and when he got nervous.

"I ain't his keeper," Elle returned. Another good song title, that.

"Dammit, Elle," Arlo yelled, and Elle flinched. The crows in the willow screeched. For all their quarrels, Arlo had never raised his voice.

"Forget his name, forget what you saw, forget I sent you there." His neck went garnet. "I screwed up, is that what you want to hear? A thousand apologies."

"I don't want your apologies," she said. "I want you to tell me the truth."

"The truth, Elle?" His voice skipped an octave, and spittle clung to his mustache.

"It's just you and me."

His mouth hung open, gaunt and desperate. "The truth is you need to disappear for a while. No good will come of this. Forget a second album, forget your way here."

Elle balked at the shock of it, the only sound between them the tweet of a finch in a nearby nest. Instantly Arlo had come undone, and finally Elle understood. This was the real Arlo, protecting something—or someone—he loved.

You got people relying on you, Elle? he'd said on the day he offered her a record deal. *So do I.*

Arlo sniffed, then began to mount the steps. His shoulders drooped. He couldn't have been born more than ten years before Elle, and yet, for the first time, he looked old. Skin hung from his jaw, his lips struck downward in a frown. His success was stealing his years away. Three children, a mansion, and a new wife. He'd lived a hundred lucky lives while Elle fought to make it through her first—and Elle knew then she'd never trade her life for his.

Hunger, perhaps, was not the worst thing after all.

Charmlessly ready to abandon her, Arlo yanked on the studio's heavy door, his cigarette a smear of ash against the steps. He didn't look back until Elle called out his name.

You can't make me disappear. She steadied herself. *Not today.*

"Arlo." She pointed toward the stoop. "Sit."

He glared, he blinked, he complied. Elle strapped on her guitar, sat down in the parking lot, and crisscrossed her legs. A crack in the asphalt grew between them where a clover had shot through. The split ran all the way from the brick steps to the far end of the lot, parting the stone sea. *All these cracks no one notices,* Elle told herself. *One day they'll break open the world.*

Just like her.

She played her new album for Arlo from beginning to end, reliving the rage and ecstasy and letdown it had caused. Elle ended with her favorite song, freshly written when she'd pulled over halfway to Nashville so she could write the chorus.

Faithful are
Wounds from a lover
Deceitful are
Kisses from an enemy
And I, no, I
Never once knew the difference

This album was no longer some treasure hunt about stolen music, but about what Elle had stolen from herself. Elle had been her own tragic lover, her own beloved foe. She had no mercy, no amnesty, no mirth. Elle was easily fooled by others because of how desperately she fooled herself.

But Elle couldn't see that this was the most moving and meteoric thing about her—the way she welcomed a stranger into her dungeon so they'd be set free from their own. No one felt lonely listening to an Elle Harlow song because she gathered that loneliness under her wing. She made it soft and pliable until it took to the wind. Elle never hid from the truth in her music—she allowed others to hide themselves within it instead.

As she sang, the song hurt and held her, it loved and lost. When she'd finished, the sun cut through the willow branches and made Arlo's face plain. If he'd appeared old before, Elle's music had turned him pure and childlike. His cheeks were slick from his tears.

"Elle Harlow, listen to me," Arlo said, even as the guitar's final note haunted the air. "This is the album you will always be known for."

He'd offered the words as a compliment. Arlo meant to say he'd been stunned by her. She'd undone, then remade him by the day's early light. But by declaring what Elle Harlow would be known for, Arlo only sealed the fact of what she already knew. The *Merry* album would never be hers. It was an act of erasure so easy and graceless that Elle decided she truly deserved it.

"What do you want to call the album?" Arlo asked.

Elle hadn't thought about it, but the answer was clear. Elle was the same as she'd always been—an offering, the darkest meal at the feast.

Believe Me, Honey

Arlo was right. *Wounds from a Lover* went platinum in early 1973, briefly outselling Waylon Jennings, Willie Nelson, and Olivia Newton-John. The outside world, itching for gritty lyrics and a strong downbeat, figured Elle Harlow had reinvented herself. They thought she'd become someone new instead of returning to someone old. *Folk music has a new queen,* one newspaper hailed. *A dark, brooding mistress of an album,* a reviewer wrote. *Where has the real Elle Harlow been hiding,* asked another.

Elle had no idea how prophetic those words would soon become.

Still a country girl beneath her thick skin, even Elle was not exempt from the wheels that turned Music City. After she returned from the woods and recorded the *Wounds from a Lover* album, she was starker, funnier, sadder, bolder. She said no to the steel guitar and yes to her own solo accompaniment. Elle refused skirts and heels in favor of red lipstick and denim with boots. Clothes make the man, so they say—and Elle now knew they could unmake a woman. She would no longer stand for being forced to wear a dress, only not to be taken seriously because she did.

"Look alive, y'all! Here comes the queen!" the studio songwriters said of her when they met at Tootsies for noontime gin after Elle's album topped the charts.

A man in a gray army-navy shirt and a pair of faded camouflage pants stumbled toward the jukebox. He was day drunk, but so were the studio writers, and they watched him like he was Moses hoisting the Ten Commandment tablets. Elle knew what they were thinking. Would this brawny, muscled chunk of a man choose one of their songs with his five cents?

He leaned on one boot, then the other. Flipped forward, then back through the slots. They clicked. One of the writers sighed.

"For shit's sake, it ain't like you got to marry it," he said under his breath.

The nickel fell; a clank filled the air. A moment of silence, then the whirring of a mechanical arm as the record was chosen. "Believe Me, Honey" swirled across every tabletop toward the bar.

"Aw, hell," Hal said. "Josie always beats every one of us out." He cast Elle a glance. "Except maybe you."

Elle didn't smile or act as if she'd heard. None of the writers ever suspected she'd written those words instead of Josie.

"Whew, doggies," Hal said when he looked Elle over a second time. She wore a tight blue flannel, worn bell bottoms, thick boots with golden toes. Her hair was tousled, parted down the middle, and her lips glared red.

"What part of the cycle are you on now?" Hal asked. "Love, marriage, or divorce?"

"Cycles ain't for love," Elle grunted. "They're for laundry." She twirled a finger in the air. "Let it spin, and pour me some gin."

Someone at the end of the bar rolled a pen toward her. "Write it down!" he called.

Elle didn't bother. Instead, she practiced her signature on a bar napkin by crafting a heart from the double *l* in her name.

"Will you look at that?" Hal asked, knocking back his third glass. "Fellas, our Elle is about to go big time."

They cheered and clapped her on the back, as if she were one of them. What lonely camaraderie to be so accepted by this cohort and yet so misunderstood. They championed her success, but if they were to write a song for her, it would surely return to a syrupy missive about man worship and she-devils, pistols and hot earth steaming from a grave. That was how men like them saw the world. Country music, as Elle had heard over and over, was "three chords and the truth." Elle believed that, down to her marrow. But she wondered—whose truth was it?

The question called to mind her old friend Leo, whose trilling banjo had graced legions of songs, even as he was erased from them. Exactly as the machine of popular music intended, Elle had lost track of her friend. This tradition knew how to take a song and claim it belonged to everyone, unless it belonged to a white man.

Elle bade goodbye to country music and ran into folk's open arms. It was free terrain there, rich for pioneering. Few rules, fewer fenced-in pastures. Elle didn't give a lick what they called her ballads. Country, folk, this new term "Americana"—it was all the same to Elle. Let the men in Cadillacs squabble over it. All that mattered now was that it was hers.

It could have been argued that Elle's music was her only great love affair. The idea held the ring of truth. The more Elle loved her songs, the more they loved her back. She could feel their delight in being written, being sung. If music couldn't be love itself, it was the conduit that allowed Elle Harlow to love the world in which she lived.

And love, she did. Everything she could no longer give any other beating heart, she gave to her songs.

Again and again, it saved her life.

Merry had healed in her own kind of way, just as Elle now healed in hers. It was Malachi in the barn, times a thousand. Concert after concert, she brought herself back to life. Each performance felt truer than the last, the stakes ever higher, until Elle's real life began to turn counterfeit. Offstage, she was a girl who ran away from home. Onstage, she was a woman who had taken her pain and transformed it into beauty.

At the end of her spring tour, she stood on an outdoor stage just south of Cincinnati. Any other artist might have felt the rote boredom of performing the same tunes every night, but not Elle. She sparked into a live wire every time she sang "Love Beneath the Mandolins," or "Shut Out the Light," or "Third Outlaw." Song by song, she watched her entire audience ignite.

After the encore, Elle set her guitar on its stand. Sweat had worked its way down her back. She was achy, tired, and satisfied.

"Play 'School Girl Crush'!" someone yelled from the darkened rows.

One meow came from the crowd, then a second, then a chorus.

"No," Elle said.

Now, more than ever, she wanted honesty.

"I hate that song," she said.

The audience laughed because they thought she was joking.

When the fans had finally filed out, the seats emptied and the lights dimmed, Elle found herself returning to that barren stage and training her eyes on a barn in the distance, searching for even the smallest hole to peer through in the hopes that Merry might be looking back at her from the other side. Elle often did this after performances when she felt dislocated and exposed, like a snake that had just shed its skin.

"Tell me what to do, Merry," Elle said softly, but it was not Merry who gave a response.

It was Elle's own phantom voice from the ballad "Sing It Slow," echoing her own longing back to her.

Knowing what you would say
Ain't the same as hearing you say it
All this music you left with me
Ain't the same as hearing you play it

Her own words: beautiful, stark, true. And painful as hell.

Elle lay flat on her back on the dirty stage and stared into the sky. *Meow,* the audience had called. All her losses were starting to look alike. She could hardly tell one from another anymore. Elle would never play a track from *School Girl Crush* again. What a sad marionette Elle had been when she recorded it. Only Weston had witnessed her cut the strings.

She and Arlo never spoke of him again after that predawn morning in the parking lot. Elle searched for his profile in every crowd, in every darkened room. He had been her audience of one, and he remained it even in a mass of a thousand.

Josie had deceived her from the start. But Weston, the thief, hadn't tricked her. Elle felt that truth as deep as her mother's love. Something had happened—but Elle couldn't figure it out. What was it about her that made people want to steal?

She hunted for Weston's Omega symbol on the back of every mandolin she saw in the studio, on stage, in every storefront. Arlo had sold them all. She'd spotted one sitting prettily in the music shop window not too far from Tootsies. Weston had made it over the summer. Elle remembered the heart-shaped knot in the wood, how his hands had sanded it, loved it, remade it. She could feel those hands on her spine as she looked at it through the glass.

Elle would have lived that summer with Weston over and over if she could have. And in a way, every time she sang the *Wounds from a Lover* album for a crowd, she did.

By the end of 1973, Elle was only twenty-two and her life swelled with snapshots of rustic beauty. She'd seen the sun rise over the mist in the Rockies and had seen it set on the beaches of California. From afar she built a new mountain school for her people; she didn't sing any more duets. She knew the dust trapped in every spotlight and the glittering of doe eyes caught in moonlight off back-country roads. She knew sleeping in station wagons and fancy hotels. She'd dined on riverboats and around campfires; she'd autographed everything from cowboy boots and guitars to the backs of envelopes for small children and their mothers. She held all these things together—the rich things and the poor, the joy and the pain. Mostly she did it alone.

Only two things remained undone.

She had yet to write another album. And she had yet to see Josie Starling.

Josie had completed a European tour over the summer and was set to return—and oh, how Arlo knew to spin a story. In any fairy tale, those who go to war must one day come home. Even though the tide had turned against America's occupation in Vietnam, Josie's *Soldier* album—or the *Merry* album, as Elle knew it—had come to represent what was stolen from a generation of men who had no choice but to fight.

Elle was woman enough to see the poetry in Arlo's lie. She was also woman enough to loathe Josie with the heat of a great fire. In the past four years, Josie hadn't dared contact her. Even Arlo, the great conspirator, shrank at the thought of a reunion between them.

As it is with all starlit beings caught in orbit, there came a time for an eclipse. An event of celestial proportions was due, and it was known in Nashville as the celebration of a hero's return.

Josie's mythical soldier was coming home.

The renowned Ryman Auditorium was a year away from closing its doors since Music City had set its sights on a flashier venue. Elle had longed to play on the Opry's famed stage, but she'd never been invited until they planned an evening to commemorate Josie Starling's only album. Word lingered of Elle's stirring rendition of "Heal Nothing."

The Opry staff had asked her to perform her own song, and she wouldn't have to pay Josie a dime. Elle knew she was of vindictive ilk. Susannah had warned her many times that bitterness would only eat her alive. And yet Elle felt a mangy alertness at the thought of confrontation. Before *Wounds from a Lover,* Elle would have shied away.

It's not the last thing you're gonna write, she'd had to whisper to herself any time she saw Josie's album in the window of the record store. Said it, but didn't believe it.

Until now.

She'd promised herself never to speak to Josie again, and she aimed to keep it. But she leapt at the chance to see Josie squirm beneath her stare.

Elle told the Opry she'd be delighted.

Her response caused Arlo to panic. "Promise me no trouble," he said.

"That sounds like the name of a song," Elle replied, "that I ain't gonna write."

On the night of the concert, Elle bit back a sour taste while waiting in the Ryman's darkened wings. Black curtains sheathed her like waterfalls as she wrestled with a stark reality. Josie had played Elle's songs more than Elle had.

For the first time since she'd performed for a boardroom of music men, Elle felt nervous. Nashville's resplendent had come out for the event, star-studded and whiskey-lit. The place was so packed that some folks had to sit on the stage itself. Elle cared nothing for the good opinion of music industry elite. She did care that her own words now felt foreign in her mouth.

She had rehearsed those lyrics, knew them frontward and back, just as she did when she was a girl writing in the smallest room of her mother's house. Elle hadn't counted on the misery of hearing her favorite musicians cover her songs. Willie Nelson sang "Leaving Song," and Loretta Lynn covered "Take Me to the River." They spoke of what this music had meant to them, how it had carved an irreplaceable cove in their hearts.

"Why record another album," George Jones quipped, "when your first is perfection?"

The audience laughed, and Elle couldn't help wondering whether she'd have received the same accolades if she'd recorded the album herself.

It wouldn't do to dwell. An audience awaited. There would be a brief instrumental number while a few props were placed on the stage: a Christmas tree, the front of an old truck that had been gutted of its engine and had a wreath on its grille. Then Elle would sing.

She dug for the guitar pick in her pocket. As her fingers closed around it, a hand grazed her shoulder blade. It was dark backstage and muffled in the curtain. Yet Elle didn't need to turn around to know who it was.

"Weston," she said into the curtain's folds.

He was so near, his chest against her back. The scent of rosewood took over her senses. Closed in.

"What are you doing here?" she asked.

"Elle," he said, and the sound of her name in his mouth made her snap.

She remembered the two of them at the fire in the woods, in the creek, singing her songs, kissing, falling to the floor. His hands all over her. Elle trembled. Then she turned around.

"Two minutes till curtain, Elle," Arlo called from the wings.

"Give it back," she found herself saying to Weston's chest. She couldn't look in his eyes; it was too dark to see him. "Give back the mandolin."

He took her by the hips. Tried to search out her eyes with his own. "Really, Elle?" He had the audacity to sound hurt. "That's all you want to say to me?"

"You disappeared." Elle couldn't believe what she said next. "You broke my heart."

"Don't you have loyalties, Elle? To people you'd do any kind of wrong for?"

She did. One was standing right in front of her.

"Give it back," she said again.

He opened his mouth—she heard her name called once more. *Curtain in thirty seconds.*

Weston took her hand. "Elle," he said. "Please."

One more *please,* one more sigh out of his mouth, and Elle was done for. She'd fall into him all over again and never be able to pull herself out.

Her heart slammed in her chest as she walked away toward her guitar, toward center stage. Sat there in the lonely dark before the curtain began to rise. She started to sweat and shake.

Don't cry, she said to herself. *Don't do it.*

Just before Elle got her cue, she kicked off her golden-toed cowboy boots and felt the grain of the wood on her bare feet. The roughness of it calmed her. This was her moment, and she wouldn't waste it. Not after everything Elle had given to be here. It would be too dark to see Josie from her wooden pew in the first row, but she knew of her presence, just as Elle knew of her lies.

Here was what she didn't know.

The curtain lifted. *Like water skipping over rocks,* she whispered to her guitar. *So you and I will be.* The spotlight flickered to life. Then Elle stepped into the tunnel of light, sensed the enchanted wood beneath her toes. It wasn't too dark to see, it turned out. Elle got a full view of Josie and who sat beside her.

It was Weston, his arm twined through Josie Starling's.

Elle hadn't been able to see the army uniform he was wearing backstage. The guitar pick fell from her fingers.

The audience watched her, silent.

Elle recalled the day she'd first heard Josie's version of "Heal Nothing" on the radio inside her mother's kitchen. It felt like another life.

She wrote these songs to remember her beloved, the DJ had crooned. *A soldier by the name of Luke.*

Here was the famed Luke, Elle realized. Luke Weston. Arlo's cousin. The luthier. Elle had never learned his first name. She thought it hadn't mattered; how wrong she'd been. Her Weston was Josie's mysterious soldier, whom Elle assumed she'd plucked out of thin air.

Don't you have loyalties, Elle, he'd asked, *to people you'd do any kind of wrong for?*

She understood everything anew in that moment, and she also understood nothing at all. Weston had been hiding out in the woods because he was supposed to be at war.

Elle's entire body warmed, and somewhere deep inside, she heard a humming. It sounded like her mother turning the dial of the radio; it sounded like Merry tuning her mandolin.

The audience still waited. Someone coughed. Weston would not meet Elle's stare, but Josie did.

All that she's taken from you, Elle said to herself. *But still, she will never have this.*

This moment. This voice. This song.

Elle made a show of being un-showed. Sniffed, bent down to retrieve her pick. She had no amplifier for the pink-and-white-gingham limited-edition guitar they'd asked her to play, no cords, no background band, no makeup. Her hair was wet, just as it had been at the festival in Texas after the storm. She closed her eyes, readying herself to perform the gritty, hard-edged version of "Heal Nothing" everyone had fallen in love with.

But that wasn't what came out.

Elle remembered the girl she was when she'd written the words, just as she recalled everything the music had meant when it was just hers. These had not been separate losses, but one twirled into the next, into the next. If Reuben hadn't died, she never would have learned to play the mandolin. If Merry hadn't died, she never would have gone to Nashville. If Josie hadn't stolen her music, she never would have fallen in love with Weston in the woods.

Her voice was mournful. Each note, its own moaning, as if she were haunting the words as she sang them. Singing, for Elle, had never been a loveless marriage between voice and throat. It was an ageless romance, a way of curving time around itself like a ring on a finger. Sometimes it came from songs and sheet music, and sometimes it lay at the gloaming beyond them.

Singing and healing were the same. They each began with a hurt that wouldn't quit.

Elle felt the aching melody reach out beyond her, filling every dirty pocket, every hollow heart, every open palm. It was the kind of echo that would remain long after she'd left, the ringing of an old lovelorn bell that Elle would never ring again.

She drew out the final chord, lifting and pressing her middle finger against the frets. No matter what came next, the notes would never be anything but perfect to her. Elle had kept her eyes shut. As her hands left her guitar, she waited for the applause to begin. She loved that silence between a ballad's end and the audience's response to it—the thrill that spanned one second and the next.

The applause never came.

Elle opened one eye, then the other. The crowd looked the same—a monstrous expanse of black, scattered with low lights on the aisles, with one empty seat in the front row. Josie had come to stand beside her. She felt Josie's hand reach for her wrist. She looked well. Plush, blush-faced, white-teethed. Elle did not smile, and the audience did not move.

"Elle," Josie said.

In another life, Elle might have asked one last time for Josie to come clean. Petitioning, it could have been called—but never begging. Elle would not do it. There might have been a parallel version of this world where Josie would hear her plea and finally concede. But that was not this place.

"Elle," Josie said again. "Help me."

She said it as if Elle were the one to fix the tear in this very public moment, as if only Elle had the power to stitch these two friends back together.

It happened so swiftly that Elle would later wonder if she had imagined it.

She hadn't.

Josie leaned toward Elle and kissed her on the cheek. Then Elle reared back her strumming hand and punched Josie Starling in the nose.

Run

Elle fled the building before Arlo could murder her. He'd never forgive her for this, and honestly—she was in no mood. It wouldn't take a prophet to see what was heading Elle's way by morning. Newspaper articles calling her a traitor to her sex. Calling her violent. A woman on the verge of a breakdown.

Maybe those articles would be right.

There would be only one version of what had occurred onstage: Josie the victim, and Elle the villain. No one would understand how easy it was to be both.

Elle had left Josie in the spotlight, hands clutching her bleeding nose. Elle knew she'd broken it. The crack her fist made upon impact sounded like lightning striking a tree. The audience had gasped, and in seconds Josie was cradled in loving arms. The backstage manager, the musicians, the crew—all of them glared at Elle. Disdain and horror, Elle could handle. She loathed being misunderstood. Elle faded into the shadows, taking only the pink-and-white guitar she had never liked. She'd even forgotten to take her boots.

Again, Elle was escaping a world she'd had a hand in building. She didn't want to live in it anymore. But also? Elle was afraid of herself.

The punch, she could understand. Could have predicted, even. Elle had always indulged a temper that screeched its way out of her body at the slightest sign of betrayal—a banshee formed from her darkest thoughts and basest instinct, ready to lay waste to whatever had overlooked her, misjudged her, used her. The demon was always chased by a shame-ridden hangover, a come-down dripping with fresh resolve to get better. Try harder. Be *kinder,* for Christ's sake.

This time, the guilt didn't come. The troubling thing was that Elle didn't regret it at all—not even one tiny, microscopic iota. The sensation of Elle's fist knocking into flesh, the startled fear in Josie's eyes shot shivers down her arm. God, it had felt *good.*

Barefoot, she ran to her station wagon, where she'd left the keys beneath the sun visor. She belted her guitar into the passenger seat, screwed the ignition, floored the gas. Elle hit Nashville city limits not even half an hour after she'd finished the final chord of "Heal Nothing." She didn't think of everything she'd left behind in her room at the boardinghouse, or how it might have taken Weston only three and a half minutes to explain his actions.

Elle called out the razor-blade version of herself, the one who could not be hurt, but only hurt others—the young girl, running. Her own words came back to haunt her—

Run from what you come from, baby
Never too far, always too fast

Mercy came in a solo gig, twelve hours from Nashville, at a bluegrass spot called Sunset Park in eastern Pennsylvania. If she could just step onto a different stage, she reasoned, she'd be able to quell the panic rising from her like steam from a dead body. Elle didn't bother to consult a map. She drove through the heartland of Kentucky, and along the Monongahela Forest in West Virginia. Her mind told her she was lost. The rest of her knew where she was headed, even though the luthier wouldn't be there anymore. It was an out-of-the-way stop that only Elle's heart knew of. A place where she hadn't been the worst version of herself. A place where she'd been lovely. Loving.

Loved.

Night had fallen, and for most of the drive, it felt as if her Studebaker were the only vehicle on the road. All was not right in Elle's mind. She often felt time thrusting itself at her as an unstoppable wind that could only be manipulated through song. That power propelled her long after she wearied, as if she'd shot herself from a catapult. Elle swore she heard a baby crying, an echo of the past. It was Reuben, the day he'd been born. No, it was Elle herself, woken in the night and in need of a lullaby.

"There's three ways to fall in love with an outlaw," she sang, trying to remind herself who she'd once been. Who she still was—a woman who wrote words so true they could steal anyone's breath away. A woman who had lived them and survived.

"The first is quick and dirty. A flash of heat on a cold night."

She sang as she hadn't in a very long time—not for an audience, not even for Weston, but only for herself. It was messy and loud and anguished, but it was her, all of Elle Harlow, unedited and complete.

Near the end of her journey, Elle felt the road swerve beneath her. A coral sun grew in the distance. The ground was covered in fog. After spotting a crooked green sign signaling gas at the next exit, she pulled off into a small, forested hamlet.

LENORA, the sign said. GAS TO THE LEFT.

She pulled up to a blue pump with a large Christmas wreath on it, heard a bell ring as she drove over a thin tube. It was early morning, and no living thing appeared, other than a chicken pecking the gravel behind the small shop. Foxes cried out from the forest on either side.

Elle grew dizzy from fatigue. She put the station wagon in park, rolled down her window, and fell fast asleep.

Her dreams betrayed her. She dreamed of Weston as he once had been, playing his mandolin in the firelight. She dreamed of the two of them in the sinking woods, their instruments like kin of their own. His eyes prowled through the dark, devouring her. His fingertips slid down the slope of her arm. He spoke her name. *Elle, Elle,* as if it were the first sound in the world, and the last.

"Elle." She heard it again. "Elle Harlow."

Elle woke with a start. A rough, warm hand took her elbow. It was a young man—muscly and chiseled with the kind eyes of a fawn—who had already started to pump gas into her tank. His flannel was rolled to his elbow, his wrist striped with grease. He gaped at her as if she were a fallen star.

She handed him a ten-dollar bill.

"Aren't you Elle Harlow?" he asked, peering at the guitar buckled beside her. "Where are your shoes?"

Elle's throat burned. She was too exhausted—from the long drive, from her relentless career, from her constant hunger—to claim herself. It was such a slippery notion anyway, pretending a name was an object you could own. As if she hadn't already been a thousand different women in a thousand different lives.

"Elle Harlow," the young man tried again, as he twisted the gas cap. "Aren't you her?"

The more insistent he became, the wearier Elle grew. "If you say so," she answered. Her voice had never been so feeble.

The station attendant begged her to wait while he fetched a permanent marker. She nodded and closed her eyes—anything to make him disappear—and that was when she heard it again.

The crying.

"Sweet Jesus," Elle said as she forced herself to look behind her.

There it sat in her backseat, a fat wicker trunk, cream-colored and cozy, that hadn't been there before. Elle was terrified to guess what was inside—but she didn't have to guess. She knew deep in her gut, just as she knew she was not the person to care for whatever living thing waited in that basket. She didn't know where it had come from, and she didn't want to. Elle had just punched the shit out of someone, and she was headed straight for destruction.

For a long time Elle had feared she was the cause of harm to anyone who encountered her. Not her music or her lyrics, but this mortal, fallible Elle who had watched too many people she loved die and forced the rest away. How toxic she'd always felt, how ruined. So she leapt from the Studebaker and hastily slid the trunk to the far side of the pump. Her heart radiated in her chest—*don't do it, don't do it*—but full-blown panic clawed through her insides.

Elle was raring to speed off, but the man returned with his marker, an unbearable flush of hope on his skin.

"Sign the pump?" he asked again, pointing the marker at her face. "My name is Abe, and I'm your biggest fan. I swear it."

"I don't think—" she started, then stopped.

"Please," he said. "It's almost Christmas."

Elle took up the marker—whether it should be in her right or her left hand, she couldn't recall—and she scrawled the two words across the side of the pump. *Elle. Harlow.*

Then, her hand separated from her mind and wrote something else:

Try to heal everything, and you'll heal nothing at all.

Together, she and the gas attendant stood back and regarded it. It looked like the truth; it felt like a lie.

"Hey," Abe said. "You all right?"

Elle fell back into the car, started it up, and fishtailed out of the lot. She hadn't felt it suffocating her—the constant touring, smiling, posing—until she stood next to Josie onstage at the Opry and realized Josie saw her presence there as a damned olive branch. Josie had pardoned herself for what she'd taken from Elle, simple as that.

But that wasn't the theft that absolutely undid her. Josie had taken Weston, too.

It was foolish of her to fall in love with him. It was also one of the most undeniably potent and honest things she'd ever done. Weston had left Elle on his own, but Josie had taken what they had and turned it into a lie.

Elle drove in what she saw as a straight line. The road before her zigged, zagged, and bucked like a steer. At last, it kicked her with such might that she flew over a guardrail at a sharp curve. She sailed through the air, the seconds stretching like a horizon before her, until the car smacked itself against the earth. The last thing Elle saw before she lost consciousness was the crumpled pink-and-white guitar with her heart-shaped signature on it, slouching beside her.

She blacked out before she realized the car had started to sink.

Sing It Slow

When Elle woke again, the front half of her car was submerged in filthy water. It rushed in through her open window, the Studebaker's tail end jaggedly lifting out of the mud until its back tires left the ground. The car shot into the river like an arrow through flesh.

Elle flailed, took hold of her vanity guitar, and tried to free herself. She undid her seat belt and gripped the door frame. Then she pulled her body up, but the water poured in with such force that it knocked her back. Elle gulped a breath and tried a second time, then a third. Kicked her legs, screamed. Thrashed, but the station wagon only sank farther down.

When the water level lapped against her neck, Elle started to let herself go. It snuck up on her like a melody. Elle had never been one to give up—not once. It occurred to her then, with frigid water flooding her out, that maybe this had been her great failing all along, and now it was time. She let her head fall below the water line, listening to the clutter of bubbles as air fled her body. It was cold and quiet and primordial, and Elle reached for the neck of her guitar so it would be the final thing she held.

But then, a strong arm grasped hers and yanked her out through the window. In a final surrender, Elle let go of her instrument. She collapsed on the bank of a sinkhole in the ground, gasping for air as the Studebaker disappeared. The water coughed and spat, and then it went still.

Elle's eyes jutted around and saw no one at first. She believed in ghosts—they lived on her mountain, same as any mortal thing. Elle blinked, and before her stood an apparition. Elle couldn't think straight. The spirit looked like someone Elle had loved long ago—a face she recognized, and a voice she'd never heard. Cheeks stained red, eyes large and black, like a crow's. Somewhere, thunder pounded. The air was gauzy, and Elle's throat had run dry.

It was Merry, kidnapping her dreams, hijacking her death.

Merry reached for a bandana from the pocket of her overalls and touched it to Elle's cheek. Here was what she'd wished for as a girl but had never found the courage to ask for. It had never been about getting healed. This was about the gossamer gift of Merry's presence—how Elle had loved it, needed it, rose in it, lost it, and longed for it so much it would be the shadow side of every song she'd write for the rest of her life.

How swiftly Elle's life had shaped itself around missing someone. After Merry had died, so many well-meaning mourners had assured Elle that she already knew what Merry would tell her, if she were still alive. As if that were some sort of comfort.

Elle had fucking loathed the thought every day since.

"*Knowing what you would say ain't the same as hearing you say it.*" Elle choked on the words, more beautiful, more beastly than they'd ever been. "*All this music you've left with me ain't the same as hearing you play it.*"

Elle felt the lyrics burning into her skin. She'd written the song for Merry, but never had the chance to sing it to her.

"I'll never get over it," Elle said. "Not as long as I live."

Merry looked at her, an urgent message in her eyes, and Elle felt the words drive straight into her chest.

There are some things we never get over.

It was so simple that Elle had never thought to put such a thing in a song.

At the riverside, a spark nicked her where Merry's cloth had met her skin. At that, Elle's world went black again. Thunder cracked, good and close now. Elle startled, found herself back in the station wagon gushing with water. She'd been dreaming of Merry, but also she *was* Merry now. Stuck in a sinking car and about to sink with it.

Not today, she told herself.

There was something here—something of Elle's, intrinsic and wounded and magnificent—worth saving. It pulsed jaggedly in her chest.

Elle shoved a leg through the window. She pulled herself free. Then she lay down on the floor of the forest and watched the remnants of her old life drown along with her pink-and-white guitar.

It was December 15, 1973.

Truth was, an Elle Harlow did need to drown that day. Elle sank the parts of herself she was desperate to leave behind, starting with her own failure of sight. She'd been so very wrong about so many things, and there were more things Elle was wrong about, even now. It wasn't Merry who had freed her, or Merry who had written her music, or Merry who had given her the life from which she was about to disappear. Elle had done those things herself. What Merry had given was her unhurried and unaffected companionship, a frankness unfailingly full of mercy, the kind of offering that could not be held down by a grave.

Elle couldn't see it, couldn't see herself as anyone other than the young girl she'd been, slinging her daddy's rifle, in need of someone to save her brother when she couldn't. She couldn't remember the last time she'd had a real life worth saving. She felt it when the water had closed in—not Elle the country starlet, but the true Elle. The hiding-in-her-room, loyal and brilliant Elle who was flawed and human. She'd wandered for long enough, searching for something she already had.

It was time to get home to her mountain.

Elle did what any city girl would do, now that she'd become one. She took the bus. It helped that she was filthy and shoeless—no one at a bus depot would expect a beloved folk singer to appear, looking as if she'd just dragged herself from a sinkhole. Elle's disappearing act had already begun.

She had just enough change in her pocket to pay for a ticket to Wheeling.

From there, she called her mother with a final dime for the pay phone while "The First Noel" played over the bus station's loudspeaker.

"Mama," she croaked. The line crackled, and Elle wanted to die.

She hadn't spoken to Susannah in months. Her mother left messages—*Elle, we love you. Elle, I'm worried. Elle, it's all right to come home.* But Elle had been consumed by a cloying need for revenge—though toward herself or Josie or Weston, she couldn't have said. She'd fought so hard to hold on to it that she'd let her mother slip through her fingers.

"Elle," Susannah said into the silence. "I know you're there."

Elle opened her mouth. No sound came out.

"Tell me," Susannah said, "what you need."

"Mama," Elle answered, only twenty-two but feeling a thousand, ageless, and part of the dust. "I need you to come get me."

"Tell me where you are," Susannah said, "and I'll come."

And that was just what Elle's mother did. Took her Dodge into the city to fetch her girl and bring her home. Susannah had never known how much Elle felt at fault for Merry's death, how much she felt at fault for just being alive when Reuben died, helpless and broken.

All her mother knew was that Elle hadn't returned to the mountain since she heard Josie Starling on the radio, no matter how many times Susannah had asked.

"It ain't that I thought I was too good to come home," Elle said as she climbed into the cab of the truck. A stash of hard tack candy was stowed in the cup holder. "Just not good enough."

"You think I don't know that?" Susannah put the gearshift into drive, eyeing the mud caked on her daughter's arms. "It's why I answered when you called."

"You didn't know it was me."

"The hell I didn't."

Elle's body flagged against the vinyl seat. She had no strength left to argue, no more fig leaves to hide behind. It was time.

"Mama," Elle said, "do you blame me for what happened to Merry?"

A hawk flew by, its shadow passing across the windshield.

"It was an accident, Elle. Everyone here knows how much you loved Merry. And how much she loved you."

That was what hurt the most, Elle realized then. How deeply, how widely, how fully she had been loved. Elle wondered how much life she'd wasted by running from the kind of love she thought she didn't deserve.

"Mama," she said, "I'll still regret it for the rest of my life."

"I know, honey," Susannah answered. "The question is—what are you going to do with that regret?"

Elle hadn't known regret could be anything other than an anvil she slung around her neck. "What should I do with it?"

"Hear me." Susannah took hold of her daughter's hand. Her hair was still as bright red, her voice as vibrant, as it always had been. "If you want to be done with Nashville, then be done with it and come home. Live your life. But don't use Merry or Josie Starling as the reason."

Elle looked at the stitching on the passenger seat. "You saw the Opry broadcast."

"I did."

"I'm a mess, Mama," Elle admitted.

"I *see* you, Elle." Susannah held fast to her hand. "If someone cannot love the Elle you were when you dug that winter grave with your bare hands, or the one who sometimes loses the battle with getting out of bed, or the one who has demons of her own—the one who's actually human, for God's sake—then they don't deserve the immaculate Elle you are who leaves an entire room spellbound with your voice."

Elle shut her eyes, breathed in her mother's scent. Her comfort. Her mettle.

"I punched her in the face," she said.

Susannah hooted. "That's my girl."

It took the sound of her mother's laughter for Elle to see that she wanted to give herself what Josie had been granted already: amnesty. The chance to forget. Elle didn't think of this as an act of disappearance, though the rest of the world soon would. Her greatest song—the story of her life—was still being written. She had only to lead herself to the door of a mountain cabin, hand in hand with her mother, and walk through it.

Long Black Veil

Elle lived with Susannah in her cabin for almost eighteen years—sometimes caring to remember her past life, sometimes not. Every once in a while, an outlander came poking around, looking for signs of the missing folk legend.

"Elle Harlow?" her distant neighbors would fawn, as if she lived only in their memories. "We ain't seen her in years."

It was true, and it wasn't.

This was how a yoke was shared among a people. Elle had cared for each of them, once. Burns, bruises, blood. In turn, they cared for her. Her heart was stained in more places than she could count. And so her mountain hid her, lied for her, trusted her, believed her. This small, secluded community—considered inconsequential and shrinking to the rest of the world—had seen Elle blossom and wither. They'd watched her die and be born again. They were her first fans and her last, the people who would not care if she ever took up her guitar again.

Everyone had a story to tell Elle when she wanted to remember who she was without adornment. Without this coronet of briars on her brow. They never shared tales of Elle, the starlet—but of Elle the girl. Elle the healer, Elle the mountaineer.

Mostly, though, she felt like forgetting.

In time, she forgot Josie. She forgot Arlo, too. She also forgot her songs, though she kept a hatbox full of mismatched lyrics underneath her bed. Like dropping petals in the river, this letting go. It was harder, she found, to hold on to things worth remembering.

In 1973, Elle Harlow was not the only woman who had disappeared. Stories ran rampant of missing women from Michigan, Alabama, Virginia Beach, and beyond. It was epidemic, the way they were taken from vacations, picnics, campgrounds, right out of their homes, sudden and final—but it was not the only way for a woman to vanish. Elle found it was more likely for a woman to get swallowed into her own life than be removed from it. Taken down the gullet of her past, her marriage, her children, her job—only to resurface one day in the place she'd remained without recognizing herself at all.

The morning after the meteor strike in 1991, Elle sat on her mother's porch and watched the sunrise as she thought about her father. Hosea had died two winters back, and she missed him most during those early hours when they'd used to hunt so long ago. He'd taken precious things from his daughter, but he'd given them, too—like a love of mornings. August dawns were Elle's favorite, the ground cold and wet, the air with a delicious hint of autumn. The sky swirled with gold dust. Susannah was baking cornbread, and its scent skated out the open window along with chatter from the small RCA television they'd perched on a wooden chest in their living room.

"Elle," Susannah called, causing her daughter to turn her head. "You've got to see this."

Together, they watched a water tower's blurry black-and-white video of a meteor thrashing through the sky, striking ground in a town called Lenora.

Lenora. A place Elle had tried to forget, but couldn't.

"Christ," she said.

The next video shone with color, two young kids playing music in the back of a Chevrolet truck. She thought of them as children, but they were the same age she'd been when she left home for Nashville. Together, they began to play. One a guitar, and the other—

Susannah gasped.

Elle strode toward the screen and squinted. Sure enough, she'd know that mandolin anywhere—the onyx tuning pegs, the broken face. Elle was so ensnared by it she didn't even notice the ball of fire barreling toward the screen before it went black. Elle's memory woke, vibrant and starved. Josie. Arlo. *School Girl Crush*. *Wounds from a Lover*. Weston.

The glory of her own voice.

My God, Elle thought. *I used to want so much.*

She'd never been tempted by jewel-studded gowns or guitar-shaped swimming pools or platinum records. Elle ached for sacrifice and love and grit and desire. In a word, music. She hadn't known she'd lost that hunger until it came tearing out of her at the sight of that deep crack running down a sanded and curved slice of rosewood. She could almost hear its melody, and it wasn't nearly enough.

"I'm going to get it," Elle said to her mother as she flew out the door.

And that was just what she did. Elle hunted down her prey, as she'd done when she was a girl.

Elle thought the starving bear in her chest would be sated once she welcomed Merry's instrument back into her possession. She'd planned to force its owner to hand it over. Pay any amount, deliver any threat. Yet Merry's healing hand continued to trick and surprise. Elle hadn't known that what she truly needed was for Marijohn Shaw—this live and gutsy girl—to refuse to give it to her at all.

On the day Elle had drowned part of herself along with her station wagon in the river, she'd fought to save something inside her that she couldn't yet name. But here it was now, eighteen years later, standing right in front of her on a very rickety porch in western Pennsylvania. A young woman claiming what she wanted for herself, daring to say it out loud, even as it scared the shit out of her.

There's me, Marijohn had said. *That's enough.*

At the words, Elle felt the most unlikely warmth humming through her body—a torrential affection for the stranger holding Merry's mandolin. A girl inconvenient, thrust in the way of what Elle thought she needed. Marijohn was brave and sad and rare and peculiar, unaware of the wonder at her own fingertips. While listening to Marijohn play, a revelation sang alongside her.

This must have been what Merry had felt all those years ago when she first looked at Elle.

"But are you *back?*" Marijohn was asking her from the porch swing, milky morning light hitting the leaves and casting a filigree of shadow on the lawn.

"Back?" Elle asked.

"Are you going to disappear again—or are you going to tell everyone you aren't dead?"

"It's plain I'm not dead." Elle crossed her legs. "No need to write a song about it."

Even though that was just what she wanted to do.

Elle was already itching to get home to her mountain, back to the dusty guitar in her bedroom. She wasn't sure she liked being so vulnerable, so visible. But she remembered how Merry had called to her when she was too afraid to step out from behind an old barn wall. Elle knew the miracle of it—Merry hadn't just changed her life. She'd saved it. It was the sending out of a baby in a basket, full of promise for the world.

"Marijohn," Elle said, "have you ever performed for anyone beyond these woods?"

Marijohn's face was bold and frank, and Elle loved it. "No."

"Then it's time. Are there any venues around here?"

Marijohn thought it over. Gave a reluctant reply. "There's a popular bar just outside Pittsburgh, maybe thirty minutes from here. They host open mic nights."

"Then that's what you'll do."

Marijohn's eyes darted around the porch. "I've never sung on my own."

"It's better than singing a duet," Elle deadpanned. "Trust me."

Marijohn blinked. She didn't look the least bit pleased.

"What?" Elle asked.

"You're coming?"

"Of course I'm coming."

"People are going to *see* you," Marijohn said. "Is that what you want?"

Elle waved a hand. "I'll wear sunglasses and sit in the back. People won't pay me any mind."

Marijohn looked doubtful, but Elle knew once the crowd heard her on the mandolin, everything else would cease to matter.

As Merry had once done for her, Elle would make it so.

That night, Elle stepped into a bar for the first time since 1973. It was jammed inside, the human decor a rhinestone carousel of belt buckles and Aqua Net and menthol lights. Elle secured her sunglasses and cowboy hat, even though no one looked her way. She was middle-aged, apparently, and so many younger starlets-in-waiting flurried around the bar, Music Row dreamers, each vying for their shot just as Elle had once done—slinging bottom-shelf booze, forcing her name into strangers' mouths. She remembered it well.

Do you miss this? she asked herself as she watched the room spin. She'd been off her mountain for less than a day and already she'd walked right up to the knife's edge of her past life. It was the kind of existence she had to take all at once—or take none of it at all.

Elle loved being all-or-nothing. Lived for it, sucked strength from it like a grizzly waking from winter sleep. It was shifting between the two—all or nothing—that often proved impossible.

The small stage lights glowed, and the speakers overhead purred like kittens. Slowly, seats filled. Drinks were emptied, refilled. The crowd hushed.

The spotlight flicked on, and Elle saw her two album covers tacked to the far wall, just like so many from the 1960s and beyond. The first was a close-up shot of her holding Hal's devilish cat, the second of her against a dark background, only the light from a meager candle illuminating her profile. No makeup, lips barely parted, eyes like jade.

A few covers down from hers, she found the face of someone familiar, holding his banjo in one hand and an L&M in the other. It was Leo, smiling wide, with his name in large block letters. *Ice Cream,* he'd titled his album.

How much Elle had missed him. How much she had missed.

The first open mic performance was a pair of very tall sisters, one of whom played the dulcimer. The instrument looked like a toy in her lap. Elle remembered Reuben, who had dreamed himself on a stage such as this. She'd once imagined sitting in his audience, just as she was sitting in Marijohn's now.

Beautiful harmonies these sisters had, as siblings often do. *Promising,* Elle thought. She noticed a man with a black Stetson to her right thought so, too. He sat up, made a note in his small pad with a golf pencil. An executive or a scout from somewhere, to be sure.

Elle remembered this hustle, the drag of it. The I'll-give-anything-I've-got energy that pierced the tiny bar. She couldn't even say she missed it, really, because that drive had never left. It was eternal, this desire to play and perform and write and be seen. Elle had gone a little dead these last eighteen years by letting Nashville take from her what she loved most, and what Merry had left her with.

The chance to sing to someone.

A fiddler came on the stage next, followed by a solo guitarist. The sound of country now was glossier than it had been when Elle left Music City. Listening to it felt like an act of window-washing. *Where is the dirt,* Elle wondered. *The heartache?*

She didn't belong here.

A heavy flank of new customers filed in, and someone spilled a bottle of Zima on Elle's jeans. It was obnoxiously loud, and the place smelled like Rolling Rock, and the sweaty stench of claustrophobia hit Elle like a squall. She hadn't been around so many people at once since the night she had performed at the Opry.

Abruptly, she stood from her chair.

"You're blocking the stage!" someone behind her hissed.

Elle shimmied through the crowd, out into the misty night. Stole a few deep breaths as she went around the corner to the alleyway. She'd lost her stamina for stuffy bars. She'd have to watch the rest of the show from the wings. Elle slipped backstage by helping a drummer carry his cymbals through the back door. Marijohn was next in line to perform, after an older man in a brown fedora played the banjo. The crowd was a swath of black beyond the stage's white orb, and a brine of sweat and dust coated the air.

Marijohn had no idea Elle was waiting behind her, and Elle didn't want her to. Performers had to bear down before their sets in just this way, to the detriment of every other living thing around them. Marijohn clutched the mandolin by the frets, its onyx tuning pegs glittering prettily against her side.

Bland applause came like an exhale, along with a single *woot* from the banjo player's sole fan. He sidled off the stage and tipped his hat to Marijohn, who nodded back.

Go on, Elle thought. *Show them what you've got.*

Marijohn edged out onto the stage. She wiped her left hand against her jeans, and then her right. Adjusted the mic. Dragged the stool out of the way. Tugged it back. Didn't sit. Someone in the audience whistled.

"I'm Marijohn Shaw," she said. Her voice sounded like a thousand memories of Elle's, a thousand wishes. "I'd like to sing for you tonight."

Elle crept closer toward the stage, took the edges of the velvet curtain into her grip. Marijohn played a soulful C, just as Elle had heard the night before. The mandolin's rose-gold tone swept over the quiet room.

Until it didn't.

Marijohn stared at the back of the crowd, scarecrow-still. Elle craned her neck to see what she was gawking at, but there was nothing, only a bunker of shadowy faces. Her mouth lulled open, yet no sound came out. The audience began to murmur and fuss, and still Marijohn did not move.

Elle squinted. Marijohn was frozen. Panicked.

Alone.

"Oh, hell," Elle said.

Someone in the crowd stood and left. Another booed. The talent scout glanced toward the exit.

"You ain't getting any younger!" a woman called.

By the time Marijohn managed to swivel her eyes to the wings, Elle was already reaching for the spare guitar. She tossed her sunglasses on the side table before slipping the strap over her head. Marijohn's expression said all kinds of things—*please, I'm sorry, help*—and Elle didn't think too much about it. She drew down the bill of her hat and strode onto the stage.

"I can't do this," Marijohn whispered.

"You can."

"I wanted to sing 'Namesake.' Then I realized everyone will just think it belongs to Laz. I'd be covering my own song."

"That's *your* song." Elle's gaze darted toward the thinning crowd. "You want to sing it, sing it."

"I—I can't."

"Honey," Elle said, her eyes not once leaving Marijohn's face. Pulling her in, calming her down. "It's just you and me. Let's play whatever you want."

Slowly, Marijohn thawed. "'Long Black Veil,'" she said.

"You know that song?" Elle asked.

"It was cowritten by someone named Marijohn Wilkin. Of course I know it."

Elle held up her hands. "Apologies."

She hit an E and waited for Marijohn to follow. The crowd settled. She strummed an E again, and blessedly Marijohn found her rhythm. Elle took the first verse. *Ten years ago.* By the time she reached *town hall light* Marijohn was singing, full tilt. Elle nodded, took one step back, then another.

"That's it," she said, even though Marijohn couldn't hear her.

Confidence bloomed, and Marijohn leaned into the microphone. Stretched out a note on the chorus, perked a little lift-up at the end of each stanza.

"Shit, Marijohn," Elle muttered. "You never told me how well you could sing."

Elle discovered she loved listening to it, getting both lost and found inside the swells of Marijohn's throat. It made her feel young again, and new in town, and alive and hopeful and unafraid. Elle closed her eyes, remembering those nights she and Josie had met in the studio in secret and sung their guts out like they'd never lost anything, and they never would. In a word, that was exactly what Marijohn's voice had to it. *Guts.*

And then Elle's eyes flew open, just as Marijohn hit her final chord and all sound died out.

How had Elle missed it? The flowing hair, the peachy lips, the pert manner. The cowlick on the crown of her head.

"You're her kid."

The music had faded just as the words burst out of Elle's mouth—loud enough that Marijohn caught a piece of it. Her head snapped toward Elle along the back wall, her brow bent in confusion. The house lights shot up, and then the scout wearing the black Stetson in the crowd stood.

"I'll be damned," he said. "If that ain't Elle Harlow."

It was Elle's turn to stare blankly into the light, her mouth bobbing open like a fish. She'd never had stage fright—not even once—and she'd long been inured to the sound of a stranger calling out her name before she'd disappeared. Marijohn sensed her panic, just as Elle had sensed hers.

"I'm Marijohn Shaw," she said again into the mic. "Awful grateful you came out."

Then she grabbed Elle by the wrist and whisked her into the wings and out the back door so fast Elle barely had time to let go of the guitar.

"I can't remember where we parked," Marijohn said, yanking her along. Elle pointed toward the intersecting street.

She had no voice, no slot for what had been revealed on that stage. When they reached the car, Elle hid in the passenger seat. Marijohn looked behind her to see if anyone had followed.

"Give me the keys," she said.

She drove Elle back to her home—cutting corners, blowing past yellow lights, screeching through stop signs. Once they reached Lenora and slipped into Marijohn's living room, she pulled the curtains.

"You smell like beer," Marijohn said.

Then she came to stand in front of Elle, who had collapsed on her couch.

"You also said something about me being somebody's kid." Marijohn's voice shot straight. "Whose?"

"I—" Elle paused. She needed to backpedal. "I spoke out of turn."

"The hell you did." Marijohn put her hands on her hips. "Tell me where you've been for the last eighteen years."

"I was living in my mama's house. I disappeared just like I wanted, all by my own hand. And that was it."

The eyeliner on Marijohn's face had started to streak. "Why did you come back now, then?"

"For the mandolin."

"Bullshit."

Elle wished she had a simpler reason. Wished that mandolin was the whole of it, but it wasn't.

"You think I disappeared in 1973?" Elle asked.

Marijohn nodded. "Everyone does."

"I was invisible to myself for a long time before that," Elle answered. "And I don't want to be invisible anymore."

Until Elle admitted it, she hadn't realized it was true.

Marijohn looked at her ball cap, her sunglasses. "You've got a shitty way of showing it."

"You don't understand," Elle said. "What this business does to you. To a woman."

Marijohn began to pace. Her profile looked so much like Josie's. "Explain it to me."

Elle had thought for many years about the act of disappearing—the anonymity, privacy, and grace it had afforded her. To reappear now would force her to reconcile with who she'd been eighteen years ago, and some things were still just as troubling as she'd left them.

"Wait a minute." Elle stood. "Where did you find the mandolin?"

"You left it, remember?" Marijohn answered. "At the gas station."

"I didn't."

"You did." Marijohn's voice sounded so much like Josie's, too. "In a wicker trunk with a note that said *Call her Marijohn*."

"Impossible," Elle said, even though it wasn't.

Marijohn pressed her lips together, looked at Elle with such need, such a desire to keep her dignity, that it broke Elle in half.

The wail she'd heard as she drove away from Nashville the final time.

The life Elle knew was hidden in her back seat that she was so terrified of maiming just like she had everything else.

"I was in that trunk, too," Marijohn said. "And all you care about is a broken instrument."

Elle couldn't speak for a moment. Here it was—the beginning of what she'd need to reckon with if she truly was to return.

"I'm so sorry," she finally said.

"This mandolin was the only thing left with me."

"And your name," Elle said.

"A lot of good it's done." Marijohn looked spent. The headstock of the mandolin perched upward on her back as she pressed the heel of her hand into her forehead. "So are you going to tell me, or not?"

Elle didn't even have to consider it.

"No," she said.

She wouldn't say a word until she had proof, unless she was sure. Even then, was it right? Elle didn't know. Marijohn shook her head, shook off the hurt that was plain on her face.

"My earliest memory is of someone singing to me in the dark," Marijohn said. "Do you know anything about that?"

Elle's nails pierced the skin on her palms. "I don't—" she began to lie. "I don't know."

"That's all you're going to give me?" Marijohn asked. "An 'I don't know'?"

The truth hung between them, heavy and unspoken.

"I didn't think someone like you could be this cold," Marijohn said. "Someone who wrote a song like 'Shut Out the Light.' Like 'Love Beneath the Mandolins.' Like 'Heal Nothing.' I know you have a heart. Where is it?"

Elle had long known she could never live up to the truth in her music. It burned to hear Marijohn plead, to hear her so easily recognize the heart Elle had to prove to herself was still her own.

"Listen," Elle said. "If you spend enough time in this business, at least one person is going to think you're a bitch. And they're going to be right."

"In that case"—Marijohn tossed a blanket on Elle's lap—"you'll understand when I ask you to sleep outside."

Elle did understand. In fact, she preferred it. She thought more clearly outdoors, beneath the stars, in the wind. One thing was certain—Elle couldn't return home to her mountain after what she'd set in motion. Not yet. Elle wasted no more time fretting over her disappearing anonymity. In her mind, anyone who deserved to know she was alive already knew. Something more precious was at stake, and it always had been.

Elle wouldn't shame Josie for not wanting to be a mother. The good Lord knew Elle had never felt fit for it. But now the baby was a young woman who very much wanted to know where she'd come from. No one could shame her for that, either. Elle was so close to having what she said she wanted—what she'd sworn would finally be enough—a silent mandolin hanging on her wall like a piece of taxidermy.

The mandolin had pulled Elle from her stupor, yet she still felt lost. If it wasn't the mandolin that she wanted, then what?

Predictably, Elle couldn't sleep. She walked along the edge of the woods until she reached the outskirts where the road began to sink into the earth and curve like a hairpin. The mangled guardrail still stood testament to Elle's car crash, where her Studebaker had drowned along with so much of her. It was early fall; a faint whisper of her breath tunneled through the air. She craved the chill, had never minded not having a warm coat. She liked denying herself the fullness of her own need, the kindness of meeting it.

Up ahead at a crest in the road, steam rose from a deer carcass in the cold of early morning. A pickup truck swerved in front of it and reversed until its tailgate met the deer. A man in flannel hopped out with a crowbar. He stood over the body for a minute. His breath mingled with the fog. Then he started to hack away at the corpse, bit by bit, until the pieces were small enough to be shoveled into the bed of his truck. When it was done, the man drove away, leaving behind a smear of red on the asphalt.

It struck Elle as laughable—though not at all funny—that so much in the world had changed, but this unceremonious removal of the dead remained the same.

Elle wasn't getting any younger. And she had a very long drive ahead of her.

For almost twenty years, Elle had grieved that Josie Starling had stolen her life's work from her. Now it was finally time to steal it back.

Fist City

Arlo's house remained grossly lavish, though the 1970s chestnut trimmings had been updated with gold-and-black accents. The house looked colder now, more diamond-encrusted leopard in the foyer, less country quilt on the corduroy sofa.

It was still ugly as sin.

Elle had parked down the road from the mansion and hopped the gilded fence. The last time she'd been here had been a soiree in 1972 for another musician she could no longer remember. That was who she'd been then—someone who attended parties at their periphery, smiled and nodded, inwardly horrified at this forgettable version of herself. Now Elle skulked along the tree line of the vast Weston grounds past the stable, a small lake, and a glittering guest cabin on the far side of it. What a life Arlo had made off the music he produced, including both albums Elle had written.

His study faced the water, Elle recalled, and she knew he liked to waste his evenings there. No matter how many wives or children he would have, Arlo preferred to be alone. Like Elle, he often couldn't fall asleep at night. He loved to play old records—Bill Monroe, the Carter Family, Roy Acuff. Anything that felt like home.

Elle sidled up to the broad windowpane and peeked through it. A fire blazed beneath a marble mantel, and the record player turned. Loretta Lynn belted "Fist City," one of Elle's favorites. Loretta always delivered the best gut-punch with a smile on her face. Elle had scanned the radio channels during the nine-hour drive from Pennsylvania to Tennessee, and she recognized not even one singer. Garth. Trisha. Reba. Alan. The current country stars had such Hollywood-sounding names, such blockbuster talent.

Her hand traced the windowsill. Inside, Arlo might have looked content on his white pleather sofa. Relaxed. Rich. Instead he was steel-faced and arthritic. Elle's fist rapped so hard against the glass that he tumbled off the couch. After he stood, creakily, he peered through the window but couldn't see her. She knocked again. He stumbled toward the French doors and threw them open into the night.

Elle stepped forward into a tunnel of light, a large shadow at her back. Hands on her hips, the heat of a supernova in her eyes.

"Mother of God." Arlo could barely get the words out around his Marlboro. "I thought my scout was seeing things when he called. I told him you were dead."

"Not today."

Standing there in his red socks, he looked her up, then down, then up again. "Where you *been?*" he asked.

"You would have known, if you'd ever cared to look."

He grunted. His thin mustache danced on his upper lip as he backed toward the door. "I ain't been the one hiding. I've been here the whole time."

"So I see." Elle strutted inside and headed for the fire. Dragged a finger along the mantel. Not a speck of dust on it. "You've been busy, I gather."

He sighed, terse and antsy. Signature Arlo. "I know what this is about."

Elle saw him for what he was—country-born, same as her. Still felt he wasn't enough because he didn't have enough, still scared to death of losing everything that mattered.

"Why didn't you look for me?" she asked.

"You mean after you punched Josie Starling in the face?"

"I mean after I gave you a hit record."

Arlo set his Marlboro in an ashtray. "I don't condone violence."

"But lying and cheating, you're square with."

He frowned into his sunken cheeks. "You going to punch me now, too?"

"Don't push your luck."

"The money," he said, ignoring her. His voice sounded like a distant echo of itself, like he'd already rehearsed his defense. "Your mother's been getting all your royalty checks, I assume."

"She has."

"Good," Arlo said, as if that ended it.

In 1970, he'd paid her to be quiet. In 1972, he'd paid her to sing. Elle saw now that since 1973, he'd been paying her to stay away. Yet there were still things the two of them owed each other that had nothing to do with money.

"That's not all," she said.

Arlo had never been her friend. He was her ally. Her boss. Her soothsayer. This was the man who had seen her at her worst, who had watched Elle revive herself. He understood her, he could tell her future. He could shape it, too.

His thin eyebrows knit into one. Elle took a breath. This was it—her attempt to stitch herself back together. The twenty-two-year-old Elle Harlow—scared and sad and spiraling—needed the older, steadier Elle to fight for her now.

"I'm ready, Arlo." She didn't quiver, didn't equivocate, didn't break. This was the fire Marijohn had relit within her when she played Merry's mandolin. The sound—both coming home and leaving it—had returned Elle to herself, fully and fervently. The desire buzzed at her fingertips. "I'm ready to come back."

At that, Loretta's song ended. All the nerves Arlo held skittered out of sight.

"I think," he said, "you'd better sit down."

She followed him past the opulent fire, which was gratuitous in the heat. He leaned an arm on the mantel and pointed toward the pin-tucked couch. Elle sat, loathing the way it forced her to stare up at him as she did when she was eighteen.

"Listen," he said. "You have no idea how popular Elle Harlow is, do you?"

"I've got a decent idea," she answered. "My mother is a very good accountant."

"You don't understand." There was no joy found in Arlo's eyes, no satisfaction. "*Wounds from a Lover* is the number one female folk record of all time."

Elle took this to mean she had a crumb of power, so she took her shot. "I've got new songs, Arlo. I'm ready. Let's record."

A faint look of dread crossed his face, like he smelled something rotten. "You misunderstand. *Elle Harlow* is popular. I mean the Elle Harlow who is just as she always was: twenty-two, troubled, gifted. Legendary."

She opened her mouth, but he went on.

"The reason *Wounds from a Lover* continues to sell is because it's Elle Harlow's final album. There ain't gonna be no more."

He said it as if she really had died.

For a moment, Elle felt like she had.

"You can't keep me from recording." She hated how soft her voice sounded against the snickering flames.

"It's true, I can't." This was a new evolution of Arlo she'd never seen. He was level-headed, logical, distant. Gone was the Arlo who pushed her, praised her, bet on her. "But I can do what I do best, and that's protect what we built, you and I. That album is perfection, Elle. There's no topping it."

"Is that what you did to Josie, too?" Elle couldn't believe she had Josie's name in her mouth. Couldn't believe she had even a wisp of compassion. "You kept her from recording again?"

"That's not your concern."

"You." Elle's voice strangled into a whisper. "You need me."

"No," he said, so gently it sliced her open. "I don't."

It felt so much like that first time she'd made demands of him—*Put my name on the songs*—and he'd placed her in a box. Gave Elle her dream wrapped in a nicely tied bow, yet inside it lay a skeleton he'd picked clean.

No, she said to herself. *You didn't come all this way, back from the dead, to end it like this.*

"How can you do it?" She threw the words at him. "Treat people this way. Disregard them without a thought."

"Without a thought?" Arlo's patience faded. His mustache was a scribble in the firelight. "Elle, I'm thinking of you and your feelings here."

It was condescending and infuriating at once. "Bullshit," she said.

"You are richer than anyone I know, other than me." The words spat out of his mouth. "This is how I take care of you. This is how I took care of you for eighteen years."

Elle's body went hungry and hot. "There are ways to care for someone that have nothing to do with money."

"Fine. You want the truth?" He stepped toward her, towering above. Still too coltish eighteen years later, still too slim.

"It's just you and me," Elle said.

"Nobody wants an album from a forty-year-old woman past her prime. Dead or not. I can't sell it, I can't package it. I'm not a magician, and your past work is the best you're gonna get. You want to compete with the memory of yourself? You ain't gonna win."

His hand trembled as he went to pour himself a whiskey. The decanter clacked against the glass.

"You"—she pointed a finger at him—"don't get to define my life. You don't get to say when this ends."

"Honey," he said, gentle again, "it's already over."

She was gutted, she was embarrassed, she was trapped. She had to get out. *Run from where you came from, baby, never too far, always too fast.* Lyrics she loved that Arlo now owned. How could he still possess so much of her, even now when he'd said he didn't need her at all?

Above Arlo's drink cart sat a shelf of his music awards. Elle looked closer. Four of them were for *Wounds from a Lover* that she'd never been able to claim. Arlo watched the fire, unwilling to face her. Without a sound, she swiped one of the golden gramophones and marched to the French doors.

Arlo had reduced Elle's entire worth into only terms he could understand. Profit and loss, young and old. Their whole relationship had been founded on the money that sprang from a secret he wished to keep.

"You won't be hearing from me," Elle said, and she meant it.

She had agreed to all of it when she'd been too young to understand. Now this version of Elle Harlow—older and unfettered and still so very much alive—was through with paying the price.

Shackle

It was a gamble, returning to the Starling mansion in the middle of the night. Josie might not live there anymore. Maybe no one would answer the door. And yet, Elle had never forgotten the coldly palatial estate that had housed generations of Josie's family, the same one she'd visited during Thanksgiving so many years ago.

Echoes called out to Elle as she parked at the end of the russet drive, her boots clicking against the laid brick. The din of voices and champagne flutes, the muted scream from a back hallway. The harsh silence after Elle had saved a life.

Elle had lived half her own life since then. She still didn't regret her decision to disappear, though the choice had robbed her of her creative spirit, chipping away at it shard by shard. The stately house looked just as it had in 1969, bored and proud, if in need of a new paint job and a fresh pruning of the holly bushes. She could see the dahlias and marigolds blooming along the mansion's outer grounds. The house felt funereal, full of flowers meant to cover the scent of something dead.

Someone lived here, though. Elle just didn't know who.

For so long Elle had found peace through the vows she'd made—never to speak Josie's name, never to revisit her music. She thought she'd healed because it didn't hurt. Yet a scab had formed over the distance she'd created between that past life and this one, and it hadn't healed.

Now, Elle told herself. *No more waiting.* She scaled the steps and banged the brass knocker three times. After a minute, she knocked again. She caught a whisper of movement behind the shades, and so she knocked a third time. When the door yawned open, it revealed a man Elle had never seen before. He was clean-shaven and reeked of peppermint mouthwash and Brut.

"Can I help you?" he asked dully, and Elle played it straight.

"I'm looking for Josie."

Half asleep, he sighed. One of his eyelids twitched. "She doesn't sign autographs, but she appreciates each and every one of her fans." He tried to shut the door, but Elle stuck her foot in it.

"Tell her," she said, "that Elle is here."

He was firmly nonplussed. "It's the middle of the night."

"I know she's awake."

The man looked at her, and then he looked closer. He left the front door open as he wandered down the hall. Elle crept into the dark foyer and waited. A few minutes later, the man reappeared, weary in his pastel robe.

"She's in the conservatory," he said. "Just through the double doors."

Elle walked through. Passing that threshold was both a chance to step back in time by twenty years and to finally take a step forward in the present. The air grew cold in the room, but the slight figure balanced on the damask settee along the wall, staring off into the moonlit manicured lawn, wore only a wisp of an off-white nightgown with flowy sleeves that reached well past her wrists. She looked like fog, like gauze, like smoke.

It took everything Elle had in her not to weep.

Elle had known she'd feel anger. Remorse. Betrayal. Spite. She hadn't expected to feel sawed in half. The rest of the world thought Elle had been missing for the last eighteen years—and only now, looking at this woman who once had a turquoise stud pinned into her left ear—could Elle see how true it was. She hadn't been missing, like an absence. What a slippery word it was, *miss*. All this time, Elle had been missing her friend.

Elle didn't say Josie's name or announce herself. Went only to sit beside her and look out into the glittering stretch of Orion's Belt.

"I knew you weren't dead," Josie said without looking Elle's way. Then she lit a Virginia Slim.

"And you," Elle returned, "didn't get written out of the will after all."

"As you can see"—Josie gestured to her withered frame—"it agrees with me."

Elle leaned forward. "You're unwell?"

"I'm fine. Down a few pounds is all."

"Not to worry," Elle said dryly. "I'm sure it's just loss of bone density."

"Funny."

Josie took a drag, looking like a bad drawing of her old self. She had none of her former bounciness, none of the drive. Her hair was mousy and bleached, her nails bitten to the quick.

"So," Elle tried. She couldn't help feeling that she was staring into a part of herself that might have been. A phantom limb. "You're an heiress now?"

Her face was blank. "I live here with my brother. He's the one who let you in."

Elle couldn't help it. "My royalties weren't enough to survive on?"

Josie's head whipped toward her, and ash spilled from her cigarette. "So this is what you came back for? After all this time?"

It was dismissive and callous and made Elle feel small. How she wished that Josie had never been one of the few people she loved.

I still think about the way you backed away from me when I had your sister's blood on my hands, Elle wanted to say. *Like you loathed the real me.*

"I want to know why," she said instead.

Elle wanted so much more from Josie than an answer. She wanted her friend back—wanted that mutual invincibility from their secret studio days that granted them sanctuary from what fame had turned them into—and she knew she would never get it.

"Why what?" Josie asked.

Elle almost admired her gall. "Why you stole my music."

"Because, Elle." Josie was impatient, as if they'd had this same argument a hundred other times. "You'd already choked."

This response, among all Elle's imagined iterations of this moment, had never crossed her mind.

"You sang your music for Weston Studios, and they said no. To *you*." Josie's words were pointed and deadly. "And then you left."

It was true, and it was false. Factual, and somehow still incorrect. Wasn't it?

"So you just took it?" Elle asked. "Like it was yours?"

"We sang those songs together so much they might as well have been mine. They were rough when you came to me, Elle. Undone. You slapped together some verses and a chorus. I refined them and gave them polish. Made them real. Made them *good*." Josie shook at the volume of her own voice and settled herself with a pull from her cigarette. "You didn't want it as much as I did, anyway. You never would have done what it takes."

The room shrank around them as the starlight got caught behind a cloud.

"How can you say that?" Elle's skin was mottled, her hands drawn into fists. "I recorded two other albums after the one you stole."

"Because Arlo took pity on you. You were a liability he had to manage, and he turned it into a profit."

Elle had known this was true. Arlo made no secret of it. It still killed her to hear that Josie had seen it, too.

"You quit this game," Josie added. "Twice."

Elle hated how Josie threw the truth at her like a blade.

"And what have you been doing that's so different?" Elle asked.

"That's just it," Josie said. "You act like we aren't the same, like you can claim the moral high ground. As if that isn't a lie."

"I own my part in how we fell apart, Josie, but not in the way you think." Elle came to her feet. "You *fed* off me till I had nothing left, then told me you didn't like the taste."

Josie had wanted Elle's wildness, her brilliance, her intuition, her art, but none of the mess that came with it. None of the West Virginia mountains, none of the darkness. None of who Elle really was without her music. Her anger took the wheel, and she couldn't control it. She wanted to strike deep, to make Josie feel even a fraction of the desolation she'd caused.

"I'm here with news about your daughter," Elle said. "The one you gave away."

She regretted it before the words fell out of her mouth. Josie looked so instantly ruined, not by the words themselves, but because Elle had said something so cruelly beneath her. It made Elle hate herself.

"How did you know?" Josie asked, after a minute had passed. Gone were the insults and accusations. Josie sounded unsure, vulnerable, and young.

"She sings like you." Elle waited, wishing Marijohn didn't have to hang in the balance. Wishing she weren't so immediately undone by the hurt she felt in Josie's presence.

Josie's eyes slid toward her. "You've seen her?"

"Yes."

"How?"

"What do you mean, how?" Elle could have laughed, but it wasn't funny. "You left her in the back seat of my car at the Ryman."

Josie looked at her as if Elle had lost her mind. "I did no such thing."

"Bullshit."

"When would I have had the chance after you punched me?"

Elle still relished that memory, though not the wreckage that came after. "If it wasn't you, then who?"

"Oh my God." Josie lifted a hand to her nose like it still ached. "Arlo."

"Arlo? Why?"

Josie sat wasting away, a stencil of herself. Her mind had already flown elsewhere.

"You asked Arlo to give the baby away," Elle led.

"I wasn't myself. I couldn't handle being a mother. I never thought he'd give her to you." Josie paused, leaden. "Is she—all right?"

Elle told her the truth. "She's amazing."

"You—" Josie looked as if she didn't want the answer. "You raised her?"

"I didn't." It surprised Elle to realize she wished she had. "But her father kept the name you gave her."

"Marijohn," Josie said, a remnant of the studio nights she and Elle had spent together.

"It's a beautiful name," Elle said, but Josie didn't hear.

The two of them were locked together forever now, not by the love they'd once had, but by the death of it. By the way they'd seen each other—bloody and true—on the Thanksgiving night that set the rest of their lives in motion, their choices, their hurts, their vows. They'd both been running from it since 1973.

It was Josie who spoke next.

"I can't escape the feeling that I've spent my whole life looking for the secret everyone else has to surviving—to being fucking *all right*—only to find there is none," she said. "You ever feel like that?"

Once again, Elle caught a glimpse of herself in Josie's mirror. "All the time."

They sat in a strange quiet for a while. Elle wasn't quite ready to leave, and Josie didn't ask her to. Again, Elle recalled the last time she was a guest at this house.

"How is Jaclyn?" she asked.

"She's dead." Torment stained Josie's face. "She died right after I had the baby, and I wanted to die, too. No matter what I did, I couldn't keep my sister alive. How could I be responsible for a child? That night at the Opry when I told you I needed help? I meant it."

Elle felt a brush of shame that wasn't hers. "I'm the last person you should have asked."

"You're the last person I wanted to."

"What about Marijohn's father?"

The slanted look Josie gave Elle suggested she didn't know who the father was.

"*Try to heal everything and you'll heal nothing at all*, isn't that right?" Josie tapped her cigarette. "You tell me that lyric isn't lifted straight out of my life."

Josie had also learned that no amount of money would resurrect someone who had died. Elle knew that bled-out feeling, had grown up inside it.

"I'm sorry," Elle said, meaning it, "that Jaclyn is gone."

"Join the club. But I have to warn you, it's lonely as hell here."

Elle thought of Marijohn, who seemed lonely as hell, too. There was too much of that feeling in the world, and no good reason for it. "Your daughter would like to hear from you, I think."

Without warning, Josie's mood turned from melancholy to suspicion. She stood, but her voice lost its nerve.

"Let me guess. You came to confront me about it out of the goodness of your heart?" She laughed, wily. "Please. Blackmail is beneath you. You know it, I know it, so just ask for what you want."

Elle's body went taut. She couldn't tell if Josie regarded her as a mirror, seeing only her darkest self when she looked at her estranged friend, or if they were truly similar. Here it was, the vengeance Elle so desperately wanted within her grasp like a golden apple dangling off a tree in the garden of Eden, and it was poisoned.

"Let me make it easy for you, then," Josie said, hitting her pack of cigarettes with the heel of her hand. "I'll give you a choice. You get to play God, which you seem so eager for. I can contact my daughter—" She paused. "Or I can sign a document returning the rights to your music. Which one, Elle? What do you pick?"

It was a game, part truth, part dare. Elle couldn't make sense of it, not when Josie had offered everything Elle wanted for the taking.

"It doesn't have to be an either or," she whispered, though she knew better.

"That's not the choice I gave you," Josie said.

Elle didn't need a choice. She'd made her vow long ago.

It hadn't been a vow for revenge, though she'd made one of those, too. It went further back, to her time with Merry. A vow to help, a vow to heal.

Elle had not known then what it would cost.

"Josie," she said. "Forget the music. You should contact your daughter if you want to."

At that, Josie dropped her armor.

"Marijohn won't want to see me," she said.

"She will."

"It's too late."

"It isn't."

"How would you know?" Josie scoffed. "Neither of us is fit to be a parent."

"I don't disagree with you."

Josie went brittle, like kindling. "Why won't you just take your music rights and leave me alone?"

Elle stood firm. "Because I don't want them this way."

"But you still want them."

"Of course I do."

"And that"—Josie pressed her Virginia Slim into the ashtray before lighting another—"is why you and I are exactly alike."

She walked to the credenza, pulled out a sheet of her personal letterhead. Scribbled something and signed it with a flourish. "You want your music back? Take it. I don't fucking care anymore."

Elle drove through the Belle Meade streets for hours after she left the Starling mansion, the signed letter burning a hole next to the stick shift. For a long time, Elle had imagined Josie living a charmed life. Getting everything she desired. Yet she was just as miserable as Elle was, determined to chase the one thing she'd never get, and it had nothing to do with money.

It had kept Elle from living the fullness of her life, this envy of Josie's imagined contentment. She'd been jealous of something that didn't exist. This revelation would never alter the past, yet the question remained of what Elle ought to do now.

Who she ought to become.

If Josie had signed such a decree twenty years ago, Elle would have run through the streets with it. Screamed about it from the top of her lungs. If it was right to expose Josie's theft, why did it feel vindictive and petty, so absent of any true justice? Elle wouldn't celebrate it because she saw it for what it was: nothing but the drawn-out demise of a friendship. Elle had thought only her music hung in the balance between her and Josie, but now there was someone stretched between them, desperate for one of them to hold on.

Marijohn.

Josie had given her up. Arlo had hidden her. Elle had left her at a gas station. The three of them were responsible for the chaos they'd created, and Elle knew she was the only one who would even attempt to repair it.

She was getting so crazed over it that she swerved into a Texaco station and dialed her mother from the pay phone. It was five thirty in the morning. Susannah was making biscuits, and Elle could picture her standing at the stove, the phone nestled beneath her ear.

"Mama," Elle said, "I got what I came for. I'm holding it in my hand."

She could hear Susannah gasp.

"You got the mandolin back?" she asked.

Elle had already forgotten where her journey had started: a meteor, a missing mandolin.

"Even better than that," she said.

"You got Josie to admit it?"

"I did." Elle heard a certain kind of devastation in her voice. This had been a battle, badly won, without any real victor—other than Arlo. "Josie gave it to me in writing."

Susannah waited, sensing her daughter's unease. "And so?"

"So why does it feel like I never had these songs at all?"

A Chevy Beretta zoomed through the gas station, and Elle pressed the phone against her ear.

"I'd wager"—Susannah threw dough into her cast-iron skillet with a hiss—"that you got what you wanted, but it ain't what you been looking for."

It felt true, though Elle still had no idea what it meant. "What have I been looking for?" She paused. "And don't tell me I have to figure it out for myself."

"You know how hard everyone was searching for Elle Harlow, back when you first disappeared?"

Elle nodded. "I remember."

"We had people poking around our hills so much it seemed like it would never stop. And then one day, it just did." Susannah hummed in thought. "They weren't the only ones who stopped looking for the real you. You stopped, too."

"Those album covers were never the real me."

"Weren't they?" Dough sizzled as Susannah flipped the biscuit. "You need to reclaim all the parts of yourself—especially the parts you take pride in. It's no feat of strength to wallow in your shortcomings, even though you excel at it, Elle. There's wisdom in harnessing your power, too. Riding it bareback in the rain."

"What if—" Elle felt a tear creep out of her eye, and she wiped it with the ridge of her hand. "What if it turns out I'm not very much at all?"

Susannah didn't hesitate. "Then I'd say you're just like the rest of us. Human. Make your peace with it. It ain't half bad, most of the time."

Elle laughed. She might have felt embarrassed being forty and still needing to ask her mother how to live. But all she could feel was the heat of Susannah's outstretched hand as she stood on the other side of something Elle had never wanted to face until now. This never-being-enoughness, the beauty in it, the rest.

"Mama," Elle said, "Josie had a daughter. And I wish she was mine."

This feeling went beyond envy, beyond any sense of ownership or possession. It was a north star, a healing balm, a song that had been waiting to be written.

"I can see why," Susannah said. "Children are like violets. They don't solve anybody's problems, but they're the most beautiful things in the world."

Elle's time on the pay phone was about to run out—so she said goodbye to her mother, finally clear-eyed for the first time in her life about who she was without music, without Merry, without even her mountain.

She had always been her mother's beautiful thing.

Elle took the long way through town. Past the new Opry, past the old, abandoned Ryman, past Tootsies. A few of her favorite haunts had closed down, and Elle realized she now carried the hallmark of a person in midlife and beyond: *I remember what stood here before*. After an hour, she ended up turning right by the Methodist church, into the back lot by Weston Studios. The willow boughs had deepened over the last eighteen years, and they kissed the ground. Now Elle needed a special pass to park, otherwise she'd be ticketed. But Elle pulled in anyway, let the engine idle, and didn't even try to sleep.

Arlo was late coming in that morning. The sun perked up the sky, and it was past time to catch him by surprise. Arlo—the human equivalent of a dry shave—spotted her and sauntered over with his arms crossed.

"Thought I wouldn't be hearing from you." There was no gloat in his voice, only a bleakness.

"I've been breaking a lot of promises lately."

Elle spoke to him from the driver's side window. He stroked his mustache a single time before he strolled around to the passenger seat and climbed in. Together they stared at the willow's fat trunk.

"They need to cut it down," offered Arlo, pointing at the tree. "The roots are messing with the asphalt."

"Even that tree is too old for you, is it?"

He didn't answer her but ran his hands over the Dodge's dash. "Been a long time," he said, "since I been in one of these."

"Ah," Elle said. "So old cars, you like. Just women your own age, you don't."

"What do you want me to say, Elle?" He fingered the collar at his neck. "That I got kids half your age lined up to record, one that's already been on television? Of course I do."

Elle had a decent idea who Arlo meant, and it pissed her off. "I should have known if anyone could make money off a meteor strike, it would be you."

Arlo was in no mood for jokes. "Tell me what you want, Elle." The pearly buttons on his shirt strained as he twisted in his seat. "Also, it's possible to make appointments through my secretary like a normal person."

"You were nervous when you saw me last night," Elle said. "And not because you thought I was dead."

Arlo said nothing, so Elle continued.

"Tell me why you left Josie's baby in the back seat of my car."

She looked at him, his face owlish and pinched. Arlo was a maze of contradictions. He'd stolen from Elle, and he'd also given her something that wasn't hers. He'd kept her from recording her own music, yet he'd also sent every single one of her royalty checks on time. She wondered now if that had been because he thought she was caring for a child.

"I didn't know you were going to disappear." Arlo rested his head against the seat. Creases dug deep into his forehead. "I heard you that night at the Opry, backstage with my cousin, whispering like you thought no one could hear you. But I did, Elle. And I could tell Luke was stupid enough to throw away everything for you."

"I don't see how that has anything to do with a baby."

"Josie was a mess," he went on. "Didn't want to perform, didn't want to step on stage, didn't want to be a mother. I had a crying infant I didn't know what to do with and a woman who needed a distraction. *You*. I thought Josie's panic would last a week, tops. Then she'd want the baby back. So I gave the baby a nice, big bottle and put her in your car."

"You are an absolute lunatic."

"The windows were down."

"Why would you do that to me? To her?"

"Because you were solid, Elle. You care well for things. For people."

"I—"

Arlo lifted his hand.

"Stop," he said. "You've always seen yourself as some dark beast that needs to be caged. But in this I know you better than you know yourself."

Her words died in her throat.

"I knew you could handle it," he went on. "Josie just needed some time, I thought. You had done everything I said without a hitch, up until then."

Elle hated being seen as some mindlessly obedient soldier. "Why couldn't *you* care for the baby?" she asked.

"Be serious."

"I am." Elle felt the sun on the side of her neck. "Arlo, this is the worst thing you've ever done."

"You think I don't know that?" He looked irritatingly boyish then, a naughty heir who wanted to be congratulated for half cleaning the giant mess he had caused. "You got your royalties, and so did Josie. I was going to talk to you about it, by the way, before you punched her and lost your mind."

"I'll remind you," Elle said smoothly, "that I don't take criticism from assholes."

She was ready to shove him out of the car. Arlo caught her glare and fastened his seat belt.

"This is your fault, Elle." He held out his hands to her. "People *hated* you after that night. They thought you were insane, and even I couldn't save you. Honestly? Playing dead for almost twenty years was the best thing you could have done for your career. The troubled starlet, I could promote. Not the angry, vindictive woman. Not Josie Starling's runner-up."

Elle clamped her hands on the steering wheel. She hated that his assessments of her had always been so chillingly accurate. How much she'd gotten because of this man, how much she'd forfeited.

"I couldn't let you break up the fairy tale I'd started," he said. "I still thought Josie would record again after that."

"Let me guess." Elle's nails cut into the wheel. "Your songwriters couldn't come up with anything to top what I'd already done."

He ignored her. "That night at the Opry I could see it all crumbling, so I took you out of the game. Just for a little bit."

"With a *baby*, Arlo."

He rolled down the window with his fist and lit a cigarette. "I know you hold on to grudges, Elle. But I also knew you'd take care of a child. After that night, you disappeared, and I never tried too hard to find you." He shot his eyes toward her. "Luke did, though. He combed every bit of that mountain searching for you."

It hurt, the hopelessness of it, the effort. The love.

"Where—" Elle tried to keep her hands from shaking. "Where is he now?"

"He lives on my property, and that's where you're going to leave him." Ash fluttered from the end of Arlo's Marlboro. "It took him too long to stop looking for you."

"And no one ever knew to look for Marijohn."

"Who?"

Other cars filled the parking lot. People gave Arlo alarmed glances, as if he might need to be rescued from a ghost. He stared straight ahead.

"Marijohn was the baby," Elle said, "whose whole life you left up to fate."

"Fate?" Arlo laughed. "Fate is for motherfuckers, Elle. Not people like us. If we left it to fate I'd be working in a mill somewhere trying not to lose a hand, and you'd be married with six kids." He swiped at his mustache. Forgot about his cigarette. "Tell me I'm wrong."

He didn't wait for an answer. The Marlboro fell from his fingers onto the asphalt. "A year before that Opry performance, Josie came to me in a panic, saying she was pregnant with a baby she didn't want."

"So you fixed it?"

Arlo looked proud, almost. "Faked a European tour, Josie had the baby in a private medical facility, and you know the rest."

Elle lifted up Josie's signed letter. "Josie signed over the rights to my music, Arlo."

She wanted him to know how it felt to have a future toyed with, a legacy flushed down the drain.

Arlo took a cursory look at the note, and then he laughed. Laughed so hard he made the whole car shake.

"Shit, Elle. You really are an idiot, still. This will never hold up in court. Josie doesn't own that music. I do."

Elle had found herself in this position with Arlo too many times to count. She felt helpless, felt the need to claw at anything that might turn him vulnerable and weak. "You know Weston would never forgive you for this."

Arlo closed his eyes. "There's already a lot he hasn't forgiven me for." He sniffed. "I don't like surprises, Elle. And after twenty years, that's still all you're giving me. Now there's none left."

"So Marijohn is just collateral damage," she said. "And so am I."

He opened his eyes. "Just the opposite. You're free now. You want to guide your career so bad? Think you can do better? Have at it." Arlo looked at himself in the sideview mirror. "But Weston Studios still owns the rights to Josie's album, all your music, and your next record. So let it go, Elle. Live your life, do what you want. I'll make money off you still."

Arlo undid his seat belt and cranked open the door.

"Arlo," Elle said before he stepped out.

He looked at her one last time.

"I will *bury* you."

He shook his head, almost laughed—because he had no more use for her. And then he walked away, back inside Weston Studios, returning to the safety of the kingdom he had built.

Both Ways

Two months after Marijohn played her mandolin with Elle Harlow on her porch, that night turned into a ghost. Marijohn hadn't heard from Elle, and no word of her reappearance had made its way into the nightly broadcast news, but Marijohn still felt her just beyond reach. An apparition, a lack.

She didn't know what else to do with a ghost but sing for it. Wait for it to sing back.

Rumors hit the tabloids—Elle Harlow had been spotted behind the windshield of a car in Kentucky, at a municipal building in Tennessee, onstage at a dive bar in Pennsylvania—but no one paid attention. These headlines were no different from the ones that first ran in 1973. The idea of disappearance still had a romantic violence to it—as if an imagined kidnapping, a brutal and untimely end, turned Elle more beautiful. More urgent. More prophetic. As if it were better than letting her age. Letting her live.

Marijohn knew better now.

Singing with Elle that night was the most moving, confusing, tectonic act Marijohn had ever been part of. Before it, she'd been a motherless daughter—a shape she knew well. After it, she'd turned into a mound of loose clay where Elle had left an imprint of her bootheel. Absent but present. Marijohn had told herself for a long time that she'd survive just fine never knowing her mother. Now, she felt such a restless ache for her she couldn't sleep at night. Couldn't even play her mandolin.

Marijohn wanted to tell Lazarus all about it. She wanted to tell him all the things she understood now—that her constant state of unknowing had been an addiction. That getting sober from it felt like death. That maybe she'd confused death with destruction, and they were not the same.

She'd never been lonelier.

In early November, Laz released his new single. He'd been gone for almost ten weeks. Marijohn heard his voice on the radio one night while washing the dishes after dinner.

It's the last night of the world
For you and me, for you and me, girl

Marijohn threw her wet sponge across the counter. The song was so—happy. Jaunty. Gross. She'd always thought of their music as twin headlights coming at her in the dark. Not menacing, but bold. This song was a dead engine, and Marijohn hated it. It didn't sound like Laz at all.

She hadn't heard from him, and she wasn't sure she would. Neither of them had known that August night the meteor hit would be their last time in the woods. He'd have to return to Lenora sometime, but Marijohn didn't want to be right where he'd left her when he came back, like a wartime wife waiting to see if he'd come home.

She could tell Lazarus hadn't written that song himself. "Namesake" hadn't been a ballad the record company wanted—and they hadn't wanted his love songs, either. It was what Marijohn had hoped for, that her music would remain her own. And yet she wanted it both ways—for "Namesake" to stay in her private sanctuary, and for it to be beloved by many, for it to curl around a stranger and hold fast. She still felt herself standing at the edge of the ravine at summer's end—staring up into the smoke, not sure what she was looking for or whether she'd already missed it.

So she wrote a song about it. A good one, too. But she figured "Both Ways" would never get played on the radio because she was too afraid to send it out into the world. She had no idea how to, anyway. Laz had said she was the bravest person he'd ever met, but Marijohn didn't believe him. Courage required movement, and she was stuck.

I want you to say you're mine
You're waiting on miracles divine
But I've always wanted it
Both ways, both ways

It was a ballad about wanting too many things. She wanted her songs on the radio. She wanted to know her mother, and she wanted her best friend to call.

"I can't do this without you," he'd said to her the last time they spoke.

And he was right. He couldn't. Laz was quiet and thoughtful and private and cautious. Performing over and over again would skin him alive.

Marijohn could see the outline of his future, and it gave her no joy. His album would live just like the meteor that preceded it. It would burn bright, and then it would be gone. Lazarus, the real one only she knew, would disappear—no new lyrics, no nights spent back-to-back in the woods. No Jolly Ranchers, no corner of his mouth digging into his dimple while they dissected death and everything that came before and after. No one—except for Marijohn—to know he was missing.

Then he sent her a letter.

Just before Thanksgiving, it arrived as a curious and clean rectangle written in his careful hand. Her father left the envelope on the counter at the gas station, the same spot she used to leave faux Elle Harlow memorabilia for her father to revel in. How swiftly the roles between them had switched since the meteor struck.

"Read it if you're ready," Abe had said. "Or I can put it away until you are."

Marijohn could not wait. She clawed at it the same way her father had opened that package from Kentucky with the rhinestone cat barrette inside. It had only been a few months since then, but she was someone else now. Someone who understood that sometimes a dream was a person, and sometimes you had to let that dream go.

The letter from Lazarus contained guitar tabs for a chorus he'd written:

I never told you I loved you
Girl with the old mandolin
Its broken neck you loved true
I want you now just like I did then

Lazarus had always been a master at writing down what he couldn't say plainly with his mouth. He also wrote a note, five words in handwriting she'd recognize anywhere—

I want to come home.

What else was there to say? Marijohn had stopped believing love could heal her wounds. She took every single feeling, every longing, every speck of love, and clamped it. Laz had said he wanted to come home because he wasn't going to. Marijohn threw the letter away.

She didn't want to be someone who waited anymore.

After Thanksgiving passed, Marijohn showed up late to work on Monday morning. She'd been coming in later and later, leaving earlier and earlier. Mercifully, Abe's business had picked up. Suddenly the world was ripe for his kind of care—soft and genuine, thorough and slow.

Abe Shaw had a way of bringing about miracles for humans and vehicles alike.

When Marijohn arrived at the station, there was Elle Harlow—as if she'd never left—standing over Abe's glass case of artifacts. She inspected them as Abe stood beside her.

"I definitely wore that earring," she said, pointing at the turquoise stud plated in gold. "I left it in a drawer in my room at the boardinghouse."

Abe's face lit. "I knew it!" he cried.

She pointed to a linen napkin with *Jaclyn, in her iris fields* scrawled on it, stained with dark red. "The napkin isn't mine," she said softly. "Neither is the blood."

A thick quiet filled the shop until Elle spotted a tube of red lipstick.

"Rose pearl," she called it. "My mother's favorite shade."

The door clanged as Marijohn shut it, and Elle glanced up. She looked bright and peachy. Marijohn was haggard and petulant. She promptly turned around, flew out the door she'd just entered, and started to head for the woods.

Elle followed her.

"I'm not giving you the mandolin," Marijohn called over her shoulder, pulling her jacket close. "So don't even ask."

"I won't," Elle said, and Marijohn slowed her pace.

They walked together in silence until they reached the edge of the farmer's meadows. The meteor's wide stripe in the field had turned brown, and the cows grazed around it like an altar.

Suddenly, Marijohn stopped in the roadside dust. Then she tipped her chin to the sky and screamed. Yelled her guts out for a full minute, throaty and needy and nude.

When she'd finished, a cow flicked its tail. Another stamped its hoof, then settled into the grass.

"Feel better?" Elle asked.

"I feel like shit."

"You're getting close, then," Elle said.

"To what?"

"To what matters. Leaning into the heart of something will always hurt."

Marijohn pulled her hair into a ponytail and fastened it with the band around her wrist. She felt unkempt and wild, as if she couldn't keep all the pieces of herself in one place.

"Can I ask you something?" she hedged as she took an old stalk of wheat and held it in her grip. "Was it everything you dreamed it would be, making it as a musician?"

They started walking toward the trees as a scarlet leaf from a maple tree floated to the ground.

"It was everything I dreamed of, and nothing I expected," Elle said. "It made me not want to live in the world I had created."

It was a cryptic answer, and on any other day with any other woman,

Marijohn wouldn't have minded. She liked loose ends and mysteries and complicated truths—except when it came to her mother.

"Did you ever think," she asked, "that the world you made still needed you?"

Elle's hair looked coppery in the light. "No."

Marijohn marveled at it—the ability, the guts, the ambition to build a world of your own and then abandon it.

"Since I was young," Marijohn said, "I've had two memories. This voice in the darkness, singing to me, and that broken mandolin. I tangled them up so much in my mind because I thought my mother must have wanted me to have that instrument. I've been playing it since I could hold it up, trying to make those two memories into one. Trying to form a true version of myself out of it. And I failed."

She meant the open mic, the video half the country had seen, even her attempt to convince Elle to tell her the truth.

"You didn't fail onstage at the bar," Elle said. "You just needed a little company."

Marijohn pinched the grain between her fingers. "You never needed any company."

"You'd be surprised." Elle tilted her head to the sky. "Is that really what you wanted to ask me?"

Marijohn twisted the wheat, then dropped it to the ground. "You're really not going to tell me who my mother is?"

Elle shut her eyes for a moment. Somewhere, a bird sang. "I've been thinking on it, and the secret isn't mine."

Marijohn wanted to tear every tree by its roots from the ground. She wanted to scream again, to curse, to find a way to force someone who could not be forced. Perhaps this was her first measure of adulthood—to look at the living face of her own disappointment, to thrust all her power against it and witness how unyielding it was.

"I thought it might be you, you know," Marijohn said. Her voice was dry. "I hoped it was you."

If Elle had been her mother, every part of this sad story would have made sense. The meteor wouldn't have just been a random rock falling through the sky. Abe's Elle Harlow collection wouldn't have been the hoarding of a fairy tale. Marijohn's life would have been a folk song with a beginning and an end.

"Oh, honey," Elle said, touching Marijohn's shoulder. "I wish it was, too."

They stood in a place halfway between here and there, halfway between resolve and regret—the gas station where Elle had left Marijohn, and the river where Elle's Studebaker had sunk.

"The more I thought about it, though," Elle went on, "the more I realized that even if it's not my secret, it certainly is yours."

She unhooked her satchel from her shoulder and pulled out a folder she'd brought. Elle handed it to Marijohn, and she opened it. Inside was a sheet of paper with a name and date.

Marijohn Jaclyn Starling, born July 2, 1973.

It was a copy of her birth certificate.

"How did you get this?" Marijohn asked. It was the first tangible piece of her past she'd ever held, other than the mandolin.

"It took some doing, but let's just say there's someone at the records department in Nashville who is a huge Elle Harlow fan," Elle replied. "And she's happy I'm not dead."

Marijohn felt a flash of verve. Of mercy. Relief.

"As happy as my dad is, though?"

Elle grinned. "No one is as happy as your dad."

"My mother." Marijohn's eyes scanned the document. "She's Josie Starling."

Elle didn't confirm or deny. "Your mother never meant for you to be abandoned. She only wanted you to be cared for in the best way, that's all."

Marijohn had been given a little, and she was ready for more. She was so ready for her life to begin.

"Do you think she wants to meet me?" she asked.

"She ain't ready, honey." Elle looped her arm tightly through Marijohn's. "I'm not sure she ever will be."

Marijohn looked at the earth under her feet. Steady, unbending. "I see."

"That doesn't mean it's wrong to want it. Only that she might not be able to give it to you."

Marijohn's green eyes settled onto Elle's. "You saw her?"

"I did."

"So she also knows you're alive." Marijohn watched her. "Didn't you want to stay gone?"

"Some things are worth coming back from the dead for." Elle looked toward the tree line. "I'm sorry I abandoned you, too."

"You gave me to my dad," Marijohn offered quietly. "I was so well cared for, Elle. Always."

She'd never realized until then that her love for music didn't rest only with her mother. It had come to life because of Abe.

Elle made to head back the way they'd come, but Marijohn stopped her.

"Elle," she said, solemn, "I don't know how I can ever repay you for this."

"I'm in your debt," Elle said. "Hearing you play that mandolin gave me something I thought I'd never get back."

That seemed to be the miracle of this meteor, now buried beneath a river. It hadn't brought things back from the dead; it revealed what still lived.

"I know what you mean," Marijohn said.

They continued walking the road in silence until they reached Marijohn's porch, where her mandolin perched on the swing.

"Thing is, Marijohn," Elle began, "there is something you can help me with."

Marijohn cast Elle a wary glance.

"What's wrong?" Elle asked.

"I don't want your pity."

Elle couldn't stop herself—she laughed. "Well, shit," she said. "You might not be my child, but I feel like I'm about to have a fight with my younger self."

"Pity isn't funny," Marijohn countered.

"'Believe me, honey.'" Elle quoted her own song title. "'Pity is the last thing I feel for you.'"

Something deeper grew there between them, half hidden, for which neither of them yet had a name. It wasn't a mirror, or a family tree, or a resolution of any kind. It was a joining of hands, a fire in the night. A harmony born in the well of a throat.

Elle spoke her next words with care. "You remember the *Merry* album we sang through a few months ago?"

"I remember."

"I'm making a live recording of it. As *mine*." Marijohn could see how much Elle cherished the way this admission felt in her mouth. "I want you to play this mandolin." She took up Merry's instrument. "And sing with me."

Marijohn didn't say anything for a moment.

"You want me to *perform*?" she asked.

Elle nodded.

"You don't, though," she cautioned. "I have stage fright."

Elle blinked. "Some of these singers do, too."

At that, Marijohn began to trust herself again, the smallest bit. "Why me?" she asked. "You could have your pick of the best musicians in Nashville."

"I'll tell you why." Elle cinched her hips with her hands. "I swore off duets, but hearing you play reminded me why I first learned to sing. It was for someone I loved, with someone I loved. I've forgotten my own lifeblood, and I need you to remind me. Can you do that?"

At that moment, it was the only thing Marijohn wanted to do.

"I can."

It was true—Elle Harlow had reappeared, but she was still working on coming back to life. On understanding what it meant to carry her past with her but not be held down by it. Elle would always wish that she'd been able to record the *Merry* album as hers in 1969. It would have changed the trajectory of her entire life. But if she had, the album never would have had Merry's mandolin played on its tracks. Now, it would.

In the final weeks of 1991, Elle and Marijohn rehearsed her comeback album in the run-down cabin where Elle had spent a summer with Weston. She liked the mood inside it, Elle said, eerie and romantic. She and Marijohn traveled the long way by boat to avoid the woods' shifting ground. The cabin was cloaked in dust and wood shavings. Tools and old blankets. Elle held the bird's-eye tendrils between her fingertips, and Marijohn swept away the cobwebs. They opened the windows and let in the cold.

"I spent a whole life here once," Elle said.

They brought their instruments and a portable heater. Rehearsals only took two weeks. Elle already held the music, the lyrics, the harmonies—all boarded up inside her chest. All she had to do was teach them to Marijohn.

Her plan was equally angelic and devious. On December 15—eighteen years to the day since she'd disappeared—Elle was going to record a live performance on the wide expanse of Arlo's lawn with the sound equipment hoisted in the back of Abe's truck. She'd play through the *Merry* album with Marijohn by her side. Elle had taken out ads in five different newspapers, and everyone on her mountain was coming in a caravan in three days' time.

Elle hadn't said a word to Arlo, and she wasn't going to. He'd hear about it in the paper, or when a clamoring crowd overtook his property—Elle didn't care which. Just as she'd done when she was eighteen, she would make certain that Arlo Weston could not look away.

It was a twice-in-a-lifetime thing—not the concert itself, but the story being lived inside that luthier's cabin. Their voices held everything Elle had experienced with Merry—the joy, the hunger, the healing—and they held something new, too. A spark, a heat, the kind of electric current so strong its thunder would sound for miles.

They both felt it.

"What would you have done if a meteor never struck?" Marijohn asked Elle on their final day of rehearsal.

"I don't know." Elle put a hand over her heart and pressed it into her skin. It was cold, and her breath smoked in the air. "You need to understand," she said, "the best songs I've written are in here, whether anyone hears them or not."

It seemed like a lesson Elle had learned not from a mountaintop, but from a pit.

Elle caused Marijohn to question what a song was if it went unsung. Where it went, what secrets it held. The air outside the cabin burned like ice. Marijohn felt the magnitude of what they'd done—she and Elle were bringing a woman back from the dead through her music. Bound together in ballads no longer than three and a half minutes each, they'd created something timeless. The snow-covered earth beneath them looked like it had been swept by a tide—as if it were slowly disappearing underneath their feet—and yet they stood still.

"Tell me about Merry," Marijohn said.

All at once, Elle looked troubled. "What would you like to know?" she asked.

"What did you love about her?"

Elle looked out the window, past the old remains of a campfire buried beneath the snow. "She was the kind of person you could sit in silence with and feel seen."

"I don't think I've ever felt that," Marijohn said.

Elle ran her fingers down the neck of her guitar. "Even after all this time, Merry represents the best things I've ever done. And also the worst."

She set down her guitar, tucked her pick beneath the strings. Elle was tired not in body, but in spirit. She knew what it was to run. Now she was relearning what it meant to stay.

"I've worked you hard enough for one day," she said. "I'm going to walk by the river awhile."

Once Elle had gone, Marijohn practiced "Shackle" in the cabin by herself. Elle had asked for a lick between the first verse and the chorus that she wanted to get just right. After Marijohn played for an hour, she turned on her portable radio and searched the stations until she found Lazarus's song.

It's the last night of the world
For you and me, for you and me, girl

She listened to it the whole way through. Then she scanned the stations till she found the song again, and again. She wanted the pain of it, the longing. The company. After the sun began to set and Elle hadn't returned,

Marijohn strapped her mandolin to her back and went in search of her. When she opened the cabin door, she found that Elle had been waiting for her in the dusk.

She looked suspicious and cold.

"This Lazarus, who sings the song you keep listening to," Elle said. "He's a friend of yours?"

"Yes."

Elle frowned. "It's a shitty song."

"I know."

"Does he have your music?" Elle asked flatly. "In Nashville?"

"He does."

Elle took a step closer. Her boot sank into the snow. "What's stopping him from stealing it?"

"He wouldn't." Marijohn shook her head. "Besides, the record company doesn't want it."

Elle laughed, bleak. "I've heard that before."

"Elle," Marijohn began.

"He'll ruin you," Elle interrupted without preamble as she began to hike toward the boat. Her profile grew harsh in the paltry light, as if her bones had feasted on the rest of her face. "You know that."

Marijohn didn't know it, and she didn't want to. "You don't need to protect me."

Elle's chin touched her shoulder as she looked back. "No one else is going to."

"Listen," Marijohn tried again, "it isn't your fault."

Elle stopped at the water's edge. It was crusted in ice. "What isn't?"

"It isn't your fault that I ended up in your back seat. Or that Josie cheated you, or that Music Row used you. Or that you fell in love."

Elle's guitar slipped off her back. "I wish I believed that."

Marijohn joined her at the river's edge. "What do you believe?"

"I believe that love is good while you're making a record," Elle kept on. "But it has to die for the music to live."

"That can't be true," Marijohn said, even though she knew Elle would not lie to her.

"I want you to know what you're up against, Marijohn."

Marijohn crossed her arms in the wind. "Why?"

Elle didn't equivocate. "So you'll be better than what became of me."

The boat stood in the near distance, rocking softly in the water.

"You survived," Marijohn said.

"Barely."

"You must think I'm weak." Marijohn stepped into the boat, faltered for a moment until she found her balance. "Because you think you're weak, too."

"Weak?" Elle followed after her. "No. Your heart is the strongest muscle you've got, Marijohn. Just like mine."

A compliment and a criticism, all in one.

"You want this life?" Elle said, not unkindly, as Marijohn started to row. "Then you'll pay. You can't even imagine the ways you'll pay."

As Marijohn pulled them through the water, she found herself wanting to ask what had really happened to Elle after her summer in the cabin in 1972. Something about what she'd left behind was tormenting her, even though Elle still acted as if that time had been wiped clean.

"Elle?" Marijohn asked as she rowed down the river. "Did you ever see Weston again?"

"No." Wind rushed across the river, tossing her amber hair.

"You never wanted to find him?"

Elle pulled on the collar of her coat. "I know where he is."

"Where, Elle?"

"He lives on Arlo's property."

Horrified, Marijohn laughed. "You went all the way to Nashville and didn't even see him?"

Elle blinked and set her jaw. Her earrings jingled as the boat swayed.

Marijohn pulled the oars toward her. "Because you're afraid it won't be the same between you as it was almost twenty years ago?"

"The opposite," Elle answered. "I'm afraid it will be."

Marijohn let the oars rest against the bottom of the boat. "Who told you that you only deserve flashes of happiness and nothing else?"

Elle's gaze snagged in the tree line where the meteor had crashed, and Marijohn knew the conversation had ended.

"What song would you like to hear?" she asked instead.

Elle cast her eyes back toward the bottom of the boat.

"'Shackle,' then." Marijohn handed her the oars. "There's a new run I'd like to play for you."

Elle began to row as Marijohn picked a melody with her fingers. The sound of her mandolin traveled the river's current.

When she finished the ballad, they'd reached the far dock where Abe's Sierra was parked. Then they climbed into the cold cab and Marijohn turned the ignition.

"This is the real me, Marijohn," Elle said. "There are some things I'll never get over."

Marijohn waited for a moment with her hand on the stick shift, watching her. And then she put the truck in reverse.

"I understand," she said. And she did.

"My Marijohn," Elle said her name again, "remember you are more than what any man can make of you."

"Ah." Marijohn smiled as she turned onto the main road. "You're an expert, based on your track record with men?"

Elle failed to see the humor in it.

"Maybe," she said to Elle, "you just need closure."

"Closure," Elle said back, "can kiss my ass."

Marijohn drove through the coming night until she reached her yellow house with the green shutters and Elle stepped inside. Then Marijohn sank onto the porch steps and tried to slow her heartbeat. Elle had seen her own ghosts running through Marijohn's life, and it made Marijohn fear that something dangerous lay ahead for them both.

Rest never befriended the brokenhearted, did it? Elle kept an eternal vigilance, watching over a sore that had never healed. She'd sworn she remained out of exile to help Marijohn find what she was looking for—but that night, Marijohn started to suspect Elle Harlow had reappeared so that Marijohn could shepherd her toward something greater, too.

Something deep, something wide. Something that had nothing to do with music. Her whole life, Marijohn had remained right where she was, always waiting, meteors and missing folk singers be damned.

It was time to move.

She stepped off the porch and lay down in the tall, snowy grass. Stars shone above her like bits of spun silk. It was beautiful there just outside the woods, lovely, and sad, and true.

Sometimes, Marijohn could catch the future coming at her from around the corner—like the moment Elle walked into her life and her mother walked out of it. Other times, though? The past hurled itself straight toward her, spinning around like a broken timepiece.

Marijohn felt a presence before she could see it: the heat of an engine, the heaviness of someone lingering in the trees. A change in the wind, bringing the scent of wood smoke. The air was ripe with it. He must have been waiting for her a long time.

"Dad?" Marijohn said, even though she knew as the word left her lips that it wasn't him.

She sat up, and a bold shadow she knew as well as her own hovered over her.

It was Lazarus.

Hear Me Out

"Lazarus," Marijohn said. "What are you doing here?"

She stared at her best friend. His cheeks were flushed from the Chevy's heat, and his hair had lost some of its summer blond. He smelled like a different city. Laz looked familiar and far away and firelit, his brown eyes cast in a smoky glow from the distant porch light.

"I just came from the gas station. Your father told me where to find you." He bent down to meet her, his knees in the snow.

He stared back at her for a moment, his bottom lip caught between his teeth, as if he'd forgotten what he'd come to say. His eyes hunted hers as if she were the one thing he wanted to remember.

He blinked. "I've been recording—"

"Laz." Marijohn looked to the sky, flickering and vast. "I know you've been recording."

Everyone knew he'd been recording.

"I overheard something at the studio," Laz went on. "Elle Harlow is *alive*, Marijohn."

"I know."

His nose bloomed red in the cold, and so did his hands. "How?"

Marijohn reveled in what she said next. So many times over the last months she'd wanted to run to Lazarus, tell him everything, and now he'd run to her.

"Elle Harlow is upstairs," she said.

His eyes flew to the dark window of the guest room, the mossy shutters that framed it. "Holy shit."

"Wait a minute," Marijohn said. "How did *you* know?"

"I'm recording with her old producer. He saw her ad in the newspaper and his cigarette singed a hole right through it."

"You're recording at Weston Studios?"

"Yes." He blew into his palms, rubbed them together. "I've been staying at Arlo Weston's house. Why?"

"That motherfucker."

Hours ago, Marijohn had said she didn't need Elle's protection. She'd never imagined that Elle might need hers.

"You were in the middle of recording," Marijohn said, "and you just up and left?"

"Yes."

"To tell me about Elle?"

Laz went shy at the sound of his actions repeated out loud. He cuffed the back of his neck with his hand. "You never pick up the phone."

He knew that about her, and so many other things, too. He knew she liked her eggs over easy. That she wrote songs in her underwear. That she had wanted to touch that meteor so badly because she feared it would be the most monumental thing ever to happen to her. That no matter how she tried to hide it, she'd always be desperate for any clue that might be connected to her mother.

Marijohn stood and shook the snow from her back. "Laz," she said. "I need you to go somewhere with me."

Laz came to his feet after her. The knees of his jeans were soaked through. "Where?"

"Back to Nashville."

"I just came from there."

"I'll drive," she said, undeterred. "You can sleep on the way."

She reached for the keys, but Laz kept them in his grip.

"*You* want to drive?"

"I said I would."

"Have you ever driven outside the state?"

"Don't be a dick," she said, heading for the driveway. "Of course I have."

"*Other* than Ohio?"

She stopped short and glared at him over her shoulder. "Tonight is the perfect time."

"But you get super tense behind the wheel," he pointed out.

"I do not."

"Yes, you do," he said.

And that was how Lazarus and Marijohn left home in the middle of the night—by fighting. Before they drove away, Marijohn wrote a note for Elle and slipped it under her door.

Please wait for me—I'll be back.

The letter took less than a minute to write, and it held every good thing her mother's hadn't when she'd left Marijohn with Arlo. A plea for patience, a promise of return. It was such a simple act. For a long time, Marijohn had wondered if she'd ever be able to give someone what she'd never gotten enough of. Love. Constancy. Faith.

Turned out, she could.

The only thing Marijohn took with her was her mandolin. She and Lazarus said nothing as they drove through the night. Lamps lit the highway like fits of comets until they hit the Ohio state line, and everything went black. For a while, it seemed as if they were the only car on the interstate. Marijohn used to love that feeling when she and Laz tore through Lenora's back roads.

She imagined Elle driving this route almost twenty years before, following Arlo's map toward a chance to escape. It was before she'd met Weston, before she'd written the *Wounds from a Lover* album, before she'd disappeared. Elle had been only four years older than Marijohn was now, just twenty-two, so much heartbreak in her and so much life left, too.

Marijohn was determined to help her live it.

The night was navy and cool, a thin billow of heat blowing from the vents in Lazarus's old Chevy. She'd ridden in this passenger seat a thousand times. The cup holder still overflowed with pink and green Jolly Ranchers. The leather cushions had cracked, the window's hand crank had busted, and there was no guitar sitting between them.

There was no music between them at all.

It was a nine-hour trip to Tennessee, and Lazarus's chin drooped another fraction of an inch with every mile marker they passed.

"You need to let me drive," Marijohn said. "You're exhausted."

He ignored her and leaned his foot on the gas.

"Lazarus," she said as the engine revved.

He scrubbed his face with his hand before pulling onto the side of the highway. The truck's engine ticked as they sat there in the dust. Neither of them moved.

Laz took off his glasses and leaned his head into the wheel, looking wrecked. The time they'd spent apart coiled around them, bringing their last moment together with this one.

"Marijohn," he said.

What an ageless melody it was, hearing the person she missed call out her name.

In the dark, she stole a glance at him. After only a few months, Lazarus loomed larger now, stronger, harder. His long blond hair fell over his eyes.

"What?" she asked, but he didn't respond.

All at once there seemed so much to say. Marijohn didn't know where to begin. He hadn't come back because of Elle, or Arlo, or some concert. He'd come back to look for something he'd lost.

"I didn't like your single," she said.

Lazarus laughed, lifted his head off the wheel. "Neither did I."

"That girl you sang about." She paused. "She's nothing like me."

"No." He exhaled like it hurt. "She isn't."

"Is it—" She bit the inside of her cheek to tamp down the envy in her throat. "Is it everything you dreamed, getting a record with your name on it?"

"No." The sadness in his stare ran like a bloodstain. "I never wanted any of that without you. I hate it, Marijohn. I've hated every single minute of it."

His left hand held the steering wheel as his fingers rippled against it. For anyone else, it might have been an absentminded motion. But Marijohn knew he was playing a chorus in his mind, digging his hand into the imaginary frets as he strummed a chord to calm himself. She wondered if the song he heard when he closed his eyes was the one he'd written for her.

I never told you I loved you
Girl with the old mandolin

She wanted to hear him sing it. Press her palms to his shoulders. Push him hard, just to see if he'd push back. Laz didn't hate the music in Nashville, or singing, or even being away from home. What he hated was performing.

Lazarus was still himself, and she loved him for it.

This was the first time Marijohn didn't want things to return to what they'd once been between them before the meteor. What they had was real but sequestered; it had never had the chance to breathe on its own, until now. She wanted Lazarus to give her this tension—the awkwardness, the ugliness, the mess. The fight.

Faintly, Marijohn stepped out from behind the shadow the meteor had cast.

Lazarus gripped the steering wheel again, then released it. With a sigh, he put his glasses back on and turned to look at her.

"What do you want?" she asked quietly.

"I already got everything I want, according to you."

"And you're miserable, performing music that you hate."

She caught the golden flecks in his eyes before he answered. "I'd rather make music no one hears in the woods."

She eyed him. "Really?"

He nodded.

"But you went to Nashville."

"I told them no."

"But then you went."

"*You* told me to go." He raised his hands. "I did it because you wouldn't get the chance to."

She softened then, but he didn't. His silhouette festered around her, crowding every empty space.

"You gave up on what you really want," she said. "What is it?"

"I didn't give up." The crease in his forehead deepened. "This wasn't my dream. It was yours."

To that, she had no argument. Lazarus had known it, even when Marijohn hadn't.

"Every time I set foot in the recording studio, I kept thinking of that cassette I have of my mother playing the piano. My dad listens to it all the time, right?"

Marijohn nodded.

"I always thought it was because of the hymns." He blinked back the frustration in his eyes. "But now I see he loves it because it's hers. It's something they share, just the two of them. My mother loves to play, and he loves to hear it. That's what I want. Something like that."

Marijohn said nothing. She didn't have to tell him he wanted something he already had.

"I also want to be an accountant," he said.

"No, you don't."

"Yes, I do. Don't you see it, Marijohn?" He threw open the truck door and flew out into the night. "You are the one who gave up."

She trailed him into the roadside ditch.

"How can you say that?" She thrust a finger into his chest. "I wrote the song that got you where you are."

"Oh?" Lazarus crossed his arms in the chill. He had no jacket, no hat. "So who's performing 'Namesake,' then? Not you."

"I see." She nodded. "You think I let you down."

"Why didn't you just sing with me on that stupid recording?"

"Because you didn't kiss me back."

She said the words before she could stop them. Lazarus and Marijohn had bled out for their music, and for each other on that video. There was no changing it now.

She looked up at him. Laz stood close, impenetrable, hurt. Hungry.

The same as her.

"I should have kissed you back," he said, his eyes boring into the bend of her shoulder.

"Why didn't you?"

"I told you why. Because you'd already been left behind once, and I didn't want to make it twice."

"What about now?" she asked.

"Now?" He'd driven so long through the night that he started to lay his burden down.

"I think I'm an idiot," he said.

Slowly, Laz took her by the hips. Gently pressed her back against the side of the truck, his forehead into hers.

"I fucking missed you," he said.

He slid his hands into her hair, and then Lazarus let himself go. His lips fell onto hers, searching her, calling out for her, his thumbs dipping into the sides of her neck. Marijohn reached for him, and he pulled her close. Laz kissed her as her fingers slipped over his shoulders.

They wanted each other just as they were—without words, without woods, without warning. They kissed like they were final and fatal, bruised and brilliant, like they were writing a song that had no chords, no beginning, no end.

It happened so fast that Laz had to stop to catch his breath. He ran a thumb across her cheek as if he'd imagined doing it a hundred times before. Then he closed his eyes and leaned into her, resting his lips on the rise of Marijohn's collarbone. His exhaustion had stripped him of so many things—his need for perfection, his penchant for performance, his ability to pine without reward.

"I don't know what to do," he said.

He meant in Nashville, in Lenora, and everywhere in between.

Marijohn pointed to the Chevy's passenger seat. "Get in," she said. "And get some sleep."

He climbed into the passenger side and closed the door behind him. Marijohn crossed the truck's headlights, pulled herself into the cab, and checked the darkness in the rearview mirror. They were cloaked in it. Daylight was still a long way off.

Good thing was, she didn't mind driving past midnight and onward. She liked seeing the day turn itself over, struggling to start. When they reached Nashville's city limits, the sky had pinked. One by one, the stars went out. Lazarus still dozed beside her, and she took out a map to guide her the rest of the way.

By the time Marijohn pulled up to Arlo Weston's mansion, Lazarus was still asleep. His head tilted against the window, his jaw slackened, and his glasses fogged. Marijohn had never seen him sleep before. It felt bundled and safe there in the cab of the truck, as if when they stepped out they'd find they hadn't traveled anywhere new at all.

She remembered one night early last summer when the two of them had settled into the back of the Chevy, graduation less than a week behind them. The end of the summer felt distant and impossible then.

"Been thinking," he'd said, his arms tucked behind his head, "that maybe life is just a collection of the beds you've slept in. Like maybe you reach the end of it all and see a set of them, just lined up in a row."

Marijohn turned on her side to look at him. "You're afraid of how many there will be?"

"No," he said, his chin to the sky. "I'm worried there will only be three. The crib I was born into, the bed I sleep in now, and the bunk in my dorm room."

"You can buy yourself another bed, Laz."

"That's not what I mean." He turned toward her, pain in his face. Fear. "I mean what if I never go anywhere that's so far, I can't return before dark? What if I never need to spend a night in a bed that isn't my own? It'll mean that I had no adventures."

"Maybe adventures are a privilege," Marijohn had said then, mostly because she was already dreading the day Lazarus would leave.

"Maybe so."

Now she felt the crisp thrill of traveling somewhere she'd never been before, far enough away that she couldn't see Lenora in the rearview mirror. Marijohn's idea of home was finding new definition, even from the passenger seat of Laz's old Chevy: a place to miss, a place to return to.

She left him with the engine running so he wouldn't get cold. Her visit wouldn't take long.

Before her stood a gilded gate with a colossal *W* welded to it.

"Woof," Marijohn said.

She'd never seen wealth of such gleaming magnitude. It was ominous and a little funny, especially since a bird had shat in one of the *W*'s divots. Marijohn launched herself over the same fence Elle had hopped months before and landed into a dry tuft of grass. There was no snow this far south, just the deadened ground of winter. A lake tipped with ice, horse stables battened down until spring.

She followed the trail toward a small cabin with a thick wand of smoke pointing out of its chimney. It was firmly tucked away and snug, the kind of place that would have a clothesline in summer. When she knocked on the door, a hand pulled the window curtain aside with callused fingers. Marijohn saw him then for the first time—

Weston, green-eyed, russet-haired, strong-armed. Alone.

He opened the door and peered at the mandolin she carried on her back. A dish towel was slung over his shoulder, and the air smelled like hickory. A dusting of flour had swiped itself across his cheek.

Marijohn could see what had drawn Elle to him. His whole being thrummed with the heart of a good country song, the kind written on a lonely night beneath a half-moon.

Handsome, too.

"You having trouble with your instrument?" he asked, by way of greeting.

"See for yourself."

She slid her mandolin off her back and held it out toward him. Its crack caught the light, a lightning bolt trapped in rosewood. Weston eyed it, and then eyed it again. There was no other mandolin like it. She knew it, and so did he.

"Sweet Jesus," he said, running his fingers along the instrument's grain. "Where did you find this?"

He waited, still as stone, while Marijohn wondered if she could trust him. Elle had, once upon a time.

"Can I trust you?" she decided to ask.

He scratched his jaw. "If you couldn't, I ain't sure how you'd know."

Marijohn had come here for Elle. But when she opened her mouth, she couldn't stop what poured out. It was the question of her heart, the one she carried with her always.

"My mother is Josie Starling," she said. "Did you know her?"

His eyes drew lines around her, searching for features he recognized. "I did," he answered. "A long time ago."

Weston opened the door wider and invited her in. They sat together on his worn leather couch. In the kitchen, bread dough was rising in the oven.

"Can you tell me about her?" she asked.

"I ain't sure what to say," he began. "Josie and I lived a lie together. It wasn't a good way to know someone."

"Is there a good way?"

"I wouldn't know," he answered. "My life's been full of bad ones."

"I don't believe that."

The edge of his mouth dipped. "You should."

"You knew Elle Harlow," she said. "Once."

Weston let out an aching sigh. "If Arlo sent you back here to play some kind of joke on me—"

"He didn't," Marijohn said.

"Then how could you know about Elle and me?" He leaned toward her, ardor in his eyes, his jaw ticking slightly to the left. "No one knows about that."

"Tell me this first," Marijohn said. "Are you the third outlaw?"

"No." His forehead crimped. A whole lifetime without Elle was etched into the creases in his skin. "I've loved Elle longer than I had her, and all that makes me is a fool."

"So you're still Elle's Weston, then."

"Is she—" He paused, his body rigid. It was forever, this thing between them, whether living or dead. "Is she alive?"

"Yes."

Weston came to his feet. "You've *seen* her?"

Marijohn nodded. She'd seen so much of Elle—her unassailable prowess, her stark heartbreak. Her predatory regret. This was why Marijohn had come.

"Is she—all right?" Weston asked, such beseeching misery in his words.

"She still loves you, but she won't let herself."

"Impossible." Weston ran a hand across his brow. "That woman does what she wants."

In his heart, he was holding up his hands in surrender to her. He'd been holding them up for almost twenty years.

"Does she?" Marijohn asked.

It was an insidious misperception, this idea that a strong woman was somehow able to do what she wanted when truly her strength came from doing the opposite.

Weston pressed his fingertips into a faint scar on the inside of his wrist. "Maybe not."

"Listen," Marijohn began, "we're performing the *Merry* album for the public in a few days. Here, on Arlo's property."

Weston laughed. The sound was winsome and warm, with a fleck of pain. "Arlo is going to bust a nut."

"If he tries to stop it," Marijohn spoke directly, her hands holding tight to her mandolin. "You can't let him."

Weston shook his head. "Arlo can get anyone to do anything. It's been like that since we were kids."

"There's got to be at least one person who can get Arlo to change his mind. Someone he owes. Someone he trusts." Marijohn slid her hand down the neck of her instrument. "And I figured that might be you."

Weston's shoulders sank into the couch behind him. "You overestimate me."

Marijohn remembered the ecstatic longing in Elle's eyes when she spoke about Weston, every time she played one of the songs she'd written for him. "I don't think I do."

He sat up, leaning his elbows onto his knees. "Does Elle know you're here?"

Marijohn twisted a tuning peg with her hand. "No."

"She's gonna be pissed," Weston warned.

"I think"—she played one E string, then the other—"this will be worth her rage."

He grinned at her slowly, a hook digging into the side of his cheek. "Do you know what you're doing, taking on the great Elle Harlow?"

"Absolutely not."

He laughed again, deep and loud, as if he'd just come a little back to life, too.

"Never, in my wildest dreams." He pointed at the mandolin. "Will you play for me? I've never heard it."

Marijohn strummed a B minor, the first note of "Heal Nothing." She played through the ballad, a flicker of Elle, Josie, and Merry—a marriage of all three.

"Your mother would be proud of your moxie," Weston said when she'd finished.

Marijohn strapped her mandolin to her back. "You think I got it from her?"

"No," he said. "I think it's all yours."

Marijohn stood, met Weston eye to eye. "When we come, be ready," she said. "And not just for the concert."

"You're hard to refuse." His eyes were softly green and constant, like Marijohn's favorite oak trees in the woods. "Anyone ever tell you that?"

"I need one more thing," she added as she headed for the door. "An address."

Back in the Chevy, Lazarus had woken up. When Marijohn climbed behind the driver's seat, he stretched his arms behind his head. His muscles tensed beneath the thin cotton T-shirt he'd somehow managed to keep crisp and white. He felt nearer to her now than when she'd left him.

He felt like the person she belonged to.

"Lazarus," Marijohn said, "Elle told me who my mother is."

He sat up so fast the tiny silver cross on his rearview mirror began to sway. "Who is it?"

"Josie Starling."

He scanned his memory for the name. "The recluse?"

She nodded. "I just got her address."

"And you want to go." His eyebrows lifted. "Right now."

"I do."

It felt like searching for that meteor before it sank into the river, not wanting to miss out on a miracle, a holy answer to the questions she'd always had.

"Marijohn," he said. "This might be a terrible idea."

"I know."

Laz turned it over in his mind, and she witnessed a shift in her friend. It didn't matter where he went—Nashville, college, or beyond. He still belonged to her, too.

"You navigate." He pulled out a map. "I'll drive."

The distance that had spanned between them since the meteor struck had only strengthened all the ways they were good together—Laz, the one who spoke caution at the edge of oncoming danger. Marijohn, the one who dove in without looking back.

They drove from the new-money section of Nashville toward the old-money. The Chevy passed curb-lined streets, mailboxes made to look like wooden ships, wrought iron gazebos, trees that arced overhead like holiday wreaths.

When they pulled up to the Starlings' brick drive, Laz put the truck in park and shut off the engine. For a minute, he tapped his fingers on the armrest. His brown eyes took in Marijohn's face, settling on her lips for the briefest moment before meeting her stare.

"Do you want me to come in?" he asked.

She did.

"No," she said. "I want her to see that I'm fearless."

Lazarus pulled himself out of the truck and met her in front of the

Chevy's grille, leaning toward her as she stared at the giant house. Parched boughs of holly hung above the shutters.

"This house is spooky as shit," Laz said.

His mouth hovered just over her shoulder.

"What if she doesn't want to see me?" Marijohn asked.

"Hold on," he whispered.

Laz leaned in through the Chevy's driver's side window. She tried not to look at the strip of tan skin between the hem of his shirt and the belt of his jeans. He grasped the mandolin by the neck, then handed it to her. The strings chimed beneath his touch.

"For strength," he said.

"Thank you." She held her instrument close. "For coming."

"I'll be here waiting," Lazarus said.

After he climbed back into the cab, the air grew quiet. Marijohn peered at the stand of willows around the side of the house, ancient and still. She thought she saw an apparition wandering through the trees.

At the front door, she rang the bell. Nobody answered, so she rang again. When no one answered after the third attempt, she walked around the broad side of the mansion. There, beneath one of the willows, stood a striking woman in a soft pink dress ill-suited for winter. She was too thin and too tired, and she was real. As she leaned against the willow's trunk, she startled at the shush of Marijohn's feet in the garden.

She turned, and they beheld each other for the first time in eighteen years.

Marijohn held her mandolin in front of her, as if it were a bouquet. "I—" she began, and then she stopped because the woman at the willow looked like she'd seen a ghost.

"Marijohn," Josie said.

"I just—" Marijohn was sweating, and shaking, and trying to stand her ground.

"Elle told you." There was a tremor in her cheek. "To punish me."

"Punish?" Marijohn's heart galloped beneath her ribs. "She doesn't even know I'm—"

"Do you need money?" Josie cut her off. Her voice had flatlined, even as she started to claw at the belt on her dress with her fingers.

Marijohn was stunned. "No, I—"

She couldn't finish whatever it was she had wanted to say. The strings of her mandolin shrieked as it slipped in her hands.

Josie inspected her with a clinical gaze, as if seeing a foal being born. "You look like her," she said.

This was it—an answer to Marijohn's questions. She wanted them all. "Who?" she asked.

"Jaclyn, my sister." Josie's voice was frayed. "Your aunt."

"I didn't know you had a sister." Marijohn took a step toward her. "What is she like?"

Josie withdrew, first knocking into the tree trunk and then staggering back. A faded blond curl fell out of place. "I—" She searched the ground as if she'd lost something, then turned toward the house.

"Wait," Marijohn called out, flinching at the desperation in her throat.

Slowly, Josie turned.

"I need to know. Did you—" Marijohn took a breath. "Did you ever sing to me?"

Everything Marijohn held in her heart hung between them. Every dark hope, every question, every dream.

"No," Josie said, her face the likeness of defeat. "I didn't."

She shifted toward the house.

"I'm sorry," Josie said, without looking behind her. Marijohn could see the ridge of her spine through the back of her dress. "I'm so sorry."

"Wait," Marijohn called out. "Please—"

But Josie fled out of the garden, through the mansion's back door, and shut off the light. The willows' branches bent in the soft breeze.

When Marijohn returned to the brick drive, Lazarus stepped out of his truck, and the slap of the driver's side door rattled the stillness. She had her mandolin on her back and her head in her hands. They stood together for a moment in front of the Chevy. For all the summer nights Lazarus and Marijohn had spent together, he'd never seen her cry. She buried her face in his chest, and he held her close. It was perfect between them then, two halves broken and bright.

"She didn't want to see me," Marijohn said.

"It's not your fault," Lazarus replied.

"I shouldn't have come. It wasn't fair to her."

"This isn't fair to either of you, Marijohn."

She pulled back to look at her friend. This was paining him. His face was drawn; his hands clung to the belt loops at her waist. The hush between them felt ominous, like they could no longer ignore that they were fully grown.

"Marijohn," he said. "Tell me what you need."

She knew the answer right away. "I need my dad."

Laz nodded, said not even one word about repeating the long drive. They climbed back into the truck and drove away, the Starlings' gray and monstrous house in the rearview mirror.

Hours passed before either of them said a word.

They hadn't talked about it—the letter he'd sent, the lyrics, the way he'd kissed her against the side of the truck. Lazarus was still so lovely, and still felt locked away.

"Why did you send me that letter?" she finally asked when they reached I-79.

The darkness around them felt sepulchral, each star a burning flame a million miles away.

"I wanted to tell you before too much time passed." His eyes were trained on the yellow lines stretched ahead. "I did love you. I do."

The confession twirled her around. It glimmered with consolation and condolence, both.

She felt it falling around her then, the dust of a dream that hadn't come true. The parallel in how she'd offered herself to her mother in the same way she'd offered herself to Lazarus at the end of the summer. Palms open, heart out. Nothing left to lose.

Getting pushed away.

"I see it now," she said. "Why you didn't kiss me back."

The silver chain on Laz's rearview mirror glimmered against the dashboard light.

"It wasn't because I didn't want to."

"You aren't anything like my mother," she said. "You know that."

The trees parted ways for them as they cut through the night.

"I'm one of the few people who can really hurt you, though," he said. "And that scares the shit out of me."

"Hurting isn't the worst thing."

"You've had enough of it, I think."

"I can decide that for myself."

"I love you, Marijohn." His hands twisted on the wheel as his eyes shot toward her. "But I can't stay in Lenora," he said. "And I don't know how to leave without hurting you."

"You act like it's inevitable."

"Because it is. We aren't kids anymore. Waiting for me is just going to hold you back. I'm not worth waiting for, anyway."

It had always been safe, trapping their feelings inside their music, where they'd never have to separate. But Marijohn didn't want to be safe anymore.

"Why do you always look in the mirror and see only the worst of yourself?" she asked.

He had no answer, and Marijohn had no strength to press—not when her mother hadn't wanted to see her. Not when Lazarus didn't think the two of them would keep.

It was after midnight by the time Marijohn returned to the edge of her woods. If it were summer, mosquitoes would have swarmed the yellow house's porch light. Their buzzing had been the score of every summer she'd spent here. The sound used to lull her to sleep. Now the snow lingered around her like a quiet scream.

She hadn't slept in more than twenty-four hours. Elle was asleep, and so was Abe. Marijohn found him slouched on the sofa beneath a flannel throw and the buttery yellow sheen of an old floor lamp. He'd left the light on for her, just as she knew he would.

After pulling the blanket over Abe's shoulder, she climbed two flights of creaky stairs to her dusty bedroom in the attic. The night was frigid, but the room felt hot. She thrust open the window, inhaled the breeze. All she wanted was to sing herself to sleep.

Marijohn closed her eyes, and a fresh melody came. Like water spilling through fingers, a steady pulse in the curve of a wrist. No thundering emotion—not regret, or fear, or anger—could slay her while she held that mandolin. The strings spoke a veiled language that lay deep in the inner courts of her spirit. She didn't need to understand the mystery. She only had to honor it.

A new song lay waiting for her in her fingertips, even though her body was weary. The mandolin's strings sighed against the frets. She rested her head on the window frame as she started to write a song for her mother.

Finally, Marijohn finished it.

There's something you should know
All I ask is that you hear me out
I know I can't make things grow
But you turn every sure thing into doubt

I have a place for sorrow
I hold a place for yours, too
You can love someone and miss them
Even as they stand right in front of you

I saw you last beneath your willow tree
And there my whisper grew to shout
It's one thing to say you hear me
And another one to hear me out

The best songs were always the ones that hurt, Marijohn and Lazarus believed. And this one hurt like hell.

A Little More

The next morning, Marijohn came down the stairs late in the day. She had a poured-out feeling in her chest from the song she'd written the night before. Abe had already left for the station, and Elle sat at the kitchen table, a Garfield mug of tea in her hand. Her hair was swept away from her face with two clips, and Marijohn caught a pensive luster in her expression as she tunneled her gaze into the tablecloth pattern. So often Elle appeared trapped between two places. She was metamorphosis incarnate, both the moth and the cocoon.

Outside, a rhythmic thwacking resounded from the far side of the house. Marijohn thought it must have been a lone lumberjack taking his chances in the woods until she saw Lazarus chopping firewood.

Barebacked and glistening, Laz worked outside the bay window by the table where Elle brought tea to her lips. He wasn't wearing his glasses.

"Christ," Elle said when she caught sight of him. "He's at it again."

Laz glanced at them through the window, a frown curving his lips before the axe sliced the air. At one time in her life, Marijohn would have told herself she could survive an era on those looks alone. She'd taught herself to need very little and to ask for even less. But that was before she'd stood in front of her own mother with her hands open in supplication, and Josie had walked away.

Miracle was, Marijohn now stood on the other side of it, still breathing.

She took the seat next to Elle and arched her back. Her whole body ached.

"He must be wanting to catch a glimpse of you," she said, looking at Laz.

"Trust me," Elle returned, "it ain't me he's here to see."

"How do you know?"

Laz stacked half a dozen logs against the side of the house, his hair tangling in the wind.

"I went out and asked him what the hell he was doing," Elle replied. "He said he wanted you to know he's trying to find the best version of himself."

No matter their fights or the distance between them, Lazarus would always come back to her. It was the kind of devotion people wrote songs about. The kind worth holding on to once it was found.

"So I told him," Elle added, "that our best selves rarely manifest before seven in the morning."

"You've been up for a while then," Marijohn hedged.

"I have." Elle touched the globular mound of melted dolls' eyes on the center of the table. "Trying to figure out what the hell this thing is."

"It's a paperweight," Marijohn answered. "I made it in metal shop."

"Let's make sure blacksmithing is not your plan B." Elle peered at the blob. "It looks sentient."

Marijohn laughed. There was something about Elle that made her feel gutsier, bolder. More like herself.

"I'm sorry I disappeared on you." Marijohn took the gold necklace at her throat and ran her finger along the pendant.

"You didn't disappear." Elle set down her mug. "You left a note."

Her kindness made Marijohn feel prodigal and unworthy. Exhausted, she pressed her forehead into the tablecloth. The embroidery sank into her eyelids. "I did something really stupid, Elle."

A scrape filled the kitchen as Elle pulled her chair closer to Marijohn's. "My best stories start that way."

"I went to see Josie." Marijohn just came out with it. "Even though you told me she wasn't ready."

Elle was silent for so long that Marijohn lifted her head from the table. Elle was watching her keenly, her face a flickering time capsule of all the selves she'd been. Marijohn could see the Elle from her album covers—the fire, the confidence, the grit. She could also see the Elle from the mountain—the one who understood a chronic case of sadness. There was even a third Elle now emerging in their shared quietude, one who no longer ran from brutal confessions but knew how to hold them, how to beckon them out of the dark.

"I shouldn't have done it," Marijohn said. "She didn't want me there."

Elle placed a hand on her back. "That doesn't mean what you did wasn't brave."

"It was stupid."

"If there's a line between bravery and stupidity"—Elle tugged on a strand of Marijohn's hair—"no one knows where it is."

Outside the window, Lazarus stacked the last of his firewood and threw his axe into the stump. Then he looked at Marijohn and raised his hand. Marijohn lifted her hand in return, and Laz nodded. Then he hopped into his Chevy and drove away.

"I woke up in the middle of the night"—Elle twirled her teabag around a spoon—"to the sound of the loveliest mandolin."

Marijohn leaned back, her eyes toward the ceiling. There was a crack growing there, the smallest hint that this house might be sinking like everything else in the woods. "I wrote a song," she said. "I'm not sure if it's any good."

"A warning, if I may." Elle pushed back from her chair and stood to place her mug in the sink. "People in the music industry are always going to tell you they know what good music is. And they don't."

"I'd still like to know what you think."

Elle watched her the way she might have with a daughter, if she'd had one.

"Show me," she said.

Marijohn took her to the attic, where they sat together on the window seat. Frigid air blew from the open window as Marijohn played an A minor followed by a G chord on her mandolin. The strings sounded lofty and rueful, like water dripping from leaves after it rained. It had been a long while since she'd sung for anyone on her own.

I have a place for sorrow
I hold a place for yours, too
You can love someone and miss them
Even as they stand right in front of you

"You know your story doesn't end with a mother who left you behind," Elle said, her voice bone-dry as the sound of the mandolin faded into the wooded air once Marijohn had finished. "This is only where it begins."

Marijohn leaned her head against the window frame. "It seems like it's already over."

"Trust me," Elle said. "Whatever you think is the end probably isn't."

Lazarus's firewood sat in a neat stack outside the window on the lawn, and a robin flew toward it.

"How do you do it?" Marijohn asked. "Write and sing about your most painful things?"

"You don't get over them," she answered. "That's the key."

"I don't want this song to be about her," Marijohn said, feeling the nakedness in her words.

"Honey," Elle said, shielding her eyes and looking across the forest freckled with balsams, "I don't think you get to choose."

Tomorrow, they'd have to leave for Nashville. The day after that, they'd bring Elle back from the dead by way of Arlo's royal lawn. But today, the afternoon spreading wide open before them, they didn't play any Elle Harlow songs. Elle pressed into Marijohn as a songwriter in her own right instead.

"The part of you that you think is so unlovable, so ugly, so broken?" Elle said. "That's what people need to hear in your music."

Slowly, Marijohn told Elle all her secrets. They both knew there was no separating the song from the story that inspired it. She told her about meeting Josie, about Lazarus, and the circles it had sent her in.

"I still can't decide if it was right or not," Marijohn admitted. "What I did."

"Right or not," Elle echoed. "That's good. Write it down."

This was Elle's way of life—sharing history, breaking down pain so she might rebuild its rhythm. Elle and Marijohn worked together late into the night, the chill of winter at their backs. Marijohn wrote down her lyrics while her breath clouded the air, while no stars hung in the sky, while snow crowned the trees, and while early-morning fog eventually drifted across the fields. Elle pushed her like they'd never have this time together again.

"Say more about less," she said.

"It's harder to write about the good things," she said.

"You should title your first album *Meteor*," she said.

"If you've written one song," she said, "you can write another."

Elle had put her life into the music she made, and she taught Marijohn to do the same.

"It was you, wasn't it?" Marijohn asked as she tucked her mandolin back into its case, just as the sun appeared on the far side of the woods. "The voice in my memory, singing in the dark."

Marijohn had been stowed in Elle's back seat through a night not unlike the one they'd just passed together. She started to understand then that though she'd had emptiness in her life, she'd also found so many divine melodies to fill it. Perhaps Elle had been the first person to sing to her, once upon a time.

"We'll never know for sure," Elle answered. "But I hope it was."

What happened next, the rest of the world knew. Elle Harlow reappeared on December 15, 1991, alongside Marijohn, and together they served a feast of music to a hungry crowd. Ardent fans flooded the grounds so fully that people perched on top of the stables and floated in the canoes on the lake. Abe had rigged the microphones and instruments with cables connected to the portable recording console in the back of his truck, which he'd plugged into an outlet on the side of the house. Arlo barricaded himself in the confines of his study, kissing a Marlboro and nursing a sloe gin fizz at the window. His sprawling lawn was blanketed with folks bundled up in the cold, their bodies giving off a heat, a hope, a hum.

Marijohn and Elle stood together on Arlo's tiled patio, an ocean of music fans waiting before them. Elle threw her gaze out across the audience like a fisherman casting a line. When she'd stepped out of Abe's truck, the tousled crowd went still at the sight of her. The last time she'd stood in front of a gathering this large she'd punched Josie Starling and run away.

Now Josie's daughter stood beside her for the first time in front of such a throng—and it would not be her last, Elle knew. They lingered in the silence, and Elle almost felt a slither of stage fright not for her music, but for the arrival of her full-blooded self. It was time to let go of her own disappearance, and she didn't know how to begin.

"Elle!" someone in the first row called out. "Where you been?"

Marijohn must have sensed Elle's hesitancy because she strummed a B minor. They'd planned to start with "Heal Nothing," the last song Elle had sung before she vanished. The chord resounding from Merry's mandolin steadied Elle's heart, and they began.

I watched you bleed from behind the door.

Elle's whole life had begun when she lived that lyric. And now, the rest of Merry's songs took flight right after.

Elle nailed the edgy melancholy of the young woman she'd been at eighteen when she wrote those songs, now colored by the command of living half a lifetime since. Marijohn played like the marvel she was, her voice branding its harmony on every single heart let loose in Arlo's tall grass.

Yet Elle would remember most what she didn't do that night. Elle didn't state the album was hers. She didn't lament that it had been stolen. She didn't confirm or deny her own existence, and she didn't compete with her younger self in a match Arlo had determined she'd lose. Instead, she brought all her flaws and scars with her, in every iteration.

Elle wanted the world to hear her music her way.

The ease of it shook her. She'd been hunting for a grand gesture of epic scale to prove to the world that Josie's *Soldier* album belonged to her—a dead quail offered at the family table, a grave dug in unyielding ground.

No one gets out of here alive
So let's do a little more than try to survive.

But Elle discovered then, while singing through "A Little More" with Marijohn beside her, that Merry's legacy never would have been found in a single momentous action anyway. It would endure in the sum of small ones. That was how women's songs had spread for generations—from one heart to the next, to the next.

Elle and Marijohn ended their performance with "Take Me to the River." Even though "Heal Nothing" was the album's most popular ballad, this one had always been Elle's favorite. It called to mind her final moments with Merry, the weight of what she'd done. Since she'd left her mountain, Elle believed the most important truth about her was how Merry had died. Now that Elle had met Marijohn, she knew it was no longer true. The most important thing was how Elle chose to live.

Applause sounded from every hollow on the Weston property—from the lake all the way to the tiny cabin by the woods.

"Play 'School Girl Crush,' Elle!" someone called out from the expanse.

"Play 'Love Beneath the Mandolins'!"

The crowd begged for an encore, and Elle gripped the neck of her Taylor. There were many circumstances in Elle's life that she'd change if she could—the deaths of her brother and Merry, and the outcome of her time with Josie and Weston, both. But Elle would never trade one second of her time with Marijohn. The young woman had done as she promised—she reminded Elle why she loved to sing.

Marijohn was bright and wry and oh, so serious. Elle got a kick out of never quite knowing what would come out of her mouth. She'd never been prouder to perform a duet. If there was any eventuality Elle feared deep in the canals of her mind it was that if there ever came a time for Marijohn to step out on her own, she would not do it. Elle wanted to share Marijohn with the world just as much as she wanted to share Merry.

The audience kept on, frantic for more.

"Marijohn." Elle stepped back from the mic. "It's your turn."

Marijohn went seasick. "You know I can't."

"Yes, you can."

"Will you sing with me?"

"I'll be right here. Just sing it slow till you find your groove."

Marijohn nodded, timid for a moment before stepping closer to the front of the patio.

"Y'all," Elle addressed the crowd, "this is my mandolinist, Marijohn Shaw. She's an incredible songwriter, and she's going to sing one of her own tonight."

Elle hit an A minor, and Marijohn began.

There's something you should know
All I ask is that you hear me out

Elle stayed back as Marijohn played so she could watch the crowd fall in love with her. On the periphery of Arlo's mansion, right at the corner, Elle caught a flicker of movement. She turned and found Josie there, watching her daughter sing. Marijohn couldn't see her, and it struck Elle then what bravery it had taken for Josie to come bear witness to her beautiful child in full bloom. She wasn't ready now to know her daughter, and perhaps she never would be. But maybe one day she would.

When the encore ended, it took over five hours for everyone to file out. Elle stayed longer than anyone, greeting each fan who waited in line. When the last of them had gone, Elle took in the vast grounds before her. She was alone—Arlo's house was dark. Marijohn and Abe had left for the motel hours earlier. Once again Elle found herself in that liminal moment between a performance and real life, but this time it anchored her. The letdown, the release, the breeze.

Since the chance for sleep had gone, Elle went for a walk. A small cabin shone in the distance, its own vivid planet. There was a campfire lit—and a line of mason jar luminaries glowing along the path to the lake.

Elle was certain those lights hadn't been there before the concert ended.

She wondered then what kind of example she set for Marijohn when she sang about love onstage but never kept it anywhere else—if it cast a shadow over her young friend instead of letting her shine. Letting her love. This felt more urgent now than it had two hours earlier, before Elle stood in front of a crowd and declared herself not only alive but aging. Herself but better. Hungry but strong. And yet Elle still grappled with the daily tide of growing older. No one lived forever the way a song would. Always, Elle woke in the morning, asking herself what she'd do if today was the day she could no longer sing.

She trailed the path toward the water, just as she might have done as a girl, wishing to get closer to the river, to fall into anything that shook with life. There had always been power in it, a girl walking. A girl driving. A girl moving. A girl leaving. What remained was what had always been—stones and sand, water and women singing their sorrows and their strength.

The same was true of Elle Harlow, a woman now forty, whose life had only just begun.

She strode down the dock, freshly aware of how hot she felt. The night had cooled, but she was burning.

Quickly she shed her clothes in the dark. Her breath made a column of smoke in the air. Then she launched herself off the dock, crashing into the frigid water. She sank down, down, seeing nothing, her hair floating around her like the body of a serpent. She liked this ache on her skin, the slap that reminded her she could still feel pain.

If she could hurt, she could still love. And if she could love, she could still sing. Elle had proven to herself tonight that Arlo, no matter how powerful, could never take that away.

Elle took her time floating to the surface, suspending her own weight for a blessed moment. When she finally pushed through, the glow of a lantern awaited her at the edge of the dock.

Finally, she thought. *Arlo came to say his piece.*

She squinted in the light, wiped water from her eyes as she treaded.

"Elle," the light bearer said, and she grew hot all over again.

It was not Arlo who had found her. It was Weston.

Love Beneath the Mandolins

Elle covered herself, even as she sank below the waterline. "What are you doing here?" she hissed.

"What are *you* doing here?" Weston repeated, the lantern casting a glow across his face that made his bold features look hazy and shaded. Elle caught the stark green of his irises, the tremor in his lip. The flushed skin near his pulse.

"I thought I'd never see you again," he said.

"So sorry to disappoint."

Elle had meant to snap at him, but her heart had no stamina for it. Not when he stood in front of her, still looking at her like she was the only woman in the world. Her words just sounded true instead.

"Don't joke about that." His whole face was gutted. "I looked *everywhere* for you, Elle."

"You didn't." She spoke as if it had wounded her, as if she had never wanted to be lost.

"I did." His voice fell into the water like rain. "No one on that mountain would talk to me. Not even your mother."

Weston felt deeply deceived, just as Elle did, and she wondered what her life might have been if she and Weston had never left the woods. *Wounds from a Lover* wouldn't exist, but she'd be holding none of the hurt it had caused.

"Can you get out?" he asked. "It has to be freezing in there."

"No."

"Elle," he said. "Your lips are blue. Get out."

"No," she answered, clinging to the paltry boon of her own dissent.

"Fuck it," Weston said, and set the lantern down. He began to unbutton his shirt.

"Don't you dare," she said.

His pants fell to the ground, and the clang of his belt buckle hitting the dock sliced through the night. Elle forced herself to look at the sky.

"You give me no choice," he said.

Within seconds, a splash broke the still water and a wave pushed toward her. Elle closed her eyes and tried to dampen the heat of the past between them—the desire, the betrayal, the pain. When she opened her eyes again, Weston swam before her, wild-eyed and furious and freezing. The cold clasp of water was so scathing that Elle couldn't stop herself.

She splashed him.

Elle splashed Weston so hard he began to cough, and he shielded his face with his arm. Then he splashed her back. The two of them went on this way for three full minutes until Elle's eyes stung and Weston swam away to catch his breath.

"I told you," she said, waves slapping against her neck. "I told you everything about Merry. And still you went and did this."

This. Lied to her. Used her. Made her love him.

"Elle," Weston said.

How long she'd wanted to hear him say her name. How it tore at her now.

"You never let me explain," he said.

"What does it matter?" she asked, even though it did.

She'd known for a long time that Weston had stolen something more precious to her than the mandolin. Only now did it have a name. *Faith*.

Elle once had so much faith in Weston, and in who she was with him. The ruins of it swirled around them, a dark and endless current.

"Please," he said. "Come inside." He looked at the cabin on the other side of the water.

"You live here now." Elle's teeth chattered. He'd seemed so in love with the Pennsylvania woods, once upon a time. He'd made her fall in love with them, too. "With *Arlo?*"

"I've always lived here."

"There is so much I never knew about you." Elle's heart sagged. "And somehow you knew me better than anyone."

Both of Elle's albums had been the result of meeting someone incandescent who broke open her life. Merry and Weston. It surprised Elle that she no longer ached for that kind of inspiration. Instead, she wanted to be that spark for someone else. She longed to be monumental not for a generation, but for one single, enduring heart.

"That's how you knew me, too," Weston said. "I promise you."

Elle treaded water, and her fingers went numb. She didn't want to admit it, but she was cold. Her lips parted as she shivered.

"I don't forgive you," she said.

He pointed toward the ladder by the dock. "I won't ask you to."

Weston averted his eyes as she climbed up the ladder and put on her clothes. After he did the same, they walked side by side down a dirt path that led to the cabin. It might have been a nice night, the moon like an opal in the sky, but Elle could no longer tell. Was it winter of 1991, or summer of 1972? She could smell it already—the wood shavings, the glue. The curly maple. The leftovers of their season in the woods.

Her steps faltered on a rock, and Weston steadied her by the elbow. His hand gripped her with that familiar vigor, the kind she'd witnessed when he brought his mandolins to life. Elle waited a moment before she took her arm away.

It had been years since anyone had touched her like that.

Weston's cabin was warm and bright, thick quilts on the old leather sofa, his woodworking tools lined up against the wall next to his mandolin. He lived in a single-room structure with a four-poster bed by the fireplace, a kitchenette with a loaf of bread on top of the stove. The air smelled like cinnamon.

He'd made a life for himself here. A home.

Elle considered what she'd built over the last two decades, and the answer was nothing. She didn't deem that choice as a fault—it was a necessary undoing, like a field lying fallow or a flame tamped so it didn't burn the whole house down. Yet even fallow fields get turned over, in time. Even ashes could be made into something new.

Weston poured her a cup of tea. She watched the flex of his back as he turned away to change his shirt, the way his navy Henley clung like a second skin. Elle's hands used to know those muscles as well as her own. She'd once traced them in the rain with the tip of her finger.

She used to think of her body as a traitor for clinging tightly to every memory she was desperate to forget. All it had been, though, was the most faithful reflection of everything she wanted but would never allow herself to have. Elle had been so young when she and Weston were together, yet she'd felt so old. Now, she didn't feel old in the least.

She blinked, realized Weston was watching her. *Weston.*

"I called you by your last name," she began, "when I really should have been calling you Luke."

He eased himself onto the opposite end of the couch.

"Is that why you never told me your name? Because of Josie?" Elle still hated saying her name aloud.

His beard was trimmed, his eyes were emerald. "I never told you because you never asked."

"Bullshit."

"You didn't tell me who you were, either," Weston argued.

"You already knew."

"I thought you didn't want me to," he said. "That's why you were hiding."

"So were you."

Weston leaned his elbows onto his knees, his head resting in his hands. "You know how you told me once that Arlo understood you because he's got family?" He looked up at her. "That's me. I'm the family that needed him. When my father injured his hand and couldn't work anymore, it was

Arlo's parents who took us in. Weston Studios provided for my family once it opened." He lifted his mug, and then he set it down. "Listen, I know Arlo is ruthless about money. And an asshole. But he's not so self-serving as you think."

Elle didn't attempt to empathize. Didn't want to have even one thing in common with Arlo Weston anymore.

"All Arlo needed was 'Luke,'" Weston said. "So that his story was tied to a real person. He never released my last name so no one would dig too deep to find me. Once I got to the woods to lay low that summer, I didn't want to leave. My life had gotten too backward on Music Row. Too toxic. So I took my time, had nowhere else to be for once. And then you came." His hand gripped the cushion as he turned toward her. "Everything between us was real, Elle. All of it. It was everything else that was fake."

Elle looked toward Weston's mandolin sitting in the corner, the same one he'd played every night at the campfire that summer. "The war," she said. "You didn't get drafted?"

"They didn't want me." Weston's finger trailed the seam of the couch. "I have a bad heart."

"You don't have a bad heart," she said, too quickly to stop herself. Elle pulled her knees to her chest. "The morning you left. Why didn't you say goodbye?"

"That mandolin, Elle." He avoided her question, but not her stare. "I know you didn't want me to touch it, but it was rotting. You were just watching it die. And maybe I shouldn't have taken it. Maybe I should have asked—but you treated that instrument like a rotted thing was all you deserved, and it's not true. It never was."

He waited for her to speak, but she couldn't.

"I wanted to restore it for you," he went on. "Fix it so it could actually live. So you could hear it again. I thought once you heard it, it would change everything."

Elle had started to cry, and she didn't care. She didn't want to be impenetrable anymore. "What happened?"

"I needed some supplies from my main workshop off I-79—where I was supposed to be. When I got there, Josie was waiting. The time had come for me to play my part, and Arlo had sent her. Said we needed to get our stories straight if we were gonna convince anyone we were in love. I could have gotten in her car and left, or I could have brought her back to the cabin. And I couldn't do that to you, Elle. I didn't want you to see me with her."

Elle's cup trembled as she held it in her hands. "So you let it happen on live television instead."

"I brought the mandolin with me that night," Weston pressed on. "And put it in your car. All I had was a big wicker trunk. Then when I saw you and the instrument was all you cared about, it killed me." He ran a hand through his hair. "I'm not proud of it, all right? I was mad at myself for being hurt by something that was my own doing. Something I could have fixed. Then you punched Josie in the nose and no one ever heard from you again."

"Somehow," Elle said slowly, "you're making this my fault."

"What I'm doing"—Weston kept his voice even, his eyes desperate and keen—"is letting you know I always meant to give it back."

They were talking about the mandolin, and they were talking of other things, too.

"That's not all that was in that trunk," she said.

Doubt crossed his face. "What do you mean?"

"There was a baby girl in that trunk, too." Elle's cup clattered as she set it down. "She played with me tonight."

He covered his mouth with his hand. "Marijohn."

"You were right when you said hearing that instrument again would change everything. It brought me back to life."

He still clutched his jaw. "So you think it was meant to be."

"I don't believe in 'meant to be.'"

"Neither do I." Weston leaned into the pillow next to him. "You know that mandolin didn't have any magic in it, right? It never did. That magic was you."

Elle looked out the window, where Arlo's mansion presided in the distance. Weston came closer, ever so slightly. He smelled like wood and autumn and precious things that were lost. He stared at her, and Elle felt like she might melt away.

"What are you staring at?" she said.

"Your hair." He reached out a hand toward her. "It has a lot of knots. From the water."

Her hand flew onto her head, where she found a nest of tangles. "From your splashing."

"You're the one who jumped in and wouldn't get out." He stood and stalked toward his dresser.

"Where are you going?"

"To get a brush."

"You have a brush?"

He gave her a look over his shoulder. "I've got hair, don't I?"

Weston sat beside her. Elle reached for the brush, but he held it out of reach. "Let me," he said.

"No."

"It's going to hurt," he said.

"I know it's going to hurt."

"Elle." His voice was so candle-soft it could have burned the house down. "Please."

Just as she hadn't been able to eighteen years ago, she couldn't say no.

She slid down to the floor, and Weston settled himself behind her, a knee on either side. He set down the brush beside him and gently took her hair into his hands. His fingers grazed the nape of her neck, and she bit the inside of her cheek. Elle had missed him. Missed him so much she couldn't stop herself from shaking.

He took a section of her hair in an easy grip and began to brush. Slow and smooth, like music.

"Where have you been, Elle?" he asked.

Hurt laced his voice. He'd thought she was dead, and she'd wanted him to. All this time she'd meditated on what he'd taken from her without any thought of what she'd taken from him. She felt it there still, the electricity between them. Not just longing or lust, but a loyalty. A kind of love Elle had felt only once in her life, with him.

"I wanted to disappear on my own terms," she said. "Instead of somebody else's."

"And now?" He took a new section of her hair between his fingers.

She leaned her head back and closed her eyes. "Now Arlo thinks nobody will want me anymore."

He combed his fingers against her scalp. His skin was warm where hers was cold. "That crowd tonight suggests otherwise."

"My music isn't like these singers now. Upbeat and lively. Sophisticated. Produced."

"I'm not talking about your songs." He slid the brush down the crown of her head. "You think you don't have anything to offer anyone outside of your music, but you do."

"You sound like my mother."

He pressed on, his hand settling at the back of her neck. "Is that why you were gone so long? To see who you were without your songs?"

"That's just it." She felt his skin on hers like a bracelet of heat. "There is no me without them. The best songs I got, nobody's even heard."

"I'd like to hear them." He set down the brush, and Elle turned to look at him.

"I don't want to play the guitar anymore tonight." She finally felt herself shedding an old shame, wanting to feel free, the way she once had with him in 1972.

"What, then?"

Weston's eyes slowly traced the whole of her. He was hungry and real, as exposed as he'd ever been. Just like Elle. This night already spoke of a thousand impossibilities, a glimpse into what no longer was.

"Josie." Elle said the name again after not speaking it for years. "What happened between you?"

"We were never in love. It was a favor to Arlo, and nothing more."

What he called "nothing" still stood like a gravestone at the head of what might have been. As he once did, Weston knew what she was thinking. "Just ask."

"Did you ever kiss her?"

He shook his head.

"Sleep with her?"

He met her stare. "No."

Tears slid toward Elle's jaw.

"You want to know my secret?" Weston bent toward her, somehow too close and not close enough. She could feel the soft scrape of his beard on her neck as he spoke. "Here's what I never told you. That album? The one they call *Soldier*? I played backup instrumentals on it. I fell in love with every single word and knew even then there was no way Josie Starling had written those songs. And that was when I felt done with it. Sickened by every fake thing I'd help build in that town. So I went to the woods when Arlo asked. When I told you everybody in Nashville wants to turn you into someone you're not, I meant it."

Weston touched her chin just barely with the edge of his finger. "That voice in the songs I fell in love with? It was yours."

He'd said everything and nothing Elle longed to hear. Weston didn't wait for her to respond. "I know that I ruined us, and it's too late now to fix it."

"We had such a short time together," Elle began, rising onto her knees in front of him. "And somehow I loved you so much."

He made to speak, but she stopped him. "I wasted so long feeling like a fool for it, and I'm done with that now."

His thumb traced her jaw and his eyes traveled her skin, like he'd never get enough. "So many times I thought about what I'd say to you if I ever got the chance," he said. "You told me once you'd never been anybody's beautiful thing. But you were mine, Elle. From the moment I pointed that stupid rifle in your face. I never should have made you believe you weren't."

Elle stopped nodding. Apologies held no magic. They couldn't undo the past; they couldn't promise a future. But they did return something lost to this right-now moment, the one neither of them would ever have again.

"Please," he said, "tell me what you're thinking."

She reached out and ran a hand through his hair, still rusty and thick. "You said you wouldn't ask me to forgive you."

He closed his eyes, just for a moment. "I'm not." He leaned into her palm. "I'm telling you that when you asked me to leave with you, I wish I'd said yes."

She took his face in her hands, his skin rough and hot. He met her halfway and brought his lips to hers. They both startled, as if their minds only now recalled what their bodies had never forgotten—how well they fit, how good it felt for his teeth to find her lower lip, her earlobe. The sigh she'd only ever made when she was with him. Weston threaded his hands into her hair. She wanted to feel all of him against all of her. It was a need that drowned out reason, remorse, and even fear.

"Elle," he said into her neck as he fought to catch his breath. "You have no idea how—"

"Yes," she cut him off. "I do."

His hands traced her thighs until they found her hips. He pulled her even closer, pulled her shirt over her head. Weston looked at her bare skin like he wanted to eat her alive.

"Fuck, Elle," he said, sliding his lips across her shoulder. "The things you do to me."

She might have cried then, if he hadn't been kissing her everywhere and praising every part of her and coming apart on his own, if she hadn't felt the same way—that here was *her* Weston, her in-the-woods Weston, come back to her, everything he used to be and so much more.

They did no talking after that. He lifted her to his bed, undressed her and then himself. She took what she wanted, while digging her nails into his chest. It was rough, then it was tender, then they were one.

"I never forgot you," she said to him and to the night at the window, the fullness inside her, the sensation that promised the best was still on its way.

"Never," Weston said, his back slick with sweat. And as he said it, she felt that he meant it with all his body, all his heart.

This was how Elle knew sex was created for a woman in her forties, in her fifties, and beyond, after she was told her desirable days were gone. How wrong Arlo had been. For the first time, Elle pitied him, because surely he'd never felt abundance anywhere close to this, no matter his riches or his power.

Weston kept on, for a second time, then a third, then collapsed against her and fell asleep. Her back molded against his front, the gold chain on his neck cool against her shoulder blade. He held her like she might never come back, like he never should have let her go.

What truly bound two lives together? It wasn't just blood, or time, or secrets. Sometimes it was forged in the unlikely inheritance of lost objects. Found histories. Mistakes and regret reborn into second chances in the early-morning light.

Wounds from a Lover

Marijohn couldn't escape a gnawing dread as she waited the following morning at her motel in Nashville and didn't see Elle's truck pull into the lot. The concert had passed like quicksilver, the flash of a camera so swift she could have blinked and missed it. Marijohn waited all day, her eyes fixed on the Christmas trees strung with bright lights around the property, and then the next day, too.

On the third morning, the motel's housekeeper let her into Elle's room, and it stood just as she'd left it—her hairbrush, her gold necklace, her favorite boots. Marijohn could hear her voice, rasping like trees in the wind, singing—

No one gets out of here alive
So let's do a little more than try to survive

This was how Marijohn knew what Elle had done—because even after less than a few weeks together, Marijohn knew her. Elle was mercurial and flickering, a song in the wind. And of all the things Marijohn would never understand, she still knew that this was what losing someone felt like.

A day later, her truck was found abandoned on the bank of a river. For the second time in her life, Elle Harlow had disappeared.

• • •

Three months after she'd gone, the Opry hosted a celebration of Elle Harlow's body of work—all three albums' worth. It was meant to be an apology for the reunion concert they'd held for Josie Starling and her wartime love in 1973—even though Elle Harlow herself was nowhere to be found. The live recording of the *Merry* album was an instant success. Curiously, Arlo had come around after all. The record played on both country and mainstream radio stations, and music stores sold out of their cassettes and CDs overnight. Marijohn's telephone in Lenora was already ringing with producers keen to work with her.

Her dream had found her, even as she'd run from it.

Some fans still claimed that the Elle Harlow who appeared on Arlo's lawn that night was a fake, that the whole thing had been staged as a money-making endeavor, even though Elle had put on the show for free. Others insisted the album was still Josie's. Josie Starling, remaining true to her reclusive life, said nothing.

After Elle never showed at the motel, Marijohn didn't know where else to go but home. Spring arrived, snow melted, and she couldn't remember the last time she'd played her mandolin. Instead, she lay on the floor of her father's living room in front of the television, perusing a pamphlet about apartments outside of Nashville.

That night, folk and country singers alike gathered at the Opry in honor of Elle's career. Marijohn, too, could have spoken eloquently about Elle, if only she hadn't loved her as much as she did. They'd asked her to sing "Love Beneath the Mandolins," but she couldn't lift herself off Abe's fraying carpet to make the trip. She didn't want to watch a remembrance for Elle Harlow when an everlasting one already lit her from the inside out.

The phone rang. Instead of watching the live broadcast of Elle's work, she took the call. It was Lazarus.

"Come somewhere with me," he said.

He picked her up in his old Chevy, and together they drove their worn path toward the cliff at the edge of the woods. It was the end of March, and the temperature had risen in the past week. A thin layer of vanishing ice crusted the edges of the hemlocks. The forest had lost the lush bloom of last summer, but it left a stark, crystalline beauty in its wake—the kind of nakedness a landscape reveals only to those who have always loved it.

After the new year, Laz had returned to college to continue studying accounting. He'd canceled his deal with Weston Studios. When his spring break began, he returned to Lenora—and Marijohn was his first telephone call.

"Laz," she said, when his steering wheel cut to the left and the tires skidded over a patch of ice. The bluffs stood just beyond them in the dark. "I don't have my mandolin."

"You don't need it."

He reversed as far as he dared up against the edge of the cliff. Its lip had softened, slowly crumbling into the ravine beneath it. She hopped out of the truck, rounded the side to pull down the tailgate. The sky was clear, the air in her lungs crisp and sharp.

"Wait," Laz said, as his breath mixed with hers. "I want to show you something."

He took her elbow and together they strode toward the tip of the cliff. Then Lazarus kept walking until he stepped right off the edge of it onto the steep hillside below.

"Laz," she said. "What are you doing?"

His hand grasped a sapling to steady himself. "The ground is going to fully thaw soon," he said. "If we're going to do this, we need to do it now."

She took hold of the sapling and climbed down after him. After ten paces or so, Laz took a flashlight from his back pocket and shined it against the ravine. She crouched beside him, her knees sinking into the cold earth.

"There," he said, training the light on a patch of dirt.

"What is it?"

He took her palm and pressed it against the ground. "Feel that?"

Her hand vanished into soil up to her wrist. Then her fingers brushed against something jagged and hard. She started to dig.

Laz held the light as she uncovered the expanse of a rock with a gunmetal sheen, an onyx hue. An outline that had been seared into shape as it shot through the atmosphere.

"The third piece of the meteor," she said. "You found it."

He nodded. Where scientists and woodsmen and hunters had failed, Lazarus Wright had triumphed. And true to his nature, he never flaunted it.

"Why are you showing me this now?" she asked.

He regarded her in the scant moonlight, his eyes honest and imploring and relentlessly brown.

"Because I'm sorry about Elle," he said. "And I wanted you to know—sometimes lost things are never truly lost at all."

She didn't know what to say, so she said the truth. "You should write that down."

He let out that blithe laugh of his, the one she longed to hear on New Year's Day and the Fourth of July and every other moment marked for fireworks after night had fallen.

"So." His chin jutted toward the rock. "Do you want to take it, or leave it?"

She didn't hesitate. "Leave it."

The third piece of the meteor was no less of a story, even if no one knew what had happened to it. Marijohn had come to believe in a different kind of knowing—one of intangibility and intuition—that lived in the echo it created.

She and Lazarus climbed out of the ravine and sat side by side on the tailgate of his truck. Marijohn wrapped herself in one of the blankets he still kept in the back.

The wind blew, collecting a crew of blackbirds into a balsam.

"There's something I still can't understand," Laz said. "Why aren't you trying to record 'Namesake'? Or 'Hear Me Out'? I know studios are calling you."

Beside her, Lazarus waited in earnest for her reply. She didn't have a good answer.

"Can I tell you what I think?" Laz asked, long after the heat from the truck's engine had gone cold.

When she nodded, he said, "I think you're afraid those songs will never be any better than they were when we first sang them in the woods, or when you sang with Elle." He stretched his arms behind his head as he gazed toward the stars. "And you know what? They won't be."

"You give shitty pep talks," she said, but she turned toward him and found his steady gaze locking onto hers.

"Nothing will ever be better than you and me singing to each other, with no one else around to hear it. But that's why people love a good song," he said. "They know it was lived."

Distant stars sparked in the night above them, and the air filled with the trickle of ice beginning to melt.

"Look at you, being so smart." Marijohn pinched the sleeve of his shirt. "Now that you're getting a college degree."

Laz pushed up his glasses. "Just remember when you start making your millions, you're going to need a good accountant." He winked. "And you better give me a call."

That was the moment Marijohn knew this story between Lazarus and her was a long one. She wanted it slow—one word, one lyric, one note at a time. She didn't know how it would end, but it wasn't over. Theirs was a tale still being told, a song still being sung.

By the time they left the cliff and Marijohn returned home, Elle's concert had ended. Since she'd missed it, Marijohn decided to hold one of her own remembrances instead.

On her VCR, she replayed the video that had entranced an entire nation six months earlier. No one who had seen this footage truly knew her. They didn't know she felt naked without her mandolin and had molten songs in her blood. They couldn't feel or see the power she had. She hadn't disappeared when the meteor struck—she lay there in the truck bed, beneath Lazarus's body. Just like Elle had been for eighteen years, just as she felt now, Marijohn was invisible.

But she wasn't lost.

Laz sang on film, and then came a flash of brightness like they'd never seen. A streak in the sky. The video cut out just after Lazarus reached for her and held on. This video, less than three and a half minutes long, had been enough to bring Elle Harlow out of hiding.

Now Marijohn knew that the meteor was drawn to them—not to Lazarus and her, but to her and Elle. The two of them had their own gravity, strong enough to pull something out of the sky. They were the miracle born from that night, the phenomenon.

As she watched the footage, Marijohn took up her mandolin. For the first time, she wrote a song about the shooting star.

I was there when a star struck the ground
My heart broke and I still hear the sound
Nothing left but lost things getting found
I'll wait for you to come back around

She'd never forget the way the ground shook that night. She'd thought it was the meteor—now she heard the sound for what it truly was.

It was the sound of herself, breaking through.

A week later, Marijohn packed a box full of her keepsakes to take with her from her father's house. She was heading back to Nashville to record music of her own for an indie label with women, by women—just as Elle Harlow had taught her.

Even though she was gone, Elle had granted Marijohn everything she'd had when she was eighteen and sang for Arlo in the back of an old parking lot: a voice, an instrument, and guts. All Marijohn had to do was try.

They hadn't had enough time together, Elle and Marijohn. How much could ever be enough? Elle had written as much on a scrap of paper trapped in glass at the center of Abe's shop.

Blood holds memory, same as the mind
Easier to shed, harder to find
You took her voice and left me behind
Carving a wound that ain't the bleeding kind

Elle hadn't set it to music yet. The song was incomplete.

But this piece of her had not disappeared, only because Marijohn remembered it. Her father—who would follow her to Nashville as soon as he'd boxed up his relics and sold the station—taught her how to become the keeper of someone's past once they'd gone.

"One day," he said, "if you're lucky, someone will become the keeper of yours."

He'd done that for Elle—kept his love for her like a picture in a frame in case she ever came back. Marijohn's mother taught her there would always be something left undone. Like Elle's third outlaw, whose identity she never truly discovered.

Or did she?

Elle had never told Marijohn who the third outlaw was, but this didn't mean she never revealed it. When Marijohn replayed the song in her mind, she heard Elle's history resounding in every note. The first outlaw was Josie, quick and dirty. The second was Weston, smoldering slow. And the third outlaw was a different kind of love, the filial affection an older woman feels for a younger one. It had begun with Merry, but Elle had also loved Marijohn from the moment she saw her holding Merry's mandolin.

Elle had been Merry's keeper. Now, Marijohn was hers.

This was why Marijohn took her father's boat to that forgotten cabin deep in Lenora's woods a final time before she left town. When she arrived, she saw it had been swept clean. No trace of the luthier's workshop remained—not his tools, not the sawdust on the floor, or the coils of spare strings hanging from pegs on the wall. Only one item remained, and it sat on the plain carpenter's table in the heart of the room.

It was that old pink-and-white piece of plastic with Elle's signature heart right in the middle of it. The one Marijohn had rescued from the sinking woods, the one she'd given to Elle on the night they met. Beneath the gingham scrap was a note much like the one Marijohn had left when she'd needed to set off on her own. The swatch of paper had three words written on it, in Elle's hand—

I'm coming back.

It had taken almost twenty years for Elle and Weston to find their way back to each other. What might happen next for them, no one knew. Like a ballad written to mark the end of a long absence, they'd become part of a larger unmasking, a wider unknowing, a deeper undoing.

If Elle were standing inside this hallowed room, close enough to embrace, Marijohn would have told her one thing. The last time they'd stood outside Weston's cabin, Elle had said that love had to die for music to live. Marijohn knew now that was the only lie she ever told. The evidence of it hung in the air around her—like a flame kissing sky, a comet scarring night, a hand setting bone.

Some wounds are worth it.

TRACK LIST

MERRY

1. Hunger
2. Water Is a Woman
3. Shackle
4. Heal Nothing
5. A Little More
6. Take Me to the River
7. Leaving Song
8. Believe Me, Honey
9. Sing It Slow
10. If Only

WOUNDS FROM A LOVER

1. Daughter to Wife
2. Ruined Hearts
3. Shut Out the Light
4. How Do You Sleep (All Right at Night)
5. Dark Swim
6. Run
7. Third Outlaw
8. That Don't Mean You Ain't Lived
9. Wounds from a Lover
10. Love Beneath the Mandolins

Heal Nothing

by Elle Harlow

Bm   A
I watched you bleed from behind the door
D   A
Rain came down, didn't care what for
**   Bm   A**
Your gaze held mine till I felt the scar
D   A
Those we can't save tell us who we are

CHORUS:
Am
Try to heal everything, and
F
Try to heal everything, and
C   G
You'll heal nothing at all (x2)

Bm   A
I'll write you letters when I'm gone, though you won't write to me
D   A
A message in a bottle, getting lost inside your sea

Bm **A**

No pretty words will keep you, no picture on the wall

D **A**

Try to heal everything, and you'll heal nothing at all

Chorus (x2)

Hear Me Out

by Marijohn Shaw

Am
There's something you should know
G
All I ask is that you hear me out
Em
I know I can't make things grow
F
But you turn every sure thing into doubt

Am
I have a place for sorrow
G
I hold a place for yours, too
Em
You can love someone and miss them
F
Even as they stand right in front of you

Am
I saw you last beneath your willow tree
G
And there my whisper grew to shout

Em

It's one thing to say you hear me

F

And another one to hear me out

(x2)

Acknowledgments

Writing this book and bringing it into the world has been a truly wild, challenging, and glorious ride, and I wouldn't change one bit of it. I'm beyond grateful for my meteor of an agent, Meredith Kaffel Simonoff, who believed in this story from the beginning and never wavered. She is the reason this book is in your hands. My editor, Deb Futter, has the best eye and the best heart there is, and this story became the best version of itself once it hit her desk. Deb, you have created an environment where your authors can flourish personally and creatively, and I love getting to work with you.

The extraordinary team at Celadon is my favorite part of publishing a book. Huge thanks to Rachel Chou for steering the boat with such acumen and joy. Margaux Kanamori holds everything together and is a whip-smart, kind, and thoughtful editor, to boot. Thank you also to Anna Belle Hindenlang for always being publicist extraordinaire, Jennifer Jackson, Jaime Noven, Rebecca Ritchey, Gregg Fleischman, Anne Twomey, Ryan Doherty, Christine Mykityshyn, Carla Benton, Morgan Mitchell, Erin Cahill, Liza Buell, Christina McDonald, Yelizaveta Rogulina, Susie Brustin, and Emily Radell.

Deep thanks to The Gernert Company for being so steady and

wonderful. Rebecca Gardner and Nora Gonzalez, I'm so grateful for your care of my books here and abroad. To true phenom and friend Michelle Weiner at CAA, your love for this story gave me so much encouragement right when I needed it. Thank you for your expertise, your drive, your huge heart—and this book's perfect title.

I'm also indebted to countless authors and documentarians who captured life in Nashville in the 1970s so well. A few of my favorites include *Finding Her Voice: Women in Country Music* by Mary A. Bufwack and Robert K. Oerman, *In the Country of Country* by Nicholas Dawidoff, and of course the fantastic *Country Music* miniseries from Ken Burns. Tootsies Orchid Lounge is a real spot close to the Ryman Auditorium, and very famous for what it's done for songwriters and musicians who were just starting out. Tootsie was known to do for young performers just what she did for Elle—provide a beer and a meal and a place to call home.

Weston Studios is very loosely inspired by RCA in Nashville because Studio B has an incredibly rich history. There are a lot of stellar documentaries on it as well. Arlo Weston is a character all his own, but I pulled a few fun details from Chet Atkins's life. Similarly, Hal, the head songwriter, was inspired by songwriting dynamo Harlan Howard, who famously coined the phrase "three chords and the truth" to describe country music and was known to write his song lyrics on napkins.

In terms of the meteor, I pulled many details from a Smithsonian report of a 1938 meteor strike in western Pennsylvania, where I'm from. That report is a fascinating read on its own, and it's where I first found the idea for the missing third piece of a meteor. That meteor, as it stands in real life, was never located.

I couldn't do any of this job I love without the dedicated booksellers, librarians, podcasters, Instagrammers, and readers who populate the beautiful and vibrant book world. I'm deeply grateful for you every single day—this writing life I have is because of you.

What would I do without the companionship and support from my writing group? Sara Sligar, Katie Gutierrez, and Julia Fine, you are the best of friends to me and have held me up on my darkest days. I love you more than words can say. Anica Mrose Rissi, thank you for walking miles and miles with me and always listening to me say, "I'm giving this book one more shot." Dear friends and writers Ellen O'Connell Whittet, Kimi Cunningham Grant, and Celia Laskey also gave such helpful feedback.

To keep these acknowledgments from becoming a novel of their own, I've focused here on book-related gratitude—but to my cherished friends and family, including my wonderful husband and our two sweet kids, the reason I have anything worthwhile to say is the love and grace you have always shown me.

Lastly, the inspiration for Elle Harlow comes from my beloved mentor and friend Louise DeSalvo, who once said to me, "Whatever you think is the end probably isn't." She said it about writing, but it applies perfectly to life, too. After she passed away in 2018, so many people told me I still had her with me because I knew exactly what she would say. At the time, it just wasn't good enough to ease the ache of not being able to talk with her. So I sat down with my notebook and wrote two phrases:

Knowing what you would say
Ain't the same as hearing you say it.

It took a few months to realize what I had written were song lyrics, and that was the moment Elle Harlow was born.

ABOUT THE AUTHOR

AMY JO BURNS is the author of the memoir *Cinderland* and the novel *Shiner,* which was a Barnes & Noble Discover Pick and an NPR Best Book of the Year. Her novel *Mercury* was a Barnes & Noble Book Club pick, a Book of the Month selection, a *People* Book of the Week, and a *New York Times* Editors' Choice. A western Pennsylvania native, she lives in New Jersey with her family.

Founded in 2017, Celadon Books, a division of Macmillan Publishers, publishes a highly curated list of twenty to twenty-five new titles a year. The list of both fiction and nonfiction is eclectic and focuses on publishing commercial and literary books and discovering and nurturing talent.